DEMON OF THE DEEP

BRIAR BELMONT

This is a work of fiction. All names, characters, events, places, organizations, and incidents portrayed in this novel are either products of the author's imagination or are used fictitiously. No identification with actual persons (living or deceased), places, buildings, and products is intended or should be inferred.

DEMON OF THE DEEP

Cover Art by: María Arteta https://marosar.carrd.co/

Typography and Illustrations by Amphi https://www.amphi.studio/

Map By: Isaac Jordan

ISBN 979-8-9905007-1-6 (hardcover)

ISBN 979-8-9905007-0-9 (paperback)

ISBN 979-8-9905007-2-3 (ebook)

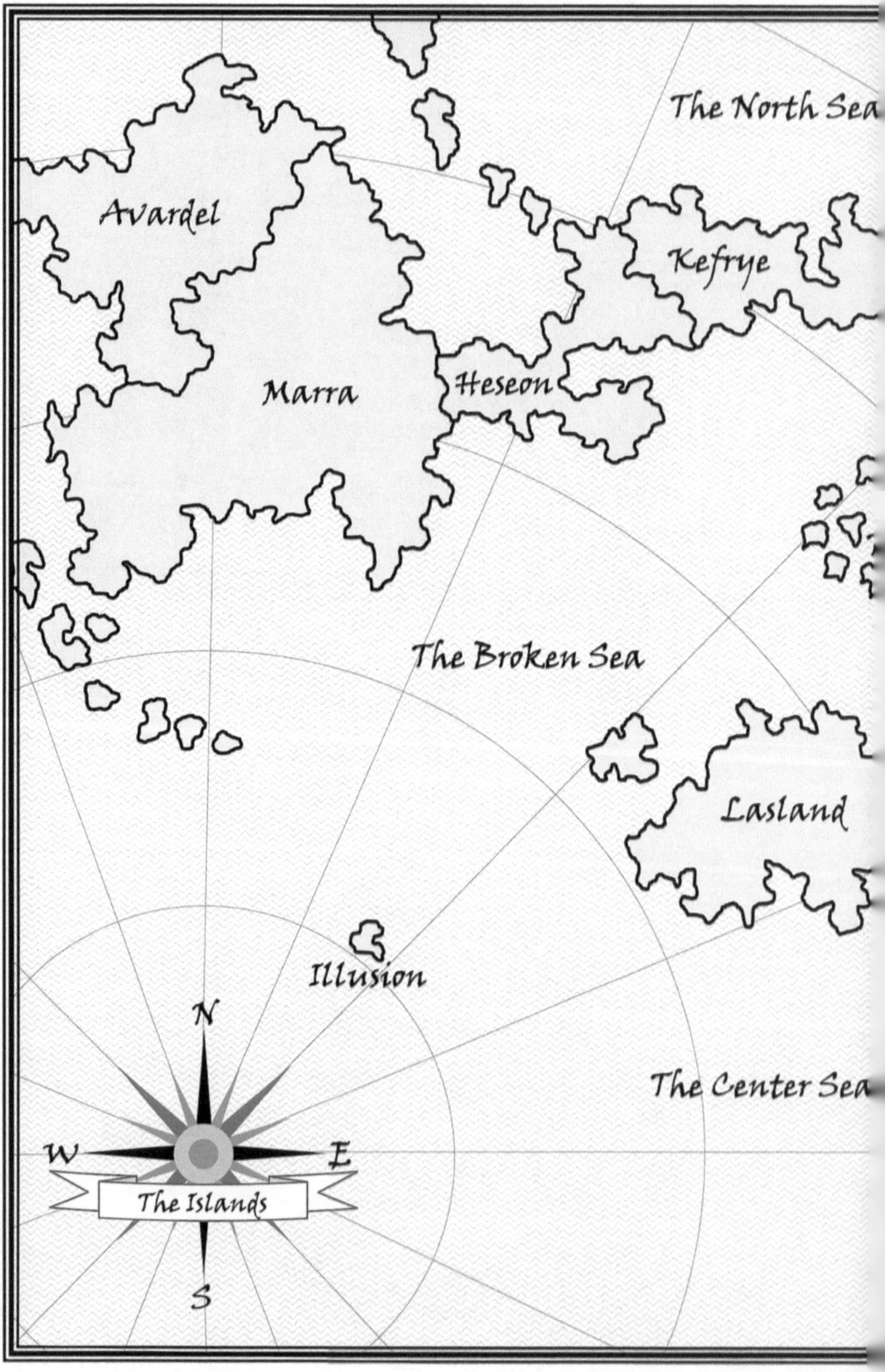

The North Sea
Avardel
Kefrye
Marra
Heseon
The Broken Sea
Lasland
Illusion
The Center Sea
N
W
E
S
The Islands

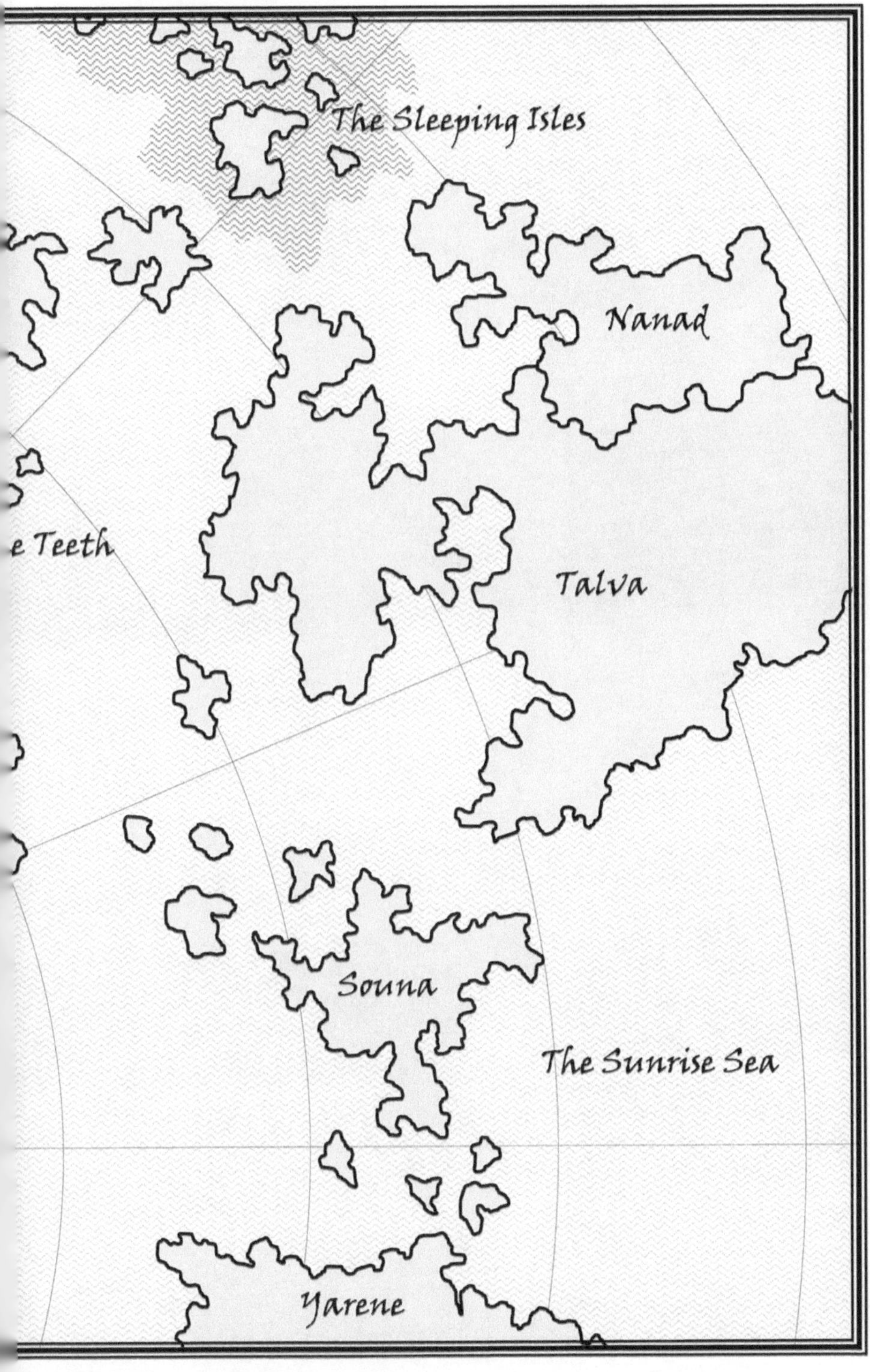

The Sleeping Isles
Nanad
e Teeth
Talva
Souna
The Sunrise Sea
Yarene

PRONUNCIATION GUIDE

CHARACTERS

- Rowan Faine: RO-ən / FAYN
- Yves Francios Lesauvage: EEV / FRAHN-SWA / Læ Saw-VAWG
- Fox: FAHKS
- Logan Crowder: LO-gən / Krow-derr
- Nephele: NEHF-ə-lee
- Henri Wells: AHN-REE / WELZ
- Gaël: GA-EHL
- John Hakon: JAWN / HAA-kon
- Robin Beckett: RAWB-in / BEHK-it
- Old Joe: JO
- Ana: AHN-ah
- Cyrus: SIE-rəs
- Nia: NEE-a
- Zanta: ZAHN-tah
- Admiral Batteux: - BAHT-oh
- General Batteux: BAHT-oh
- Silver Stroud: STROWD

COUNTRIES

Marra: MAR-uh
    Talva: Tal-vuh
    Avardel: Av-AR-del
    Kefrye: KEH-free
    Souna: SOO-nah
    Gosoya: Gos-OY-uh
    Lasland: LASS-land
    Yarene: Yah-RHEEN

~

SHIPS

Siren Song: SAI-ruhn song
    Kraken's Fury: KRAA-kn's FYUOR-ree
    M.W.S. Wolf: WULF
    Monsoon: mon-soon
    K.S. Glorieux: Glor-ee-oh
    K.S. Vaillant: Vahl-ahnt

AUTHOR'S NOTE

For the sake of my own sanity and the vibes of this book, please suspend your disbelief about a few key factors for this world. We are going to pretend that STIs don't exist and that these pirates all bathe regularly. Agreed? Agreed.

Content Warnings can be found in the back of the book or by following the QR code below.

For my wild and wonderful friends:
Stay delusional.

PART 1

DEEP WATERS

CHAPTER 1

JULY 29TH, 1666

Salt air stung Captain Rowan Faine's throat as he watched the horizon of the Broken Sea. His fingers tapped a faint rhythm on the rail of his beloved ship, the *Siren Song*, the fastest and most agile pirate ship in the Islands. Yet it had lain at anchor in the shipping lanes between the Broken and Center Seas for a day and a night, waiting. Above, the red and white cross of distress snapped in the wind beneath a false Laslandish flag.

Rowan licked salt from his lips and tucked a wind-whipped strand of blond hair back into its tail. He was no good at waiting and neither was his crew. He could feel them growing restless at his back, eager for some unsuspecting ship to fall into their trap. The *Siren* was an angler fish, and those flags were their lure.

Well, that and...

"Captain!" Fox bounded up the stairs to the quarterdeck, adorned in a voluminous skirt and lace kerchief over his usual clothes. His wavy brown hair was half tied up in a tail with pieces falling across his brow. His once pale Laslandish complexion was now tanned by years of piracy, but the freckles splattered across his nose still stood out, giving him a half-innocent, half-impish air. Despite the heavy skirts that had once belonged to some rich lady they'd robbed, Fox made it up the stairs in a few long strides and skidded to a stop before Rowan.

Rowan pinched the bridge of his nose between thumb and forefinger.

"Fox, I told you. You don't have to wear the disguise until a ship is in sight."

Fox's face split into a grin, and he framed his chin between his hands. "But I look so pretty!" He fluttered his lashes, then did a little twirl to emphasize his point, the skirts flaring out around his ankles.

"Very pretty," Rowan's first mate Logan Crowder agreed from his station near the wheel. He wore a blue wide-brimmed hat squished down over his mop of golden curls, protecting his fair skin from the sun as much as a seafarer could. Rowan glowered at him, but he just shrugged. "What? It's the truth."

This was the other part of the lie, appearing as least like pirates as possible. And what better way to do that than by keeping a trunk of fine ladies' dresses aboard?

Out here on the open sea, Rowan was hoping to catch something big. Something that would satiate the crew's restlessness and provide enough funds to get them through the winter. It was a risk to be out here after all. They were encroaching upon the territory of the Deep Water Demon, the most brutal pirate on the seas and captain of the former Talvan warship, the *Kraken's Fury*.

Well, that bastard had started it.

Or had Rowan?

Rowan narrowed his eyes at the waves beyond Fox's head as Fox chattered on about how the blue skirt brought out the green of his eyes. Rowan couldn't remember when his rivalry with the Deep Water Demon had begun. Maybe it was when the Demon had started hunting Rowan's territory along the coast, or before that when Rowan had swooped in to take a prize the *Kraken* was too slow to catch. Or before that, or before that. Rowan could still hear the bombardment echoing like thunder through the clear night the last time the *Kraken* had snatched another prize from him. The flash of cannons lighting up the darkness. The Demon's reputation of ruthlessness was well earned.

But in all the years of taunting, Rowan had never come face-to-face with the Demon himself. The Demon was known for his raw power and expensive tastes. He hunted the deep waters of the open sea, targeting big game like treasure ships and loaded merchants ferrying goods and gold from Marra's and Talva's colonies to the greedy maws of the two empires. Rowan had to admit he admired the man for that. Pirating was a risk in and of itself, but going after real treasure was the stuff of legends. And with every legend Rowan heard, with every prize snatched from the sticky fingers of the empires or Rowan himself, his sense of rivalry and curiosity grew.

Was this a factor in Rowan's decision to sail directly into the Demon's own territory? Maybe. This season had been a particularly lean one because of him, and Rowan was determined to grab some of the Demon's glory and riches for himself before they had to go to ground for winter. Besides, what was life without a little risk?

Fox had begun twirling again, giggling at the way the skirt flared out and caught the sea breeze. Thank the gods he was wearing pants underneath. Last time they'd used this ruse, Fox had fought the whole battle in nothing but his skivvies after tearing off the restrictive disguise. Rowan's and Logan's eyes met over Fox's shoulder and Logan smiled ruefully, thinking the same thing Rowan was.

"How much longer do we have to wait?" Fox whined. "I'm bored."

"If you're bored, maybe you should do something useful," Logan admonished him gently.

"Yeah, but—" Fox stopped twirling, his eyes widening over freckled cheeks as something caught his eye. "Hey! Is that a—"

"Ship!" the lookout called down from the crow's nest. Rowan spun and searched the horizon, finding three tall masts cresting over the waves. Rowan's hunting hawk, Nephele, a gorgeous gray creature with a speckled breast, spiraled down from her roost near the lookout post and alighted on Rowan's leather-clad shoulder.

"Go organize the others," Rowan ordered Fox. Fox dashed away to get other crew members, including a few actual women, into their feminine disguises. They needed to make the *Siren* look as innocent and civilian-like as possible, and what would be more innocent than rich ladies?

Rowan extended his spyglass and looked out over the water but couldn't make out the flag the other ship was flying. She was large though, much larger than the *Siren*. Perfect, they'd lure the unsuspecting ship under the pretense of needing help, then when they got close, turn on them and rob them for all they had.

The ship sailed nearer, following the wind that would carry them to the northeastern shores of Lasland. At this rate, they would pass by. Rowan raised his spyglass again, taking in the sight of the other ship. He couldn't make out details yet, but he could tell it was well-made and lacked many visible gunports. A merchant then—by the red, black, and white flag flying on its mast, a Marran one. A thread of disdain for his former homeland twisted through Rowan's gut. Finally he would snatch a prize worth having.

"Looks like they're going to pass us by," Logan said from his side, short nose wrinkling with disappointment. The rest of the crew milled about the deck pretending to work, or in the case of the gown-clad pirates, pretending to be in distress at the fact that their ship was not moving. "Should we give chase or wait?"

Rowan lowered the spyglass, glancing up at the lookout who signaled confirmation of what Rowan had observed. A Marran ship with little in the way of firepower. If they decided to chase, to swoop in under full sail, appearing like a hawk skimming the waves, then the jig would be up, the ruse abandoned. They had a good chance of catching the larger ship that way, even if they would lose the element of surprise. But if they waited, there was a chance the ship wouldn't come to investigate their distress signal, and it would all be for nothing anyway.

Rowan glanced at his first mate, and Logan smiled back, waiting for orders. Rowan needed this prize, not only for the crew but also his own restlessness that had been tugging at his insides since the last few run-ins with the Demon. He needed this. Needed to know that he was as good as, if not better than the most notorious pirate on the seas.

He turned his eyes back toward the other ship just as it diverted course, prey falling into his trap.

"We wait."

~

THEY DIDN'T REALIZE they'd been tricked until it was almost too late.

Rowan and his crew waited patiently as the larger ship approached, trying to seem innocent and in need of help. It was hard, considering he and the rest of the crew were practically vibrating with energy. But he kept his spyglass trained on the other ship and waited. Even if they clocked the *Siren* as a pirate vessel, the smaller ship would easily run them down.

Sunlight glinted off the other ship's figurehead, preventing Rowan from seeing it clearly until it was close enough to make out with the naked eye.

A kraken, its glass-embedded tentacles twisting back along the prow in ominous waves. It was no merchant vessel that sailed toward them under the Marran flag, but none other than the *Kraken's Fury* in all its murderous glory.

"Fuck." Rowan turned to the crew waiting below. "It's the *Kraken*! Battle stations!"

A jolt of energy ran through the crew as they discarded their disguises. Half of them rushed to battle stations while the other half swarmed into the rigging to unfurl the sails. They could wait like sitting ducks to see if their ruse had worked on even the Demon, or they could try to outrun the larger ship. But what was the fun in that? The anticipation of this unexpected but not unwelcome challenge tightened Rowan's muscles. Finally he would be able to test his mettle against his rival one-on-one. Brute strength against cunning quickness.

A slow, malicious smile spread across Rowan's face. His eyes raked across the other ship, assessing the manpower and guns as Fox whooped in excitement and threw off his skirt, rushing to grab his rifle and climb into the rigging with the other sharpshooters. Nephele took off from Rowan's shoulder with a screech, soaring up to circle the sky.

Upon seeing the action of the *Siren*'s crew, the *Kraken* finally dropped its own pretense of innocence. The Marran flag came down, replaced by a white tentacled skull on a black field. Dark blue sails dropped down over the plain white ones, the same tentacled skull symbol emblazoned on the mainsail. A simple hourglass graced its bony forehead, signaling to anyone unlucky enough to cross its path that their time in this life was up.

Rowan strapped his cutlass and pistols to his side, his mind whirling through strategies even as he began giving orders. Above, the sails unfurled and caught the wind. Now that they were under sail, the crew descended into silence as they worked. Rowan had carefully chosen and trained his crew to work in near silence when engaging in battle. Not only did it keep the enemy from gauging their next move, but it also unnerved them. Rowan retrieved his bosun's whistle from his pocket and slipped the chain around his neck. Then, assessing the *Kraken*'s position and speed, piped directions to the crew to adjust their course.

The *Kraken* was bearing down on them quickly, but Rowan's little ship had the advantage when it came to maneuverability. All along the *Kraken*'s sides, Rowan could see hidden gunports opening. The *Siren* banked to starboard. The *Kraken* definitely had them outgunned, but did they have them outsmarted?

Now that it was clear the *Siren* wouldn't run, the *Kraken*'s momentum slowed and they turned broadside, revealing just how many cannons they really had. Two entire decks sported ten gunports each, and that wasn't counting the numerous cannons they had on the main deck—over twice as many guns as the *Siren* had overall.

The *Siren* swooped close, taunting, and the first volley of cannon fire thundered across the water, crashing just short of the *Siren*. The *Siren* darted toward the *Kraken*'s bow. If they were going to be in range, it might as well be somewhere that wouldn't be susceptible to the full force of the guns. The huge ship wouldn't be able to turn fast enough to deliver another broadside.

As soon as the *Siren* pulled out of range of the *Kraken*'s portside guns, they swooped even closer and fired a volley into the *Kraken*'s hull. Above, Rowan heard the shots of his riflemen picking off members of the opposing crew. Cannonballs crashed into the pristine wood of the *Kraken's Fury*, one splintering the ornate blue and gold lettering that proclaimed its name.

Rowan assessed the *Kraken*'s damage, contemplating whether the Demon would give up before he'd have to completely obliterate the ship. He hoped there would be something left to salvage by the end of this. It really was a beautiful ship. The kraken figurehead was ornately carved and painted, its blue tentacles trailing along the foredeck rails with little bits of glass embedded in the wood to reflect the sun. Both beautiful and practical, the same glass bits had flashed into Rowan's eyes, preventing him from realizing it was the *Kraken* early enough to have an advantage. Everything looked like it had been cleaned just that morning. If he didn't know any better, he'd have thought it belonged to the navy instead of pirates. It was too big. Too clean. Too beautiful.

He whistled the order to switch the top guns to a payload that would target the crew, not the ship itself. The *Kraken* might not be his style, but he could get good money off it if it was still seaworthy when he captured it.

The *Siren* turned as they reached the open water in front of the larger ship, cutting them off. On the *Kraken*'s deck, orders were being given, but Rowan couldn't quite make out what they were as the *Siren* fired another volley. The cannonballs and chain shot raked down the length of the *Kraken*'s deck, one hitting the foremast directly. The small projectiles fired from the top guns wreaked devastation on the *Kraken*'s crew.

But the *Kraken* was ready. Hatches within the coils of the wooden tentacles opened, exposing additional forward-facing guns. Their shots hit the *Siren* broadside, taking out two of their cannons.

Rowan smirked. It was just like the Deep Water Demon to counter Rowan's agile maneuvers with simple might. He didn't need to rely on clever little tactics when he could deal maximum damage from any angle. Rowan signaled to Logan, and the *Siren* began to pull out of range.

"Fire!" The order echoed across the water, crystal clear, and a volley of flaming arrows arched over the gap between the two ships, whizzing through the *Siren*'s rigging and setting one of the foresails alight. Another arrow cut through the ropes securing a cannon to the deck. Rowan and several of the crew barely managed to dive out of the way as the loose cannon rolled backwards when the *Siren* banked sharply starboard. Rowan rolled to his feet, blue eyes searching the sky for Nephele. The screech of her call pierced the air, and he found her wheeling high above, blessedly out of arrow range.

The smaller, more nimble *Siren* was literally running circles around the *Kraken's Fury*, causing their crew to constantly shift focus, but that didn't mean the *Kraken* was unprepared to deal with their antics. Every tactic Rowan tried was met with brute force. Any advantage either ship might have had was canceled out by the other's strength.

The *Siren* darted close again to rake the deck with more cannon-shot, but the spreading fire in the sails slowed them, filling the air with thick gray smoke. The bombardment from both ships boomed constantly over the water, cannon-shot and splinters flying in every direction. Rowan stalked across the deck, embers of flaming canvas falling around him.

The flames swarmed across the upper rigging of the *Siren Song*, chewing through the sails and ropes. There was shouting in the rigging as some of the crew evacuated to the deck, and the others tried to cut away the flaming foresail before the fire began to eat up the mast. The *Kraken* was becoming equally as hindered. Many of its crew members were down with injuries, and its once pristine sides and masts were peppered with cannon damage.

"Go help with the fire. I'll take over here," Rowan ordered Logan, taking the wheel from his hands. He would've liked to go himself, but he knew Logan would scold him for acting without thinking. Rowan liked to be in the thick of the action, but in a battle like this, he knew he needed to keep his head.

"Aye Captain." Logan started down to the main deck, then stopped and turned to look at Rowan over his shoulder. "Don't get carried away."

Rowan nodded, and Logan disappeared down the steps.

Don't get carried away. Logan knew his captain too well. Knew the gleam in Rowan's eye. Knew that his blood was up with the exhilaration of battle against the man who'd been a thorn in his side for years, and he was likely to get riled up and end up making a stupid decision.

The *Siren* rounded the back of the *Kraken,* and Logan made it to the base of the foremast just as the flames ate through the last of the lines and the foresail snapped free. Logan and several other crew members jumped away as the heavy lump of flaming canvas thumped to the deck.

Rowan grimaced but held the *Siren's* course firm. They could still run before they were completely destroyed, but he had not yet given up hope that they could succeed. There had to be a way to win.

Rowan looked away from the deck where his crew swarmed to put the fires out and continue their bombardment now that they were almost side-to-side with the *Kraken* again. Everything in Rowan's instincts screamed at him to turn the *Siren* away. To run toward the open sea. But he needed this. His gaze raked across the *Kraken,* trying to find any weakness he could exploit.

The sight of a man standing still amidst the chaos on the *Kraken's* quarterdeck stopped Rowan in his tracks. He knew instantly it was the Deep Water Demon. The man was tall, raven haired, and broad shouldered. He stood with a rifle resting over one shoulder and a saber at his hip as his crew worked in ordered chaos around him. He seemed unbothered by the way the battle was going. Confident. Maybe even bored.

A cannonball thundered through the rail to the Demon's right, splinters flying all around him. But the Demon did not flinch. He gazed at the *Siren Song*, cool eyes assessing.

Then his gaze found Rowan.

Something stirred in Rowan's guts as he locked eyes with his rival. Hatred? No. Grudging admiration? Certainly. But that was not all. There was something more. Something deeper and more twisted that he had no name for.

One hand still on the wheel, Rowan raised his pistol, aiming straight for the Demon's heart. The man just looked back at him with an intense curiosity. If Rowan killed the Demon here and now, would he win? Would the legend of the Ghost Hawk surpass that of the Demon? Would his lust for adventure finally be sated?

He doubted it. A simple death would be an unsatisfyingly swift end to their one-sided rivalry. He wanted the Demon to know who had bested him. Rowan would win somehow, but it wouldn't be like this.

He lowered his pistol just as the Deep Water Demon raised his gun, cocked it, and fired one single shot. It whizzed over Rowan's shoulder, scoring across the leather.

It seemed the Demon didn't feel the same way. Rowan took aim again but the Demon was lowering his gun, satisfied that his point was made. Then, resting the still-smoking barrel on his shoulder again, the Demon raised a fist.

All activity on the *Kraken's Fury* ceased with startling immediacy. Barely an extra shot was fired. It was eerie, how the Demon had complete and utter control of his crew.

Rowan piped the signal for a ceasefire on his whistle, and his crew obeyed. The fierce battle came to stillness and silence in a second.

It was time to see what the Deep Water Demon was made of.

~

THE TWO CAPTAINS stared at each other for a moment. The only sounds the crackling of the flames and the rush of waves. The Demon cocked his head in question, and Rowan felt an inexplicable tug behind his navel. He stepped away from the wheel, trusting that one of his crew members would take hold of it in his absence, and strode toward the center of the ship. The Demon matched his pace. Rowan collected Logan on his way, and soon found himself standing at the rail between two cannons, gazing up at the *Kraken* as the two ships maneuvered closer until Rowan could almost have spit onto the *Kraken*'s deck from his position at the rail. Fox definitely could've. In fact, Fox dropped down from the rigging right beside Rowan and looked like he was working up a mouthful to try.

Logan stopped him with a calm hand on his arm and a minute shake of his head.

The two crews were hushed, staring at each other across the gap of blue water. Behind them, the wounded were being helped by their comrades, and the fire in the *Siren*'s sails was almost extinguished.

Sensing that the danger was over, Nephele swooped down to settle onto the rail of the quarterdeck.

The Demon stood calm as ever at the rail opposite. His eyes raked over the *Siren Song* below him and once again lit on Rowan.

"The Ghost Hawk." He said Rowan's alias evenly, raising one manicured eyebrow. "You don't usually stray so far from the coasts. When I realized it was you, I half expected you to live up to your name and disappear."

There was an insult in his tone, but all Rowan felt was a thrill of satisfaction that the Deep Water Demon knew him. And yet now that he got a closer look at the man himself, he frowned.

The Demon wasn't demonic at all. He was handsome.

The Deep Water Demon was dressed immaculately in a long cream coat with stitching in red and gold, a wide leather belt accentuating his trim waist. The tops of long black boots with brass spurs met the hem of the jacket. He still held the rifle over his shoulder, an ornate saber strapped to his hip. His alabaster face was angular, with onyx hair and deep black eyes that sparkled with the reflection of the sun on the waves. This was a man who enjoyed finer things—a man who'd become a pirate for riches and fame, and had achieved both. But good looks on top of that?

Rowan was almost offended.

"Why are you out here Hawk?"

Rowan smiled pleasantly. As if this bastard didn't already know the answer. He'd been driving Rowan out of his own territory all summer.

"I'm sure it's no concern of yours, Demon. Considering you abandoned this territory to invade mine."

A slight smile tugged at the corner of the Demon's lush lips.

"It wasn't my intention to offend you. But since you're here—"

"We might as well negotiate your surrender," Rowan interrupted him.

The Demon's laugh was melodic, with a slight wheeze at the end, and a ripple of shock passed through the *Kraken*'s crew. From the stories Rowan had heard, their victims were usually too terrified to do anything but grovel and beg for their lives, but Rowan got the sense that they were just as shocked at their captain's laugh as they were by Rowan's audacity.

The Demon stepped gracefully up onto the rail of the *Kraken's Fury*, and Rowan realized the two ships had drifted very close indeed.

"If you will allow me to board," the Demon said quietly, in a conspiratorial tone just for them, "we can have a nice discussion about who will be surrendering to whom."

Rowan nodded his assent. The Demon handed his gun into the waiting hands of a crew member, then dropped lightly down onto the deck of the *Siren Song*. He landed as if stepping from a stage, graceful and effortless.

"Captain," a crew member called over the gap. The Demon spared a glance back over his shoulder, to which the man raised his eyebrows. He was a white man of average height and build but with an intensity in his deep-set eyes that said he was not to be messed with. The Demon turned back to Rowan.

"My first mate seems to think I'm too reckless," the Demon said, a hint of mirth in his twinkly eyes. Rowan had no doubt that even alone, this man was fully capable of murdering his way out of a bad situation. Barehanded if he had to.

"Will you allow me some company?"

He was being annoyingly polite. Rowan nodded. "Two."

With this, the first mate signaled to another man, an enforcer by the looks of his muscle-bound frame and sharp jaw, and they boarded as well.

"Search them," Rowan commanded. His crew descended on the trio, patting them down and confiscating weapons. "I will allow one knife each, in accordance with the parlay code." His eyes met the Demon's and found the man was already looking at him, unbothered by the hands digging through his clothes for hidden weapons. A slight shiver ran down Rowan's spine. Not fear exactly, but the sense one got in open water when something big and dangerous lurked just beneath the surface.

∼

THEY PARLAYED in the captain's quarters. Luxurious and comfortable by Rowan's standards, but the Demon's gaze swept the room, unimpressed by the modest size, Rowan's unmade bed against the far wall, and the shelves packed with trinkets, weapons, and books. The first mates accompanied them, leaving Fox and the Demon's enforcer in the hall to guard the door.

Rowan took a seat next to the small table at the center of the room, and the Demon sat across from him without being invited, long legs crossed, spurs glinting in the light from the windows. They drew their knives at the same instant, stabbing them into the scarred wood of the table between them. The Demon's knife, intricate, beautiful, deadly, with a carved ebony handle and a pommel inlaid with gems. Rowan's, well-made, plain, and serviceable.

Their hands stayed on the hilts of their blades for a moment, and Rowan noticed a knucklebone tattoo peeking out from behind the ring on the Demon's right middle finger, indicating he'd survived a shipwreck. Rowan had a feeling the Demon wouldn't be easy to kill. But then again, neither was he.

"I think some refreshments are in order," Rowan said, not taking his eyes off the Demon. They both released their grip on their knives and sat back.

"I am a bit parched," the Demon agreed. "Too much smoke."

Logan had a quiet word with the men outside the door.

When the wine arrived, Logan poured two glasses. The deep red of the liquid sloshing in the glass reminded Rowan of blood. The Demon waited for Rowan to drink before sipping his own glass. Rowan held back a smile, secretly pleased he'd kept a few bottles from the crate they'd stolen off a merchant ship a few months back. The Demon twirled the stem of the glass between his fingertips, seeming content.

It seemed that neither of them knew quite how to begin.

Rowan took a bracing gulp of the wine, then set his cup back on the table, leaning forward to glare at the Demon.

"So about your surrender—"

The Demon's eyes scythed up, cutting him off.

"A bit audacious to assume I'd surrender to a man whose name I don't even know," he said coolly.

Annoyance stirred again in Rowan's chest. They were here to negotiate, weren't they? Was the man just going to sit here drinking Rowan's expensive wine all day?

"Why would you need to know my name?" Rowan asked.

"I like to know who I'm dealing with."

Rowan frowned. "A name can't tell you who I am."

The Demon's gaze flicked to the side where the first mates were watching their captains warily.

"Shall we have this conversation privately?" he said. When Logan tensed, he added, "I have no intention of harming your precious Ghost Hawk; you have my word on that."

Logan did not look comforted.

Rowan knew it was a bad idea to face an enemy with no backup. Worse that it was an enemy such as this. But a wild recklessness had overtaken his body, an intense desire to see what the legendary captain would say and do next. All sense of logic and self-preservation had fled, and the Demon saw the resolve in his expression.

"Mister Hakon." The Demon looked to his first mate. "Step out into the hall, will you? We'll be fine here."

Giving his captain a skeptical look, Hakon left the room. And after a few reassuring words from Rowan, Logan followed.

The Demon sipped his wine again, wiping a stray droplet from the corner of his lip with his thumb. Rowan simply watched him, waiting to see what he would do.

The Demon stood and began to slowly wander the room, examining its contents as if they were mildly fascinating. Rowan stayed seated, determined to appear unbothered and unaffected. He had a feeling this man would pounce at the first sign of weakness.

"Now that we're alone I'd like to know your name." The Demon's back was to Rowan, examining his meager shelf of books.

"Why?" Rowan scoffed. "Will it make it easier to give up?"

"That remains to be seen. It's just that I'm curious about you." The Demon ran a finger down the spine of a book.

A silent thrill ran through Rowan's body. He struggled to keep his voice calm.

"Me? What do you have to be curious about?"

The Demon finally turned to look at him again.

"I've heard the stories, the rumors. And you've been quite a nuisance as of late." He walked slowly back toward the table. "I want to know more. I want to know the truth." He reached the table and settled one hip onto the top, leaning down to look more closely at Rowan's reddening face.

"I'm the nuisance?" Rowan scoffed, trying to keep a cool head. "You're the one who invaded my territory first. If anyone is the nuisance here it's you. I came out here to land a juicy prize, yet here you are instead."

The Demon seemed amused by this. "Am I not juicy enough for the Ghost Hawk? You wound me." He placed a delicate hand over his own heart as if Rowan had snatched one of the knives from the table and driven it into his chest. Rowan glowered at him, and the Demon's eyes narrowed in return.

"You are out here because I drove you out. I provoked you to sail into my deep water because I want to see the man behind the ghost."

Rowan just stared at him, wide-eyed, barely clinging to the nonchalance he'd tried so hard to cultivate. All this time Rowan had thought himself clever, invading the Demon's territory in retaliation, but that was what the Demon had wanted all along, so he could spring a much larger trap.

"And what do you see?"

The Demon smiled, leaning fractionally closer, his large hand moving from his chest to brace on the table. So close to their knives. Yet Rowan didn't move.

"Tell me your name."

"You first."

The Demon blinked, as if he hadn't expected that.

"Yves," the Demon said after a moment. "Yves Francois LeSauvage."

"That's a lot of names for a pirate."

"It is. And all of them are false but the first one."

A chuckle bubbled up between Rowan's lips. What Rowan had said was right. One could not know the truth of a man simply by knowing his name. Yet the name Yves had chosen for himself spoke of a desire for luxury, for greatness. It spoke of a man hungry to escape a lowly past.

"So Yves it is then."

"Now it's your turn."

"Rowan Faine," he answered.

They did not shake hands.

"Now, shall we negotiate our truce?" Yves asked. He seemed satiated by the name somehow, as if knowing it put him at ease.

"I thought this was a surrender," Rowan countered, "and you didn't answer my question."

"Then I'll answer both. I do not surrender, but I'm willing to offer very reasonable terms that have us both surviving this encounter. You saw our crews, the state of our ships. If this goes on..." He shook his head, redirecting his focus. The smell of blood and burning sails still clung to them. "I offer this because I see a spark in you that will burn us both to the ground. I have you outgunned, and you have me outmaneuvered. Given the chance, we would obliterate each other."

All the while, he'd been leaning nearer and nearer to Rowan. But Rowan hadn't moved a muscle, mesmerized by the other man's words.

Yves reached across the short distance between them and wiped a smear of ash from Rowan's jaw.

His touch was a lightning bolt that seared through Rowan's nerves right down to his groin. He leapt to his feet, the wooden chair toppling to the floor behind him.

Logan and Hakon burst into the room.

"Cap..." Logan started.

"It's fine," Rowan almost snarled, embarrassed to be caught... what? Having a conversation?

Yves waved the first mates away, and after more strained reassurances from Rowan, they reluctantly retreated back into the hall.

"I didn't mean to startle you," Yves said, almost poutingly.

"You didn't."

Yves's sharp gaze traveled down Rowan's body slowly.

"I see that."

Color rose to Rowan's cheeks. "It's not—"

But Yves slid from the table and stalked toward him and Rowan couldn't help but stumble away until his back bumped against the boards of the wall, Yves's tall body between him and the door.

How had he let himself get into this position?

"I'm curious," Yves murmured, "I want to know what makes you tick..." He smirked as Rowan squirmed under his gaze. "Or, what makes you purr."

Rowan pushed him hard in the chest, causing Yves to stumble back a step. He didn't know why he'd done it. Only that this feeling building in his body was overwhelming and he'd needed to *move*, to do *something* with this energy. He regretted it as soon as he'd done it, feeling Yves's absence like dropping into the bowl between stormy waves.

But the Deep Water Demon was back before him in a second, strong fingers pressing deep into Rowan's throat.

"I'm not into force," Yves snarled, barred teeth just inches from Rowan's nose. "But I won't be disrespected." His sparkly eyes now burned with a deadly fire, and Rowan felt himself grow harder even as he struggled to breathe around the strong hand. He leaned his head back against the wall, keeping his eyes on Yves's face.

He saw the moment Yves felt Rowan's hardness against his thigh. The violent fire in his dark eyes reduced to a smolder. His fingers eased until there was only a slight pressure against Rowan's neck.

"So that's how it is," Yves purred, his body pressing closer, examining Rowan's face for answers. Rowan's breath hitched as he felt Yves's own hard length against his hip. A slow, feral smile spread across Yves's full lips.

"Do you know the other reason they call me the Deep Water Demon?" Yves murmured, his lips brushing Rowan's ear.

"No," Rowan gasped, anticipation coiling through his chest.

"You're about to find out."

CHAPTER 2

JULY 29TH, 1666

Something finally snapped.

Rowan wrenched Yves around by his hair, crushing their lips together in a hard kiss. Yves deepened it. His tongue tasted heady with wine, and Rowan moaned quietly as Yves's hands slipped beneath his coat. Then the coat crumpled at their feet, and Rowan's fingers curled into Yves's hair again. Demanding and insistent. Their kissing grew more frantic. Yves grabbed Rowan's waist, grinding their hips together. Rowan was breathless, already dizzy with sensation.

They broke apart for just a moment to catch their breath. Yves's hair and clothes were uncharacteristically rumpled. He grinned, looking nothing like the cool-headed captain that had stood unfazed as his ship was shot to pieces around him.

Rowan had done that.

A sudden possessiveness overtook him, a need to devour every inch of this beautiful man. A need to make it so the Deep Water Demon would never forget him.

He grabbed the front of the black leather belt, pulling their bodies back together.

"I'll ruin you," he rasped, teeth catching the shell of Yves's ear.

Yves flashed him another dazzling smile.

"We'll see."

Then Yves was on his knees, ripping Rowan's belt from his waist and tossing it aside. He freed Rowan's cock from his pants, stroking it. Rowan leaned his head back against the wall, still keeping his gaze on Yves as the man licked up the length of his cock. His sparkly eyes never left Rowan's face. A shiver ran through Rowan's body as Yves continued teasing with his long tongue.

Yves stopped after a moment, looking up at Rowan, eyebrows raised. Waiting.

"P-please..." Rowan stuttered.

He moaned as his cock penetrated through Yves's plump lips, tongue swirling expertly around the shaft. Rowan felt a slight resistance and expected progress to stop, but Yves kept going until his nose was nestled in the blond curls of Rowan's pubic hair. Yves swallowed, his throat tightening deliciously around Rowan's cock.

"Yves—" The name left his mouth before he could stop it, but he didn't care how desperate it made him sound. Yves's mouth retreated until only the tip remained inside. Rowan's fingers fisted in Yves's hair, but Yves pushed his hips firmly back against the wall before he could do anything. Rowan's pants and boots had come off at some point; he didn't know when.

Yves deliberately locked eyes with Rowan as he took him back in. Agonizingly. Deliciously. Slowly. His tongue hitting all the right places—it felt longer than it had any right to be—until Rowan's cock was deep in his throat again.

Then he began in earnest, sucking and licking till Rowan felt like he would go mad if he couldn't move. His hips bucked forward, fucking into Yves's mouth, his hand securing Yves's head in place.

His mind was so full of the sensation of Yves's luscious mouth around him that he didn't even notice Yves's hand wandering until one finger brushed his opening. He shivered.

The Demon locked eyes with him again, releasing his cock with a flick of his tongue.

"I told you I don't surrender," Yves said, the fire back in his eyes. "It has to be you."

On his knees with Rowan's dick in his mouth, he certainly looked like he was surrendering.

But Rowan didn't want this to end. He'd do anything to have the Deep Water Demon.

"I've never..." It had been a long time since he'd slept with anyone, and he'd only ever topped.

Yves was on his feet, one hand palming Rowan's wet cock, the other caressing Rowan's cheek. He looked down at Rowan with half-lidded, lust-filled eyes.

"I can't promise gentleness," he murmured, "but you will beg for more."

Rowan kissed him fiercely in response, releasing the shiny buckles of Yves's belt with quick fingers. He undressed Yves until he was standing there in nothing but his trousers, all hard muscle and flawless skin except for an old bullet wound over his heart.

Still kissing, Yves ripped Rowan's shirt down the front then wrenched him away from the wall to throw him onto the bed. He landed sprawled on his back and looked up to see Yves shedding his remaining clothing. His cock springing free.

Fuck. He was in for it.

That thing was enormous.

Yves pounced on him, devouring his mouth in a crushing kiss. Rowan reached down to stroke him, his hand feeling tiny in comparison. A small spark of anxiety flickered in his belly. There and then gone, replaced by building pleasure as Yves ground against him. The friction of their cocks together making both of them moan. Then Yves stood, produced a vial of something from the folds of his discarded coat, and returned to the bed. A faint coconut smell filled the room as he uncorked it.

"Spread your legs."

Rowan did as he was told, and Yves knelt between them. Yves removed his rings from one hand and spread the sweet-smelling liquid over his fingers. His lips found the tip of Rowan's throbbing erection, and he bobbed his head down, shallowly at first, building Rowan's anticipation. Then he went deep, eliciting a moan as his finger breached Rowan's entrance, the knucklebone tattoo disappearing inside of him. It hurt, but Rowan couldn't bring himself to care. Yves hummed, his throat vibrating around Rowan's aching cock. Rowan's back arched slightly as Yves's long fingers began to loosen him. The strange sensation warred with tingling pleasure. The wave of fire built, and he almost couldn't take it anymore until Yves's fingers found a certain spot, and he saw stars. His back arched, and he came, hot liquid gushing down Yves's throat.

Yves wasted no time—he pounced on Rowan, wiping a dribble of cum from his lip just as he had with the wine. He kissed Rowan deeply, tongue tasting of wine and salt. Then threw Rowan's legs over his shoulders before Rowan could come down from his bliss and slammed into him.

Rowan screamed as Yves plunged in up to the hilt, hitting his prostate and sending a shiver of intense pleasure and pain through his whole body. He was already getting hard again.

There were *many* reasons to call him the Deep Water Demon.

Yves withdrew slowly until just the tip was still in, then pounded back in, angling their bodies to reach even deeper. He set a punishing pace that left little room to even breathe. Rowan clutched onto Yves's broad shoulders, scrabbling for purchase. Something to ground him in this tsunami of sensation.

Yves bent to kiss him almost tenderly, groaning into his mouth. Then pressed a hand to his lower belly, crushing Rowan's guts around his cock to heighten their pleasure.

"F-fuck..." Rowan moaned. He said it so many times he lost count. The whole ship had probably heard them by now, but he didn't care one bit.

Yves withdrew and flipped him over. Rowan found he didn't mind being man-handled either—his limbs felt like jellyfish. Yves ran a hand lightly up his spine under his ripped shirt, cock poised at Rowan's entrance. Rowan squirmed, feeling horribly empty. Wanting more. Yves leaned close to his ear, wrenching his head back by his ashy blond ponytail.

"Do you want it?" he growled.

Rowan bucked his hips back, trying to take matters into his own hands. Or ass, so to speak.

Yves stopped him, pulling his hair harder till his scalp tingled.

"Naughty." He tsk-ed in disapproval.

Rowan wasn't used to being scolded or giving up his power.

He liked it.

"Answer my question."

"Yes..."

"Yes, what? Tell me what you want."

"Please..." Rowan whined. He could feel Yves's cock at his entrance, if he could just...

"Fuck me," he pleaded. "I need you... I want your cock inside me—"

Yves penetrated him suddenly, pushing his head down to the

mattress at the same time and holding it there as he pounded mercilessly into him, abusing his prostate. Rowan tried to move his hips with Yves's rhythm, letting the friction build. His cock was dripping, throbbing, aching for another release.

He felt the sting of Yves's fingernails digging into the meat of his ass, Yves's other hand still pressing the side of his head down into the mattress. His vision went fuzzy around the edges, but a low growl brought him back to his senses. His gaze flicked back, seeing Yves's elegant face twisted in ecstasy. They locked eyes.

"Come for me, Rowan."

The tsunami broke, crashing through him so hard that for a moment he felt like he may actually be drowning in the unparalleled pleasure. His second orgasm spurted onto the sheets below him, and he felt the hot rush of Yves's release filling him.

"Rowan..." the taller man moaned.

They collapsed into the bed, panting. Yves was still inside him, Rowan's head pillowed on his muscled arm. Yves tucked the other around Rowan's waist. Rowan's back was enveloped by Yves's still heaving chest. Yves's thundering heartbeat reverberated through him; his ragged breath stirred Rowan's hair. Rowan's eyes fluttered closed. Exhausted.

He'd never felt so satisfied, nor so content.

Eventually calmed, and Yves unseated himself from inside Rowan, allowing him to turn over so they were face-to-face. Yves planted a long, lingering kiss on Rowan's lips, stroking his sweat-soaked hair away from his face.

"So shall we negotiate our truce?" Yves asked as their kiss broke apart.

Rowan, still slightly shivering with aftershocks, had completely forgotten about their original purpose for meeting here. He opened and closed his mouth like a caught fish. Unable to think of what to say.

"Did I fuck the thoughts right from your brain?" Yves laughed, his voice slightly hoarse from the abuse his throat had taken. "I hope they come back soon. I liked them."

"What are your terms?" Rowan managed to say, struggling to

think business while they were still naked, sticky, and cuddled together in his bed.

"I'm prepared to replace your burned sails and rigging, have one of my physicians tend to your wounded, and..." He eyed the shirt still clinging in tatters around Rowan's shoulders. "I'll give you a nice new shirt from my own wardrobe."

These were generous offers. Rowan waited for the other shoe to drop.

"If..." Yves continued, pausing to pinch Rowan's chin between his fingers, bringing their faces close so their lips almost brushed. His shiny eyes became smoldering embers again. "If I can see you again."

Somehow Rowan wasn't expecting that, and for a moment he was stunned speechless. The Deep Water Demon had just given him the best sex of his life so...

"Yes."

Their deal was sealed with another languid kiss.

CHAPTER 3

JULY 29TH, 1666

Fox was jittery, pent up, and spoiling for a fight. So when he first spotted the sails of a huge merchant ship on the horizon, it was like all his prayers had been answered.

But now, sitting in the rigging of the *Siren Song*, looking down the barrel of his rifle, he could feel only regret, a sinking feeling that reminded him of the first time he'd been seasick. It was like time had slowed when he spotted the man on the deck of the *Kraken's Fury*. Fox considered just shooting him. Just doing his job. He had the shot. He aimed. His finger found the trigger. Then the man looked up with that all too familiar face, and his gaze seemed to find Fox in the rigging.

Gaël.

Fox took his finger from the trigger. Despite his hatred for the man, he couldn't do it.

Then everything was suddenly on fire, and he lost sight of Gaël in the smoke and chaos. He scrambled down the rigging but didn't get very far.

"Fox!"

Henri's deep voice barely reached him in a lull between volleys of cannon fire. He looked over and saw Henri through the smoke, his large frame dangling from one hand on the lowest yardarm. His rifle was on the deck twenty feet below, and one long leg was tangled in a bit of rigging. The sail crackled with fire. Dangerously close. Fox climbed out onto the yardarm, the fire hot on his face.

"Hen—"

"Help," Henri croaked. His clothes and dark skin were streaked with ash.

Fox grasped the back of his shirt and tried to haul Henri back onto the yardarm. He was much bigger than Fox, and between the smoke blowing into his eyes and the rolling of the ship, it was next to impossible.

A tongue of flame jumped from the sail to his pant leg, and Henri shouted in pain. He couldn't move away, tangled as he was in the ropes.

"Cut me free! Cut me free!" He was panicking, wriggling and writhing to get away from the fire.

"But—"

The ropes slackened, burned through, and Henri's body weight suddenly swinging free was too much. His grip on the yard slipped. Fox surged forward, but his fingertips just brushed Henri's outstretched hand. He watched in horror as Henri plummeted to the deck, tongues of fire following him down. He bounced off a bundle of stowed cargo and thudded to the deck itself. Several crew members rushed to him, immediately putting out the fire on his clothes.

Henri's eyelids fluttered and opened. He looked up into the rigging and gave Fox a shaky thumbs up.

Fox scampered down, determined to help his friend. But by the time he made it there, the battle seemed to be over.

Fox's feet hit the deck as the *Kraken's Fury* drew up beside them, and Logan motioned Fox towards where he and Captain Rowan stood at the rail. A spark of anger lit inside him as he saw Gaël's face in the crowd. The Deep Water Demon had trapped them...hurt his friend... Fox worked up a wad of saliva in the back of his throat, wanting to see if he could spit the distance. Logan's gentle hand on his arm stopped him.

The two captains began talking, but Fox couldn't pay attention. His eyes found Gaël again. Gaël stared back at him, expression blank, almost surprised.

Good. Fox hoped seeing him again after all these years was a very unpleasant surprise. He scowled over the gap between the two ships.

Then Gaël was coming aboard, and they found themselves

walking side by side, following the captains and first mates. Before Fox knew it, he was being left to guard the door alone in the hallway with his ex-best friend.

Fox tried his best not to look at his former friend. But his eyes kept straying to that once beloved face. The years since his abrupt departure from Fox's life had been kind to him. He was taller, his shoulders broader, body more muscled. He looked confident. Composed. Deadly.

But he was familiar too. His cheeks had filled out with adequate food, but his broad, high cheekbones still underlined his angular eyes, and his jaw was sharp enough to cut.

He looked like he hadn't smiled in a long time.

Gaël's magnetic gray eyes slid sideways to look at Fox. He swallowed, as if he was about to say something.

The door to the captain's quarters opened, and Logan stuck his head out.

"The captain wants wine." He looked back over his shoulder to where the Deep Water Demon was lounging in a chair as if he owned the place. "The good wine."

Fox caught a passing crewman and sent him for the wine.

The hallway was plagued by silence. Fox thought about Henri. How badly was he injured? The burns were nasty enough, but he couldn't have come out of that fall unscathed either. Fox itched to go check on his friend.

The delivery of the wine interrupted his thoughts.

"Henri's fine," the crewman said, seeing Fox's frown. "Just a few burns and a broken leg."

Fox thanked him, feeling some of the tension in his shoulders lighten. He knocked on the cabin door and handed the wine to Logan.

Silence again. Fox refused to look at Gaël.

"How have you been?"

The question caught Fox off guard, and he whipped his head around, long brown hair getting in his eyes. Gaël gave no indication he'd even spoken.

"Fine," Fox muttered.

Gaël looked over at him, those fathomless storm cloud eyes boring into him.

"We need to talk."

"Oh? Do we?" Fox leaned back against the wall, crossing his arms. "What is there to talk about?"

"You know," Gaël said in a low voice.

He did.

"I'm sure I don't," Fox lied. His characteristic obstinance coming out. Let Gaël say it. Let him acknowledge exactly what had happened.

Gaël swore under his breath. He looked away and ran a frustrated hand through his black hair.

Fox felt a little bad for a moment, then scolded himself for it.

He wasn't the reason for all of this.

"If you really don't want to talk to me, I'll respect your wishes," Gaël said, his voice wavering slightly. "But I have some things to say that would be better said in private."

"Who says I'll listen?"

"Only you."

This was...strange. Fox didn't quite know what to do. He was used to people getting angry at his stubbornness, not this defeated acceptance. He examined Gaël for a moment longer.

"Come with me."

Fox led Gaël down the hall to the small cabin he shared with Logan. He didn't like being in such close quarters with his former best friend, but it couldn't be helped. He stood with his back to Gaël, staring at the stacked bunks, trying to prepare himself for whatever it was his ex-friend had to say. He heard the door close.

"Spit it out then—"

When he turned around, Gaël was on his knees, head bowed in contrition.

"I'm sorry." Gaël bowed further, forehead resting on the floorboards between flat hands.

Fox backed up a step, sinking heavily onto the edge of the low bunk.

"What?" Early on, he'd imagined this a thousand times, all the cutting, cruel things he would say if he ever got the chance. But now his brain felt sluggish.

"I'm sorry," Gaël repeated.

The past came crashing back to Fox all at once. The hurt. The confusion. The betrayal and feeling of worthlessness that had haunted him since that day.

Fox and Gaël had been best friends since they were children. Nearly inseparable. Gaël's merchant parents from Gosoya, in the far east, had died when he was young, leaving him an orphan. No one in the little Laslandish port town wanted to take him in as their own, so he ended up working on Fox's family farm.

Fox's father was not a kind man. If he had no love for his own son, he had even less for the foreign kid he'd hired off the street. And when life at home became unbearable, they'd run away together. They were so young they didn't even remember their family names. All they knew was that they had each other.

First they became gutter kids. Then thieves.

Eventually they'd gotten work as powder monkeys on a privateer ship. It was good for a while. They were warm. Fed. Together. But their relationship changed, and one night after a bit of drinking in a sleazy dockside tavern, they'd ended up in bed together.

Fox realized he was in love the moment Gaël's lips touched his. And when the kiss broke, Gaël confessed his love in the most gentle and quiet voice. A voice that spoke as if these feelings were the most obvious and natural thing in the world. *I love you, Foxy. I always have and I always will.* Fox couldn't quite remember what he'd said in return, but Gaël's words were eternally branded on Fox's heart, an open wound he tried to soothe with the attention of others.

It was all a lie in the end. In the morning Gaël was gone, leaving him in a strange port city where he had no friends, little money, and barely spoke the language. The only thing Gaël had left behind was the broken remnants of the leather bracelet Fox had made him when they were younger and living on the streets.

Fox's heart ached at the memory, old hurts he'd thought long buried rushing up to the surface. He'd stolen and starved for a while after that, unable to get honest work until Captain Rowan saw him get into a street brawl one day and took Fox under his wing.

Fox had tried to sink all that hurt, all that worthlessness, to the bottom of the sea. But since then he'd been a little more loose with his favors than he'd like to admit. He'd slept his way through a good portion of the Islands and the *Siren*'s crew. Men or women, it didn't matter. Sometimes it was fun, sometimes it only served as an attempt to drown out the memory of Gaël's touch. But no matter what he did, he couldn't forget the betrayal of his best friend and first love.

This hurt that he'd been carrying inside for so long felt insurmountable now. Like it was a vital part of him.

"Why?" His voice came out quiet and small.

When Gaël looked up, he had tears in his eyes.

"I was afraid."

"Afraid? AFRAID?" Hurt turned to rage in an instant, spreading like fire. "Don't you think *I* was afraid when I woke up and you were gone? Don't you think I was afraid, being left alone in a strange country? I hoped you were *dead*. At least then it wouldn't have been your choice to leave me." He was shouting now, but his voice caught on the last word, turning into a sob, unable to stop the hot tears coursing down his face.

Gaël wouldn't look him in the eye.

"There's no excuse that will take away what I did," he said.

"That's right," Fox agreed, angrily dashing the tears from his cheeks.

"I don't deserve your time." It didn't feel like a guilt trip. It felt honest, like Gaël truly believed he was the lowest scum to walk the earth.

"Then leave," Fox spat.

Gaël began to stand, but the ship rolled suddenly, sending him back to his knees at Fox's feet.

Gaël looked up into his eyes then, fat tears rolling down his sharp cheeks. And some of Fox's anger dulled to a faint, familiar ache.

"I just wanted you to know I regret it," Gaël said, his eyes searching Fox's face as if to memorize his features. "The moment I ran, I regretted it and still do. But I was afraid of what happened, afraid of my feelings and"—he gulped—"afraid you would hate me."

His words ached as a constant thrum in Fox's chest. But he couldn't look away from the face of the man he'd once loved, that he might love still.

"I looked for you," Gaël continued. "I kept trying to get back to Wave Harbor to find you again, but by the time I returned, you were gone...and I'm so ashamed that I failed you, that I didn't have the strength to face my fears for your sake." His hands trembled, and he brought them up to his lips as if to stop himself from saying anything more.

Fox's heart cracked a bit at that, seeing the pain in Gaël's face, hearing the shame in his voice. And that small crack exposed the part of his heart long buried.

His hand twitched in its place on the edge of the bunk, itching to touch Gaël.

"What do you want? Forgiveness?"

"I don't think I can hope for that. I want to know that you are happy."

Fox took a steadying breath. "What would you do? To make me happy?"

Gaël's eyes widened. "Anything."

"Would you betray your captain?"

Gaël flinched. "Yes."

"Would you jump into the sea?"

"Yes."

Fox was silent for a long time.

"Would you kiss me?"

Gaël sat back on his heels. "Is that what you want?"

What Fox wanted was to see if that old spark was still there. If he had the capability to set aside the past and give himself back to Gaël.

"Yes."

Gaël straightened up so they were eye to eye. He leaned forward slowly, giving Fox ample time to change his mind. When their lips were about to touch, he whispered, "Are you sure?"

Fox didn't answer. He acted.

The kiss was tender. Hesitant. But it was full of something that no kiss since that night had ever had. Gaël made a small noise in the back of his throat, and pulled away but not far. He searched Fox's expression, a small desperate hope in his eyes. And slowly the red fire of rage and hurt that had been burning for so long began to soften to its old warm glow.

Their lips were still only a whisper away, and Fox could tell that Gaël was desperate to touch him again. But he held back, waiting for Fox to make the next move, to push him away. To tell him to leave and never come back.

But Fox didn't want that. He wanted more. He wanted to be closer. He moved, and Gaël flinched like he would hit him, but Fox's hand curled gently around the back of his neck. His grip was firm, so Gaël could not pull away.

"What do you want?" Fox asked softly.

"I already…"

"No. What do *you* want? Right now at this moment."

Gaël looked almost afraid. As if telling the truth would break this moment's spell. He gulped, trying to work up the courage to answer. Finally he looked Fox in the eye.

"You."

"And what will you do if you have me?"

"I won't run away again. I won't let fear cost me more years with you."

Fox pulled him forward so their lips met again, more insistent this time. Gaël hesitated for the briefest moment before his eyes slid closed and his lips parted for Fox's tongue. Fox moaned, letting his hand slide down the back of Gaël's neck and under the collar of his shirt. He was already turned on, his skin hot and the front of his pants tight. Gaël leaned further into the kiss, his hand running up Fox's thigh. He was growing bolder, finally accepting that Fox wanted him. His fingers brushed Fox's cock through his pants, and Fox gasped. Then Fox was on his back on the bunk, Gaël's hard body pressed against him. Gaël's lips left a trail of fire down his neck and over the swallow tattoo on his collarbone. Gaël's fingers slid beneath the hem of Fox's shirt and over his burning skin. He pulled Fox's shirt off, then his own. And continued kissing a trail down Fox's chest and stomach.

His palm rubbed over Fox's cock again. Fox moaned quietly. Now he knew why he had never been able to forget Gaël's touch. The shivers of his body remembered. It was like nothing else he'd ever experienced. Whether it was rough or tender, it was somehow right, full of some quality Fox could never fully understand. He arched his back as Gaël unbuttoned his pants. Then Gaël paused, looking up at him questioningly. Waiting for permission to continue. Fox took this opportunity to turn the tables; instead, he flipped Gaël onto his back.

He gazed at Gaël for a moment, taking in his sculpted body, muscles mounded beneath honey-brown skin like desert dunes. He ran his tongue up the center crease of Gaël's abs while slipping Gaël's pants down over his muscled thighs. Then he licked up the underside of Gaël's cock. Gaël cupped his chin between thumb and forefinger, tugging his face up so their eyes met.

"You don't have to…"

Fox batted his hand away playfully and swirled his tongue around the tip of Gaël's cock while still making eye contact. Gaël's hand dropped back to the bed, and he groaned, letting Fox continue doing whatever he wanted. Fox vowed silently to himself to drive Gaël insane. He was eager to show Gaël just how much he'd changed too.

He teased him with his tongue until Gaël's hips began to wiggle in impatience. He paused, lips poised on the tip of Gaël's cock for just a moment.

"Please," Gaël gasped. Fox bobbed his head down, flicking his tongue over the tender underside of his cock and sliding down until he couldn't go any further. Gaël moaned, and Fox bobbed his head a few more times before Gaël lifted his head.

"Fox, let me..." He drew Fox up to kiss him. He began to remove Fox's pants. Fox pulled away momentarily.

"Do you want to stop?" Gaël asked.

Fox shook his head. Last time they'd been together, Fox had been on the receiving end. And since then he'd been with all types of people in all types of situations. He was perfectly capable of giving as good as he got. But his feelings were still a little raw, and he couldn't quite bring himself to be *that* vulnerable with Gaël just yet. He needed to maintain a little control, or he would unravel back into those distrusting feelings.

"Gaël..." He didn't quite know how to broach the subject. "I need...I need to be the one in control this time."

A brief flash of guilt crossed Gaël's face. And Fox was afraid he would pull away completely and call the whole thing off. Then Gaël seemed to compose himself and bumped his forehead gently against Fox's.

"Of course."

Fox caressed his cheek and kissed him tenderly, wriggling the rest of the way out of his pants. Gaël rolled his hips forward gently, the friction of their cocks rubbing together causing both of them to moan. Fox ran his fingers down Gaël's broad back to cup the curve of his ass, simultaneously pulling a vial of clear liquid from beneath his pillow. Gaël's muscles tensed.

"Relax," Fox murmured, his tongue brushing over Gaël's lips.

"Sorry"—Gaël chuckled—"it's just that I've never done this before."

Fox smirked. "Don't worry. I know what I'm doing." He went to kiss Gaël again but Gaël pulled back slightly, eyebrows knit together with a slight frown. Was he hurt that Fox had slept with others in the almost seven years they'd been apart? Had Gaël *not* slept with others?

"Gaël..." Fox tried to broach the subject gently. "Have you slept with anyone else since me?"

Gaël's frown deepened. "Have you?" he countered.

"A lot," Fox confessed with a bashful smile.

Gaël bit his lip. "Then I guess I'm in good hands."

"You're not going to answer?"

Gaël looked away and then back again, fiddling with the frayed edge of the pillow. "I tried once, but I felt too guilty."

A pang of unexpected jealousy and pity touched Fox's heart. Gaël looked at him nervously, and Fox smiled.

"You don't have to feel that way anymore."

Gaël's frown smoothed a bit, and he reached out to run his thumb over Fox's bottom lip.

"I'm jealous, but I can't blame any of them. You're everything anyone could want."

Fox blushed, pleased at the sweet words and lack of judgment. A small, affectionate smile spread across Gaël's lips as well, revealing his dimples.

Oh, those dimples. They'd been Fox's downfall all those years ago.

Fox kissed him again.

"We don't have to," he whispered. But Gaël pulled him closer still, grinding their hips together and deepening the kiss. After a while Fox let his hand wander down to part Gaël's thighs.

"Ready?"

Gaël nodded, and Fox slathered his fingers in lube. He hooked one leg over Gaël's to keep them spread and nibbled his ear.

Gaël hissed as Fox's finger entered him. Fox moved a little, gentle but firm. He stroked Gaël's insides, letting him get used to the feeling.

When he added the second finger, Gaël turned his face away and bit his knuckle.

"Are you okay?"

"Keep going," Gaël murmured around his knuckle.

"Tell me if you want to stop."

Gaël nodded.

Fox continued working; methodically loosening Gaël and searching for the spots he knew would make Gaël feel good. Finally he found what he was looking for.

"Ah..." Gaël's hole tightened, his body tensing like a drawn bowstring. Fox massaged the same spot again, eliciting a deep moan from the other man. Fox smiled, watching Gaël's lips part as another moan escaped. He was almost ready.

Fox planted a lingering kiss on Gaël's mouth and worked his way down his body until his lips found Gaël's quivering cock. He licked up its length and then bobbed his head down to take as much of it into his mouth as he could. Gaël groaned, his fingers tugging on Fox's hair.

Fox continued to loosen him as his mouth slid over Gaël's cock, veins bulging against his lips.

"Ah...Fox..."

Fox released him, sliding his fingers out as well. He leaned over Gaël's quivering body to capture his lips again. Gaël already looked half delirious, but his dark gray eyes found Fox's. His strong hand slid over Fox's cock, guiding him to his entrance.

"I want you," he breathed.

Kissing him again, Fox repositioned himself between Gaël's thick, muscled thighs. He spread more of the lube over his cock, then slowly entered Gaël, sliding his lubed hand up over Gaël's cock at the same time. Gaël gasped, clutching Fox's arms. Fox kept going until his cock hit the spot he was looking for.

Gaël's hands tightened around Fox's biceps. Fox pulled back, then rolled his hips forward again, harder this time.

"Ah..." Gaël shuddered beneath him. It was a sort of exquisite torture seeing him like this. Vulnerable and quivering. Fox wanted to wreck him, take his revenge one thrust at a time. Still he held back, trying not to cause any pain. But his own need was building as he moved, and it was getting more and more difficult. Gaël's gaze suddenly sharpened on him.

"J-just fuck me..." he gasped as Fox's hips rolled forward again. "Fuck me harder, please..."

The self-restraint he'd been holding onto frayed. There was no time to be tender now; he felt his cock grow a bit harder, and he pulled out until just the tip remained inside.

"Look at me."

Gaël did.

Fox bucked his hips forward, burying his cock as deep as it would go. Gaël let out a feral growl that only served as encouragement. Gaël braced his feet against the underside of the bunk above, giving Fox a deeper angle and more leverage. Fox pounded in again, his hand working over Gaël's throbbing cock. He couldn't take his eyes off Gaël's gorgeous face. Watching his expressions change with every thrust. Watching him come apart. Fox loved seeing the effects of his touch. The pleasure he caused. It was even better now that it was Gaël under him and not some stranger he didn't care about.

Gaël's eyes half closed, his lips parting to beg for more. Then his head tilted back against the mattress. Seeing that exquisitely muscled body laid out beneath him, sucking him in deeper and responding to his every touch was almost more than Fox could bear.

"Gaël..." he gasped. Gaël moaned wordlessly in response as another thrust hit his prostate. Fox's hand pumped Gaël's cock faster. He wanted Gaël to come first, but Gaël's sounds of pleasure and the fucked-out expression on his face were driving Fox crazy.

"Yes...YES..." Gaël's hips moved to take Fox in more, faster, deeper. The palms of his hands were braced against the wall above his head. "Fox...yes..." He threw his head back, mouth open, but no sound came out as his cum spilled through Fox's fingers onto his own stomach. His insides clenched deliciously around Fox's cock, and Fox's last thread of self-control snapped, sending him over the edge with no time to pull out. He could feel every beat of Gaël's racing heart as his cock throbbed out his orgasm inside Gaël.

Gaël's legs dropped, wrapping around Fox's waist to keep him inside. He pulled Fox down into a needy kiss. When the kiss broke, Fox buried his face in the crook of Gaël's neck, tasting the salty sweat on his skin.

"Fox." Gaël's voice sounded deeper than before, a bit raspy. Fox turned his face to nuzzle Gaël's neck more.

"Hm?"

"I love you."

Fox couldn't help the grin that spread across his face. He felt like laughing from the sheer joy of hearing those words again. He wiggled his hips playfully, causing Gaël to moan and bite his lip.

But he couldn't say it back. Not yet.

He didn't know how to receive love. Gaël was the only person in the world who'd ever cared about him that way. But he'd left, and that wound hadn't closed with time. The balm of Gaël's touch had instead scrubbed it raw.

Gaël planted his hands on either side of Fox's face, pushing him back a little to look at him fully.

"You don't have to say it back. It's enough for me that you're here," Gaël whispered.

Fox had never really been romanced before. It had all been flings and one-night stands. So having sweet words said so sincerely was new to him. He didn't know what to do.

He pulled out gently, not missing the slight wince that Gaël tried to hide. He tucked himself under Gaël's arm, head on his firm chest, one leg thrown over Gaël's hip. Gaël's fingers traced a lazy path up the two knotted tattoo bands that ran diagonally around Fox's upper thigh, little waves and foxes frolicking through the intricate strands.

"You got tattoos," Gaël observed.

"Mmm." Fox relished Gaël's fingertips tracing over his skin. He readjusted his head on Gaël's chest.

"Do they mean something?"

Fox looked up, letting his lips trace across the edge of Gaël's jaw.

"That one is me," he said, indicating the intricate bands beneath Gaël's fingertips, each detail representing an important event in his life. He wiggled around so Gaël could see his chest.

"This one"—he traced the line of the soaring bird's wing across his collarbone—"is a swallow. It's for good luck." He looked up at Gaël from beneath his lashes. "And it means I swallow."

Gaël stared at him for a moment in bewilderment, then burst into disbelieving laughter, his beloved face transforming with joy.

"Never change, Fox." He kissed the tip of Fox's nose, and Fox settled his head back onto Gaël's firm chest. The muscled mounds of his pecs still glistened slightly with sweat.

"You don't make a very good pillow," Fox grumbled jokingly.

Gaël's lips pressed against his hair.

"Sorry." The word sounded sleepy. Fox wanted to ask what would happen next. Would Gaël leave the *Kraken's Fury* for him?

Would the Demon let him? Would Gaël still be here the next time he added a knot to his tattoo?

But he shook those thoughts from his mind as Gaël's thumb rubbed over his cheek. He didn't want to disturb the small pocket of peace they'd created. Sooner or later, someone would come looking for them.

Yet he found himself unable to rest or even close his eyes. His fingers fidgeted with the edge of the sheet. Listening to Gaël's heartbeat.

"I'm right here," Gaël murmured sleepily. "I'm not going anywhere."

Fox sighed and stopped his fidgeting. He was tired from the fighting, but he still couldn't relax. Gaël's breathing grew slow and even, a small snore escaping every few minutes. Gaël's childhood habit of hugging something while sleeping hadn't changed. Fox felt safe snuggled into the warm embrace, but that was a problem. His mind wouldn't let him fully forget that feeling of waking up to nothing but a cold, empty bed.

Maybe in time, if he spent enough mornings being crushed to death against Gaël's hard chest, he would forget it had ever been any other way. So he closed his eyes and let himself enjoy the sensation of being wanted. But he did not fall asleep.

CHAPTER 4

JULY 29TH, 1666

"Where the hell are they?" Logan grumbled as he reluctantly left the captain's quarters. Fox and the scary-looking crewman from the *Kraken's Fury* were supposed to be guarding the door, but they were nowhere to be seen.

The first mate of the *Kraken*—Hakon, the Demon had called him—leaned casually against the wall next to the closed door of the captain's quarters, one foot propped up on the wall. Logan started down the corridor.

"You're leaving?" Hakon said, stopping Logan in his tracks. "Seems like you don't mind leaving your precious captain all alone." His eyes darted to the door. "Two against one if things go wrong."

He was right of course, but...

Hakon saw his hesitation. "They're fine," he said nonchalantly. He struck a match on the rough wall, watching its flame waver with his deep-set eyes. "Gaël may look scary, but he's basically a kitten." His eyes met Logan's as the flame went out. "Me, on the other hand..."

Logan scowled at him but took up a position on the other side of the door.

There was silence for a while. Logan tried hard to hear what was happening inside, to no avail. He sighed, opening his mouth to attempt to make small talk, but one glare from Hakon silenced him before any words could leave his mouth.

He watched Hakon out of the corner of his eye. He was of similar height to Logan, and his short hair was the color of a chestnut, shiny brownish red, and there was a faint dusting of stubble on his chin. He wore a dark jacket that looked like it had been stolen off some unlucky Marran naval officer, a faded gold braid epaulet gracing one shoulder and one sleeve a stark, bright red instead of the usual black. His build wasn't particularly intimidating, but his eyes were intense. Shrewd. He gave off an aura that you should be afraid of him.

Something crashed in the captain's quarters, and Logan burst in, followed closely by Hakon, both ready to defend their captains. They stopped short on the threshold.

Captain Rowan stood with his back to them, his chair on its side behind him. The Deep Water Demon sat with one hip settled on the table.

"Cap..." Logan started.

"It's fine," Rowan snarled. He never spoke to his first mate that way. Rowan looked nervous and the Demon looked surprised. The Demon waved a dismissive hand at them, but Logan wasn't about to leave by his order.

"Captain?" Logan asked.

"I said it's fine Logan, go back outside." With one last regretful look at his captain, Logan followed Hakon out again. His stomach knotted with anxiety. Something was wrong. Despite Rowan's reckless streak, Logan would usually trust his judgment. They'd grown up together since the age of nine, after all. Logan knew Rowan would always have his back, just as Logan always had his. When Logan had been turned away from his family home after he finally escaped the navy, Rowan had been there waiting for him, hand extended in welcome. Their own families didn't want them, so the closest thing they had was each other, and Logan would never think to abandon him, no matter how reckless he was. But when it came to the Deep Water Demon, Rowan was different. This rivalry he had built up in his head had become more like an obsession, and it was consuming him slowly.

Another awkward silence out in the hall. Hakon lit another match and flicked it away when it was spent. After a while, a noise came from behind the door. Logan tensed.

Hakon's brown eyes slid toward the door, then to Logan's face.

"You know they're probably fucking in there," he said wryly.

"What—"

Rowan's familiar voice interrupted him, moaning a name.

Panic twisted in Logan's chest. He gripped the door handle, ready to burst into the room. Hakon caught him by the arm, his hand like a vise.

"If I'm right, is that really something you want to interrupt?" he said calmly. Rowan's voice moaned again from the other side of the door. "Sounds like he's having fun."

All the fight went out of Logan in an instant. He let go of the door, and Hakon released him.

"Relax." The ghost of a smile crossed his lips. "The Demon won't hurt him."

Somehow Logan believed him. He would have to trust in his captain.

More sounds drifted from the captain's quarters. Logan closed his eyes, trying to block them out. Really, he wished he could just leave them to it. The sounds coming from the other side of the door were not for his ears, but he couldn't bear the thought of leaving his captain to the mercy of these two rogues if something went wrong.

"Here."

When Logan opened his eyes, Hakon was sitting on the floor, holding out the bottle of wine he'd swiped from the captain's table.

"We can't abandon our posts like those other idiots, so we may as well drink. I'm John by the way. John Hakon."

That name was familiar but Logan couldn't quite place it. He slid to the floor beside John and took the bottle.

"Does this happen often?"

John shrugged. Logan took a deep gulp of the strong wine.

"Seems a bit different this time," John said.

Logan passed the bottle back as they heard the deeper voice of the Demon. John raised a salute and drank.

They stayed drinking in silence until the sounds in the captain's quarters died down. John's dark gaze slid toward him again, head lolling against the door.

"I have a feeling we'll be seeing a lot of each other."

～

THEY'D FINISHED the bottle of wine by the time the Deep Water Demon emerged from Captain Rowan's quarters. He smoothed his black hair back from his forehead, looking like a self-satisfied cat, and glanced between the two of them on the floor.

"Come in."

Logan and John scrambled to their feet and followed him into the room. Everything looked as they had left it. The chair had been righted; the bed was made for once. Logan zeroed in on Rowan sitting at the table. He was fully clothed but looked a bit disheveled, and his black shirt had been replaced by a white one with lace at the cuffs. Logan's eyes swiveled to the Demon, whose jacket was slightly open over his chest, no shirt underneath. The man was practically glowing.

"We've reached an agreement," Rowan announced. He twirled his dagger in his fingers, looking at Logan directly. Rowan quickly laid out the terms, which seemed to greatly favor the *Siren*. What was the Demon benefitting from this? Was the sex enough for him? Logan narrowed his eyes.

"Hakon." The Demon leaned back against the edge of the table. He was looking awfully comfortable already. The tension between the two captains seemed to have mellowed for now. "You're acting captain of the *Kraken* for a few hours. Go and fetch Mister Beckett, and see that he knows the terms."

John, for his part, looked completely unaffected by the wine, even as Logan's head swam slightly. He nodded in agreement.

Rowan tilted his head to look past the first mates into the corridor, eyebrows raised.

"Where's Fox?"

"I don't know," Logan admitted.

Rowan rolled his eyes. "Probably off causing problems," he muttered. "No matter. Logan, see that the physician—Beckett, was it?—gets settled in the infirmary, and take stock of our damage and casualties. I'll be out shortly."

"Yes, sir."

Logan and John left the room, Logan looking back as he closed the door behind them. He caught sight of the Demon moving toward Rowan as if to embrace him, mumbling something too low for Logan to hear.

Logan did as he was told. He escorted John back to the *Kraken* and waited as he gave orders to the crew and handed over a tall man carrying a bag full of medical supplies. Logan appointed a few crew members to receive the supplies the Demon had promised. All the while, his mind whirled around and around what was happening. He didn't trust this. It was too easy. He loved Rowan dearly but couldn't imagine that he'd be so good in bed the infamous Deep Water Demon would give them such favorable terms without a catch.

He escorted the physician down to the infirmary, got a report from their own ship's doctor—an old man who wasn't quite up to the task anymore—and checked on the injured men.

After doing everything he'd been ordered to do—and delivering his report to Rowan, who was still holed up talking quietly and closely with the Demon—he went to search for Fox and the missing *Kraken* crew member. He had an inkling of what they were up to and hoped he was wrong. But it had been hard to miss the immediate tension between the two men as soon as the *Kraken* crew member stepped aboard. He checked the galley first. No luck. So he made his way to the cabin he shared with Fox.

It wasn't strange knocking on his own door. He was used to Fox entertaining guests in their room. Logan had spent many a night bundled up on a fold-out cot in the corner of Rowan's room as Fox entertained another in an endless string of lovers.

Fox answered the door, rubbing his eyes. His shirt was askew, and when Logan looked past him into the cabin, he saw the *Kraken* crewman pulling on his trousers.

Well, he'd found them at least.

"Captain wants you," he said, pointedly not looking at the other man.

"Right." Fox didn't even have the grace to look embarrassed about being caught fraternizing. Fox was never embarrassed.

"Now," Logan said.

Fox glanced back into the room where the other man had managed to finish dressing.

"Lead the way."

"Everyone's lost their damn minds," Logan grumbled as he led the pair down the short hall to the captain's quarters.

～

THE CAPTAINS TOOK one look at Fox and the other man and seemed to know exactly what had happened.

A wry smile twitched at Rowan's lips. "I see you've kept yourself entertained while you waited," he quipped.

The *Kraken* crew member blushed, but Fox only tilted his head, a lock of wavy brown hair falling into his eyes; he too had clocked what the captains had been up to in his absence.

"I need you to keep an eye on the physician we have on loan from the *Kraken.*"

"Aye, Captain." Fox looked a bit ridiculous, his shirt still rumpled.

There was a beat of silence. The Demon's cool gaze flicked between Fox and his crewman.

"Gaël, stay aboard and assist Mister Beckett in his duties," he said smoothly, glancing briefly at Rowan for approval, to which he received a slight nod.

"Yes, Captain," Gaël replied, trying to keep a smile off his face.

"Unbelievable," Logan muttered under his breath.

CHAPTER 5

JULY 29TH, 1666

Henri blinked slowly from his place at the far end of the infirmary as Logan entered, followed by a tall stranger carrying an expensive looking leather bag. Logan strode over to Old Joe, the *Siren*'s doctor, looking annoyed and had a quiet word with him. The stranger remained near the door, his eyes shyly but keenly sweeping over the patients.

Old Joe had given Henri something for the pain, but it was mostly just making him drowsy and a bit nauseous. Other people were being tended to before him. Open wounds took precedence over burns. He knew that, but it didn't lessen the pain. The burns on his leg were screaming, and there was a deeper pain radiating up his leg that he didn't want to think about just yet, all of it only slightly dulled by the drug.

Logan finished speaking to Old Joe and stepped back over to the door.

"Everyone, this is Mister Beckett," he said in a voice clear enough to carry through the room but not loud enough to wake the patients who were already sleeping. "Our captain has come to an *agreement*"—there was a strange emphasis on that word, but Henri couldn't place why—"with the captain of the *Kraken*, and they have loaned us their fancy ship's physician as part of it." With that, Logan gestured the physician forward and left.

Mister Beckett remained at the door for a moment, his fingers twisting the handle of his leather bag nervously. Then he stepped over to where Old Joe was cleaning a wound.

"Where would you like me to begin?" he asked politely, looking over the stooped man's shoulder.

Old Joe looked up from his work with rheumy eyes, as if he'd already forgotten why the man was there.

"Anywhere, anywhere," he muttered, flipping one bloody hand dismissively. A drop of blood flicked off his fingers to land on Beckett's cheek. "I already bandaged most of 'em. The ones that survived anyway." The last words held a not so subtle accusation, as if Beckett himself was personally responsible for the actions of the *Kraken*'s captain and crew. Beckett stepped back, then seemed to find his resolve and made his way slowly from bed to bed, checking on Old Joe's work and assessing the most dire cases. Henri watched him between heavy eyelids as he made his way closer. There was a faint smile on the man's face as if he was pleasantly surprised, or mildly amused, by the old ship doctor's work. He adjusted a few things here and there. And finally he made it to the hard cot where Henri lay.

Henri blinked up at him, trying to focus on his features through eyes bleary with pain and whatever drug Old Joe had given him. The doctor had a round, pleasant face, framed by sandy, brownish-blond hair that fell over his forehead. He was tall. Probably even taller than Henri's considerable height and his skin was paler than any seafaring man had a right to be. He was the cleanest person in the room by far, as if he'd spent the entirety of the battle safely tucked away like a pearl in an oyster shell. In contrast, Henri and the other *Siren* crew members were streaked with gunpowder, ash, and blood.

Unfortunately, Henri was intimately familiar with the infirmary after a battle. He'd always been a bit accident prone, and living on an active pirate ship only exacerbated that. His mother had never wanted him to follow in his parents' pirating footsteps, but they were both gone now, and he was here.

Henri's mother would have scolded him if she saw him in this state, lying on a cot in the belly of a pirate ship, all drugged up against the pain, his clothes fire blackened around the edges. He was sure a few of his locs were singed at the ends too.

Beckett tilted his head, hazel eyes meeting Henri's brown ones, gaze soft but assessing. Then he saw Henri's leg.

"Good god man, have they not even cleaned this?" Shocked, he took in the raw burns across Henri's skin between the scorched edges of his pant leg. He reached out, fingers hesitating for just a moment before prodding the edge of one of the burns on Henri's shin.

Henri hissed in pain, and Beckett's gaze flicked back to his face.

"Broken too, I reckon. We'll have to clean and splint it carefully if you don't want to have a limp. I think there will be some scarring though."

He retreated to grab his bag and a pot of boiled water. He set both to the side and pulled out a pair of wicked looking sheers. Henri flinched, remembering for the first time that this man was technically an enemy.

"I'll have to cut away your pant leg," Beckett explained. Henri stayed tense but nodded to show he understood. Beckett's straightforward demeanor put Henri a bit more at ease, despite his current circumstances.

"What's your name? Mine's Robin."

Henri opened his mouth to speak but found his throat unbearably dry and raw. All that came out was a pathetic croak.

"Smoke inhalation too." Robin Beckett shook his head. He left for a moment and returned with a cup of water. "Can you sit up?"

Henri was able to raise himself to his elbows, the fracture in his leg flaring painfully with every movement. Robin hovered like a worried hen, then seemed to decide something. He cupped the back of Henri's neck with one hand to steady his head as he held the cup up to his lips. Henri took a few grateful gulps before collapsing onto his back once more.

"Henri," he managed to rasp.

"Okay, Henri." Robin's voice was deep and gentle. "Here's what we'll do..."

~

THE PHYSICIAN expertly cut away Henri's pant leg up to his thigh, leaving him feeling a bit exposed. But as soon as Robin touched a damp cloth to the burns to begin cleaning, Henri forgot all about modesty. Excruciating pain shot through his raw nerves as Robin meticulously cleaned the burns and set about picking bits of scorched sailcloth and pant threads away from his skin with tweezers. He spread a bitter smelling ointment from a jar over the skin and bandaged it thoroughly.

Then it was time to set the bone.

"This will hurt badly." Robin warned him, handing Henri a leather strap to bite down on.

Robin grasped his leg. Henri's fingers gripped the edge of the hard cot and he nodded. With a deft movement Robin realigned the bone. Pain, as deep and terrible as any he'd ever experienced shot up Henri's leg. And everything went black.

~

WHEN HENRI CAME TO, Robin was sitting beside him, dabbing his forehead with a cool damp cloth. Henri's eyes fluttered open, and the physician's face was the first thing he saw. His gaze flicked down to where his leg was neatly splinted with two pieces of wood that snugly fit the contours of his leg from ankle to just below the knee.

"Water..."

Robin seemed almost startled that Henri was awake but fetched a cup of water swiftly. He helped Henri sit up with a firm hand on his back. Henri's head swam with vertigo, but he managed.

"Don't you have other patients?" Henri asked when he'd managed to get his voice back. It was still raspy and smoke damaged.

"I attended them already. You were out for quite a while."

Henri's eyes swept through the small infirmary, realizing that about half the injured men were no longer there, and neither was Old Joe. Apprehension spiked in his gut as he remembered that despite Robin's gentle demeanor, he worked for the Deep Water Demon.

"Old Joe is resting, and the others have been patched up and sent back to their quarters." Robin explained quickly, seeing Henri's perplexed expression. He was only one of four patients now, the other three sleeping. His face heated.

"There's no shame in passing out," Robin assured him, seeming to read his mind once again. He frowned. "A broken leg is no small thing. You'll be out of commission for months. I hope your captain is the patient sort."

While some pirate captains would ditch injured and non-useful crew members at the first opportunity, the Ghost Hawk, despite his fierce reputation, was not like that. He cared for his crew like family. Better than family, for Henri was the only pirate among them who had been raised well and with love. One had only to look at Old Joe, a man who was well past his prime as a doctor, to realize that. Soon enough it would be the crew taking care of Old Joe, not the other way around, and they would be happy to do it.

Captain Rowan had been searching for a replacement doctor at every port for a while now, so Old Joe could enjoy his retirement. But not just any old sawbones would do. Rowan wanted someone competent and caring. Someone who wouldn't be quick to condemn an injured man. Someone who actually washed his hands with some regularity, which was a concerning rarity in the seafaring world.

Henri let his gaze sweep over Robin when the man wasn't looking. It seemed that they had found one such physician, if only temporarily.

Before he could respond to Robin's worries, another man he didn't know swept into the room. Robin scrambled to his feet as the man made a beeline for him.

"I need you." The man was not as tall as Robin but held an air of elegance and superiority. His black hair was slightly rumpled, but his coat was immaculate, and he wore a large ruby in one earlobe.

Robin frowned slightly, his eyes sliding to Henri then back to the man. His posture straightened up even more.

"Captain," Robin said before the other man could continue. Henri flinched, realizing this was the infamous Deep Water Demon, freely walking around their ship like he owned the place. What kind of deal had Rowan struck? "With all due respect, I have patients to attend to. So unless you've seriously injured this one, I don't have time to care for your conquests," Robin finished.

"Conqu—" Henri choked, sitting up quickly, causing his leg to flare with pain. "What the *hell* did you do to our captain ..." His head swam with sudden dizziness and Robin guided him back down to the cot with a gentle hand on his shoulder.

The Deep Water Demon watched him with sharp mirthful eyes.

"Nothing horrible," he said nonchalantly, "I expect he'll be down to check on you once he can walk again." He smirked at the flare of rage in Henri's eyes.

Then his attention turned back to Robin. "At least give me something for his back. A hot water bottle maybe. Everything seems quite calm now." Robin nodded and busied himself with preparing a hot compress. When the Demon got it in his hands, he swept from the room without another word.

Robin sat heavily on his stool next to Henri's cot.

"That was the Demon?" Henri asked incredulously.

Robin nodded.

"Why's he here?"

Robin looked distinctly uncomfortable for a moment, mulling over how he should answer.

"I, ah... It seems our captains have found a common ground." He sighed, running a frustrated hand through his hair.

"Being mysterious bastards?" Henri guessed.

Robin's surprised laugh was like sunlight in a storm. Henri didn't know how, but they seemed to have become fast friends. His earlier anxiety dissipated the more he talked with Robin.

"They're lovers," Robin answered after his laughing fit had subsided.

"What?!" Henri's shout cut off with a coughing fit that had Robin rushing to get him more water. Several of the other patients stirred but did not wake. Henri's mind was reeling. He'd never known Rowan to take lovers, let alone his arch rival who he'd been determined to sink to the bottom of the ocean just earlier today.

Before Robin could answer, the door burst open, and Fox barreled through dragging yet another stranger by the hand.

"Henri!" he screeched, before noticing the other patients and lowering his voice. They must have been on some great drugs if they hadn't woken up by now. He stopped beside Henri's cot, his fingers twined with the stranger's. "I'm glad you're okay!" His gaze swept over Henri's bandaged and splinted leg. "Or...are you okay?"

"I'll survive," Henri answered, his brows furrowing in confusion. There was so much happening, and he was so tired. He wished he could go back to his own cabin and sleep for the next week. But Fox's familiar, wide smile was a balm to his pain. His friend's sunshine-y energy could always brighten his mood.

Fox turned to the stranger. "This is my friend Henri," he said, his free hand furling out to present Henri like a kid showing off a partic-ularly interesting rock he'd found. The stranger nodded in greeting, looking a bit overwhelmed by Fox's enthusiasm. Fox turned back to

Henri. "And this is my..." He paused for a moment, mouth open. "...Gaël," he finished.

"Nice to meet you," Gaël said with a wry smile on his face.

"You too," Henri croaked.

Fox's eyes slid to Robin. "You must be the doc."

"I'm Robin Beckett." Robin held out his hand for Fox to shake, but Fox's fingers were still entangled in Gaël's, so Robin dropped it.

"We've been assigned to keep an eye on you," Gaël explained to his crewmate.

"The hardest part is over," Robin said. "That fellow over there has a fever, and Henri will need help getting around and frequent bandage changes. It's mostly just maintenance from here on out." He paused. "Am I staying?"

"Seems like it," Gaël said. He and Fox shared a look.

"Logan is taking your room for a little while," Fox piped up to Henri.

"What? Why?"

Fox looked at Gaël again and smiled. A small spark of realization flickered in Henri's mind. It seemed the captain wasn't the only one who had gained a lover from the *Kraken*.

"Never mind."

CHAPTER 6

JULY 29TH, 1666

Rowan stayed holed up in his cabin for longer than was strictly necessary. As soon as his clothes were back on and the post-coital bliss had faded, he'd faced the prospect of going back out and being captain with the knowledge that the crew had probably just heard him get absolutely wrecked by the pirate captain he'd always professed to hate. It was just too embarrassing.

He'd never really had a lover before. And that's what Yves seemed to be getting at with the terms of this truce. Rowan didn't know how to act. He'd had flings and one-night stands of course, and Fox had certainly made no secret of flirting with him over the years they'd known each other. But he had a personal policy against sleeping with his crew. He'd kept everything discreet and away from the ship. Now the whole crew knew the details of his sex life, and it was mortifying but not enough to cast Yves aside.

At some point Yves left and returned with a plate of food and a heated compress for Rowan's back. He set the food down on the table and handed the compress over as he settled across from Rowan.

"Your men seem to be on the mend," he said, picking up an olive and popping it into his mouth. When Rowan raised a questioning eyebrow at him, he clarified, "I stopped in at the infirmary to get something for your back."

Rowan placed the compress against his lower back, then took a biscuit from the plate. The soreness in his back twinged. Yves barely hid his amusement at Rowan's wince. He'd never bottomed before, so he wasn't sure if this was normal. But Yves didn't seem overly concerned, so he resolved not to worry about it. Besides, every time the pain twinged it reminded him of the reason behind it.

Rowan took a bite of hard biscuit and wished they hadn't run out of jam a few weeks ago. They sat in silence for a moment, both nibbling at the food. Rowan was surprised there was no awkwardness between them. Sure, he was still wary of the Demon's intentions, but it almost felt comfortable just sitting here in silence.

While Yves was gone, Logan had brought Rowan's hawk Nephele in, and she was now resting on her ornate brass perch near the bookshelves. Yves looked over to her to find the golden hawk eyes already fixed on him. She cocked her head. Then, seeming to decide she didn't like him, puffed up her feathers.

"I have to ask," Yves said, not taking his eyes off Nephele's threatening display. "Did your name come before the hawk? Or did the hawk come before the name?"

Rowan didn't have the energy to go over and soothe his pet. Yves and Nephele continued to eye each other suspiciously, both beasts of prey fighting over him as the morsel.

"The name came before the bird." Rowan chuckled. "I coincidentally ran into a ship carrying her a few months after I first got that name. I tried to free her, but she took a liking to me."

Nephele shifted on the perch and flapped her powerful wings once. Then settled.

"Looks like she's no fan of yours however," Rowan said.

Yves rose from his chair and strode over to the perch.

"Pretty but deadly." He reached out as if to let the hawk sniff him like a cat, and received a snap of her razor-sharp beak instead, only pulling his hand back just in time to avoid losing a finger. Yves turned back to Rowan, eyes shining. "She suits you."

He returned to his seat, and Nephele settled again, keeping a wary eye on the suave intruder.

"So what are your plans?" Yves asked once he'd settled. He leaned forward, bright eyes intent on Rowan's face.

Rowan thought for a moment, trying to parse what exactly Yves meant. Finally, he settled on the obvious.

"I'll have to dock in Lasland and make repairs." Rowan sighed. He really hadn't planned on making port again for a while, but between the damage from the cannons and fire, he didn't have much choice.

Yves's sparkly eyes held a hint of mischief. Or maybe anticipation?

"I know a place." He was looking at Rowan so intently, and his fingers twitched as if he wanted to reach for Rowan's hand. "Would you come with me?"

It seemed a simple enough question, but Yves's body language told him it was not simple at all. There was some hidden depth to it, something serious that Rowan didn't understand.

"Where?" he asked.

A wry smile graced Yves's full lips. "It's a surprise."

Rowan eyed him skeptically. They'd known each other for less than a day and though the tension between them had turned from hatred and rivalry to sexual energy, that didn't mean he suddenly trusted the one pirate on the seas more notorious than him.

Sensing Rowan's hesitation, Yves got up from his seat and sat on the edge of the table within arm's reach.

"You don't trust me," he said. He didn't seem mad about it but nor was he happy.

Rowan shook his head.

"Good." Yves couldn't seem to keep a smile off his face. He reached to take Rowan's hand in his. "I don't expect you to trust me. Who would? But you trusted your instinct thus far and those instincts brought us together. I promise no harm will come to you." He kissed the back of Rowan's fingers, maintaining eye contact. "Plus you said I could see you again."

Rowan couldn't help the shiver that rippled through him at the other man's touch. He tried to avert his eyes from Yves's handsome face so he could think clearly. But Yves's fingers tightened around his, and he looked back up.

How much was the word of a pirate worth? Most people would say they were all liars and thieves. The Deep Water Demon was the most infamous of them all, but he'd kept his word thus far, and his crew seemed as loyal as Rowan's was. One didn't inspire such loyalty with money and fear alone.

Rowan mulled it over. Docking in a legitimate port was always a risk for any pirate, especially while they were vulnerable and couldn't sail away at a moment's notice. If the Demon had some secret safe haven wouldn't it be worth the risk of trusting him?

Besides, he was the Ghost Hawk, he could disappear if it all went south, right?

The brush of Yves's thumb across his knuckles brought him back to the present moment, and he refocused on Yves's face.

"I'll come with you," he answered. "But the moment I sense danger, we're gone."

CHAPTER 7

JULY 29TH, 1666

For the first time in years, Yves Francois LeSauvage didn't know what the hell he was doing.

As the Deep Water Demon, he was always in control. Focused. Even with his many sexual conquests, he never lost sight of who he was supposed to be. He never got attached.

So *why* had he invited the Ghost Hawk, his rival, to his safe haven?

He'd done it without thinking, simply following instinct. John would probably crack Yves's skull open with his bare hands when he heard the news. But despite the fact that it was clearly a terrible idea, Yves didn't intend to rescind his offer. His first mate would just have to trust him, just as he was asking Rowan to trust him.

Yves sat up against the headboard of Rowan's small bed. He'd convinced Rowan to let him spend just one night before he was exiled back to his own ship. He couldn't begrudge the other captain's mistrust of him. *He* wouldn't be so trusting if the situation were reversed. When he'd decided to seduce the Ghost Hawk—a strategic decision spurred on by curiosity more than anything—he thought it would simply be an extension of their rivalry. A quick fuck to get the aggression out. An outlet for the intensity between them. He had never intended to be seduced in turn. Fucking Rowan had only heightened his curiosity, and all the violence Yves had planned to

59

inflict upon him to ensure his surrender now only lingered in the darkest recesses of Yves's soul, slumbering and satiated.

Being allowed to spend the night was a victory, and Yves hadn't pushed his luck by trying to seduce Rowan again. Even though he wanted to ravish the delicately handsome captain till he was whimpering and broken, Yves knew Rowan was in no condition to do it again so soon. Usually Yves would not have cared overmuch about the comfort of another beyond how it would affect his ability to get what he wanted. But right now, the things he wanted were jumbled and contradictory. He wanted to break Rowan but not hurt him. He wanted to keep him near and throw him away. And none of it made sense. They'd known each other for less than a day, yet Yves felt like he'd been hunting this man his whole life. He wanted to peel back the layers of Rowan's exterior and chew on the meat of his essence. Perhaps if Yves devoured him, the contradictions would clear away.

These thoughts rolled in Yves's head like a rock rolling through the tide, edges smoothing over time. Yet the more Yves's thoughts were tossed, the more jagged they became. His gaze caught on the murderous yellow hawk eyes watching him from the corner. The bird seemed able to read his intent more clearly than he could. She was ready to swoop in and claw his eyes out if he made a wrong move toward her master. Yves stared her down for a moment, then looked away to the stunning man sleeping by his side.

Rowan slept like a misbehaving toddler, sprawled on his back across the bed with his legs akimbo and his arms thrown over his head. One side of his open shirt had slipped down over his shoulder, exposing the top of the tattoo that resembled the skull and wings on his flag. Yves might have thought this chaotic sleeping position undignified in anyone else, but instead he found it strangely captivating. In sleep, all the ruthlessness of the Ghost Hawk had drained away from Rowan's face and left only innocence behind. It only served to heighten Yves's confusion further.

He let his eyes trace over Rowan's face and body. He was shorter than Yves by a few inches. Nevertheless, it gave his sleeping form an aura of something tiny and fierce, like a feral kitten. Most of his skin was tanned, but for the most intimate parts which remained pale white and unscorched by the unforgiving sun. His white-blond hair, which was usually pulled into a tail at the top to expose the close-shaved sides, had come loose from its tie and was now splayed across the pillows like a halo. His cheekbones were broad and smooth, framing a pointed, pixie-like nose, and his eyebrows were expressive even in sleep.

Yves watched Rowan's chest rise and fall, remembering the feel of his naked body. His surprisingly firm chest, slender waist, and gloriously plump ass. Yves shook his head, turning his eyes away before he got to the point where he'd have to wake this sleeping menace and ravish him all over again.

Yves was never intentionally cruel to his lovers as other men with power were. He prided himself on being gentlemanly and generous. But he wasn't sweet, nor doting. There would never be someone he couldn't leave behind. Never more than physical attraction or the thrill of a challenge. Anything beyond that was impossible. Such things served only to be devoured by the darkness that threaded its tentacles through his soul. Yet for Rowan, the darkness stirred up silt with every breath, choking out any scrap of reason or calculation.

He ran his finger over the scratches Rowan's nails had dug into his shoulders. The man had certainly left his mark.

~

July 30th, 1666

The next morning, after giving orders to Gaël and Robin, Yves was exiled back to the *Kraken's Fury*. John met him in the luxurious captain's quarters. When Yves had first set foot on the *Siren Song* he'd found it quaint, but now looking over his own spacious quarters which spanned three separate rooms, he found himself missing the coziness of Rowan's room.

"I assume we're going home for repairs," John said matter-of-factly. That was what Yves liked about him. He was competent and didn't mince words; it must have been all that navy training he'd had before his disgrace.

"Yes, and the *Siren Song* is coming with us."

The first mate was silent for a moment, just staring at his captain with those intense eyes.

"Captain..." he said warningly.

"Spare me the lecture," Yves interrupted. "I know it's a stupid idea."

"And yet you're still going to do it."

Yves flashed him the charming smile that had never worked on him. "I gave my word; it's already done." He knew he was being irrational. But the thought of letting Rowan go sent his guts twisting with something that felt worryingly like rage.

"I don't think you've fully considered the danger here." John's voice was low and stern, anger simmering beneath the surface. "A secret can only remain a secret if no one talks. How do you know you can trust him, or his crew for that matter?"

Yves was starting to regret not just having a yes man who followed orders as a first mate.

"I just do." He was about to continue to lay out his feeble arguments about alliances, but John cut him off.

"You're thinking with your dick," he snarled. "I never thought *my* captain would unnecessarily risk his crew for a quick fuck with some pretty boy. I know you've followed him for a while but now you've had him. So get over your obsession and kill the son-of-a-bitch so we can move on."

Yves was stunned into silence. John had always been blunt and practical, but he'd never talked to his captain like *this*. In the five years John had been his first mate, he'd never wavered in his loyalties. But of course as the only person Yves could reasonably call a friend, he'd seen the changes in Yves since the Ghost Hawk had started sailing, even if no one else noticed.

Yves had been interested in the legend of the Ghost Hawk since he'd first heard the stories many years ago. A young upstart of a pirate. Clever, swift, ruthless. He haunted the coasts like a fox stalking a chicken coop. Despite their differences Yves had developed a sense of rivalry with the other captain. He didn't know why. They were so different—they didn't even run in the same circles. Maybe he'd seen a reflection of himself in the tales told about the Ghost Hawk. Maybe he admired him. But he'd become fascinated by Rowan before he'd even learned his name. Like him, the Ghost Hawk had started from nothing and succeeded. His legend had become almost as big as the Deep Water Demon.

And when the Ghost Hawk had picked off a prize that Yves had his eye on, something finally snapped. His rivalry morphed into obsession, and his covetous eye turned from treasure to the Ghost Hawk himself. So he set a trap. He invaded the Hawk's territory, purposely taunting and provoking him. He knew it would drive the other captain out into deeper water looking for revenge and glory. Then, Yves hunted him. He hadn't expected to be presented the *Siren Song* and her intriguing captain on a silver platter, but when he saw the little ship waiting there acting helpless, it was more temptation than he could resist.

At first he'd simply wanted to test the man. To see what the Ghost Hawk was made of. Then as the tides of battle had turned, he'd wanted to annihilate him. But when he'd finally seen the other captain face-to-face, a new understanding had hit him like a punch to the gut. He couldn't beat the Ghost Hawk. Not because he didn't have the power, but because he didn't want to. He wanted to know the Ghost Hawk, wanted to explore every inch of him, body and mind. Wanted him for himself.

The Deep Water Demon stepped in close to his first mate, glaring at him with new determination. There was no shame nor hesitation in his eyes.

"You know I never ask you to do as I say without reason. I can't explain why I am doing this, but I need you to trust me as you always have before. If my belief in him is misplaced, you can deal with it as you wish."

John stood defiant for a moment, and Yves thought he would have a mutiny on his hands right here and now. But then John took a step back.

"Okay, I'll trust you. But know I won't hesitate to put a bullet in his pretty little head if I have to."

CHAPTER 8

AUGUST 7TH, 1666

A bead of sweat dripped down Henri's temple as he sat on the wooden crate Fox had hauled onto deck for him. Pain flared up his leg as he shifted, but there was no position of comfort to be had. He just had to endure until his leg healed enough. Standing by his side, Robin shifted as well, as if sharing Henri's discomfort. Or maybe it was because of the sun currently beating down on their heads as the *Siren* bobbed on the waves, a brief respite in their journey beside the *Kraken* toward an unknown destination.

The day was much too sunny for a funeral.

Henri's mother's funeral had been sunny too. A gorgeous day in spring. And ever since then, Henri loathed being sad when the weather was good. It stirred up not-so-distant memories he wanted to forget.

The entire crew of the *Siren* stood solemnly on deck, watching as a few crew members carried the sail-shrouded body up from below. It was one of Henri's fellow patients. A man named Jacob who'd had a fever from a wound on his side. Robin and Old Joe had been unable to keep it from turning, and he'd died sometime during the night.

They placed Jacob's body on the gangplank and stepped back. Robin sniffled quietly. Henri knew he was taking this hard. Not only because of professional pride, but because he was empathetic and warmhearted, and he wasn't as used to death as the rest of them. That was more than could be said of most pirates, or doctors for that matter. Over the intervening days since Henri's injury, he'd come to understand that Robin was very different from the average pirate. He spoke softly and properly. He never complained about the constant work of healing, nor of Henri having to ask for help dressing or walking to the head to pee. He never wavered, attending to Henri and the other patients with that small smile perpetually stamped on his mouth.

With the other patients discharged back to their berths, Jacob delirious with fever, and Old Joe taking a well-deserved rest for his old bones, Henri and Robin had grown close over the week or so Henri had been under his care.

Henri's attention was drawn back to the body as Captain Rowan stepped up to the rail beside it. Jacob was wrapped in a length of blue sailcloth from the *Kraken*. The *Siren* didn't have enough of her own to spare after using the remnants of the burned sails to shroud the rest of the dead a week before. Henri had been in too much pain to go to that funeral, but he'd been determined to drag his injured ass to this one. He hadn't known Jacob well, but still his chest tightened to see a fellow crew member shrouded in the sails of the ship that had ultimately killed him.

Rowan gazed down at the body solemnly for a moment, then looked out across his waiting crew. "Today we have lost our brother, Jacob Stuart. We will not forget his valiant service. I commend his body to the sea." He laid a hand on Jacob's shoulder. "May the currents bear you home, wherever that may be."

He nodded to the men who'd carried the body, and they tipped up the head of the plank. The body slid over the side of the ship and splashed down into the sun-dazzled water, quickly sinking beneath the waves with the weight of the cannonball that was sewn into the foot of the shroud.

Several crew members said prayers quietly in their own languages to their own gods. Others dispersed back to their duties or leisure. Rowan moved through the crowd, making a beeline toward Henri and Robin.

"Glad you could make it," Rowan said when he reached them. He'd been checking on Henri and the other patients daily, maybe out of guilt for sleeping with the enemy, maybe because he genuinely cared about their wellbeing. Probably both. For all the trouble this situation had caused, their captain looked none the worse for wear. In fact, there was a new spark in his eye, though he pointedly avoided any mention of the Deep Water Demon. Henri didn't want to pry. He figured his friend would tell him in due time. But that didn't mean Henri was capable of stopping the incessant ball of questions and teasing that was Fox.

"I'm glad too," Henri replied, wincing slightly as the ship rocked. "Though I think I could use a nap."

Rowan smiled, then glanced up as a whistle sounded from the *Kraken,* hailing them. They all listened to the message, *All crew assemble.*

"I guess that means me," Robin said. In the endeavor to get Henri up onto deck, he'd forgotten a hat and the bridge of his nose was already turning pink in the sun. Robin frowned. "Let's get you back to the infirmary before I go."

"No, no. I can rope the captain into helping me," Henri joked with a dramatic sigh. He removed his own hat and plopped it on Robin's blond head. "But take this, or you'll be red as a cooked lobster when you get back. We can't expect you to take care of a burn victim if you're burned yourself."

Robin's laugh was small and creaky, barely any sound escaping. "Thank you. I'll make sure to return it in good condition."

A spark kindled in Henri's chest at the unexpected pleasure of making his new friend laugh.

A small boat had tied up to the side of the *Siren,* and the oarsman called out to Robin and Gaël. Robin waved to him then turned to Rowan. "Can you help him get back to the infirmary, Captain?"

Rowan blinked, seemingly startled from his thoughts. "Of course. Best not keep the Demon waiting."

The Demon. Even his own crew called him that. Henri wondered if Rowan knew his actual name.

Robin patted Henri on the shoulder and loped off toward the waiting boat. Henri felt his absence more keenly than he'd expected, but Fox sidled over soon enough. The space beside him looked strangely empty without Gaël there to fill it.

"Need help?" Fox asked, and both Henri and Rowan nodded. It was all well and good being helped around by Robin, who was of similar height to him, but Fox and Rowan were both quite a bit shorter, and he was still very unsteady on his feet. He needed all the help he could get. His two friends took up positions on either side of him, bracing their shoulders beneath his arms, and hauled him to his feet. They made their way slowly below deck, sharp pain shooting up Henri's leg with every step. Finally they made it to the infirmary and deposited Henri safely onto his cot.

"Do you need anything before I go?" Rowan asked. Henri shook his head and Rowan ducked out of the infirmary.

Henri winced as he lifted his leg onto the cot, massaging his knee above the top of the splint to ease some of the tension. Fox hung back, looking a bit lost.

"Well, we've both got nothing to do. Might as well keep each other company," Fox said, producing a deck of cards from his pocket.

The journey onto deck and back had wiped out Henri's energy, and all he really wanted was to take a nice long nap till Robin came back. But Fox and Gaël had been taking their infirmary-minding duties very unseriously in the past week, often sneaking off to do gods knew what. And Henri had barely had the opportunity to talk with Fox alone. So he nodded.

They settled in to play cards sitting on either end of Henri's cot. Henri's leg still hurt, so he extended it in front of him, his foot elevated on Fox's lap.

They'd played several hands, Fox cackling like a banshee whenever he won, when Henri finally broached the subject.

"So...Gaël..."

Fox's already bright face lit up at the mention of his new lover.

"Jealous?" Fox joked, but Henri could tell he was pleased he'd brought it up.

"Terribly," Henri said, trying to keep a straight face.

Fox patted Henri's foot comfortingly. "You had your chance," he said smugly.

It was true, when Henri had first come to the *Siren Song* almost three years ago, Fox had been all over him, and Henri had turned him down. After that, Fox had diverted his endless energy into becoming friends.

"So anyway," Henri continued his line of questioning, "you seem to have become close with Gaël pretty fast. Are you finally settling down?"

"Well I knew him before..." Fox seemed suddenly shy, which was unlike him.

"Before? Like before the *Siren?*"

Fox nodded, concentrating on his cards.

"Wait..." Henri leaned forward, trying to catch his friend's eye. "He's not *that* bastard is he? The one who left you in Wave Harbor?"

Fox pursed his lips.

"Fox..."

"Yes, yes he's that bastard," Fox admitted. "But he apologized!"

"I'll kill him," Henri growled. He tried to rise from the cot, but Fox leaned forward and planted his hands on Henri's shoulders, forcing him back down.

"You'll hurt yourself!"

They stared at each other until Fox finally seemed to decide that Henri wouldn't hobble off on a mission of revenge any time soon. He leaned forward and pecked Henri on the tip of the nose before settling back into his spot and repositioning Henri's injured leg.

"He apologized," Fox said again.

"And you forgave him?"

Fox blinked at him innocently. "Well...um...he apologized *really* well."

Henri had never known Fox to be the bashful sort, but the man was blushing fiercely, which made Henri blush in turn. It really must have been some apology to erase so many years of resentment.

Gods, everyone seemed so sex-crazed these days. This was supposed to be a pirate ship, not a pleasure cruise.

"Let me shoot him just once," Henri argued. "I won't hit anything vital; I just wanna teach him a lesson."

"You don't think the captain would eviscerate him if he hurt me again?" Fox asked.

"The captain is...distracted right now. I'm not."

Fox raised a skeptical eyebrow but said nothing.

"So it's settled," Henri said. "I'll shoot him."

"But I love him!" Fox blurted, his hand immediately clapping over his mouth in horror as if he'd just admitted something unbearably embarrassing.

They went back to playing cards, the awkward silence stretching.

"Let me at least punch him," Henri said after a while, smiling at his friend.

Fox looked up and smiled back, taking this statement for what it was, a grudging acceptance of his relationship.

"As long as you don't damage his pretty face."

"Deal."

~

F OX WAS CALLED AWAY before Robin returned, and Henri grew bored exceedingly fast. His healing skin itched under the bandages, but he knew he'd get scolded if he scratched it. So he laid back and stared at the ceiling, trying to keep his mind occupied by tracing the ripples and whorls in the boards.

It seemed everyone was finding love in unlikely places these days. Or if not love, then at least something beyond mere attraction. Henri chewed his bottom lip. He'd never been in love, never really even thought much about it. But now two of his best friends were preoccupied with their lovers, and Logan was no doubt busy putting out all the fires the other two caused. All while Henri was stuck here with a broken leg staring at the ceiling. For the first time he could remember since joining the crew of the *Siren Song*, Henri was lonely.

When the door to the infirmary cracked open and Robin slipped through, Henri couldn't help the smile that spread across his face.

"You're back."

Robin smiled back, padding across the wooden floor like a puppy returning to his master. "I am," he confirmed. "How are you? How's the leg?"

"You haven't been gone that long. I'm not going to perish from an itchy leg," Henri chided.

Robin busied himself with gathering supplies. "Maybe not, but it is time to change the dressings."

Henri nodded, taking the supplies that Robin handed to him and laying them out next to his leg on the cot. Robin settled onto the end of the cot that Fox had recently vacated.

Henri only winced a little as Robin began to remove the bandages from the burns. The first few days of this had hurt a lot. But now it wasn't so bad. Robin's hands were careful and practiced. He liked watching Robin work. When Robin was concentrating, the tip of his tongue slid to the left corner of his lip, where it stayed for the duration of the task.

The burns were looking a lot better. A lot less angry. Robin bent low over Henri's injuries, examining them for any sign of infection or other problems. Satisfied that he was healing nicely, Robin wrung out a cloth from the pot of warm water on the stool next to him and began to wash Henri's skin. He cupped Henri's heel in one hand, gently turning his leg back and forth, patting it with the damp cloth, careful not to jostle Henri's still healing bone.

"I can do this, you know," Henri said quietly, trying not to disturb the doctor's concentration too badly. He suspected Robin was babying him a bit, feeling guilty for having lost one of his crew members. "I've watched you do it enough times."

"What would I do then?" Robin murmured, not looking up. He placed the cloth to the side and began spreading the healing ointment over Henri's skin. Henri bit his lip as Robin's long fingers brushed the underside of his knee where the burns didn't reach. His leg twitched.

"Did that hurt?" Robin asked.

"No." He usually didn't like being touched much, but somehow with Robin it was okay. Even nice.

Robin moved on to bandage the burns and then carefully replaced the splints to restabilize the broken bone. Finally he looked up.

"I think we should try to get you walking more," he said. "I found a crutch while I was over on the *Kraken*. It would make you more mobile."

Henri felt a slight pang of apprehension at the thought. If he was more mobile, then he could go back to his quarters and Robin might go back to the *Kraken* for good.

He nodded sullenly.

Robin fetched the crutch from the hallway and handed it over.

"Try to stand up using it to support your bad leg," he instructed. "Don't put any weight on the leg yet."

Robin held Henri's arm to help him stand, thumb rubbing over one of the sea serpent tattoos that banded both of his forearms just beneath his elbow. Henri tucked the crutch under his arm on his bad side, swaying a little.

"I'll be right here," Robin assured him. "If you lose your balance, just grab me."

They took a few tentative steps away from Henri's cot together, Henri resting his weight on the crutch when he had to.

"Doing good," Robin encouraged. "Let's try to make it to the door."

It was slow going, and halfway across the room the ship hit a swell, sending Henri violently off balance. The crutch clattered to the floor as he grasped for Robin's supporting arms. But Robin had been knocked off balance too, and they both went down. Henri landed jarringly on his side, covering his head instinctively. Bracing for the impact of the other man falling on him. But it didn't come. Henri uncovered his face and turned to see Robin had caught himself just in time, hands braced on either side of Henri's body. He was hovering, a worried expression on his face. When Henri turned to him they were face-to-face, their noses almost touching.

Robin's ears flushed a deep red, and he scrambled up, careful of Henri's injury.

"Are you okay?" he asked, holding out his hand to help Henri back to his feet.

Henri didn't know. His hip hurt a little bit from its impact with the floor, and his burns were stinging, but there were more pressing matters on his mind now. Namely, why Robin had been so blushy and embarrassed just now.

"I'm fine."

~

AUGUST 10TH, 1666

Henri couldn't seem to shake Robin's blushing face from his mind. Ever since Robin had gotten flustered at their proximity the day they fell, he'd been a bit skittish. And that made Henri want to know more about his new friend. But every time Henri steered the conversation toward Robin's personal life, he found it turned back on him. It left him slightly unsettled but even more curious than before. He lay awake late two nights in a row, listening to Robin's steady breathing a few cots away. Wondering where he'd come from. How had he become a doctor, and why was he now a pirate? He had many questions and no answers.

One morning while they were eating breakfast in companionable silence, Henri's curiosity finally boiled over. He wiggled in the chair, leg propped up on a stool, looking at Robin sitting on the edge of the cot opposite. They'd spent so much time together, talked about so many things. Yet Henri knew nothing of Robin's past, and Robin knew nothing of his.

"You're such a good doctor," Henri began, taking a contemplative bite of his porridge. "You're too good to be a ship doc. How did you fall in with the Demon's crew?" That question in particular had been nagging in the back of Henri's mind for a while. The truth was that most pirates became pirates because they were running from something. This seemed especially true for someone as ill-suited to violence as Robin was.

Robin's head snapped up, eyes wide like a cornered rabbit.

"I—I didn't mean anything by it," Henri quickly backtracked, seeing the near-terror on his friend's face. He hadn't been expecting such a visceral reaction to the question, and Robin's expression sparked a new thread of anxiety in Henri's gut. "I just meant that you're so nice. And you seem so educated..." He knew he was digging himself back into the same topic that had spooked Robin in the first place, but he couldn't seem to stop talking. "You don't have to tell me though," he added.

Robin sighed and placed his half-full bowl on the cot beside him. He looked down, rubbing the back of his neck nervously.

"I was top of my class," he started sheepishly. Glancing up and seeing he had Henri's full attention, his face flushed.

"You don't have to—"

"But I want to," Robin interrupted him. "Only the captain and John know where I came from and...it would be nice for someone else to know too. Besides, we're friends, right?" He cleared his throat, not looking at all like he was sure of this decision, but he plowed ahead anyway. "I come from a wealthy family in Avardel. They sent me to the medical school in Hallenburgh, and I was the top of my class. But my parents had plans for me that I couldn't fulfill." He wasn't looking at Henri any longer; his eyes were on his own hands clutched tight in his lap. "They betrothed me to this woman. She was beautiful, rich. She was even a minor noble. Everything they wanted for me but...I couldn't go through with it. I couldn't stand the thought of marrying her, having children with her, living a lie with her. So last year I ran away." He chuckled self-deprecatingly. "The ship I was on got captured by pirates almost right away. The Demon was going to ransom me back to my parents, but I convinced him to take me on as a doctor instead. Most of my pay goes right back into his coffers to pay off the ransom he would have gotten for me. As long as I earn my keep I won't have to go back."

Henri's mouth hung open in shock, and he didn't seem able to close it. Of all the stories he had come up with in his head, running away from a seemingly perfect life and marriage hadn't been one of them. The wealthy had very few real problems in this world, but Robin's voice was so desperate, so hopeless, when he spoke about the life he'd almost had. He'd gone so far as to run away from all the worldly comforts he could ever want. And he'd rather put himself in danger on the world's most notorious pirate ship than live a lie beside a woman he didn't, maybe couldn't, love.

Would Robin go back to a normal life if he could? He seemed so ill-suited to the violence of piracy. While Henri had chosen this life and taken to it quickly, having been raised on his father's tales of piracy, Robin hadn't had a choice, not really. He was basically an indentured servant to the Demon. If his ship hadn't been captured, he would have settled down in some cozy seaside town by now, healing innocent villagers instead of murderous pirates.

"I understand," Henri said quietly. Maybe he could never truly understand it. Just as Robin could never understand the struggles he'd grown up with either. But they'd both ended up here for one reason or another. They'd both chosen this life. One because he couldn't go back to his family, and one who had taken to the sea in search of family. So right now they were the same.

Robin smiled that small, rueful smile of his.

CHAPTER 9

AUGUST 13TH, 1666

A faint sound woke Henri in the middle of the night. He didn't open his eyes at first. Then the sound came again. A soft grunt. He turned his head and opened his eyes, worried that someone had come to the infirmary with an injury.

But no one was there. And in the soft light of the half-shuttered lantern that was always kept burning by the door, he saw Robin lying facing away from him two cots down. He must have been covered up at first, but the blanket had now slipped down past his hips. It took Henri's sleepy mind a moment to process what he was seeing. Robin's pants were down around his thighs, his deft doctor's hands fingering his own ass.

Another soft moan issued from the doctor, and Henri turned his face away, willing himself to fall asleep and forget he'd ever witnessed his friend in such a private moment. But something stirred deep in his gut, impossible to ignore.

The next gasp was desperate and hushed, but it sounded like *Henri.*

For a moment Henri was afraid that he'd been caught awake, but...his eyes snapped open. He hadn't been caught. Robin was whispering his name for an entirely different reason. Despite himself, he was getting hard listening to the quiet sounds Robin was making. He turned his head back toward him.

"Henri..." Robin moaned, the sound muffled against the pillow as he worked his front with his other hand.

Henri bit his lip. It felt wrong to be watching, but he couldn't take his eyes off Robin's fingers and what they were doing. He was obviously aware that some men liked other men, that was the reason Robin had run away after all, but he'd never thought...well it had never really occurred to him that he might be one of them. Then again, he'd never really been into women either. Yet here he was getting turned on at the sight of his friend masturbating to him.

But maybe that was the point. Maybe the strong response of his body was because he already cared for Robin so deeply.

"Robin." The name was out of his mouth before he could stop himself. Robin's fingers stilled, his whole body frozen. The orange glow of the lantern light fell just right across Robin's arched back, the curve of his ass... Henri sat up, his erection already weeping precum under his pants.

"Robin," he said again, and the other man snatched his hands away from his own body like it had burned him. Then slowly turned to look at him. His face was flushed, expression terrified.

"Come here," Henri said softly, trying not to frighten him. Henri swung his legs over the side of the cot as Robin rolled to his feet, hitching his pants back up around his hips. He trudged to Henri's bedside like a condemned man going to the executioner. He stood at the edge of the cot, unable to meet Henri's eyes.

In the dim light, Henri saw one single tear roll down the taller man's cheek. Did he think Henri was angry? He reached up to wipe it away, and Robin flinched as if he was about to be hit. But as Henri's hand settled gently against his skin, he finally looked up.

"I want to kiss you," Henri whispered. Robin's eyes grew wide, his fingers came up to tentatively touch the back of Henri's hand where it rested on his cheek. Henri guided him down till their lips were only a breath away. "Can I?"

Robin was trembling, but he closed the distance between them, kissing Henri chastely.

The light pressure of Robin's soft mouth against his was overwhelming and at the same time not enough. Henri wanted more. He tilted his head to deepen the kiss, but Robin pulled away. Skittish.

"Henri..." he started hesitantly but didn't continue.

"This is why you ran away from that comfortable life," Henri said, searching Robin's expression.

Robin nodded, unable to speak.

"I like you, Robin." He paused, letting the words sink into both of their minds. Robin looked startled by the confession, but Henri continued before he could chicken out. "Let me finish what you started." His other hand slid down Robin's waist.

Robin looked perplexed for a moment. As if he couldn't quite bring himself to believe what Henri was offering.

"You don't have to— Just because— I mean—" he stammered, tongue tripping over the words. Not knowing what he wanted to say.

Henri's fingers tightened their hold on the side of Robin's face. "I want you," he managed to breathe. "I've never wanted anyone like this, Robin. Is it so hard to believe you're desirable?"

Robin blinked rapidly, still processing. Henri was beginning to grow impatient.

"Please," he begged quietly, "please understand." He wasn't begging for his own release; he needed Robin to know that he was desired. That he was loved. Because clearly, he had been rejected again and again, told he was wrong, that no one could love or desire him as he wished.

Robin's gaze suddenly cleared. "You want me..." he repeated, almost awestruck. Henri was starting to understand the depths of Robin's self-denial. He'd run from his family, his career, his whole life because of how he loved, but he hadn't been able to free himself from his family's expectations and shame.

Then Henri couldn't think anymore, because Robin's mouth was pressing against his again. The kiss was slow. Testing. Exploring. Henri could almost taste the sweet yearning as he let himself be kissed. He didn't want to scare Robin away, yet he needed to taste more.

"Mmmhm." He couldn't restrain the moan that rumbled up his throat when Robin's tongue stroked into his mouth. Something was building inside Robin, making him more confident, and before Henri knew it, Robin was in his lap, straddling his hips. Their bodies pressed close, and Henri couldn't keep his hands still. He let them rove over Robin's body, feeling every detail of him beneath his rumpled clothes. His body had the softness of someone who'd grown up well fed. Henri too had been like that once.

Henri kissed a slow, meandering line down Robin's throat to his collarbone, letting his hands wander even lower until he was cupping Robin's ass. Robin rocked his hips, the friction making them both gasp. His fingers found the hem of Henri's shirt and pulled it off, then his own. Henri continued his exploration of Robin's body, licking down Robin's exposed chest and then taking his hard nipple into his mouth.

Robin threw his head back, fluffy hair falling away from his face, even more golden in the lamplight. Henri slipped his fingers beneath the waistband of Robin's pants.

"Tell me what to do," Henri groaned. "I want to make you say my name again."

Robin's breath hitched. "But your leg…"

"Don't worry about it, chéri." The pet name from his homeland rolled off his tongue, as natural as breathing. "Just tell me how to please you."

"Take off your clothes."

There was a brief struggle as Henri tried to take off his pants over the bulky splint, but with Robin's help, he accomplished it. Robin stripped off the rest of his own clothes and pushed Henri down onto the cot to straddle him again. He leaned low over Henri, giving him a lingering kiss on the lips, savoring every touch as Henri's hands found his cock. Henri enclosed both of their cocks in one large hand and began stroking.

The sensation went straight to his head. Robin moaned, his hips bucking involuntarily into Henri's hand, his arms circled around Henri's broad shoulders.

"Shit," he mumbled, his lips in Henri's short brown locs. "I want you, Henri. I want you inside me."

"Tell me what to do," Henri begged again. His hand came down in a swift stroke that had Robin choking on his next words.

"I'm already prepared," Robin answered breathlessly. "Please just…"

Henri laid back against the blankets and slid down until he was positioned correctly. His fingers found Robin's already loosened hole, still dripping with whatever he'd used for lube. He positioned his cock at Robin's entrance, bracing his good leg against the cot and letting the other hang off the side so he wouldn't be tempted to use it.

"Ready?"

"Yes...please..." Robin moaned. He was already stroking his own cock, surrendering to the desires he'd denied himself for so long.

Henri guided Robin's hips down slowly, gasping as Robin's slick walls closed around him. He wanted to go faster. Wanted to lose control. But he needed to please Robin more, to show him the pleasure and rightness of all they could do together.

Robin had other plans. He sank down quickly as soon as Henri entered him, impaling himself on Henri's already throbbing cock. His moan sounded filthy in Henri's ears, and his hand began to move faster.

Henri grabbed his slim hips, taking control. He pulled Robin slightly off him then thrust up into him again and again. Growing stronger and more confident with every dirty sound that escaped Robin's lips. The pleasure was building uncontrollably, but Henri sought Robin's pleasure before his own. He rolled his hips at a different angle and thrust harder, deeper, hitting a little knot of nerves that had Robin's head tilting back, a trembling cry emanating from his throat. Henri smirked up at him, but he didn't see. His eyes were closed, lost in bliss.

Henri pounded into him, thrusts growing slightly sloppy as he started to lose his control. But Robin was even more lost than him, coming apart at the seams.

"Yes...Henri..." he gasped, his hand pumping faster on his own cock. Henri almost lost it right then, but he held it together for a few more strokes until Robin cried his name again, painting Henri's chest with his cum. His insides clenched around Henri's cock so deliciously that Henri's orgasm wasn't far behind. His last thread of sanity snapped, and he came into Robin's tight hole, letting his hot release fill him up.

Robin collapsed against him. Lips finding the racing pulse at his throat.

"Henri." His body shuddered. "Oh my god."

Henri's hand stroked Robin's messy hair.

"I like you," he whispered, and Robin sat up a bit to look at his face, his expression halfway between bewilderment and bliss. "I like you a lot."

"I..." Another tremble wracked him. "I like you too. I..." Sense seemed to wash over him all at once, and he sat up fully. "Is your leg okay?"

Henri laughed and pulled him back down into a deep kiss. "If it's not then you can heal me again."

PART 2

ILLUSION

CHAPTER 10

AUGUST 13TH, 1666

Rowan paced the edge of the quarterdeck like a caged wolf. It had been nearly two weeks since the two infamous pirate ships had begun sailing together toward their unknown destination, and Yves still refused to say where they were going. The *Siren Song* simply followed the *Kraken's Fury* through the endless waves of the Center Sea. Rowan could tell roughly where they were by the stars but it made him anxious to not be in control of his own ship.

Now that Yves had gone back to the *Kraken*, Rowan's mind seemed to have cleared from some sort of fog. He had flashes of paranoia that this was just an elaborate trick. The infamously cruel pirate was surely leading them to certain death, and more than once, Rowan contemplated turning tail and running. The *Siren* was more than capable of outrunning the *Kraken*, even in its current sorry state. Robin and Gaël were still on board, but he could deal with that later.

But something always stopped him. A flash of memory of the way Yves had kissed him after. Or the *Kraken* would drop back beside the *Siren* and he would find himself making eye contact with Yves across the blue water.

Rowan stopped pacing and turned his eyes to the ship sailing peacefully ahead of them.

"Logan."

The first mate was by his side in a moment, following his gaze to the *Kraken*.

"Captain?"

"Should we run?"

Logan tilted his head, contemplating this familiar question.

"What does your gut say?"

Rowan finally tore his eyes away from the other ship and looked at his first mate instead.

"It's telling me a lot of things."

Logan smiled ruefully.

"Well it's rarely steered us wrong before," he said thoughtfully. Then his smile brightened. "I guess the Demon messed with your guts a little too much."

His smile widened even more at Rowan's startled bark of laughter.

"I trust you, Captain. I know you'll make the right decision."

Just like that, some of Rowan's anxiety cleared. With Logan's trust, and the support of his crew, he could see this through. Wherever it might lead them.

Rowan had become a captain quite young, even for a pirate. His mother died when he was just nine years old, and his father, not willing to care for him alone, had sold him into indenture as a cabin boy for the Marran navy, where he'd met Logan. Rowan had been a clever kid and he'd quickly made himself an invaluable asset.

It hadn't been so bad. He'd fallen in love with the sea, and most of the sailors had been kind to him. They raised him to be daring and brave. And when his indenture was over when he was seventeen, he'd left to avoid involvement in Marra's invasion of Kefrye and subsequent war with their rival empire Talva.

He joined a series of expeditions before landing a spot on a Talvan merchant crew. But he soon realized the company ran a human trafficking operation under the table. Rowan bided his time, making friends on the crew who would be loyal to him above all else. And after getting some key crew members drunk and dumping them in alleys, he was able to lead a successful mutiny against the scum captain, free the captives, and was officially declared a pirate by most of the kingdoms that made up the Islands. When Logan had been released from his own navy indenture, Rowan had recruited him as first mate and renamed the ship to the *Siren Song*.

If Logan trusted him, he had no choice but to trust himself.

∼

AUGUST 16TH, 1666

It was late afternoon when they finally spotted land. The *Kraken* immediately signaled for them to meet. They anchored, and the Demon was rowed over to the *Siren Song* on a boat.

A small smile twitched the corner of Yves's mouth as he stepped onto the deck. He was wearing a long blood red coat trimmed at the shoulders and collar with glossy black fur. The signature ruby earring gleamed in his ear. It was as if all of Yves's clothes had been made just for him, whereas Rowan had to steal nice things off the backs of those unlucky enough to cross his path. Rowan looked like a rogue, while Yves looked every inch a dashing and dangerous gentleman.

Rowan's stomach gave an undignified flutter, and he looked away, trying to school his expression to neutrality.

"Our destination is just on the horizon," Yves said. "It can be a bit tricky getting in, so I'm here to guide you." His shrewd eyes flicked over the crew on deck. "I'm going to need you to reduce the amount of crew on deck. Only those you trust the most should be up here."

"I trust my crew completely." Rowan scowled.

Yves stepped in close, lowering his voice.

"Look..." His tongue pushed against the inside of his cheek in annoyance. "You've made it abundantly clear that you don't fully trust me. But this place is a *very* well kept secret. I have more at stake than just my crew if it gets out. It's not just you taking a risk here; it's both of us."

Rowan let out an exasperated breath.

"Fine."

∼

THE SUN WAS SETTING orange and pink as they approached a small island. Ahead of them, the *Kraken* ran up a signal flag that Rowan couldn't interpret. Who were they signaling? The place looked uninhabited, black volcanic cliffs rising out of the water, topped with lush green trees. Rowan watched Yves at the wheel of the ship. The man was turned away from him, sharp profile lit by the dying light. He was beautiful, a sculpture carved by a master hand. It almost took Rowan's breath away.

The *Kraken's Fury* maneuvered slowly between spikes of rock that rose up from the waves. Yves followed, steering the *Siren* with a deft hand.

"Yves..." Rowan murmured nervously as they passed especially close to one of the rocks. "We'd better..."

The *Kraken* disappeared.

At first Rowan thought it was a trick of the light. They'd swung portside toward the cliffs, and then they were gone. And now the *Siren* was heading for those same cliffs.

"Yves, wait—"

Yves turned the wheel sharply, and the *Siren* banked hard to port. He seemed pleasantly surprised at the ship's nimbleness. But Rowan was no longer looking at him.

The black cliffs seemed to open before the *Siren's* bow like gates to paradise, revealing a hidden cove of deep water. The *Kraken* already sat at anchor, blue sails purpling in the rosy light. Beyond it, several smaller ships were moored. And beyond that, the faintly twinkling lights of a village lay between the trees.

Rowan looked from the lights to Yves and back again, mouth hanging open in astonishment.

"Welcome," Yves said with a sweeping gesture that encompassed all that lay before them, "to Illusion."

Damn. Rowan had known the bastard was rich but not *that* rich.

Yves was smiling at him, watching for a reaction. "Now do you see why it's a secret?"

Rowan laughed in disbelief, feeling a bit giddy. "Yes."

The crew was swarming over the deck now, dropping anchor next to the *Kraken* and preparing the landing boats to take them to shore. Rowan eyed the two other ships anchored in the cove, as well as a small fleet of fishing boats secured to the docks. The ships were smaller than both the *Kraken* and the *Siren*. Neither sported the iconic blue sails nor any other symbol of the Deep Water Demon.

"I didn't know you had a fleet, let alone a whole island," Rowan commented.

"We do a bit of legitimate trade." Yves smirked. "Mostly supply runs and laundering our plunder. In fact, you've poached one of my merchants before."

A blush rose up Rowan's neck, and he was grateful for the rosy light. He didn't know why he felt flustered by this. He hadn't known those ships belonged to the Deep Water Demon. If he *had* known, he probably would have gone after them even harder. But now that they were reluctant allies, he felt a bit ashamed of it.

ROWAN COULDN'T HELP his wide-eyed wonderment as Yves walked them through the small village. Besides the few guards he'd left behind on the *Siren*, the whole crew was with him. Rowan's nerves were calming now. He'd somehow been expecting a fortress or a pirate island full of murderers and thieves. But this was...peaceful, almost idyllic. People stood around on their porches chatting and laughing. Most of them didn't look like pirates at all; they were just normal people living normal lives.

The villagers watched the crew of the *Siren Song* curiously, but they didn't seem worried about the extra ship moored in the harbor or the swarm of strangers that were suddenly on their island. A few kids ran up to greet members of the *Kraken* crew and were swung up onto shoulders as those crew members broke off from the group. One by one the crew of the *Kraken* began to split off, going to their homes for a much needed rest.

Pirates with homes to go back to. What a novel idea.

A large house stood between the towering trees at the top of the sloping lane. It looked like an old manor house and was completely out of place in the overgrown street filled only with one story white-washed cottages, a smithy, a carpenter, and a building that looked like a tavern. The manor house itself was three stories tall, its exterior walls a faded pink like the inside of a seashell, as if their intended color had long since worn off and exposed something hidden beneath. A stone carved monogram stood over the double doors, its lettering completely obliterated by a chisel. Nephele swooped up to settle on the iron-railed widow's walk on the mansion's roof. Yves glanced up at her, then opened the large wooden doors and led them into a well-appointed, if a bit shabby, foyer.

"John, see that the *Siren*'s crew is fed and settled." Yves's eyes slid sideways to Rowan. "Have Cook leave dinner outside my door. The Ghost Hawk and I have business to discuss."

John rolled his eyes almost imperceptibly but began issuing orders to the remaining *Kraken* crew. They dispersed with the *Siren* crew in tow. Yves met Rowan's eye and twitched his head for Rowan to follow up a curving flight of stairs.

They hadn't yet made it to their destination on the second floor when Yves grabbed Rowan's hand. It was the first time they'd touched since Yves had gone back to the *Kraken*, and it sent tingles racing up his arm.

"What is this place?" Rowan asked.

"Does that matter right now?"

He'd asked mostly to distract himself from Yves's touch, but he was also curious beyond belief.

"A little, yes."

Yves sighed, but didn't release his hand.

"It was a summer estate for some rich bastard a long time ago. It was abandoned when the wars started. The family died, and this place was forgotten. I found it a few years ago, after..." He stopped in front of a door with an elaborate brass handle. "Well, after some things happened. But that doesn't matter now." He opened the door, revealing an ornate room within. Light from the final dregs of sunset cascaded across a lush bed draped in crisp white linens.

Yves dragged Rowan into the room, slamming the door behind them. His lips were on Rowan's in an instant, hungry and devouring. And Rowan couldn't help but melt at his touch. In all his anxiousness, he hadn't realized how eager he was to be touched by Yves again.

He moaned into Yves's kiss, letting his tongue explore. Letting instinct take over. His fingers fumbled with the onyx buttons of Yves's red coat. Yves tilted Rowan's head to the side, teeth grazing the earrings that lined the shell of Rowan's ear.

"Have you recovered?" Yves growled, sending shivers down Rowan's spine.

He nodded, finally releasing the last button and slipping his hands under the coat to frame Yves's trim waist. Yves unbuckled Rowan's belt, lips wandering down his neck. Then it was a blur of undressing. They stumbled toward the bed but didn't make it there. Rowan was too impatient and pushed Yves to the floor. He knelt on the plush rug and trailed kisses down Yves's bare torso. He palmed

Yves's already hard cock, and Yves moaned, his back arching. Rowan's lips reached Yves's hip.

"Rowan..." Yves's voice was rough. Rowan went to lick his cock, wondering how it would taste.

Yves's fingers closed hard on his jaw, forcing his mouth away.

"No," Yves said, eyes hard. The room was mostly dark now, the sun having finally dipped completely below the horizon.

"Okay," Rowan agreed. He wouldn't question it, but he was curious why Yves didn't want head from him.

Yves sat up and raised Rowan's face until their lips were only a breath apart.

"You are my guest," he whispered, and Rowan could see the fire of passion rekindling, burning away the stormy expression. "So let me treat you right."

"Do you get this close with all your guests?"

Yves flipped him onto his back, hand cupped behind Rowan's neck so his head wouldn't hit the floor. "I never have guests. Besides, you're—"

Yves cut himself off, instead kissing Rowan hard. Rowan's head spun. Yves's tongue swirled into his mouth, and he arched his body into Yves's touch as his hand left his neck and trailed over his fevered skin. Then he heard a clink, and his own leather belt was being secured around his wrists. He tugged at them. The binding was firm but not tight.

"What are you doing?"

"Instead of my guest, you're now my prisoner," Yves purred. Rowan's anxiety spiked for a moment before Yves smirked and added, "Just for tonight." Now that he was back in control, his voice was honey smooth.

Rowan relaxed into his bonds. He must have been crazy for continuing to trust this man, but even if he was nervous, he was power-less to deny the pull he felt towards the other pirate. And the vulnera-bility of having his hands bound was turning him on even more. Yves crossed the room and came back with a bottle of the same coconut-scented lube they'd used before. His lips looked kiss-bitten, and one lock of ebony hair fell in front of his eye. Rowan looped his bound arms around Yves's neck and dragged him back down to the rug. He hooked one leg over Yves's hip, pressing their bodies together. Their cocks slid against each other, and he gasped. Yves reached down to grasp both of their members in one hand, his tongue still exploring Rowan's mouth. Rowan moaned and arched his back again. Thrusting into Yves's grip.

"Eager, are we?" Yves purred, his hand pumped down onto their cocks together. "Did I make such an impression last time?"

"Shut up," Rowan mumbled, smothering Yves's words with another deep kiss. Yves was charming, a master of flirtation and teasing. But Rowan was done with words now. All he wanted was for Yves to wreck him again.

Yves did as he was told. His hand moved expertly, the delicious friction of their cocks together matching the slight chafing of the belt around his wrists. Rowan was losing his mind already. But of course Yves had more in store.

Yves disengaged from Rowan's arms and guided him onto his elbows and knees. Yves's large hands spread Rowan's buttocks wide, and he felt a wet tongue at his entrance.

"Yves..." he moaned. He was desperate to be filled, desperate for as much as Yves would give him. Yves licked around the rim, teasing. His hand wandered to Rowan's cock again. Then his tongue breached Rowan's entrance, pressing against his walls. The thought of what Logan said rose unbidden to his mind. The quip about the Demon messing with his guts. But his giggle turned to moans as Yves's freakishly long tongue licked his insides.

Yves added a finger, slick with lube, and began stretching him. Rowan winced slightly, his body remembering the soreness. But the stretching was easier this time, and soon Yves withdrew his tongue and added a second finger, then a third. He rubbed a hand over Rowan's lower back, soothing him even as he excited him.

"Ready?" Yves's voice was rough again.

"Yes," Rowan gasped.

Yves's fingers withdrew, replaced by the press of his cock at Rowan's entrance. In one motion, he grabbed Rowan's hips and yanked him back, his thick cock opening Rowan wide.

"Aaaaggh..." Rowan groaned, an edge of pain in his voice, but he was already desperate for more. He bucked his hips back, taking Yves in fully. Yves growled, fingers tightening bruisingly on Rowan's hips. He withdrew slowly. Agonizingly slowly. Then his hips snapped forward again, grinding into Rowan's buttocks. His cock pressed against Rowan's prostate, sending a heady tide of pleasure through his entire body.

Rowan bit down on his leather bindings. Yves thrust deeply again. Rowan screamed through clenched teeth as Yves set a punishing pace. His arms trembled in an effort to hold himself up as Yves rearranged his guts for him.

"Rowan," Yves moaned. His nails dug into Rowan's skin, and he bent to lick a bead of sweat from Rowan's back. His fingers tripped up Rowan's spine and wrapped through his blond hair. He pulled Rowan up off his elbows, tilting his head back to expose his throat. His other hand slid down Rowan's slim stomach, pressing below his navel, feeling his own movements deep in Rowan's guts. Then he slid lower to wrap his fingers around Rowan's throbbing cock.

Rowan wavered on his knees, unbalanced and dizzy from the overwhelming sensations coursing through his body.

"Don't get tired just yet," Yves whispered in his ear.

"Yves...please..." Rowan couldn't keep the desperation out of his voice. His wrists strained against the bonds. He didn't know what he was begging for. To be untied? To come? All he knew was that he wanted more of whatever Yves would give him.

Another ripple of pleasure tingled through him. Everything was too much and yet not enough. Yves's hand pumped on his cock in counterpoint to his thrusts. Tingles built deep in the pit of his stomach, and with one more hard thrust, Rowan came into Yves's hand. Yves didn't pause even for a moment. His hand kept moving, squelching with cum and overstimulating Rowan to the point his vision went blurry.

Rowan's whole body trembled, and Yves released his hair. His arm snaked around Rowan's chest to support him. A few more stuttering thrusts and Yves came as well, cock throbbing, gushing into Rowan's clenching insides.

They were still for a moment, Rowan's body shivering.

"Is that enough, darling?" Yves asked, stroking Rowan's sweat-soaked hair back from his forehead.

Rowan laughed breathlessly. "Maybe the bed next time?"

Yves withdrew and picked the smaller man up almost effortlessly, carrying him bridal-style to the pristine bed. He laid him down very gently, attentive where he had been rough only moments before, and unbound his hands. Then laid down beside him, dragging his swollen lips over the red marks the belt had left. Rowan's breath shuddered.

Yves watched him, drinking in his reactions. He trailed a line of kisses up Rowan's arm, lingering at the pulse point of his wrist and the crook of his elbow, savoring Rowan's thundering pulse.

Rowan didn't know what to say. He was exhausted already, but he wanted more. Sex with Yves was like a drug—it muddled his mind, and the more he had it, the more he needed.

Yves's lips pressed to his shoulder and traveled over his collarbone to the base of his throat. Rowan rested his palms against Yves's smooth chest, fingers rubbing the scar tissue of the old bullet wound.

"Where'd you get this?" he asked. He had more than a few scars himself and didn't always remember where he'd gotten them. But Yves's skin was much too pristine for a pirate.

"Mmm," Yves mumbled, too focused on the task at hand. But Rowan persisted. Suddenly getting an answer seemed very important.

"Who shot you, Yves?"

Yves looked up at him. "What?"

"I asked where you got this scar." He rubbed his fingers over the puckered skin again. This was Yves's only physical flaw as far as he could see. He wanted to know who had the audacity to wound the Deep Water Demon.

Yves blinked at him. He placed one hand over the spot where Rowan's hand rested on his chest.

"Planning to avenge me?" Yves teased.

Rowan's nose scrunched up, but he said nothing.

"It's nothing. It was my first year as a captain. I was young and stupid. I thought I could take on a Marran navy ship." He chuckled, but his fingers tightened around Rowan's. "We barely made it out. I almost died."

"That doesn't sound like nothing," Rowan said. Yves was acting nonchalant, but Rowan could sense a darkness just below the surface.

Yves's lips twisted into a rueful smile. "That was before I got my bearings. I was just a kid." He kissed Rowan's jaw.

"So was I," Rowan murmured.

"Hm?"

"What was the name of the ship?" Rowan propped himself up on his elbow, eyes searching Yves's face carefully.

"Why?" Yves asked.

"Just tell me."

Yves bit his lip in concentration. "*M.W.S. Wolf*, I think."

Rowan couldn't help the grin that broke over his face.

"It was me who shot you."

Yves stared at him, bewildered for a moment. Then he grinned back, looking like a wolf himself.

"How old were you?"

"Seventeen."

"Ha! Me too." Yves gazed at him wonderingly, as if some piece of a cosmic puzzle had fit into place.

"I got a commendation for it," Rowan admitted.

Yves tilted his chin down to capture Rowan's lips in a lingering kiss.

"So you're the little shit who marked me like this," he murmured. "I always wondered what became of him. I hoped he made a name for himself. I suppose he did...Ghost Hawk."

"Glad I didn't disappoint." It felt a bit strange to be having this conversation laying stark naked in bed together. But nothing about this situation, or their lives, was conventional.

"Thank you," Yves said earnestly.

"For what?"

"This wound." Yves placed Rowan's hand back over the scar. "That battle changed me, hardened my resolve. It was an important step on the journey that made me into the Demon. I wonder why..." He shook his head as if dismissing the next thought.

His other hand came up to cup the side of Rowan's face, rubbing his thumb over his cheekbone. Then he pulled him close suddenly.

"However," he purred, a smoky edge in his voice, "you still gave me this scar." His tongue flicked out to lick the corner of Rowan's mouth. "How will you atone for your sins?"

A spark of renewed passion kindled in Rowan's core.

"I don't know," Rowan said carefully, "but I'm sure it will take a very long time."

CHAPTER 11

AUGUST 16TH, 1666

When Henri had woken after he and Robin's first night together, Robin was no longer squished into the thin bed with him. He came back soon after with breakfast for them both. But when Henri reached for him, Robin avoided his touch.

In the days following, Robin acted as if nothing had happened between them. Henri was confused. He'd never had a romantic interlude before; he'd never had a one-night stand either. The only reason he'd felt safe sleeping with Robin was because he'd developed feelings for him and thought Robin felt the same. Yet now he was adrift and abandoned. Was lust all Robin felt for him? Now that they'd slept together was that all there was? There was a tightness in his chest that wouldn't go away no matter how much he tried not to think about it, no matter how much he tried to accept it. The only time Robin touched him now was out of medical necessity, yet even that clinical touch woke feelings in Henri he wished had remained sleeping.

Henri didn't know what to do. Ask Robin why he was acting like this? Just let it go? He waited to see if Robin would come around, but nothing had changed by the time Fox visited the infirmary days later.

He skipped in excitedly, for once without his muscle-bound boy toy, and made straight for Henri's cot, ignoring Robin.

"We're here!" Fox exclaimed, flopping onto the end of Henri's cot, narrowly missing his injured leg.

"Where?" Henri hadn't been paying much attention to what was going on with the rest of the crew, not being mobile enough to leave the infirmary often and also being quite distracted by the situation with Robin.

"The Demon's mysterious island of course!" Fox said, sitting up. He explained what had been happening while Henri was convalescing.

"So I came down to help," Fox finished, looking between Henri and Robin. He seemed to suddenly sense the tension in the air and raised an eyebrow at Henri.

"We're to stay until the repairs are made?" Robin cut in.

Fox nodded again.

"I came to help get this big lug into the landing boat," Fox reiterated. Robin nodded and began bustling around the room, packing up supplies.

"What's up with you two?" Fox whispered, leaning close to Henri.

Henri wasn't sure what to say. The change in Robin's demeanor was definitely due to the sex, but what did it mean? Fox was one of his best friends and very experienced; maybe he would know what to do.

Robin left the room, muttering about supplies.

"We slept together," Henri blurted as soon as he was gone.

"What? When?" Fox exclaimed, smacking Henri on the shoulder in excitement.

Henri fiddled with one of the beads in his short locs, suddenly embarrassed. "A few nights ago."

"And this is...bad?" Fox prompted, seeing his friend's troubled expression. "I thought you liked each other?"

Henri had never admitted that to Fox out loud, and he doubted Robin had either. But Fox had always been good at reading people, especially when it came to sex.

"We do... I mean, I like him. He said he liked me, but he's barely talked to me since."

"Wow, you were that bad, huh?" Fox joked, trying to lighten the mood.

"Maybe." Henri sighed miserably.

Fox's expression softened, and he placed a comforting hand on Henri's shoulder.

"Just talk to him," he said gently. "You'll never know how he feels unless you ask."

～

HENRI WAS the last to leave the landing boat as the rest of the crew made their way from the docks toward the peaceful village beneath the trees. He didn't have the energy to ponder the implications of the Deep Water Demon owning a whole island. The process of getting Henri from the *Siren*'s deck to the boat had been an exhausting ordeal, and he just wanted to go to bed and deal with his problems in the morning.

Fox hopped onto the dock and turned back to help Henri over the gap. But Robin was already there, elegant hand extended. Henri took it and allowed himself to be hauled over onto dry land. When his feet hit the dock, it jostled his splint, and he hissed in pain. Robin grasped his arm to steady him. But when Henri regained his balance, Robin didn't let go right away. His hand lingered on Henri's arm, grip softening.

"You okay?" he asked, glancing at Henri, then away. The words seemed like he was asking about more than just Henri's leg. Robin's face was tinged peach in the dying light of the sunset, and his touch—shy as it was—was almost comforting. Like maybe he did have feelings for Henri after all. Or maybe Henri was reading too much into it, and Robin was just being a good doctor.

"I'm fine," Henri answered.

Robin let go, and Henri was adrift again.

"I'll go on ahead," Fox cut in, handing Henri his crutch with a wink. It was obvious he wanted to give the two of them ample alone time to talk. "You'll be fine, won't you, doc?"

Before Robin could answer, Fox bounded away to catch up with Gaël, who was waiting on the shore.

The walk through the village seemed so long. And though Fox had given him a good opportunity to talk to Robin, he couldn't think of what to say. He was completely out of his depth when it came to matters of sex and romance. And he couldn't quite bring himself to show Robin just how hurt he was by the sudden distance between them.

By the time they reached the large, slightly rundown manor house at the top of the lane, the rest of the crew members were already dispersed. Only the *Kraken*'s first mate, John, remained, waiting for them in the foyer.

"I'm to assign quarters to all the *Siren* crew members," John said when they arrived. He glanced at Henri's leg. "Does he still need to stay in the infirmary?" he asked Robin.

"No," Robin answered, and Henri felt a pang of loss. The infirmary, and Robin caring for his injuries, were the last connections they had to each other. "But he should stay nearby," Robin added.

"Third door on the left," John said. "Get him settled, will you? I'm going to find dinner." Robin nodded, and John left them in the foyer.

"This way," Robin said, still avoiding Henri's eyes. He led Henri down a hallway, walking slowly to match Henri's pace. They reached the door of Henri's new room in no time, but Henri didn't want Robin to leave. He wanted more time to come up with the words that would close the awkward gap between them.

"The infirmary is right down there," Robin said, pointing to a door near the end of the hall with a faded white cross painted on it. "And I stay right next door to it, if you need anything." He lingered for a moment, scratching the back of his neck awkwardly. Then he turned to go.

"Wait." Henri caught his hand, but his mind was still blank. He still didn't know what to say. The silence stretched in the empty hallway. Robin was looking at him expectantly, almost as if he dreaded what Henri would say next, but he didn't remove his hand from Henri's grip. Henri swallowed reflexively.

"L-let me stay with you instead," Henri stuttered, already cursing himself for his boldness. "I don't know what I did wrong, but I want to be near you. Please."

Robin bit his bottom lip, gaze lowering to where their hands were clasped between them.

"You didn't do anything wrong," he muttered, almost too quiet to hear.

Henri wanted to step closer, but he felt like he'd fall if he did. His fingers tightened around Robin's. Robin looked up at him, still biting his lip till there were red marks on his skin.

"Please. Just talk to me. I..." The tightness in Henri's chest moved up to his throat, and his voice trailed off.

"Come with me," Robin said, seeming resigned to this conversation. He extricated his hand from Henri's grasp and walked down the hall towards his room. Henri followed, his crutch thumping against the floor with every step.

Robin's quarters turned out to be a single room which looked like it had once been a small study. Shelves lined one wall, packed with all manner of medical texts and well-worn notebooks. Four small brass bells hung on the wall opposite, rigged on curled metal springs with wires running through the wall into the room that housed the infirmary. An over-large desk sat pushed against the wall beneath them, and a double-wide bed with a brass headboard was pushed against the far wall beneath the window.

Robin lit an oil lamp on the desk and closed the door behind them, dumping their bags in the corner by the bookcase.

"Take a seat," Robin said, pulling out the desk chair. "Your leg must be hurting."

Henri had been too distracted by everything going on to realize it, but his leg *did* hurt. So he sat, leaning the crutch on the edge of the desk. Robin stood a pace or two away, fidgeting. There was nowhere else to sit besides the bed.

Henri was getting anxious again, not wanting to push Robin too hard but needing answers more than ever. When it became clear that there were no answers forthcoming, he took a deep breath.

"Why aren't you talking to me?" Henri asked, trying to keep the desperation out of his voice. It seemed like the easiest question to ask but might be the hardest answer to hear.

Robin hung his head, picking at a cuticle. "Is your leg hurting?" he asked instead.

"Yes," Henri admitted.

"Stay here." Robin retreated to the other room and returned with new bandages and a jar of ointment. He knelt in front of the chair and took Henri's heel in his hand. He removed the shoe and moved Henri's foot to rest in his lap. He began unraveling the old bandages in silence.

"Don't you like me anymore?" Henri blurted, immediately flushing when Robin's hands stilled.

"I do," Robin said quietly. It was like he had to force the words out. His head was still down as if focusing on his task.

"Then why won't you look at me?"

Robin finally looked up, eyes shiny in the light of the oil lamp.

Henri was gripped by a sudden urge to touch him. Despite the hurt and confusion Robin had caused him the last few days, he was still undeniably drawn to him, and seeing tears in his eyes pulled at Henri's heartstrings. He reached down and brushed a lock of hair from Robin's brow, full of all the tenderness and affection he'd felt during their only night together.

"Did I do something wrong?" he asked again quietly. His fingers traced down the edge of Robin's ear. Robin inhaled sharply at the contact.

"You didn't." Robin's voice was thick with emotion, and his fingers slipped up to the back of Henri's knee beneath the hem of his rolled-up pant leg. "You're perfect. It's me. I...felt ashamed." His lips thinned to a line. "Not because of you, but just... I was raised to believe that what we did is wrong, and I felt like I shouldn't drag you down with me." He bit his lip and looked up at Henri with warring emotions, like he hoped Henri would both understand but also reject him.

"You said you liked me," Henri whispered. His feelings were at war within him too. Maybe he shouldn't have moved so fast when he discovered Robin's feelings. He'd had an inkling that Robin had grown up that way. That he'd been raised to reject who he was.

A tear slipped down Robin's cheek. "I do, but I'm disgusted with myself for it."

Henri threaded his fingers through the back of Robin's hair, leaning down so they were face-to-face.

"Does this disgust you?" he asked. He was amazed with his own calmness. In all twenty-four years of his life, Robin was the first person he'd ever felt romantic or sexual feelings for, and he didn't want to let him go, especially not when he was hurting. But his heart was breaking that this beautiful, sweet man had so much hatred for himself.

Robin closed his eyes and took a deep breath, as if centering himself.

"You're amazing," Robin murmured. "You could never disgust me."

"But you don't want me." It was a statement more than a question.

"I..." Robin's voice trailed off.

"I care about you," Henri said, as if the words would awaken the truth in Robin's heart. "I want to be with you. What we have and what we are is not wrong. Forget the past, and say yes."

Robin blinked back tears, and for a moment Henri thought maybe he would give in to his self-hatred and turn away. That he would give up the possibility of a happy future for the traumas of his past.

Suddenly, Robin closed the gap between them, catching Henri's lips in a trembling kiss. Henri froze, unsure if this was a kiss of acceptance or goodbye. His fingers were still threaded through Robin's fluffy hair. He wanted to pull him closer, to deepen the kiss and never let him go, but he feared doing so would push Robin even further away.

Instead, he waited. He closed his eyes and relished the feel of Robin's soft lips, committing it to memory in case this was the last time he could taste them.

Robin pulled away all too soon, and Henri braced himself for the imminent rejection. But nothing happened. The silence unfolded, broken only by their shared breath. He opened his eyes.

The flame in the oil lamp guttered, throwing shifting shadows into the corners of the room. Robin gazed up at him in the flickering orange light. There were still tears in his eyes, but an expression of serenity had stolen over his face. Henri sucked in a deep breath, readying himself for anything.

That sweet, familiar smile broke across Robin's mouth. He seemed to have made a decision that lifted a weight from his conscience.

"I care about you," Robin confessed. Henri's held breath rushed out with relief. Somehow he hadn't expected this outcome, and still waited for the almost inevitable *but...*

"I'll try my best to make you happy," Robin continued, his voice low and sincere. "If it's for you, I think I can learn to accept who I am."

"Can I kiss you?" Henri asked. He felt lightheaded and couldn't quite believe this was really happening. But he wanted to make sure he wouldn't scare Robin away.

"Yes."

Henri's fingers tightened in Robin's hair as he drew him closer. The kiss was chaste at first. Until Robin's tongue slipped between Henri's lips. Henri's foot still rested in Robin's lap, and he felt Robin's cock harden slightly beneath the bare sole of his foot. He didn't want to move too fast, but their bodies seemed to have other ideas. Robin moved Henri's foot off his lap and sat up further between Henri's legs, hands running lightly up his thighs. Blush was high in Robin's cheeks, and Henri's face felt hot as well.

Robin's thumb rubbed Henri's inner thigh, and he felt the blood rush from his face to somewhere else. He moaned quietly as their kissing grew more heated. But Henri still held back. The first time, he'd been so caught up in the surprise of new feelings and the need to please Robin that nervousness hadn't had a chance to get a hold of him. But now a hundred worries flicked through his mind. Could he please Robin? Were they moving too fast? Would he spook him? Would Robin go back to being a stranger in the morning despite his loving words? All of this distracted him, detaching his anxious mind from his body which only had one desire.

Sensing Henri's hesitancy, Robin pulled away slightly.

"Are you okay?"

"I just don't want to move too fast and scare you away again," Henri admitted, his voice sounding small and pathetic in his own ears.

Robin thunked his forehead gently against Henri's, pulling him closer with arms around his waist.

"If I get scared, I'll have you to comfort me," Robin said. Their breath mingled in the small space between their lips. It was intoxicating to feel Robin so close, and some of the worries plaguing him dissipated. "We don't have to do anything tonight. Just let me hold you."

Henri licked his lips and nodded. As turned on as he was, all he really wanted was to be near Robin. And besides, his leg was aching after the eventful day.

"Alright." Robin gave Henri another peck on the lips. Then to Henri's surprise, he hoisted Henri into his arms, Henri's legs wrapped around his waist, and he carried him to the bed.

"What are you doing?" Henri laughed. With his stature, he'd never expected to be carried anywhere.

"Carrying my boyfriend to bed," Robin answered innocently, settling Henri on the edge of the mattress. He knelt to one knee to check Henri's leg. The splint was still in place but the bandages over the burns were still on the floor by the chair. Robin made quick work of applying ointment and rebandaging the burns. He stood and bent to kiss Henri again. Henri could see that he was still half hard.

Robin crossed the room and turned off the oil lamp, then after propping a rolled up quilt beneath Henri's injured leg, stripped off his outer clothes and climbed into the bed. He laid back against the pillow, hair splaying like a puffy cloud, and held his arms open to Henri.

"Come here."

Henri laid back, nuzzling into Robin's chest. His feet hung slightly over the foot of the bed, but he was as comfortable as he'd ever been sleeping alone. He hugged one arm around Robin's middle and listened to Robin's slow heartbeat. Robin's hand stroked his hair soothingly.

"Sweet dreams," Henri murmured. The kindling passions of his body were cooling, and his eyelids grew heavy.

"Mmmm," Robin answered sleepily. Henri closed his eyes and allowed himself to drift into sleep to the sound of Robin's heartbeat.

CHAPTER 12

AUGUST 17TH, 1666

In the morning, Rowan woke to the sound of his own stomach growling. The night before, he'd let Yves fuck him twice more as atonement for the sin of giving him that scar before they both fell into an exhausted sleep, completely forgetting the dinner tray that was meant to be left outside the door. Now Rowan was ravenous. He sat up, the white linens pooling around his bare waist, and looked toward the other side of the bed. He expected Yves to already be awake, like the other time. But he wasn't. The other man lay on his back, one hand resting on his bare stomach and the other curled into the rumpled sheets. Gentle morning light brushed the smooth plains of his face and his plush pink lips.

He looked like a fae prince out of a fairytale.

Hunger forgotten, Rowan leaned over him, memorizing every detail of his gorgeous face. Yves sighed in his sleep, dark head turning on the pillow so his face was towards Rowan. Rowan reached out to brush away a stray lock of hair, mesmerized by the beautiful vulnerability of the sleeping Demon.

It happened so fast that Rowan wasn't quite sure how he'd ended up there. In a split second he was on his back on the bed. Yves straddled him with a fist cocked back ready to strike. Those beautiful lips twisted into a snarl. His eyes had lost their trademark stars, and without that shine, they were as dark and deep as the furthest reaches of the sea.

"Yves!" Rowan yelped. The other man blinked, dull sleep finally clearing from his black eyes as he recognized him. The fist unclenched, and Yves fell back to the bed beside him, rubbing an exasperated hand down his face.

"Sorry." Yves's voice was still roughened by sleep, but he offered no further explanation.

"It's okay..." Rowan replied slowly, trying to shake off the spike of adrenaline the sudden attack had ignited. "Next time I'll sneak off before you wake." He smiled reassuringly, but Yves frowned.

Yves turned to fully face him, touching his forearm gently and then growing bolder when Rowan didn't move away. His fingers trailed over Rowan's chest.

"Can I kiss you?"

This was very different from the Yves of last night. The man who had tied him up with his own belt and ravished him.

"That depends," Rowan murmured. "Am I your guest or still your prisoner?"

"The sun is up," Yves replied, inching closer. "You are my esteemed guest."

"In that case, let's go find some breakfast." Rowan sat up and swung his legs over the side of the bed. Yves caught his arm, a spark of something unreadable in his expression. Rowan's stomach chose that moment to make its demands known, gurgling so loudly that Rowan was pretty sure it could have been heard from the hall.

Yves's expression cleared, and he leaned in, waiting for Rowan to initiate the kiss. Rowan pecked him on the cheek.

THEY FOUND their clothes from the previous night scattered across the floor, and opened the door to the sight of two cats eating from the dinner tray that had been left in the hall the night before.

"Shoo," Yves said to the cats, a small frown on his lips. The cats loped away with their bellies full. "They keep the mice away but at what cost?" he grumbled.

"Are they yours?"

"They're everyone's," Yves answered. "But they sleep in Gaël's room most of the time."

"I'm sure Fox will be jealous."

Yves glanced at the ceiling as if to see through the roof to where Nephele roosted.

"Your hawk isn't going to cause a problem, is she?"

"She knows friend from foe. Your cats will be fine," Rowan assured him.

They descended the stairs into the main foyer and spotted another pair of pirates making their way slowly toward the mess hall.

"Henri!" Rowan hurried toward his injured crew member, feeling Yves glowering behind him. He hugged the taller man around the waist, careful not to unbalance him as Mister Beckett hovered close by. Henri patted his captain's back with his free hand.

"You look much better," Rowan said, pulling away. He usually wasn't a very touchy person, but Henri was one of his closest friends, and it was a relief to see him up and about.

"I feel much better," Henri agreed.

"His burns are almost healed," Beckett piped up, "but the break will still take several months to heal."

Rowan nodded. "Thank you for taking such good care of him." Rowan released Henri fully and extended his hand to shake.

"My pleasure. He's been a model patient," Beckett replied as his large hand enveloped Rowan's.

The three of them made their way toward the mess hall, with Yves trailing moodily behind.

The mess had likely once been a ballroom, but was now full of mismatched tables and chairs that had clearly been looted from the various ships that had fallen victim to the *Kraken's Fury*. It was already half full of sleepy-looking pirates from both crews, eating their breakfast. A few of the *Siren* crew quieted when they spotted the Demon, but he ignored them. He gathered a plate of food for himself and Rowan. Beckett settled Henri at a table in the corner and went to get them some food as well. Rowan sat across from him, and with a sigh, Yves joined them.

"Do you not usually eat with your crew?" Rowan asked, raising his eyebrows at Yves's haughty attitude.

"I was hoping to spend a bit more time alone with you." Yves's voice was pitched low so the others wouldn't hear.

A blush climbed up Rowan's neck, and he turned his face away to hide it.

"Captain!" Rowan looked up to see Fox bounding toward them,

his perpetual muscled shadow, Gaël, following behind carrying their plates. Fox's hair was a mess, as if he'd just rolled out of bed after some morning activities. He crashed into the chair beside Rowan, knocking Rowan's shoulder into Yves's. Rowan had never understood where the younger man got his boundless energy, but it never failed to either elevate or exasperate his mood. Rowan, Henri, and Gaël all smiled at him fondly as Gaël placed their plates on the table.

"So, how long are we staying?" Fox asked, shoving a large forkful of food into his mouth.

"Just until the ship is repaired," Rowan answered. He felt Yves tense beside him. What was wrong with him this morning? He seemed particularly on edge. Maybe he was regretting bringing Rowan and his crew here after all.

"So soon? There's going to be a party for the autumn festival. It would be a shame to miss it," Beckett cut in. Yves tensed again as the tall doctor passed behind him to set a plate in front of Henri and settle in beside him. They seemed close. Rowan supposed that spending weeks being taken care of by someone would cultivate friendship quickly.

"Did you two make up?" Fox asked innocently, but with a hidden smirk that told Rowan he was intentionally stirring something up. Beckett and Henri exchanged a look.

Oh, so it was like that with them too.

"Yes," Henri answered, as Beckett's ears turned red. Fox beamed, and Gaël slipped an arm around Fox's waist.

Yves had remained silent throughout this exchange, but now he rested one hand on Rowan's thigh, squeezing lightly. They finished their breakfast, listening to the chatter of the two crews mingling.

"We should talk about getting supplies for the repairs," Rowan said after they finished their meal.

Yves smiled disarmingly, causing Rowan's heart to flutter.

"Why don't you just rest for the day. We can start all that tomorrow." He leaned close, his lips brushing Rowan's ear. "Besides, your back must be hurting."

A thread of unease mingled with arousal wound through Rowan's gut, but he dismissed it as Yves took his hand. "Come, I'll show you the island."

～

Rowan couldn't help but be impressed by the marvel that was Illusion. The village was well kept and more extensive than it had initially seemed the night before. The people who lived there were the families of the *Kraken* crew and various retired *Kraken* crew members. They seemed happy and prosperous. The plunder of the *Kraken* was laundered through a small fleet of merchants and supply ships that all answered directly to Yves. The dock teemed with fishermen preparing to go out to the blue island waters for the day. Yves showed him the village, the docks, and the fields, which they'd managed to hide nestled in the thick forest that covered most of the island. If seen from a ship, they would simply look like natural clearings in the trees and nothing more.

The secrecy was astounding. No wonder the Demon was so successful; he had his own small kingdom at his beck and call.

The lot of a pirating life was to have no home but your ship. No family but your crew. And some pirates didn't even have that. Yet Yves had been able to create this peaceful haven so his crew would not have to choose between family or pirating. He had created a home for them, defended and supported by his ruthlessness.

Rowan felt his heart softening. To have a home where you never had to watch your back. Never had to make a quick escape when the authorities discovered you. It was an impossible dream, and he would be sad to leave, but Rowan was already itching to get back out to sea. The *Siren* was the only home he had. The crew, his only family. He was restless on dry land, even with the pleasant distraction of Yves by his side.

Close to dinnertime, Rowan excused himself to seek out Logan.

Logan sat at the end of the largest dock, bare feet swinging over the water. He hummed quietly to himself, occasionally looking out over the cove toward the *Siren*, then writing something down in a small notebook in his lap.

"What are you doing?" Rowan sat cross-legged next to him on the salt-weathered wood. Logan blinked at him, startled by his sudden appearance.

"Making a list of supplies," he answered. His gentle voice mixed with the soft sound of the surf. "When are we getting started?"

Rowan sighed. Every time he had brought it up today, Yves had brushed him off, steering him toward new distractions.

"Hopefully tomorrow. Yves has been a bit flaky about it."

Logan snorted but said nothing.

"What?"

"Just be careful. If this place is such a secret, is he really going to let us leave?"

Rowan had considered this as well, but he was trying not to think about it.

"We'll just have to see. I want to trust him. So for now I will. But I'm putting you in charge of the repairs. I need someone, ah...not so distracted." He was a bit embarrassed at how much Yves affected him. How easily he fell under the spell of his considerable charms.

"Do you really like him so much?" Logan asked absentmindedly, busy scribbling in his notebook again.

Rowan nodded.

"Why?"

Rowan's lips quirked into a half smile. Logan was one of the smartest people Rowan knew. He could read whether a man would be a dependable crew member with one look, but when it came to the intricacies of romantic relationships, he was a fish out of water.

"I admire him as a captain and..." Rowan trailed off. What exactly was it that drew him so strongly to Yves? A kindred spirit? His handsome face? Or was he just that good in bed? Rowan didn't know. He was acting purely on instinct. "...Well he's very handsome," Rowan finished sheepishly.

"So are you. So are a lot of people," Logan pointed out.

Rowan sighed in exasperation. Why was nothing ever easy with his crew?

"But I will oversee the repairs," Logan said, circling back to the original point of their conversation. "Just tell me when to start."

Yves frowned, watching Rowan's back retreating down the main street of the village in search of his first mate. Yves turned and closed the mansion door behind him, then ascended the grand curving staircase to the second floor. He entered his office, unsurprised to find John seated at the captain's desk.

"John."

His stern first mate looked up from whatever he was reading.

"So the moonstruck lover returns to the real world," he said, the barest hint of teasing beneath his disapproving tone. He was the only person on the *Kraken*'s crew who dared tease Yves, and then only in private.

Yves rolled his eyes. "Yes, yes. You disapprove. You've made that abundantly clear."

"So what can I do for you, Captain?" The mocking tone was still there, and he hadn't gotten up from Yves's desk. Yves chose to brush off the insult.

"I need you to delay the repairs of the *Siren Song*."

John's eyebrows rose.

"And why would I do that when I want them gone as quickly as possible?"

Yves dropped into one of the chairs, leaning his head back over the top of the backrest, long legs extended before him. The picture of a troubled prince.

"I need more time." He would never admit even this much to anyone else, but John was the closest thing he had to a friend, and it was not wise to lie to him.

"The repairs will already take weeks," John pointed out.

Yves sat up straighter, leveling his best demon gaze on his first mate.

"I know. But I *need time*."

"For what?"

What did he need time for? To make Rowan his? To devise some plan to make him stay? Yves rubbed at the scar over his heart that Rowan had left all those years ago. Rowan was the only enemy who had dared leave a permanent mark upon him.

"Just do it, and keep it quiet," he growled.

"Aye, Captain."

CHAPTER 13

AUGUST 19TH, 1666

Something wet and rough touched Fox's face. He swatted at it without opening his eyes and settled back into sleep.

Again, the warm wetness swiped across his cheek, dragging him back to consciousness.

"Gaaaaaaël," he whined. "Let me sleeeep."

Meow.

Finally Fox opened his eyes to find a slightly chubby gray cat perched on the pillow beside his head. The cat stared at him with wide blue eyes, then booped his cheek with its cold nose.

Gaël wasn't in bed with him, only the cat.

He sat up quickly, scanning the room, but Gaël wasn't there.

Fox inhaled sharply, panic instantly sparking in his gut. He'd quickly grown used to waking up beside Gaël. Being crushed in his arms more often than not. Gaël had been diligent about soothing his fears of abandonment, always waiting for Fox to wake up before getting out of bed.

Fox gathered the cat into his arms, trying to regulate his breathing and stave off the tide rising all around him. The cat mewled at him inquisitively.

Oh gods, it was happening again. Gaël was gone.

Fox blinked back tears and cuddled the cat close. His breath came fast. Hyperventilating.

The door squealed open.

Fox's head snapped up to see Gaël entering the room with a basket, his hair still messy from sleep.

"Gaël," Fox choked, trying to swallow past the lump in his throat. He scrambled to the end of the bed, discarding the cat who chirped in protest.

"Good mor— What's wrong?" Gaël noticed Fox's distress and abandoned the basket on the floor. He hurried to the end of the bed, where Fox was kneeling on the mattress, and gathered him against his chest.

"You weren't... I thought..." Fox stammered. Despite the relief that was flooding him at the sight of Gaël, panic still curled through his chest. He fisted his hands in the front of Gaël's shirt.

"Oh, sweetheart." Guilt crossed Gaël's chiseled face as he realized what had happened. He cradled the back of Fox's head in his hand, pressing Fox's face into his shoulder. "I'm sorry." He kissed Fox's hair. "I'm sorry. I shouldn't have gone. I'll never leave you. I promise."

Fox felt foolish for having such a reaction. For letting the panic overtake him so quickly. But in the moment it had seemed like the worst day of his life was happening all over again.

"I just went to get some food," Gaël soothed. He pulled Fox away from his chest to look at him, cradling his tearful face between his palms. Fox bit his lip, trying to blink away the residual tears.

"Foxy, are you alright?"

Fox nodded, and Gaël leaned in to kiss his forehead.

"Sorry," Fox murmured. "I'm pathetic."

"No. It's my fault. I should have waited."

The fact that Gaël blamed only himself made Fox feel more pathetic, even as his heart clenched with fondness.

"You can't live your whole life waiting for me to wake up. I need to get over it," Fox said quietly.

"Everything takes time," Gaël soothed. "I'll be here."

Fox smiled up at him gratefully.

"So...breakfast?" Fox asked.

"Ah." Gaël helped Fox off the end of the bed. "Not breakfast. I was hoping to take you on a date."

～

Fox FELT MUCH CALMER as he followed Gaël out of the house. Gaël hadn't let him see what was in the cloth-covered basket, and Fox was becoming increasingly more curious about what he had in store.

"Where are we going?" Fox asked, taking Gaël's unoccupied hand and threading their fingers together.

Gaël's dimples dented his cheeks as he smiled.

Fuck, Fox wished he could live in those dimples.

"My favorite place on the island," Gaël answered, swinging their hands between them. "I think you'll like it."

The day was warm and sunny, bright blue waves just visible through the trees as they walked. After an hour, Fox heard the distant rush of water growing louder. Then they rounded the corner, and the scene opened before them.

A waterfall about twice Fox's height rushed over the edge of a mossy cliff, plummeting into a sparkling pool. A clear, slow moving river snaked off between the trees toward the sea.

"It's amazing!" Fox gasped. Gaël squeezed his hand.

"You like it?" Gaël sounded pleased.

"Of course!"

They picked their way down the bank to a wide, flat rock that jutted out into the water. Gaël unpacked their picnic while Fox crouched at the edge of the rock, running his fingers through the cool water.

"Come eat," Gaël said.

They settled onto the warm rock and tucked into the meal Gaël had packed. Cheese, bread with butter, and fresh late summer blackberries.

"Mmm," Fox sighed, popping a blackberry into his mouth when he'd eaten his fill of the cheese and bread. He closed his eyes, letting his head fall onto Gaël's broad shoulder.

"Foxy."

Fox opened his eyes.

"Are you feeling better?" Gaël asked gently.

"Yeah." Fox laid back against the warm rock.

"I hope you know I would never leave you," Gaël said seriously.

"I know. It's just... I couldn't help but get scared."

"I'm sorry," Gaël apologized again for the hundredth time.

"Let's just enjoy the day." Fox sat up, a smile spreading across his lips. "Let's go for a swim."

They stripped naked and jumped into the pool at the base of the waterfall. Fox gasped as he resurfaced, the shock of cold water forcing the breath from his lungs.

"Wimp," Gaël teased. Fox splashed him, shrieking as Gaël tackled him in turn.

"No fair!" Fox yelled. He tried to tackle Gaël back, intent on tickling him into submission. But Gaël dove away toward the waterfall. Fox followed.

Gaël resurfaced beneath the tumbling water. Then reached out and pulled Fox in when he got close. Fox couldn't control his laughter—the joy of being with Gaël like this, lighthearted and free, bubbled up uncontrollably.

"Foxy."

Gaël was gazing at him lovingly, the waterfall cascading down over his head and shoulders, flattening his hair against his forehead. Fox pushed his own soaked hair out of his eyes.

"You look handsome," Gaël said.

"As always." Fox smirked. Gaël reached out to wrap an arm around Fox's slim waist, pulling their bodies flush against each other.

"I love you." Gaël's deep voice vibrated through Fox's body.

Gaël had never stopped saying it since that first day. He didn't ask Fox to return his feelings. He only wanted Fox to know he was loved. And Fox felt more loved, more taken care of, than he ever had before. His chosen family on the *Siren* and his true love were all together in one place, and the scars that held together his fragile heart were healing, slowly but surely. He'd known from the moment of their first kiss all those years ago that he loved Gaël, and he hadn't stopped loving him since. That was why it hurt so much, why he'd pushed it down and pretended it was hatred instead.

But now he was safe. Now he could bring it back to the surface.

"I love you too."

Gaël's whole face lit with surprise, then joy, and Fox felt warmth spreading through his limbs like a tropical tide. He leaned further into Gaël's embrace, lifting his face to bask in the sunlight of his beloved smile.

The kiss was slow and tender at first. Gaël's tongue parted Fox's lips gently. Fox sighed into his mouth, melting at Gaël's touch. They'd slept together countless times since their reunion on board the *Siren*. Sometimes Fox topped, sometimes Gaël. But Gaël's touch always ignited passion no matter where they were or what they were doing.

The kiss deepened, Gaël's hand slipping down Fox's waist to cup the curve of his ass. Fox flattened his palms against Gaël's warm chest. They moved through the water toward the back of the waterfall, only up to their waists in the pool.

Gaël's hard cock pressed against his skin beneath the water.

"Gaël..." he moaned.

"Here." Gaël broke their embrace, taking Fox's hand and leading him behind the waterfall. They climbed three steps that had been cut into the rock, ending up on a shelf of rock tucked behind the waterfall.

Sunlight shone through the falling water, shimmering on their soaked skin and reflecting in waves off the roof of the shallow cave.

Gaël eased Fox down onto the rock. Its surface was smoothed by decades of water wearing it away, and Fox knew better than most the changes that time could bring. Gaël's hands moved over his skin, trailing warmth and tingling pleasure. He kissed beneath Fox's jaw, moving down his throat and over his chest. Fox's soft moan was lost beneath the rushing water as Gaël's tongue circled his pebbled nipple. He arched into Gaël's touch, seeking more heat. Gaël's mouth continued over his ribs and stomach, then sank down around Fox's cock, the warmth of his tongue dragging over the supple skin.

"Mmm." Fox let his hands fall back against the smooth rock behind his head, his legs falling open to allow Gaël the access he needed. He was still a little loose from the night before, and Gaël's wet fingers sank in easily, quickly finding the small bundle of nerves at his core.

Gaël's nimble fingers moved as expertly as his mouth. Quickly building the pleasurable heat throughout Fox's body and loosening him further.

"Gaël, please." Fox wanted more; impatient heat desperately pulled at every nerve in his body. The sound of the waterfall roared in his ears, drowning out everything else. Gaël complied to Fox's begging and withdrew his fingers and mouth. Fox whined, but he wasn't left untouched for long. Gaël flipped him onto his stomach, propping his hips up and kneading the pliant flesh of his butt cheeks with strong hands.

Fox lifted himself to his elbows, hands clasped almost prayerfully before his face. Gaël's breath feathered across Fox's exposed hole, causing him to clench down on nothing.

"You're so pretty back here," Gaël murmured. His thumb brushed the pink edge, and Fox whimpered. "So pink and cute."

A shiver broke across Fox's skin as the breath of Gaël's words wafted hot over him. Gaël separated his cheeks further.

Fox's body jolted in surprise as Gaël's warm, wet tongue circled the pink bud of his entrance. He clenched again, desperate to be filled. He felt more than heard Gaël chuckle at his desperation. Gaël's tongue swirled the other direction, then gently probed into Fox's hole. Fox's hips rutted back involuntarily onto Gaël's face, and Gaël squeezed his ass cheeks harder to keep him in place.

Gaël's tongue stroked tantalizingly into Fox's interior, sending warm tingles through his body. Fox imagined he could almost feel Gaël's taste buds pressing to his soaking walls. Fox's teeth sank into his lower lip hard, stifling the pathetic little mewls and whimpers that tried to tumble past his lips. One of Gaël's fingers slipped in beside his tongue, catching on the rim then intruding further and curling down to massage Fox's prostate.

"I need you," Fox keened again. He could barely stand this cornucopia of sensation as Gaël feasted on his insides like a starving man. Drool coated Gaël's face and Fox's ass cheeks, mixing with the water that still beaded his skin. Gaël's tongue continued to lick along Fox's desperately quivering walls as his finger massaged and stretched him. Gaël was indulging himself, sumptuously lapping at the pliant pink flesh and listening to Fox's pleasured sounds.

Fox's head was fuzzy and warm with euphoria, the waterfall's roar buzzing in his ears. If he let Gaël do whatever he wanted, Fox would tumble over the edge into an orgasmic puddle before he even got the chance to be filled with Gaël's delicious dick.

"Gaël..." Fox managed to moan. The pad of Gaël's finger pressed into Fox's prostate and it was as if he could feel everything, the whorls of Gaël's fingerprints, the texture of his tongue, imprinting themselves forever on his insides. "P-please...fuck me..."

With one last indulgent stroke, Gaël's tongue and fingers withdrew, replaced by the tip of his cock teasing Fox's soaked entrance. He pressed forward slowly, careful not to cause Fox any discomfort in the absence of proper lube.

Fox bit his knuckle. He wanted to move, to take all of Gaël in. But he knew he had to be patient. Gaël liked to take his time.

"You're so tight," Gaël groaned. His lips trailed up Fox's spine, and Fox's hips pushed back just a little more, taking all of Gaël's thick cock. Gaël's teeth grazed Fox's bare shoulder, and he began to move, hips rolling like the waves beyond the horizon, powerful and fluid. The thrusts quickly grew in intensity. Fox tried to match the pace, rutting his hips back to take Gaël up to the base with every thrust.

"So perfect," Gaël praised, his hands gripping Fox's waist hard. He was always like this when he was inside Fox, worshiping him body and soul.

Fox's cries of pleasure echoed off the ceiling of the cave. He reached between his legs to wrap his hand around his own cock, pumping in time with the rhythm of Gaël's thrusts.

Gaël panted, planting one foot against the stone to get a deeper angle and now hitting Fox's prostate with every thrust. Fox's carnal need sharpened.

"Fuck. Right there," he panted, his own hand moving more desperately around his weeping cock.

"Come for me, sweetheart," Gaël moaned.

Fox was swimming in Gaël's touch, drowning in it. The ecstasy left him feeling drunk as he crested the wave of his orgasm. Gaël rode him through it as Fox's cum spilled between his fingers onto the damp stone.

"You're so perfect. So beautiful," Gaël rasped as Fox's slick walls clenched and quivered around him. "I'm gonna make you come again."

Fox's first orgasm was barely even over, but Gaël's words ramped his need back up again, moving him quickly past overstimulation and into shuddering shockwaves. Every thrust of Gaël's exquisite cock sent another jolt through him.

"I'm close," Fox panted. All he could do was brace against the rock beneath him. Suddenly Gaël pulled out, pushing Fox onto his back and burying himself in again. He captured Fox's lips with his own, and his hips stuttered. Fox's mind blanked out for a moment, filled only with the rippling sensation of his second orgasm. A moment later, Gaël's cock throbbed, and his cum rushed hot into Fox's quivering cavity.

Gaël groaned as his hips stuttered to a stop. He leaned down to nuzzle into the crook of Fox's neck, kissing the spot where his pulse thundered beneath his skin. Fox wrapped his arms around Gaël's broad shoulders, still panting as they both came down from their orgasms. Gaël's now softening cock was still seated deep inside him.

After a few moments, Gaël withdrew, but he stayed hovering over Fox, gazing at him.

"Gods, you're beautiful, Foxy." His lips brushed across the freckles on Fox's cheek reverently.

Fox's stomach fluttered. It was such a simple compliment, yet from Gaël's lips, it sounded like poetry.

Gaël sat up and helped Fox up as well.

"Was this your plan all along?" Fox asked teasingly.

Gaël's cheeks flushed prettily.

"Maybe."

"Naughty." Fox bumped his shoulder against Gaël's. Gaël just smirked back.

CHAPTER 14

AUGUST 23RD, 1666

A week passed in the calmness of the island. Repairs on both ships were well underway, with Logan and John supervising. Knowing that Logan had it well in hand, Rowan was able to relax into his time with Yves, even if he did feel a little guilty about pushing all the work onto his first mate.

Yves kept him busy both in and out of the bedroom. Rowan's back was perpetually slightly sore, but Yves cared for him well, and he didn't really mind.

Yves woke him early one morning with a kiss on the temple. Rowan shifted, wiping a dribble of drool from his chin.

"It's time to wake up." Yves's voice was still husky from sleep. And despite himself, Rowan felt the ever present attraction kindle in his gut. He groaned and felt Yves's long fingers run through his hair.

"We have something important to do today."

Rowan opened his eyes blearily to see Yves leaning over him, ebony hair falling over his eyes.

"Can I kiss you?" Yves asked. He'd asked every morning. Maybe it was his way of apologizing for the scare he'd given Rowan that first morning on the island, not that it prevented him from being rough with Rowan the rest of the time.

He moved his hand from Rowan's hair, brushing the pad of his thumb over Rowan's lower lip. Rowan sighed contentedly and raised his chin up to meet Yves's lips. Yves's fingers moved down to rub at the edge of Rowan's ear.

Rowan's cock twitched. But he was still sated from the night before. Yves knew how to please him more than any partner he'd had before.

Yves ended the kiss with a quick swipe of his tongue over Rowan's lip.

"So what is it?" Rowan asked when he caught his breath.

Yves smiled. His perfectly white teeth gleamed in the soft light from the window.

"There is someone very important I want you to meet today."

THEY DRESSED QUICKLY and simply in trousers and loose linen shirts. When Rowan went to buckle his cutlass to his side as usual, Yves stopped him.

"There's no need for that today."

Rowan raised an eyebrow. He left his sword on the bed but still kept the knife on his belt.

They left the mansion through the back, made their way through the overgrown gardens, and began walking down a well groomed path. Yves looked especially handsome today. His hair gleamed beneath the dappled light that shone through the canopy. His crisp white shirt had lace at the collar and cuffs and was tucked into a pair of tight mulberry colored trousers. The ever present ruby glinted in his ear.

Rowan felt almost ugly beside the Demon's beauty, like a barnacle clinging to the hull of a royal ship.

They walked down the path for a time, hand in hand. Nephele flew overhead, eventually diving into the trees to hunt. Yves and Rowan left the fields behind, turning down a side path that led in a direction Rowan hadn't ventured before.

"Where are we going?" he asked, thinking of his abandoned cutlass back in the mansion. It wasn't that he thought Yves would harm him. It was just in the nature of a pirate to always be waiting for the other shoe to drop.

"Almost there."

Up ahead, the trees parted, and they emerged into a sunny clearing. A quaint white cottage reminiscent of those along the main street was surrounded by a small garden full of a profusion of pink and white roses spilling over a low, white picket fence.

As they approached the gate, a woman's voice hummed a scattered tune over the white noise of the insects and distant waves. A beautiful woman knelt among the flowers, pruning a particularly lush rosebush. She wore a simple white dress and a wide-brimmed straw hat with a pink ribbon that matched the shade of the roses exactly. An abundance of onyx curls tumbled over her shoulders.

At the sound of Yves opening the gate, the woman looked up, a wide grin spreading across her gorgeous face. Yves made his way quickly down the path as the woman stood to meet him, flinging her arms around his neck in a fierce hug.

Rowan stopped at the gate, unable to make his feet cross the threshold. For an awful moment, he thought the woman must be Yves's wife. And that not only had Rowan begun an affair with the most notorious pirate on the seas, but a married one at that. Rowan might be a murderous pirate himself, but adultery was a moral line he would never willingly cross.

He tried to swallow around the lump in his throat as Yves picked the woman up and spun her around, then planted a kiss on her cheek.

When they both turned to look at Rowan, relief flooded through him. No wonder he had thought her so beautiful—she and Yves bore a striking resemblance to each other.

Yves tilted his head questioningly.

"Come in, Rowan. Meet my sister, Ana."

Ana smiled brightly, and Rowan stepped over the threshold. She held out her hand to shake, but Rowan decided to take a page from her brother's book. He took her hand and bowed over it, pressing a gallant kiss to her fingers.

"A pleasure."

"Oh? Who is this?" Ana said when Rowan released her hand.

Yves's mouth twisted ruefully. "This is Captain Rowan of the *Siren Song*. Also known as the Ghost Hawk."

Ana's dark brown eyes widened, flicking from Rowan's face to Yves's and back again. She seemed much more shocked by this news than she should have been considering her own brother was a far more infamous pirate than he.

Then she smiled knowingly.

"Of course. I've heard so much about you, Captain. It's wonderful to finally meet you."

She'd heard about him? It was wonderful to *finally* meet him? Yves's sister was either exceedingly polite or she hadn't heard of all the awful things he'd done.

But then again, her brother *was* the Deep Water Demon, scourge of the seas. And she lived on an island that's sole purpose was to house pirates. So maybe she was used to it.

There was a beat of silence before Ana said, "Well, come in! I'll put on some tea, or maybe you'd prefer lemonade?" She didn't wait for their answer but bustled back toward the house, retrieving her basket and gardening shears on the way.

"You look a bit shaken up," Yves commented as they followed her.

Rowan glanced up at him. "I thought you had a secret wife for a second there and was plotting ways to take my revenge on you."

"A secret wife? How scandalous."

As if the Demon didn't *live* on scandal and secrets.

"I mean, you do have a secret island."

"Touché."

The interior of the cottage was cozy and flooded with sunlight, furnished with what Rowan knew were the latest styles in Talvan high society. He raised an eyebrow at Yves as Ana swept ahead of them into the kitchen.

"The woman practically raised me. She deserves nice things." But there was no affection in Yves's deep voice; he stated this as if it was merely a fact. "Besides, I bought all of this fair and square." Rowan's skeptical eyebrow climbed higher. "With stolen money of course," Yves finished with a wolfish smile.

Ana breezed back into the sitting room, ushering them to sit on the hand-carved, velvet-upholstered sofa and placing a tray of lemonade on the low table. She settled on an adjacent wingback chair. Yves slung his arm across the back of the sofa behind Rowan and crossed his long legs elegantly.

Ana chatted easily with Rowan and her brother without touching on the obvious awkward questions about why Rowan was here. And why Yves's arm was practically around his shoulders. Despite her bubbliness, Rowan could sense a shrewd undercurrent beneath.

They passed the warm afternoon with cool drinks and pleasant conversation.

When Yves stepped away to refill Rowan's drink, Rowan turned to Ana.

"So, you said you'd heard a lot about me. Surely it can't have been some of the legends I've heard, or you wouldn't have let me into your lovely home so easily."

Ana smiled at him warmly.

"Rest assured I have heard those stories. I can't very well turn you away when they say awful things about my own brother. And I assure you, he's much worse than the legends. He..." She seemed to think better of what she was about to say and sipped her drink instead. When she looked back up, there was a glint of mirth in her eye. "Besides, Yves talks about you all the time."

Rowan's mouth dropped open in shock. Yves, the Deep Water Demon, had talked about him?

"What did he—" But Yves reentered the room, cutting off Rowan's question.

~

"I assume you're staying the night?" Ana asked some time later over dinner. "It's getting late."

"Of course." Yves leaned back in his chair, looking lazy and sated by both the meal and his sister's company. There was something a bit off about their relationship, and Rowan couldn't quite put his finger on it. Outwardly, Yves seemed the doting brother. Yet when Rowan looked closely, his smiles and words seemed distant, almost as if Yves's affection for his sister was simply familial duty. Yet if Ana noticed this, which Rowan had no doubt she did, she chose to ignore it.

Ana's eyes flicked to Rowan.

"And...should I make up the sofa?" she asked slowly, finally acknowledging the question she had likely been dying to ask for hours.

Rowan held his breath, wondering whether Yves would acknowledge the true nature of their relationship to his sister.

"No need," Yves said easily.

"Right." Ana flashed Rowan a dazzling smile that, on Yves's face, would have set his heart pounding. She stood and dropped a motherly kiss on the part of Yves's hair, then retreated to her bedroom, closing the door behind her. Yves gathered up the plates and brought them to the kitchen to wash.

A giggle bubbled up to Rowan's lips. He'd never imagined the fearsome Demon in a situation so domestic.

Yves flashed him a smile.

"What?"

"Nothing, nothing," Rowan gasped, getting his giggles under control. He stood to help Yves clean and dry the few dishes. When they were done, Yves led him out into the garden.

They sat on a wooden bench at the center of the garden, moonlight silvering the fragrant blooms all around them. Fireflies blinked in the dark air, and the chirring of frogs hummed in the distance.

Yves settled his arm around Rowan's shoulders, staving off the slight chill of the night. He leaned close, nuzzling the side of Rowan's neck and kissing the soft skin there.

Rowan cleared his throat. "So..."

"Hmm?" Yves kissed his neck again, breath hot on his throat.

"You told her about me."

Yves sat up straight immediately. Rowan could barely see his expression in the dark, but he thought Yves might be blushing.

"Why? What could you possibly have told her about me before we met?"

Yves's arm tightened around Rowan's shoulders. "Do you really want to know?" His tone was forbidding, but Rowan could tell it was an act. He was embarrassed by something, and Rowan desperately wanted to know what.

"Tell me." Now it was Rowan who leaned close, lips ghosting across Yves's sharp jaw. His hand moved up Yves's thigh. Yves shuddered beneath his touch.

"I..." For the first time Yves was flustered. "I may have told her everything about you."

"But not just the legends," Rowan said.

"No, not just the legends. I told her how much I hated you. How I longed to wring your neck and sink that little ship of yours to the bottom of the sea. I was..." He hissed as Rowan's teeth caught his earlobe. "I was jealous of your success."

Rowan pulled back slightly.

"*You* were jealous of *me*? But you're more successful than me by far."

"Maybe it wasn't so much jealousy as rivalry."

"So we really *were* rivals!" Rowan laughed.

Yves tilted his head, ruby glinting in his earlobe.

"Yes. We were." Rowan didn't miss the fact that they both referred to their rivalry as the past. What they were now, he didn't quite know.

"And you hated me." Rowan's hands went to the buttons at the collar of Yves's shirt.

"I did."

"Show me how much you hate me." Rowan's mouth was back at Yves's throat, his fingers unbuttoning Yves's collar and trailing beneath the edge of the fabric.

Yves gripped his shoulders, relishing the feel for just a moment before pushing him away to examine him with dark, brooding eyes. A firefly landed on Yves's shoulder, blinking lazily and lighting up the side of his face.

Yves licked his lips.

"What is it you want, Rowan?"

Rowan wasn't used to having the upper hand when it came to Yves. It both thrilled and unsettled him. He rubbed the pad of his thumb over the hollow of Yves's throat.

He didn't know the answer, so he kissed him. Yves made a small sound of surprise in his throat when their lips met. The firefly buzzed away, and Rowan pressed his advantage, tugging the hem of Yves's shirt out of his waistband and slipping his hand beneath. Yves's skin was heated as he caressed it.

"Mmm," Yves moaned. He pulled Rowan tight against his chest and tilted his head to deepen the kiss. Rowan's fingers hooked beneath the waistband of Yves's trousers. Yves pulled away just a little, their noses brushing.

"Darling...not here. It's my sister's house."

So the Demon did feel shame. Rowan huffed.

"Let's go back then," Rowan said. He hadn't meant to seduce him, but now they were both turned on. His cock was already hard, pressing uncomfortably against his trousers.

Yves's tongue poked the inside of his own cheek.

"You want to trek back through the woods in the dark just to have my cock inside you?"

"Well when you put it like that..." Rowan shifted in his seat, but it only served to increase the friction on his cock. He pressed another desperate kiss to Yves's mouth.

Yves seemed to reach a decision. He reached out to palm Rowan's cock over his trousers.

"You really want me?" he murmured.

"Yes," Rowan breathed. He didn't know when the power dynamic of the situation had shifted back to its usual balance, but he found he didn't care.

Yves's eyes flicked to the darkened windows of the cottage, half hidden by the profusion of flowers.

His fingers moved fast, releasing Rowan's needy cock from his trousers. He knelt on the gravel path and pulled Rowan to the edge of the bench. His tongue swirled around the tip of Rowan's cock, lapping up the small beads of precum. Rowan moaned softly, leaning his head against the back of the bench.

Yves worked his fingers around the base of Rowan's cock, then locked his lips around the velvety tip and slowly inched down over the shaft.

"Yves," Rowan gasped, trying to be quiet so as not to wake Ana, but Yves was making it very difficult. Yves hollowed his cheeks and bobbed his head faster. Pleasure built as Yves's throat flexed around his cock. His hips twitched, and he threaded his fingers through Yves's lush hair.

Rowan wouldn't last at this rate. A knot of heat already coiled tight in his belly. Yves looked up at him, black eyes wide and almost innocent as he took Rowan apart with his mouth. His lips met Rowan's pubic bone, long tongue snaking around the side of his shaft even as Rowan's cock was lodged deep in his throat.

Gods, that mouth was magic, and those eyes...

Rowan's fingers tightened in Yves's hair, and his hips bucked up involuntarily, chasing more friction. Chasing release.

Yves's teeth scraped lightly at Rowan's skin in warning. He shivered, and with another flick of Yves's tongue, the coil snapped, and Rowan came, hot cum rushing down Yves's throat.

"Ah..." He released his grip on Yves's hair, petting the silky tresses as Yves withdrew.

Yves settled next to Rowan again, rebuttoning Rowan's trousers and pressing a kiss to his sweat-slicked brow.

But Rowan wasn't done, not until he'd driven Yves as crazy as him. He leaned over to suck at Yves's neck, starting to unbutton his pants and slip to his knees. His head was still muddled by his recent release, and all he wanted was his mouth around Yves's hard length.

"Stop."

For a second Rowan thought they'd been caught. Yves's long fingers gripped his wrist, stopping his movements.

But they remained alone in the garden.

"Let me..." He tried to move again but Yves's fingers tightened on his wrist.

"Why won't you let me suck your dick?" Rowan asked, frustrated.

"I just...can't," Yves said quietly.

The residual fuzzy pleasure fled. Rowan sat up.

"I'm sorry."

"No." Yves shook his head, changing his grip to hold Rowan's hand gently. "It's not you."

"What..." Rowan hesitated, redirecting. "Will you tell me why?"

Yves bit his lip. They were still so close, only a breath away from another kiss. He could see the calculation running behind Yves's eyes. Rowan waited. Not moving. Not pushing.

"I..." Yves sighed and pressed a kiss to Rowan's lips as if gathering courage, the salty taste of Rowan's cum still on his tongue. When he pulled back, he seemed more resolved. "Something bad happened to me when I was younger." He swallowed nervously, glancing down at their clasped hands.

"You don't have to tell me," Rowan murmured. He'd enjoyed having the upper hand earlier, but seeing Yves vulnerable now was unnerving.

"Ana and I became orphans very young," Yves finally said. "She's only older than me by four years, and she did her best to provide for us and keep me safe, but we were on the streets most nights."

Rowan smoothed Yves's hair back from his face, lending silent support.

"She did whatever she could, even if it put her in danger. And when I was a kid, I wanted to help her out so she wouldn't have to work so hard. I got a job as a kitchen boy in a fancy house. But I was young and naive and..." He cleared his throat, leaning into Rowan's soothing hands. But after a moment a feral gleam crept into his eye. "Ana saved me. I had my revenge eventually, and now I can be the one who protects my sister." He took a deep breath. "Because of all that it's...hard for me to relinquish control."

Rowan nodded. If you were the one giving pleasure, you were in control of the situation. If you were receiving pleasure, it was easier to fall apart. After meeting Yves, Rowan knew that very well.

"I'm sorry." Rowan squeezed his hand reassuringly. The frogs continued to chirr under the trees around them, and the fireflies had congregated in the leaves and thorns of the rose bushes. "Tell me what's off limits for you."

"I don't bottom, and I don't get head. That's it."

Rowan nodded. He wanted to hug Yves, but he felt almost like the beautiful man before him had turned to spun glass.

"Let's go to sleep," Yves murmured.

The matter was closed. Rowan let Yves lead him back into the house to his bedroom. The island breeze ruffled white curtains at the open window as they slowly stripped the clothes from each other's bodies. Yves pulled him into his arms under the covers, and he fell asleep with his head cradled against Rowan's chest.

CHAPTER 15

AUGUST 23RD, 1666

The wide hallway was quiet as Logan approached the office on the second level, the only sound that of his own boots on the polished wood floors. Rowan had asked him to oversee the *Siren Song*'s repairs, and it felt good to have something to do while they were stuck on this island.

He stopped in front of the door, its panels carved with swirls of waves. He took a deep breath, gathering his courage to face the Deep Water Demon. They needed more sailcloth for the repairs, and of course he had to ask for it from the man in charge. Personally, Logan found the Demon to be a bit creepy, but Rowan seemed smitten. Logan hoped it wouldn't affect his judgment too much when it came time to leave.

Logan's fist thudded dully against the wood, and he heard a voice on the other side bid him enter. He stepped into the cool interior of the office. It was well-appointed, with a marble fireplace, lush carpets, and a large mahogany desk that had definitely once belonged to a Talvan admiral or general if the five-flower insignia carved into the front was any indication. There was a space in the center of the desk where a crest or monogram would be. But it was blank, having been destroyed and sanded over, but Logan thought he could see the ghost of an 'R' or maybe a 'B' beneath the new coat of lacquer. The Demon certainly had eccentric and expensive taste.

However, the man sitting at the desk was not the Demon, but he was just as scary.

"First Mate Logan," John Hakon said in that unknowable monotone he had. He set a quill pen down on the leather ink blotter. "To what do I owe this visit?"

Logan closed the door behind him and crossed the room, sitting in one of the empty chairs across from John.

"I was expecting the De—" Logan cleared his throat. "I was hoping to speak to your captain."

"Ah." John settled back in his chair. He picked up a glass of what looked like whiskey from among a small pile of wood shavings and a half-finished carving of a bird. "Unfortunately he is still out...what's the word...cavorting with *your* captain."

Logan snorted. "Cavorting would be a good word for it, yes."

John's smile was small. He took a sip of his drink.

"No matter what we call it. It leaves me in charge. So what can I do for you?"

John seemed to think this situation was just as annoying as Logan did. But Logan had long ago given up on talking his captain out of things. Rowan always took care of his crew, even when he led them into danger with some harebrained plan. He deserved to let loose every once in a while, even if Logan didn't approve of how he was doing it.

Or who he was doing it with.

Logan would be there to pick up the pieces when it was all over. He always was.

"I need at least ten more yards of sailcloth and a few other things for the repairs," Logan said, wondering if John's exasperation at his captain's behavior was because it was out of character for the Demon or in it. "The sooner we can get out of your hair, the better."

John glanced out the window, noting the position of the sun.

"It's almost midday. Have lunch with me, and we can discuss it."

Logan wasn't sure what exactly there was to discuss about sail-cloth. But he was hungry, so he agreed. John led him down to the main floor of the mansion and into the hot interior of the kitchen at the back of the building. A person he assumed was the cook slid a chipped china plate across to John, already loaded with chicken and potatoes. He was a man of habit then, predictable.

"A plate for Mr. Crowder too, please," John said, and the cook quickly assembled a plate for Logan as well. Logan took it with thanks and followed John out to a small walled garden, overgrown with various flowers. At the center, a round table and two chairs sat on a patio of cracked mosaic tile.

They sat and ate in silence for a little while, bees buzzing in the warm air around them.

"So what is this place?" Logan asked after he finished the last bite. He had to admit, all the food he'd eaten here on the island was delicious. He only wished ship food could be half as good. That was the one thing he loathed about sailing—no matter how good your cook was, or how well-stocked the ship, the food was always shit.

John glanced up at him as if he'd almost forgotten he was there. He looked lazily around at the garden.

"This used to be the private garden of the lady of the house." He laughed, a surprisingly cheerful sound coming from someone who looked so serious. "I guess that's me now."

"You're...the lady of the house?" Logan asked, confused.

"Well I'm second in command so close enough," John said. His brown eyes cut toward Logan. "So I guess we're both the ladies of the house right now. Unless that captain of yours is looking to take up the job."

There was an insult hidden somewhere in there, but Logan couldn't quite place it. He sat up straighter. "Do you think that's a possibility? Would the Demon keep him here?" A little well of anxiety opened up in the pit of his stomach.

"Keep him?" John took a small sip from the glass of whiskey he'd brought down from the office, wood shavings still clung to the bottom. "I don't know. He's never done something like this before."

That was disconcerting. They were all in uncharted waters here.

"Can I have some of that?"

John took a flask from the inner pocket of his jacket and handed it over. Logan took a swig of whiskey. In the heat of the day, it went straight to his head. His brain buzzed along with the bees.

"What about your captain?" John asked. "Does he fall in love easily? Would he stay if the Demon asked?"

"He doesn't fall easily," Logan admitted.

"Bunch of crazy bastards." John shook his head, and Logan knew he was encompassing the other four crew members who were now sleeping together in that assessment. They both drank again.

"I don't understand it," Logan muttered.

John sat up straighter, looking at him intently.

"You don't understand it?" Something in his tone put Logan on edge.

When Logan didn't elaborate, John pushed further. "What don't you understand?"

Logan felt hot suddenly and took another gulp from the flask.

"I don't understand how they can be so foolish. Don't get me wrong, my captain is a fool, but never like this."

"Lust makes fools of us all." John sighed.

"Wouldn't know," Logan muttered behind the flask.

John's intense eyes sliced to Logan's face, riveting him to the spot.

Fuck, he shouldn't have said that. But the whiskey and the heat had loosened his tongue.

"A virgin pirate?" John whistled. "What are the chances?"

The chances were slim, Logan knew. Yet here he was in all his virginal glory. It wasn't that he didn't have the desire or opportunity. And it wasn't that he was unschooled in the ways of sex. One couldn't share a room with Fox for years and *not* get a thorough education in the sexual possibilities. He'd just never actually *done* anything. He was too focused on more important matters, and that made him a bit scatterbrained when it came to interpersonal relationships. Then there was the fact that they were always moving from place to place—the timing was just never right.

Logan felt his cheeks flush. John tilted his head, trying to catch Logan's eye, but he stared at his plate, the delicate painted roses still smeared with chicken grease.

"So do you want some experience?"

Logan's head snapped up.

"W-what?"

John smiled at him lazily, as if this were the most natural conversation for them to be having instead of discussing the yardage of sailcloth he needed. John stood and slowly removed his jacket, revealing a subtly muscular form beneath his white shirt. He hung the jacket carefully on the back of his chair and approached. Logan eyed him warily.

"I said," John leaned down with a hand on the back of Logan's chair, pinning him. "Mister First Mate Logan, would you like to lose your virginity to me?"

Logan opened and closed his mouth like a gaping fish. It felt like every bee in the whole garden had flown straight into his brain and was buzzing around frantically, crashing against the inside of his skull.

"Ah, sorry." John removed his hand from the back of the chair. "Maybe this is more your speed." He cupped Logan's chin, tilted it up slowly, and kissed him.

All the buzzing ceased, and there was only the feeling of John's lips on his. This was his first kiss, baring the platonic pecks Fox was always pestering him with. It wasn't quite how he'd always expected it would go, but it was pleasant.

When John's tongue slipped inside Logan's mouth, a bolt of lightning shot straight to his crotch.

John released Logan's mouth but didn't release his chin from his concerningly strong grasp.

"Well?"

"I...um..."

John's eyes roamed down Logan's body to where his erection was bulging inside his trousers.

"Oh? Is this your answer?"

He waited, and Logan's brain finally caught up to the situation he found himself in.

"H-here?" he asked. The sweet pollen of the flowers mingled with the faint whiskey smell of John's breath.

"I can't exactly march you through the house sporting that." John glanced down at Logan's erection again.

He was right. And besides, Logan didn't think he could wait.

"Yes," Logan agreed simply.

John smirked as if he knew this was the inevitable outcome. "I'll go easy on you."

Somehow Logan doubted that. But he leaned forward anyway, kissing John back. John hummed, pleased, and pulled Logan to his feet. Before he knew it, Logan's back was pressed against the crumbling brick of the garden wall, crushing the climbing flowers against his heated skin.

John's tongue swirled through Logan's mouth. John swiftly unbuckled Logan's belt and a thrill of anxiety and anticipation quivered through him. John's hand slipped into his trousers, stroking his cock. Logan tried to stifle a moan, and John took that as encouragement. He broke off their kiss and sank to one knee on the cracked tiles. He pulled Logan's trousers down his hips, letting his fully hard cock spring free.

Logan watched with half-lidded eyes as John licked a stripe over the sensitive underside of his cock. Logan's eyes slid closed. He leaned his head against the wall behind him, letting the sun warm his face.

John's lips found the tip of his cock, then sank down around him, hot and soft. Logan almost came right then, but he got himself under control quickly, biting the inside of his cheek. He didn't want this to be over before it even began. The tip of his cock hit the back of John's throat, and John hummed, vocal cords vibrating.

Logan couldn't help the small, pathetic noises that escaped him as John's mouth worked him. Sucking and licking expertly. Applying friction where he needed, backing off when he needed. Fuck, it felt so good. Better than anything. Better than the delicious food they'd just eaten. Better than being on the open sea. He was struggling to keep it together. He wanted this to last as long as possible.

John's soft tongue swirled around his shaft on a downstroke, and Logan's hips bucked involuntarily. John grunted and pinned Logan's hips to the wall with one hand, his thumb massaging the tense muscle of Logan's groin. Logan opened his eyes and looked down at the man whose mouth was latched around his cock. But John was focused on the task at hand. His long lashes fluttered against his suntanned cheeks. Logan threaded his fingers through John's glossy chestnut hair, and the man finally looked up at him.

Shit, John's eyes were still intimidating, but now they just served to turn Logan on even more.

His thoughts were interrupted by a particularly deep stroke, accompanied by a lewd sucking sound from John's mouth.

"Ah, fuck..." The coil of pleasure that had been building in the pit of his stomach finally snapped. His cock throbbed as a tide of pleasure washed through him, and his orgasm spilled into John's mouth. John pulled away, spitting it into the flowerbed.

He stood, wiping a bit of cum from his bottom lip with a monogrammed handkerchief that had someone else's initials on it.

"Damn, I thought you were a virgin. Why'd you last so long?" He leaned closer, hitching Logan's trousers back up his hips.

"It just...felt so good. I wanted it to last," Logan answered innocently.

John's laugh this time was loud and genuine, showing his teeth and gums.

"Of course you did." He patted Logan on the cheek. "I learned from the best."

CHAPTER 16

AUGUST 25TH, 1666

Two days after Yves took Rowan to meet Ana, Rowan decided to check on the progress of repairs on the *Siren Song*. He felt almost as if he'd been in a dream since arriving on Illusion, forgetting his worries and responsibilities when he was wrapped up in Yves's arms. The beautiful man's company was wholly distracting and intoxicating. Before Rowan knew it, so much time had passed.

"I don't see why this is necessary," Yves said as Rowan pulled on his boots. "Your first mate seems to be taking care of everything adequately."

"I like to be a bit more hands-on. I get restless if I'm not doing something."

"I wouldn't say we've been doing *nothing*." Yves smirked, and Rowan felt a blush rising to his cheeks.

"Still, aren't you hungry to get back out into the open sea? Back to pirating? I never thought the Deep Water Demon would be complacent," Rowan teased.

A muscle in Yves's jaw twitched.

"I suppose I should check the *Kraken*'s progress as well," he sighed.

They made their way down to the docks, collecting Logan and Gaël on the way.

"Where is Fox today?" Rowan asked. Though Fox and Gaël had

never actually said they were a couple, it was extremely obvious by the way they were attached at the hip. It was almost odd now to see one without the other.

"At the tavern with Henri," Gaël answered.

The group separated into two landing boats which took them out to the waiting ships.

~

Gaël eyed his captain as they stepped onto the deck of the *Kraken*. The ship buzzed with carpenters and other crew members working on repairs. Captain Yves seemed to be in a bad mood, but Gaël couldn't think of why. The repairs were going well, and his fling with the Ghost Hawk was obviously quite active. Maybe he had the same things on his mind as Gaël did.

The captain strode through the ship with Gaël on his heels, checking up on the progress. He was cordial with the crew but they'd never been close like the *Siren*'s crew seemed to be. Gaël thought maybe he held himself aloof on purpose to lend himself authority and maintain the mystique of his position.

Captain Yves stopped in the hallway after checking on the gun decks. Gaël stopped short behind him, wondering what he was doing. There were no repairs happening here, and they were alone.

"Well? Say what you wanted to say then," the captain said without turning to look at him. He might be aloof, but that didn't mean he was unobservant. You couldn't become the most feared pirate captain on the sea without knowing how to read people. Gaël cleared his throat; there was no use beating around the bush.

"I would like you to release me from service on the *Kraken*," Gaël said evenly.

The demonic captain turned to look at him now, anger flaring in his dark eyes.

"The answer is no," he said without hesitation. Without asking why Gaël would decide to leave his home of several years so suddenly. The captain turned away as if the matter were closed.

"I think you misunderstand, Captain," Gaël said. "I am only asking your permission out of respect. But I am going to leave whether you agree to it or not."

Was that hurt he saw flicker across Captain Yves's expression? Surely not.

"Why?" he finally asked, deadly quiet.

"I want to join the crew of the *Siren* because of Fox."

"Because of Fox?" the captain repeated, as if he could not begin to fathom what the words might mean.

Gaël stepped closer, appealing. "I love him. And I promised I wouldn't leave him again. Surely..." He hesitated. "Surely even you can understand that."

"Even I—" Captain Yves's voice was full of barely suppressed rage. Did he understand? Maybe. But he would never admit it. Gaël wilted beneath his captain's intense gaze, but he did not back down.

Then just as quickly as it had sparked, Captain Yves's anger seemed to die.

"Do as you wish," he said, turning to glide down the hall once more. "I have neither the room nor the patience for lovestruck fools on my ship."

Would the captain deny himself even now? When anyone could see he was just as much a fool as Gaël?

~

THE TOWN on the island of Illusion could barely be called a town, but it had a tavern, and that was good enough for Fox.

After Gaël had told him that morning that he would be busy all day inspecting repairs with the Demon, Fox had commandeered Henri for an adventure. He wanted to make the most of the sunny day, and while Henri couldn't go exploring around the island itself, there was nothing stopping them from exploring the town. There wasn't much there—a blacksmith, a carpenter, the typical things that all small villages had. But by midday they ended up where every pirate ended up eventually, at the tavern.

The interior was packed mostly with crew from both pirate ships, having little to do while the repairs were being made. Cheers and raised glasses from their fellow *Siren* crew members greeted Fox and Henri as they entered.

They whiled away the afternoon, sipping their mugs of ale and mead and chatting with their friends about whether they would be leaving before the harvest celebration at the beginning of September.

No sooner had Henri excused himself to the toilet than another crew member slid into his recently vacated space on the bench next to Fox.

"Haven't seen you around in a while," Cyrus said, taking a gulp from his tankard. He was a gunner on the *Siren*, taller than Fox but shorter than Henri. Broad-shouldered with a face more disposed to frowning than smiling. And he used to be Fox's frequent bed fellow.

"Yep," Fox agreed. The others at the table had turned to their own conversations.

Cyrus shifted closer along the bench. Fox's back stiffened.

"So, when are you going to get sick of the new guy and go back to normal?" Cyrus asked casually.

Fox choked on his ale.

"What?"

"I said, when are you going to get tired of playing house and start sleeping around again?" Cyrus leaned forward a bit, hand resting on Fox's thigh under the table. "I'm getting impatient."

Gods, he hadn't formally broken it off with any of his ongoing flings when he and Gaël had become a thing. He didn't think he needed to. He just assumed they would get the hint. What use was formally breaking it off when they hadn't been formally together in the first place?

He picked up Cyrus's hand gingerly between thumb and forefinger, removing it from his thigh as if it were a wayward salamander.

"We won't be going back to 'normal.'" Fox laughed, keeping his tone light. "I'm with Gaël exclusively. That's the new normal."

Cyrus frowned. "You'll get over him soon enough. You never could be satisfied with just one person."

Fox's lips thinned into an annoyed line.

"No, I really won't." Now a few of the others at the table were watching them. Among them were one or two of Fox's other former flings. Did they all feel the same as Cyrus did? Just waiting for his relationship with Gaël to run its course? He scooched down the bench away from Cyrus's reach.

"I know it will be difficult to replace someone as amazing as me," Fox joked, pitching his voice so the others could hear. No use having this conversation more than once. "But you'll just have to try your best."

A few of their tablemates laughed, but Cyrus's scowl deepened.

"You'll come crawling back when we leave this godforsaken island," he growled.

"I won't be crawling towards you, however."

"You're in my seat." Henri's deep voice cut in before Cyrus could get another word out.

Cyrus looked up at the much taller man, still imposing despite his broken leg. His gaze flicked to the judgmental faces staring at him around the table. He got up with a huff, taking his drink elsewhere.

"I never liked him," Henri grumbled, retaking his seat.

"You don't like anyone I've slept with," Fox countered. Most of the others had gone back to their own conversations.

"I like Gaël."

"Really?" Fox beamed, the unpleasant conversation almost forgotten.

"He seems like a good guy, and he can keep up with you which is surprising," Henri admitted. "But Cyrus has a mean streak. You better watch out for him."

Fox shrugged. "It's not a big deal. He'll get over it soon enough."

Henri looked skeptical. "Are you going to tell Gaël?"

"Like I said, it's no big deal. There's nothing to tell."

CHAPTER 17

AUGUST 25TH, 1666

Henri slipped into the darkened room he and Robin shared. Or he tried to slip in; it was a bit difficult with the broken leg and crutches and all. He needn't have bothered with stealth though. Despite the late hour, Robin was still awake, poring over his medical notebooks by lamplight. He looked up when Henri came in, furrowed brow smoothing when he caught sight of his lover.

Henri felt an overwhelming fondness for the other man well up in his heart as the golden lamplight played across his features. He was gorgeous, especially like this, lit in the same light by which they'd first made love. Henri hobbled to Robin's side and bent to kiss him.

"Welcome back," Robin said when the kiss was broken. "Not too drunk, I hope?"

"Would I have made it back up here if I was?" Henri chuckled. It was no secret that he was a bit accident prone, even Robin knew that by now.

"Fair enough."

"I hope you didn't stay up late because of me," Henri said.

"Partly you, partly this." Robin gestured to his notebook, which was open to a page with detailed medical diagrams Henri couldn't even begin to understand.

"Maybe you should have been an artist instead. Those illustrations are amazing."

Robin blushed delicately. Henri adored making him blush,

almost as much as he adored making him smile. And both were bless-edly easy to do.

"Come here." Robin pulled him gently closer till Henri's hips were pressed to his chest where he still sat at the desk. Robin propped his chin on Henri's stomach. He wrapped his arms around Henri's waist and gazed at him.

"Did you have a good time with your friends?"

Henri hummed and nodded, carding his fingers through Robin's fluffy hair.

In the days since their reconciliation, the two of them had settled into a comfortable level of touch. But they hadn't had sex again. For Henri's part, he didn't want to push Robin's boundaries and scare him away again. For Robin's part, Henri suspected he was probably still worried about jostling Henri's broken leg.

But tonight he'd sat at the tavern with Fox until Gaël came back from the *Kraken*. They all had dinner together. Of course, Fox and Gaël were all over each other, especially when the drinks started flowing. And though Henri was happy for his friend, he was jealous too.

"What are you thinking about?" Robin asked, and Henri realized he'd been zoning out while playing with Robin's hair, which was now sticking up at odd angles like it did in the mornings.

"You," Henri answered.

Robin raised his eyebrows, prompting Henri to continue. But he didn't know what to say. There wasn't much to say really. This was the first time Henri had ever been in love, and his mind was filled only with Robin in all his waking and sleeping hours.

So instead Henri bent down, fingers still in Robin's hair, and kissed him with all the passion that had been building up for days.

Robin made a small, surprised noise, but his lips parted readily for Henri's tongue. His large hands tightened on Henri's waist, and Henri kissed him breathless.

"What was that about?" Robin gasped when Henri finally released him.

Henri lowered himself carefully to kneel between Robin's knees so that they were face-to-face. "Maybe I just wanted to kiss you."

"Maybe you should do it again."

This time, Henri didn't hold back. Their lips connected hard, and he leaned into Robin's embrace. Robin groaned softly. This hadn't been Henri's plan for the night. But kissing Robin in the lamp-light intoxicated him far more than spending the day at the tavern had. He wrapped an arm around Robin's waist and pulled him closer until Henri's waist was slotted between Robin's thighs. Robin was already half hard, but Henri still didn't want to push him too fast.

Still, his hands wandered beneath the hem of Robin's shirt, caressing the soft, pale skin of his waist and eliciting small noises of pleasure from Robin's busy mouth. His other hand slid up Robin's thigh.

"You shouldn't push yourself. Your leg..." Robin murmured between kisses.

"Don't worry so much, Doc." Henri's hand had made it to the top of Robin's thigh, and he hesitated for just a second before brushing his thumb over Robin's hard length.

"Henri..." This time it was a moan, and it sent shivers throughout Henri's body.

"Tell me when to stop."

He hitched Robin's shirt up further, exposing his stomach, and trailed kisses down the side of his neck. Robin squirmed but didn't stop him.

Emboldened, and now fully turned on, Henri pulled Robin's shirt off over his head and continued his trail of kisses down Robin's chest. His dick was already straining uncomfortably inside his trousers. He sucked at Robin's right nipple, eliciting another moan. Robin's hips twitched, his cock rubbing up against Henri's torso.

Henri looked up at him questioningly, but Robin's eyes were closed, his head tilted back.

"What do you want?" Henri asked. He desperately wanted to fuck Robin, but couldn't stand the thought of pressuring him.

Robin looked at him, eyes half-lidded and lustful. Henri's breath caught. But instead of answering, Robin stood up, helping Henri to his feet as well. Henri felt a flash of disappointment but didn't let it show on his face.

The disappointment didn't last long. Robin gripped Henri's waist in one large hand and pushed him up against the edge of the desk. He pressed their bodies close, his lips a breath away from Henri's.

"I want you so bad."

He captured Henri's lips in a fierce kiss, tongue flicking into Henri's mouth. Robin braced one hand against the top of the desk, leaning further into the kiss. He ground their hips together, eliciting low moans from both of their throats.

Henri let Robin take the lead, enjoying the warmth of his hands, the friction of their bodies pressed together. Robin's other hand slid down Henri's waist to cup the curve of his ass. He rutted his hips against Henri's again.

"Robin, please," Henri gasped. Robin's hand moved to the back of Henri's thigh and eased him onto the edge of the desk. He palmed Henri's still clothed cock, then undid the fastenings on the front of Henri's trousers and slipped his hand beneath. He stroked Henri's length twice. Then pushed Henri's trousers down over his hips, releasing his cock.

He knelt and swirled his tongue over the head.

"Robin," Henri moaned. Robin glanced up at him, eyes sparkling in the lamplight. Despite the thrill of seeing Robin's beautiful lips on his cock, his mood sobered for a moment. "Are you sure about this?"

Robin's lips left his cock. Henri bit his lip, but Robin was smiling.

"Of course." He ran his lips lightly over the soft skin of Henri's shaft. Henri shuddered and leaned back on his elbows but kept his eyes on Robin's face. That slight, perpetual smile was still on his lips as the tip of Henri's cock breached them. His mouth sank down slowly, the velvety interior dragging deliciously around Henri's shaft.

"Fuck," Henri gasped. A coil of pleasure wound tight in his stomach, and it was all he could do not to buck his hips up into Robin's mouth seeking more. Robin continued to move. The pace quickened a bit. Robin's tongue cradled the sensitive underside of Henri's cock as it slid wetly in and out of his mouth.

Gods, Robin was beautiful with his lips stretched around Henri's girth, a light sheen of sweat across his brow and the orange light reflecting off his messy hair.

Henri cupped Robin's jaw and lifted his face up. Robin released his cock and let Henri guide him into a kiss instead. Henri's other hand opened the front of Robin's trousers, and he rubbed the pad of his thumb over the weeping slit at the tip of Robin's cock.

"Fuck, Henri. I want you inside me."

Something in Henri's chest snapped. There was a flurry of activity, their clothing thrown into the corner. Henri tripped out of his trousers as he tried to strip them off over his splint, but Robin caught him, giggling. Their lips crashed back together once they were stripped down to the skin. Robin's meticulously organized notebooks scattered to the floor as Henri lifted him onto the desk. He grasped Robin's soft thighs and spread them wide. His hands slipped down Robin's inner thigh, and his thumb circled Robin's entrance.

"Do you have—"

Robin produced a small bottle of lube from the top desk drawer.

"You'll have to walk me through it. I haven't done this part before," Henri said, leaning his forehead against Robin's.

"Here." Robin was still a bit breathless. He uncorked the bottle and spread the sweet-smelling liquid over Henri's long fingers. "Start with just one finger. Go slow."

Henri did as he was told, gently pushing his index finger past the tight ring of muscle at Robin's entrance. Robin's hole clenched around his finger for a second before relaxing. He inhaled sharply.

"You okay?"

Robin nodded, and Henri pressed his finger forward again slowly. Robin kissed him, but Henri was distracted, concentrating on getting this right.

"I'm okay, love. You're not hurting me. Just move."

Henri swallowed nervously. But he pulled his finger back a bit then thrust it slowly in again, curling it up in the way Fox had told him about a long time ago. Robin moaned quietly.

"Good?" Henri asked.

"Keep moving."

Henri obeyed, gaining a bit more confidence as his actions caused little noises to escape Robin's lips. Repeating the actions that produced the best reactions.

"Add a second finger," Robin instructed.

Henri pulled his finger out and slicked it up with more lube before pushing two fingers back in. Robin's back arched when Henri inserted them.

"Open your fingers a little," Robin huffed. "Stretch me out for your cock."

Henri thought the passion of the moment would lessen with Robin teaching him. But Robin's breathless instructions were driving him insane. Telling Henri exactly what he liked, exactly how to please him. Henri scissored his fingers open as he thrust, gently stretching him.

"Good," Robin moaned.

The lube squelched as Henri's fingers caressed Robin's soft and yielding walls. When he thought he was stretched enough, he added a third finger without being told. His fingers sank in up to his knuckles, and he curled them again, finally finding the magical little bundle of nerves that made Robin clench tightly around him.

"Right there," Robin gasped.

Henri brushed it firmly again, alternating between thrusting and rubbing circles into his prostate. He basked in the wash of praise and pleasured sounds that spilled from Robin's lips.

"Fuck. Henri. Stop."

Henri's fingers stilled immediately, his eyebrows drawing together in concern.

"Are you—"

"I need you inside me. Now."

No sooner had Henri removed his fingers than Robin dragged him forward into a desperate kiss, his teeth catching on Henri's lower lip. Henri hastily slicked his cock with lube and lined it up with Robin's entrance.

He hesitated.

"Henriiii," Robin whined.

Henri couldn't hold back anymore. He thrust in harder than he'd intended, wet walls closing around his cock.

Robin gasped, his fingernails digging into Henri's shoulders.

"Sorry," Henri murmured, but his hips were already moving. Already dragging his cock back out and then thrusting deeper. Chasing pleasure.

"Don't stop," Robin moaned.

"Shit." Henri couldn't quite get the right leverage. His broken leg couldn't take much weight, and the desk wasn't really the ideal surface to have sex on.

Henri lifted Robin further onto the desk and hitched his own knee up onto the edge to relieve the pressure on his splinted leg. He rolled his hips forward, sinking deep into Robin's dripping hole. The girth of his cock pressed Robin's prostate, and Robin arched his back, eyes sliding closed. Henri leaned forward to kiss him, the movements of his hips setting a steady pace, dragging across Robin's prostate with every thrust.

"Yes! Faster!" Robin groaned. He clutched Henri's shoulders fiercely. His nails dug little painful crescents into Henri's skin. Henri hitched one of Robin's legs over his shoulder, turning his head to bite the supple flesh of his leg. He picked up the pace as instructed, thrusts becoming aggressive as he delved deeper and deeper.

The lube squelched with every thrust, but it only served to heighten the tension coiling in his belly.

One of Robin's hands trailed down Henri's chest and stomach to the place where they were connected. The tips of his fingers brushed Henri's cock as it hammered into him.

"You fill me up so well," Robin moaned. Henri bit his lip. He'd never heard Robin speak so lewdly before, but he liked it, and it was making it hard to last as long as he needed to.

Henri grasped Robin's cock with his still lube-slick hand, pumping firmly in time with his thrusts. Robin bit back a moan, back arching up into Henri's touch. His eyes rolled back in his head, letting the sensations wash over him, lips parted in ecstasy.

"Henri, I'm—" Robin's words were interrupted by a hitching breath, his fingers still feeling the way Henri penetrated him.

"Come for me, baby," Henri panted. His thrusts were getting sloppy and rough as he neared his own release. Robin's nails raked down his arm, moans growing to a crescendo before they were suddenly cut off with a strangled noise. Pearly cum spilled across his stomach. Henri fucked him through his orgasm, now chasing his own. His hips stuttered. Thrusts quickened. He moaned Robin's name, and Robin's eyes opened to watch his face as he came apart. Henri clutched Robin's leg tight to his chest, rutting into him hard. Shockwaves of pleasure shattered his control, and he came, hot and throbbing, with one last thrust deep into Robin's core.

Henri exhaled shakily, the edges of his vision going a bit fuzzy. He squeezed his eyes shut for a moment, and when he opened them again, Robin was gazing at him blearily. Henri released Robin's leg and bent low over him, pressing their sweaty foreheads together. They stayed silent as they caught their breath, basking in the afterglow.

"Henri." Robin's voice was gentle but still a bit breathless.

"Hm?" Henri realized he'd sunk down to rest his forehead against Robin's collarbone. He pressed a languid kiss to the hollow of Robin's throat before pulling back a bit to look at his face. The lamp flame had burned low, but it still gave off enough steady light to see Robin's peaceful expression.

"I think I'm in love with you."

Henri couldn't help the smile that broke across his face. Nor could he help the slight twitch of his cock where it was still buried in Robin's ass. He pressed another kiss to Robin's lips.

"I *know* I'm in love with you."

Robin's smile lit the room, and a giddy giggle rose to his lips, stifled as Henri kissed him again.

After a moment, Henri withdrew, dropping his leg back to the floor, his knees almost buckling. Robin hopped off the desk and helped him to the bed even though his own legs quivered as well.

"Does your leg hurt?" Robin asked, brow knitting back into his worried, doctorly frown.

"A bit," Henri admitted.

"I shouldn't have let you exert yourself."

Henri pulled him down to the bed, and kissed his cheek. "Worth it," he declared.

Robin giggled. "Yes, it definitely was."

CHAPTER 18

AUGUST 29TH, 1666

Fox was hatching a plan to kidnap Gaël. First he would need a chicken...

He let half his brain wander into increasingly convoluted plans as he counted supplies and called the numbers back to Henri, who jotted tally marks down in the small notebook Robin had given them. When Robin had initially handed the notebook to Fox—seemingly forgetting that not everyone had the benefit of education—Fox had stared at it for a few seconds before informing Robin that he was, in fact, illiterate. Robin had apologized profusely, then set about drawing miniature pictures next to each word so Fox could decipher them. Ultimately though, it was Henri who could read, and Fox who could walk, so they'd teamed up to complete the inventory of the infirmary storeroom.

Fox licked his lips as he replaced the vials of some strange, green liquid back on their shelf. He called the number over his shoulder, to be met with the scratching of pen on paper as Henri recorded it. It had been a few days since Fox had run into Cyrus at the tavern, and the interaction still left a sour taste in his mouth. Since then, Cyrus had a bad habit of popping up wherever Fox was. Usually he wouldn't have even noticed. But Henri's warning and Cyrus's words about the future had been nagging at the corners of his mind.

As romantic as being star-crossed lovers on rival pirate ships sounded in theory, Fox didn't want to be apart from Gaël. How would Gaël keep his promise to stay together if the *Siren Song* and *Kraken's Fury* would be parting ways before long? Usually pirates could come and go from their crews as they pleased. But Fox didn't think the Deep Water Demon was that easygoing.

Hence the kidnapping.

Fox brought a vial of the next thing for Henri to read, only half paying attention. He, Henri, and Gaël had been assigned to help Robin take inventory and restock the *Siren*'s medical supplies for their inevitable departure. Old Joe had decided to stay on the island and retire in luxury. That left the *Siren* without a physician and the *Kraken* with more than they needed; besides Robin, that greedy bastard Demon had two whole extra doctors waiting in the wings. Fox suspected Robin would be coming with them when the time came. But nothing was official yet. He wasn't sure why he of all people had been assigned to this particular job. He suspected that Logan was just trying to keep them all busy and out of each other's pants.

"I'm going to see if Robin and Gaël need any help," Fox told Henri as he handed the vial back. "This is the last of it, and there are three vials." Henri nodded, recording the last of the numbers, then picked up a basket beside the low stool he sat on and began rolling bandages.

Fox left the infirmary and made his way down the narrow corridor that would lead him up to the deck where Gaël and Robin were unloading supplies from the landing boat.

"Not long now."

Fox cursed silently as Cyrus loomed out of an open doorway. Fox was really getting sick of seeing his stupid, gloomy face.

Fox didn't respond. He tried to slip past, but Cyrus's arm shot out to block his path.

"What do you want, Cyrus?" Fox asked, not looking at his ex-fling's face. He was done playing nice. Fox wasn't a patient man, and Cyrus had already spent any goodwill Fox might have still held for him.

Cyrus smirked. How had Fox ever thought he was attractive? His expressions were so sour, and he was a selfish lover to boot. Fox supposed it had something to do with being stuck at sea for months on end.

"I want to fuck you," Cyrus said. "I would have thought that was obvious."

"And I thought I made it clear that won't be happening. So I guess we're both bad listeners," Fox snapped. He tried to push past Cyrus's blockade again, but Cyrus stepped further into the bubble of Fox's personal space, grabbing his forearm in a bruising grip.

And not the kind of bruising Fox liked to engage in on occasion, as a treat.

No. This was the kind with a real threat of violence behind it.

"You're just a little slut at heart, Fox. A few days without that arrogant bastard once we leave, and you'll be begging me to fuck you."

"Let go," Fox said through gritted teeth.

"Or what?" Cyrus sneered.

"Or you'll have to deal with me."

They both turned at the sound of Gaël's menacing voice. Neither had heard him come down the stairs, but he seemed to have heard a great deal of their conversation. His sharp face was set in a scowl, eyes glittering in the low light. A tiger waiting to strike.

"Two against one's no fair," Cyrus joked, releasing Fox's arm. He pushed past Fox, closer than Fox liked.

"Next time your guard dog won't be here," he whispered before disappearing into the bowels of the ship.

Gaël's expression changed from murderous to concerned as soon as Cyrus was out of sight.

"Are you okay?" Even his voice was different. Gentle. He brushed his hand down the arm Cyrus had grabbed.

"I'm fine," Fox sighed. In the moment, he'd been more annoyed than frightened, but Cyrus's parting words made his chest constrict with anxiety.

Gaël's gaze swept over him, seeking evidence of his words.

"Who was that?" he finally asked.

"Cyrus, one of the *Siren*'s gunners."

"What happened?"

Fox had tried to keep this under wraps. To him, the confrontation in the tavern hadn't been a big deal. But this was. He'd had people obsessed with him before. He'd even had people fight over him. He'd never let it affect him much.

This time it was different. Cyrus had all but threatened him, and even Fox's easygoing nature couldn't push that aside. Fox didn't want Gaël to worry about him or get jealous. And despite the deep love he had for Gaël, they'd only been together for a few weeks after six years apart. He didn't know whether Gaël was the jealous type, but judging by the fierce expression he'd worn when Cyrus's hands were on Fox, Gaël *was* the type to jump in and defend his lover even at the price of his own safety.

Fox didn't want that. He wanted Gaël to be happy and safe. Fox could handle it as he always had before. He was used to it. It was just an old hookup who was unable to move on. But eventually they *did* all move on. He just wanted to focus on the here and now, on Gaël.

"It's nothing," Fox said nonchalantly. As he tucked a strand of hair behind his ear his sleeve slipped up to his elbow, revealing a red mark where Cyrus had grabbed him.

A muscle in Gaël's jaw twitched. His eyebrows drew together in worry, the exact thing Fox wanted to avoid.

"This is not nothing," Gaël said, and Fox could tell he was trying very hard to keep his tone calm. To not touch Fox and check that he was okay. "Please tell me what this is about."

Not telling Gaël about the first argument was one thing. But lying when asked a direct question was another. Fox couldn't lie to him.

He sighed, taking the tie out of his hair and running his fingers restlessly through the strands.

"He's been giving me a hard time the past few days." That was an understatement. Fox's arm hurt but not too badly.

"Your ex?" Gaël asked.

"I don't have any exes."

"What? I thought you said you'd slept with—"

"*Slept with*," Fox emphasized. "I've never been in an actual relationship before. That's not fun. Well, besides you, Gaël," He flashed Gaël a dazzling smile, trying to make him feel better. "You're *very* fun."

Gaël's stormy expression cleared just a little.

"So not an ex but…"

"A…friend with benefits?" Fox squinted, contemplating whether that was the right terminology. "Fling? That sort of thing."

"And he wants you back?" Gaël asked leadingly.

"That's the gist of it. Though he never really had me to begin with, so I don't know what his problem is."

Fox's nonchalant attitude seemed to be slowly smoothing Gaël's ruffled feathers.

"Anyone would be crazy not to want you Fox."

"Well that's very flattering, but he's being a bit of a dick about it."

"Does it hurt?" Gaël moved closer, pushing Fox's sleeve up and looking at the irritated finger marks that were probably going to bruise. Gaël scowled.

"It's not too bad," Fox mumbled. "I've had worse."

Gaël's head snapped up.

"What?"

Shit. He shouldn't have said that.

"Really, it's fine," Fox placated him. "I think you scared him off."

He could tell that Gaël was trying very hard not to be jealous. Or to storm after Cyrus right now and beat some sense into him. He cupped Gaël's face between his hands.

"You don't have to worry about him. I'm yours, and he can't do anything about that. What matters now is the future, not the past."

"The future." Gaël's thumb rubbed over Fox's skin. "I have something to tell you about our future."

Fox tensed. This was what he'd been planning for. The topic that had been perpetually on his mind. How would Gaël fulfill his promise that they would stay together?

"I asked the captain to release me from duty on the *Kraken*."

Fox sucked in a sharp breath. When they'd reunited, he'd asked Gaël if he would betray his captain for him. But somehow he hadn't expected Gaël to actually leave the *Kraken*.

"What did he say?"

A small smile twitched Gaël's lips.

"He said yes."

"What? Really?" Fox hadn't expected the Demon to give up without a fight. That's where the chicken would have come into the equation.

"Well really what he said was that he doesn't have time for love-struck fools."

Fox snorted. "He's one to talk."

"I don't think he sees it that way." Gaël removed Fox's hands from his cheeks, holding them in between both of his. "So I'm free to join you on the *Siren*, if you'll have me."

"You mean if Rowan will have you," Fox corrected. "I've already made my decision, but he's the captain."

"As if he can say no to you."

"No one can," Fox joked.

Gaël ran his hand down the sore spot on Fox's arm, and the mood sobered.

"I just want to protect you," Gaël murmured. He searched Fox's face. "I want to make up for all your hurt."

Fox heard the words he left unsaid. *I want to make up for how I hurt you.*

Deep in his chest, Fox's heart cracked a little, but was instantly mended when Gaël pressed a quick kiss to the inside of his wrist.

"You don't have to protect me. Just love me."

CHAPTER 19

AUGUST 30TH, 1666

The sharpened spurs on Yves's boots clinked as he paced the polished floors of his office. Apprehension had lodged itself deep into his psyche, and it had only gotten worse as the *Siren*'s departure loomed closer. He'd ordered John to delay the *Siren*'s repairs, and he had, for a time. But there was only so much more Yves and John could do while avoiding suspicion. Rowan wasn't stupid. Yves couldn't keep stringing him along and distracting him with sex forever, pleasant though it was. Rowan would catch on soon enough, and when he did he would leave, possibly for good.

The thought filled Yves with unexplainable uneasiness. He'd never wanted to keep a lover before. Never felt such ownership over another person. Perhaps it was simply that he didn't want to give up such an intriguing plaything before he was done playing.

His measured steps slowed at the thought. Was that all Rowan was to him? All they were to each other? There had to be more than lust between them. Infinitely more. Now that he'd had Rowan, his obsession only grew. And every moment Rowan was within his sight, he only wanted to gnaw him to the bone, to get at the heart of him and find the answers to why Rowan had invaded his every thought. But thus far the closest Yves had gotten to that unattainable center was with his dick buried deep in Rowan's supple ass. That was the only thing that momentarily calmed the raging storm within him. Yet the more he fucked Rowan, the more ravenous he became.

The door opened, and Yves whirled around, but it was just John.

"You called?" John asked, shutting the door behind him. He seemed sullen. Yves knew that John was still uncomfortable with the situation Yves had put them in. John was a private, diligent man. Qualities that had suited him well in the navy, until they hadn't. He didn't like that so many strangers now knew their little secret and would soon be going back out into the world with the one piece of knowledge that could bring them to ruin quicker than anything else.

"The *Siren*'s repairs are almost finished," Yves said. He resumed his pacing. John's deep-set eyes tracked him back and forth across the floor. "I need you to delay them further."

John pinched the bridge of his nose between thumb and forefinger, a gesture that Yves was all too familiar with.

"I've delayed them by almost a week already. They're not dumb. They'll get suspicious."

"You need to do more."

John glowered at him. "I've already done *quite* enough."

But it wasn't enough. The hungry anxiety churned in Yves's stomach, and it wouldn't go away until he'd secured what he wanted. The inevitability of Rowan's absence gnawed at him.

"Listen to me, John. You need to use more than just petty tactics. We need to sabotage the *Siren* itself. Blow it up. Sink it for all I care..." He stopped himself, regathering his composure. "No, never mind. Don't sink it. Just damage it enough to see us through till winter." Yves knew Rowan would be heartbroken if he lost the *Siren* for good. But once the winter storms set in, they would have no choice but to hole up here on the island and wait it out. That would give him enough time.

"That's *months* away!" John protested.

"Then you better think of something good," Yves snapped. John was a ruthless and competent first mate, but Yves was growing tired of all this pushback, even if he knew perfectly well that John was right. What did John care whether the *Siren* was damaged? He'd sunk countless ships throughout his career. Wouldn't it be better for his concerns over the secrecy of Illusion if they stayed here?

John mumbled something under his breath.

Yves stopped pacing to lean back on the edge of his desk, arms crossed.

"Don't tell me you feel guilty." He couldn't keep the derision from his voice, even though he knew it made him a hypocrite. "You've been spending a lot of time with Mister Crowder as of late. I thought you were just distracting him, but perhaps it's something else? Are you fucking him?"

"You sound so judgmental of that, despite the fact you can't keep your dick to yourself. But no. I'm not sleeping with Logan. We're friends." John's face was stoic, almost purposely so. Yves was about to make another derisive comment, but John continued, "You need to think this through, Captain. With your brain this time. I've indulged your whims till now, but I don't—"

Yves's hand snapped out and struck John across the face. It wasn't a hard hit. John didn't even stumble. But Yves's rings left red scratches on his skin, and the shocked look that flitted across his face instantly humbled Yves.

Still he barked, "As your captain, I order you to sabotage the *Siren*. If you don't, you will step down as my first mate." He regretted the words as soon as they left his mouth, but he did not take them back. John's eyes flashed with anger. Yves valued him as a second-in-command, maybe even as a friend, but they were both hotheaded, and if this was the only way to get what he wanted, then so be it. He and John both knew that when it came to threats, Yves was a man of his word. "It's nothing you haven't done before," Yves snarled, adding the final nail to the coffin. They both knew what he was referring to, and they both knew how much of a sore spot it was for John.

Resignation replaced anger in John's eyes, and Yves knew he had won.

"Yes, Captain." John turned to go, his shoulders stiff. He twisted the brass door handle but did not open it. He turned back to look Yves dead in the eye. "You need to think about what you're doing, Captain. The Ghost Hawk's not your enemy. Not anymore. So you should stop treating him like one. You can't keep him here forever. Eventually you'll have to decide what's more important. Our crew or your selfishness." The door thudded shut behind him.

Yves turned away from the door, fist slamming into the polished top of the desk. He hunched over it, trying to get his anger and anxiety back under control. The tide of darkness rose, devouring any sane thoughts. If he was out at sea, pirating and doing what he was meant to do, he would have let it take over. He would have sunk into its cool embrace like drowning. He would have fed the souls of his victims to the deep pit of black water inside of him.

But he couldn't. Not here. Not now.

Yves's teeth gritted, and he punched the desk again, feeling something crack in his hand. Pain shot up his arm, and he welcomed it, fed the darkness with it until it was satiated.

CHAPTER 20

Fox's bright, cackling laugh carried across the crowded lane. Paper lanterns strung along the front porches of the houses cast a warm glow on the underside of the tree canopy above. Fox caught Gaël's contented smile out of the corner of his eye. Gaël's warm hand found his, their fingers threading together as they wove their way through the party.

The lane leading up to the faded pink manor house was packed with nearly everyone on the island for the autumn festival. Both pirate crews and their families mingled and drank and ate and laughed. Someone had brought out a fiddle and was playing a lively tune from the front porch of one of the houses.

"Let's dance!" Fox dragged Gaël toward the music. They were both a little tipsy already, the honey-sweetness of mead warming their cheeks. He knew that they would be leaving soon, going back to the cold sea and the violence of pirating. But it was all okay now, because Gaël would be coming with him.

He drew Gaël into his arms, pecking the small mole on his cheek before spinning him away again. Gaël laughed, the mole disappearing into his dimples. The music picked up its pace, and they danced till they were breathless and dizzy, stealing kisses in the cooling air. It would be autumn soon, but in each other's arms they were warm and happy.

They stumbled away from the dancing still hand in hand, grabbing two more cups of ale on the way. Fox downed half of his in a single gulp.

"Slow down." Gaël giggled. "I don't want to have to hold your hair back while you puke later." His face was red from dancing and drink.

"You would anyway."

"That's true," Gaël conceded. He had a habit of pouting a little as he talked. It softened the severe lines of his face and contrasted with his outwardly intimidating looks. Fox found it unfairly charming. He wondered if anyone else got to see this side of Gaël or if this sweet interior came out only for him.

"I'll try very hard not to puke," Fox said. He pulled their bodies flush with one arm around Gaël's waist.

"Don't you have anything better to do than flirt?" They both turned to see Logan approaching with Henri and Robin trailing slightly behind.

"We absolutely do not have anything better to do," Fox shot back playfully. "Plus it's a party! That's literally what it's for. You should try it sometime."

Logan rolled his eyes, but a fond smile played on his lips.

Henri and Robin finally made it to them. Henri was still on crutches but he seemed to be moving around much easier these days. No doubt due to Robin's tender loving care. Fox smirked at them.

"I heard congratulations are in order," Robin said as Henri leaned down to ruffle Fox's hair. "Gaël works for the *Siren* now."

"Welcome aboard," Henri added.

Gaël beamed up at them. "Thank you. I was nervous that the Ghost Hawk wouldn't want me."

"Fox probably would have been a menace if he didn't get his way," Logan said. "Besides, you have a reputation as a great fighter. I'm sure you'll be a valuable asset."

They chatted for a while longer before Henri and Robin drifted away to get food and Logan went to find Rowan. Not long after, Fox felt the call of nature.

"Be right back." He kissed Gaël on the ear. "Gotta pee."

He made his way down a path between two houses, the light of the festival lanterns fading behind him. He knew there were latrines around here somewhere. Maybe he should have brought Gaël with him. He would know where they were.

"Where's your protector, little slut?"

Fox whirled as Cyrus emerged from the darkness under the trees.

"This again..." Fox rolled his eyes. In the tipsy haze of his mind, he wasn't afraid. He was only annoyed that Cyrus continued to buzz around him like a persistent fly. "Just move on, Cyrus. This is getting a bit pathetic."

Before he knew it, Cyrus was much too close.

"You little fucker," Cyrus growled. For every step forward, Fox stepped back. Till he was backed up against one of the broad trees lining the path. "You think you can call me pathetic? You think you can humiliate me? You're *my* bitch. And I'm not going to let you forget it." He grabbed the front of Fox's pants.

Fox slapped him hard across the face, but there was nowhere to go. The tree was at his back, and Cyrus's bulk was blocking any avenue of escape.

The slap seemed to have no effect on Cyrus besides angering him even more. "You'll regret that," he snarled.

Fox's hazy mind was having trouble keeping up with the situation, but the first blow across his face cleared it considerably. His head snapped back with the force of it, striking the tree trunk behind him. He shoved Cyrus in the chest, ears ringing, but he was at a disadvantage. Smaller. Drunker. Nowhere to go.

The shove barely gave him enough space to breathe before Cyrus punched him in the jaw again. A sharp pain lanced through his body. Another blow landed on his ribs this time. He couldn't catch his breath. And he thought he felt something crack beneath Cyrus's fist.

"Stop!" Fox gasped. But Cyrus didn't listen. He grabbed Fox by the throat and dragged him to the ground. His unwelcome hands pawed at Fox's clothes, ripping his shirt open and trying to drag his pants down his hips as Fox struggled. Shit. This was not how this night was supposed to go. Just a minute ago he was dancing with Gaël in the light of the lanterns, music wrapping around them. And now he was pinned to the dirt in the dark.

Fox's teeth found a stretch of bare flesh and bit down hard. Skin burst beneath his teeth like an overripe tomato. Coppery blood washed over his tongue, and Cyrus howled. The groping hands left him as Cyrus scrambled to his feet. Fox sucked in a shaky breath and tried to sit up.

"Bitch." Cyrus kicked him in the stomach and kept kicking. Fox curled up on the dirt, shielding his head and neck the best he could. Pain sizzled across his nerves with every blow. And with that pain came the sudden, crystal clear thought that he was going to die here in the dirt and the last touch on his skin had been Cyrus's, not Gaël's.

A pathetic whimper escaped his lips. Dirt stuck to the tear tracks on his cheeks, smelling of salt and leaf litter. Fuck. He was going to die.

Then, as suddenly as it had begun, the assault stopped. For a moment he thought maybe this was death. Maybe he'd taken Cyrus's boot to the head, and it was all over. He would never see Gaël or his friends again.

But the pain hadn't gone away. It was still there, stabbing every part of him. What the fuck kind of afterlife was this, where he could still feel so much agony?

Hands grabbed him again, and he yelped, striking, trying to scrabble out of the grip.

"Fox! It's me. It's me."

Fox wrenched his eyes open at that familiar, trusted voice. He found himself being cradled in his captain's arms.

"Fox are you okay? How badly are you hurt?" Rowan's voice was frantic but there was a pounding in Fox's ears. His own heartbeat. Alive. Still alive and aching. Rowan's eyes flicked over Fox's disheveled state, cataloging his injuries. Fox realized his own body was shaking violently, out of his control. His shirt was torn open, and his trousers were smeared with dirt and half down his hips. Rowan draped his own coat across Fox's exposed torso.

"Gaël, stop!" Logan rushed past them, and Fox's vision came into sharp focus. Gaël had Cyrus on the ground. The sound of his fists pummeling Cyrus's flesh was what Fox had at first mistaken for his own adrenaline fueled heartbeat. Logan tried to pull Gaël off of Cyrus, but he would not stop. His muscles bunched with every blow like a jaguar crouching over a kill.

"Gaël! You'll kill him!" Rowan was shouting. "I order you to—"

"Gaël..." His name passed Fox's lips as a sob. Gaël's body went still, fist cocked back and ready to strike. He turned his head slowly as if Fox's voice was the last thing he'd expected to hear. There was a feral-ness in his eyes that Fox had never seen before, and it frightened him. All at once, Fox's pain-addled mind comprehended that while he was lying on the dirt wondering why the afterlife still had pain, Gaël had actually thought he was dead.

"Let Logan handle him," Rowan said, his firm gaze on Gaël. "Fox needs you."

Gaël stood, Cyrus forgotten, and moved toward Fox as if he were in a dream. That ferocious, wild expression softened with every step.

Gaël dropped to his knees beside them. He hesitated for a moment, then held his arms out to Fox, Cyrus's blood still smeared across his knuckles. Fox launched himself into Gaël's embrace. Rowan's coat slipped down to his waist, exposing his aching chest, but Fox didn't care. He buried his face into Gaël's shoulder and sobbed.

Fox's BODY was still shaking by the time he and Gaël made it back to their room. Robin had checked him over, voice soft. Careful only to touch him where and how Fox said he could. Deep bruising already littered Fox's body, and Robin suspected at least one cracked rib. But there was nothing much Robin could do about that, so he sent him back to their room with orders to rest and to come get him if Fox started puking or shitting blood.

Cyrus had been dragged away to the brig somewhere. But that didn't really make Fox feel better. Everyone was treating Fox so gently, like he was some fragile little thing to be put away in a padded box and forgotten. He hated it.

Since his tears had subsided, Fox felt like he was floating. Disconnected from his body and the world. Horribly. Awfully. His mind was no longer connected to his nerve endings. No longer in control of how he moved or what he said. The pain of the beating was only a distant thing.

He observed his own flinch when Gaël touched his arm unexpectedly. Then scolded himself when Gaël pulled away quickly. They just stood there facing each other for a moment. Gaël's eyes had lost that ice-chip hardness they'd had when he came roaring to Fox's rescue. Now there was only tenderness.

Being perceived like this, beaten and weak, was unbearable. Fox's body was still numb, but it suddenly felt as though the skin had been flayed away, baring his damaged soul.

He wanted his body back. He wanted to burrow into Gaël's arms and feel everything and nothing at once.

"Hit me," Fox demanded. But his voice sounded brittle to his own ears.

"What?" Gaël took a step back. His eyebrows drew together in confusion. Concern. As if Fox had gone mad.

Maybe he had. He could feel something inside him crumbling away, and he could only think of one thing, one person, who might be capable of holding him together. In some distant part of his psyche he knew this was a bad idea. But he didn't care. What use was rationality when everything else was screaming that this is what he needed?

"Please," Fox begged. This sort of thing wasn't something he engaged in often. In any other circumstance he would never have sprung this on Gaël out of the blue. But if he didn't get Gaël's hands on him right now he was going to scream. He wanted his body to be his again, not some distant unfeeling puppet he happened to inhabit. And to do that, he had to feel the pain. He had to read the map of bruises aching across his skin.

The only thing he could feel right now was the pressure of Cyrus's hands. And he couldn't bear it, the thought that someone had marked him in violence like that, especially in front of Gaël.

Fox wanted to erase it. But that was impossible, so he would overwrite it with something he chose.

"I need..." Fox almost choked on the words. He stepped closer to Gaël, and Gaël let him draw himself into the protective circle of his arms. He'd gotten so strong during their long separation. Fox would have loved to see him grow from that nervous boy to the strong man he was today. But Gaël was holding him like he would shatter at any moment.

He hated that. Hated that Gaël and the others had to come to his rescue.

"I need you to erase him. Please, Gaël."

"Fine," Gaël growled, misunderstanding Fox's words. "I'll go right now and—"

"No. No, that's not what I meant." Fox was desperate. His cock was already painfully hard and throbbing at the prospect that Gaël might say yes to his request. But for all his desperation, he didn't miss the implication that Gaël was perfectly prepared to murder a man in cold blood for him.

"What is it then, Fox? I'll do anything. Just tell me what you need." Gaël's whole body was tense in their embrace. Fox felt a faint flicker of guilt that Gaël might come to regret that promise soon.

"I need you." Fox just couldn't think of the words to convey it. His head was still so far away in the fog. So he did the only thing he could think of. He grabbed Gaël's hand and pressed it to his hard dick, rutting against it involuntarily.

Gaël froze. Then his other hand went to Fox's hip to stop him from doing it again.

"Fox..." His storm cloud eyes searched Fox's face. "What's going on?"

Fox almost sobbed in frustration. How could he explain in a way that wouldn't sound absolutely insane?

"I need you to touch me," Fox said urgently. "Erase what happened. Bruise me too so that when I feel it later, I'll think of you and not him."

Gaël blinked back tears. Was it pity? Fox couldn't tell. He laid his forehead against Gaël's shoulder so he wouldn't have to look.

"Fox, you're not okay," Gaël said softly.

Fox let out a pent up groan before pulling away to look into his face.

"I will be."

"Not this way. It's not a good idea."

Fox leaned forward for a kiss, but Gaël turned his face away. Fox desperately did not want to show Gaël this side of him. The side that had always been, and always would be, a little bit broken. Not because he thought Gaël would reject him, but because he didn't want to hurt him with his brokenness.

He rested his hands lightly on Gaël's broad chest, shame for so many things washing through him. Shame for his weakness. For needing to heal like this. For asking Gaël to do this for him.

Fox squeezed his eyes shut. The pain was starting to come back to him, and with it... No. He wouldn't let himself crumble. He would rather be detached and numb.

"I could never hurt you like that," Gaël murmured.

"It's okay if it's what I want. Please..." Fox whispered in a broken, feverish voice.

Gaël's arms came up around him, pulling their bodies against one another. Fox was still half hard, and his erection connected with Gaël's hip.

"Tell me what you need me to do."

~

"GAËL..." Fox moaned as Gaël's hard length slid inside him. His body shuddered, and Gaël's hand connected with the bruising on Fox's back. Pain radiated through his flesh, sharp and welcome. But it wasn't enough. Gaël was being too gentle with him. The blows were too light, and the glide of his dick along Fox's tight walls was too slow.

It had taken longer than usual to get Gaël up. His reluctance to accommodate Fox's request was clear. But Fox's charms and need won out in the end. Fox would feel guilty about that later.

But now he was on his hands and knees on their bed. He couldn't see Gaël's face, and Gaël couldn't see his.

"Harder," Fox hissed.

Gaël's next stroke was rough, hitting Fox's sweet spot and eliciting a deep moan. Gaël knew exactly what Fox wanted, how to touch him and please him. He gripped Fox's hips in place with one hand and the other struck his shoulder, connecting with another bruise.

"Yes," Fox groaned. He could feel his mind connecting back to his body with every strike, every bruise that rebloomed and deepened under Gaël's hands. Gaël's cock squelched against Fox's insides, pleasure mingling with pain.

"Turn over," Gaël said. Fox flopped onto his back and pulled Gaël down into a deep kiss as Gaël reentered him. Gaël pressed one hand firmly against an indigo bruise on Fox's chest, then moved down to the others that were unfurling across his stomach, careful not to touch his potentially cracked ribs. Fox imagined Gaël was creating a map of their passion on his skin. A series of lakes, cold and deep, where he could sink all his hurt and come out new.

Pleasure pulsed beneath his skin, building with every stroke. He raked his nails through Gaël's hair. Gaël's breath was ragged, his face stricken.

"I love you." Fox held his gaze for a moment. Gaël leaned his head down to nuzzle Fox's neck, kissing his fevered skin. He rolled his hips forward, and Fox arched up to meet them, chasing the ache. He palmed his own cock, pumping it quickly. He felt more awake, more alive. The carnal heat seared away everything that had come before. Gaël's hands had abandoned their bruising trail, but it was okay. Fox was here. He was connected deeply to his own body. To the man he loved. A man who would never hurt him unless he asked. Even at the expense of himself.

And now it was not pain that wove through the pleasure. That had retreated to the background. He felt only ecstasy. Only love. Deeper than the bruises that would fade in time. Deeper than Gaël inside him. It was down to his bones, written across his crumpled soul.

And he shattered. Not in a way that would destroy him. Rip him into a million shards that would cut them both. But into two pieces. Himself and Gaël.

He pulled Gaël into another crushing kiss, moaning desperately into his soft mouth. His slick walls clamped down on Gaël's throbbing cock as he came between them, painting the bruise-mottled skin of his stomach with pure milky white. Gaël's thrusts slowed to a languid pace. Slow and sweet. Until Fox was spent. Then he retreated as if to pull out. But he hadn't come yet.

Fox guided him so he was sitting with his back to the head of the bed. Fox climbed into his lap, positioning Gaël's cock at his entrance and sinking slowly down until he was buried as deep as he would go. Gaël gasped, his strong hands caressing Fox's bruised skin.

Fox wrapped his arms around the back of Gaël's neck and began to ride him. He pressed their foreheads together. Eyes closed. Breathing the same breath. Gaël grabbed his chin to hold him there, thumb pressing to the bruise that bloomed across his face. Fox could tell Gaël was getting close, and he slowed momentarily, savoring each stroke. Their lips brushed lightly. Then Fox picked up the pace, and in a few strokes, Gaël cried out, filling Fox with throbbing warmth.

They stayed that way for a moment, erections softening. Sweat cooling. Wrapped up in each other.

"Thank you," Fox whispered.

Gaël pulled away slightly, misty eyes searching Fox's face.

"I love you, Fox. I'd do anything for you." His voice was raw.

Fox felt a pang of guilt for asking this of him. Despite the clarity the act had brought him, he suddenly felt vulnerable again for having caused Gaël pain. He curled into Gaël's embrace.

"Stay with me," he murmured. He didn't know where the words came from. But there they were, out in the open. He promised himself to make it up to Gaël in the morning. But for now he simply needed him.

Gaël stroked the back of Fox's hair.

"I'm here. I'm not leaving."

CHAPTER 21

SEPTEMBER 2ND, 1666

Rowan's feet swished through the dew-cloaked gardens behind the manor house. It was early. Much earlier than he would usually be awake, but the events of the night before weighed heavily on his shoulders, and he could hardly sleep. Until finally, with red eyes, he'd gotten out of bed and left Yves slumbering soundly. In his years as a pirate captain, Rowan had dealt with his fair share of disagreements, brawls, and all manner of things between the crew, but he'd never encountered an all-out assault, especially an attempted sexual assault. He didn't know how to deal with this. His crew was close, meant to be a family, and something like this had been unthinkable until now. What was the appropriate punishment? He knew what other captains would do, everything from ignoring it to flogging. But what would the Ghost Hawk do? All he knew was that he needed to protect Fox.

He reached a one-story building made of red brick. It sat low in the overgrown remnants of the house's gardens. One of Rowan's loyal crew members sat huddled on a wooden chair in front of the door. He looked up when he heard his captain approaching and removed the chair so Rowan could enter the building.

Dim light filtered through a window at the far end. It must have been a dog kennel at one time, a row of iron barred enclosures ran along one wall. But now it only held one kind of dog.

In the middle enclosure, Cyrus sat with his back against the brick wall. He seemed to have just woken, roused by the squeal of rusty hinges as Rowan stepped into the building. His face was bruised and swollen, and Rowan suspected he had a broken nose. A flicker of hope seemed to cross his face at the sight of his captain, before he saw Rowan's dour expression and realized that Rowan was not the savior he could have been if he were a crueler man. Rowan's feet crunched over the moldering straw quietly as he crossed the room to stand before the bars of Cyrus's prison.

Neither of them said anything for a long while. Both just staring at each other through the gaps between the iron.

Finally Rowan gathered enough of his thoughts together to ask, "Why?"

Cyrus frowned. This was not the question he was expecting. The answer was probably obvious to many. But not to Rowan. He valued loyalty implicitly. And though he was a violent man, a man who lived on the wrong side of the law, he was also a man who did not understand the motive behind an act such as this.

Rowan stared at his crew member, waiting for an answer. He saw a series of calculations tick through Cyrus's mind. Whether to be honest or beg for mercy. Rowan didn't feel merciful. His fingers itched to add to the bruises Gaël had painted across Cyrus's face.

"The little slut had it coming," Cyrus finally said, with all the venom of a cornered snake.

The rage that had been simmering in Rowan's belly since the night before boiled over, consuming any uncertainty Rowan had harbored in the vain hope that perhaps he *could* be merciful if Cyrus was repentant. He couldn't. He spat into the straw at Cyrus's feet, and without another word, turned and left the caged man behind.

Rowan was halfway back to the house when Yves materialized out of the mist with the haunting call of a mourning dove accompanying him. He wore a deep green dressing gown richly embroidered with patterns of ferns and white rabbits, open over a bare chest and the trousers he'd slept in. His black hair had been raked back from his forehead by hasty fingers. He looked like a spoiled aristocrat lost in the woods.

"I don't want him on my crew anymore," Rowan growled when he saw him. There was no need to explain exactly what, or who, he meant. "I don't want him around Fox."

"I concur," Yves said evenly. He didn't seem cold, even with his slippers and the hem of his dressing gown soaked in dew. "But I'm none too thrilled about taking him on either. A man like that can't be trusted. But then again we can't exactly punish him then turn him loose. Not with him knowing about Illusion. Even if he doesn't hold a grudge, many people would pay a pretty penny to catch the Demon and the Ghost Hawk."

Rowan clenched and unclenched his hands. He'd spent a good portion of the night thinking of this very problem. They could punish Cyrus as they saw fit. But they could no longer trust him. Nor could they let him go free to blab their secrets throughout the Islands. Fox deserved justice, and it was Rowan's job to mete it out.

"So what do we do?"

"Neither of us want him on our crew," Yves said slowly, puzzling it out as he spoke. "Ana and the others definitely won't tolerate him around here. And we can't let him go. So there's really only one option. We have to kill him."

Rowan's head snapped up. The cruel lines of Yves's face were not softened by the gentle morning light around them. In fact the rosy glow that had begun to rise above the horizon sent his angles into sharp relief, enhancing the harshness of his expression.

He was a harbinger of death wrapped in a beautiful package.

"I agree the punishment needs to be severe but execution? We're pirates, not the fucking government."

"Strand him on a desert island then. Or leave him to rot in the kennel like the dog he is."

"That would be as good as murdering him. And if he doesn't die he'll *definitely* hold a grudge. We can't do that."

Yves seemed puzzled.

"Why not?"

They stared at each other for a few moments.

"I'm not in the habit of murdering crew members," Rowan said with wary eyes.

"But he's not a crew member. He's a traitor and an abuser. You don't even have to carry out the punishment yourself. Let me flog him; people die from that all the time. I *do* love a good whipping. "

The sadistic glee in Yves's eyes sent a shiver down Rowan's spine. He knew the Demon was ruthless, they all were, but his suggestions just felt too cruel.

"You're a bit soft for a pirate captain," Yves noted.

"I'm not soft. I'm just not bloodthirsty."

"How about this," Yves said, ignoring the implication that *he* was bloodthirsty. "Fox is the victim here. We'll let him decide the prisoner's fate."

"You might not like his decision," Rowan warned, thinking how unpredictable Fox could be.

Yves smiled, showing his rows of perfect teeth.

"He might surprise you instead."

"Oh, I'm sure he will," Rowan said tiredly.

THEY MET with Fox in Yves's well-appointed office. Gaël was there too. "For emotional support," Fox had said, but Rowan knew that Gaël had barely let his lover out of his sight since the incident occurred. Rowan himself had felt uncomfortable letting his friend and crew member, whose safety he was responsible for, out of his sight.

"We've come to a decision to let you decide Cyrus's punishment." Yves got straight to the point. "As the victim and with these unique circumstances, we feel it is your right. Keep in mind that the safety of this island and its inhabitants take priority over any merciful feelings you may have."

Rowan shot him a disapproving look.

"Take your time," Rowan added. "I don't mind letting him rot in the brig another day or two."

Fox's eyes flicked between the two captains before a slow, malicious smile crept across his scabbed lips.

"I want to fight him."

"Fox," Gaël protested. "You can't."

Fox silenced him with a hand on his arm. Rowan and Yves looked at him with a curious mix of expressions on their faces. Yves, intrigued and anticipatory. Rowan, worried.

"You said I could decide his punishment. So that's what I choose."

"Why?" Yves asked, leaning forward.

"I think it will deter him. I'll humiliate him in front of a crowd. Teach him not to mess with me. Then he can do a stint of labor punishment or something to prove himself worthy of being on crew again." Fox shrugged. "Besides, it will be fun."

Yves hummed in appreciation.

"It does have a certain elegance about it," he said to Rowan.

"Elegance?!" Gaël sputtered, clearly enraged by the prospect of his lover fighting the man who had just attacked him the night before. "Are you really going to allow this, Captain? It's absurd."

"We agreed he could pick the punishment," Yves said. Then turned his attention back to Fox. "Are you sure this is what you want? That you can win?"

"Believe me; I know what I'm doing." Fox smirked.

"It's up to you, Hawk," Yves said, no doubt using Rowan's pirate moniker to remind him that mercy had no place for a crime such as this. "They're your crew members. Do you approve?"

Rowan had said nothing up until now. His eyes bored into Fox, assessing.

"Approved," he said finally.

"Then it's settled," Yves said. There was a beat of silence between the four of them.

"I'll fight him in your place," Gaël insisted.

"No, you won't," Fox said. His tone was light but nonetheless brooked no argument. "I deserve my revenge."

Torches guttered around the ring of packed earth in the street in front of the mansion. It was after dark, but a significant crowd had gathered to watch the fight.

"I heard it's to settle what happened last night," one woman from the *Kraken* crew said to the man next to her. "You know, with Gaël's man? The pretty one? He got beat up something fierce by a jealous ex."

"Gods help the idiot who has to fight Gaël," the man said, making a sign to ward off evil.

Fox grimaced as he wrapped his knuckles to protect them from injury. Of course, these people didn't know him. They'd assume he would let Gaël fight his battles for him. And if Gaël had his way, he would.

The hum of the crowd got louder as Cyrus was led into the ring, his jailers unlocking his cuffs and leaving him standing in the center with all eyes on him.

Fox took a deep breath. He was rarely one to solve personal problems with his fists, but he knew how to fight. It was what had gotten him onto the *Siren* crew in the first place.

The bruises ached, the memory of pain, then the later pleasure, mapped out on his skin. Rowan had offered to postpone the match till he was healed, but despite Robin's medical advice, Fox had refused. There was a well of anger simmering in his gut and he wanted to use it. Wanted to humiliate and hurt Cyrus just as he had been.

Fox rolled his shoulders and flexed his fingers. He looked down to his feet, bare in the dirt.

"Not too late to back out," Gaël murmured at his side. Gaël's fingers brushed his arm tentatively, as if he wanted to hold Fox back but knew this was necessary. "I'll beat him six feet underground for you."

Fox pecked him on the cheek.

"So gallant, but no."

"It's time," Rowan said. His blue eyes swept Fox from head to toe, and Fox suddenly felt as if he were back in Wave Harbor again, fresh off a fight with a man who'd bought him dinner and expected something in return. This new stranger's eyes watching him from an alleyway, judging him worthy of *the* Ghost Hawk.

Rowan clapped a hand on Fox's shoulder. "Show them."

A shocked murmur rippled through the crowd when Fox, not Gaël, stepped into the dirt ring. He divested himself of his shirt, revealing the myriad of bruises dappled across his skin. He wore them like a badge of honor. Like a king's robes. A few people gasped in the crowd. He practically felt Gaël flinch, no doubt guilty that some of those bruises had come from him. However consensually and enthusiastically Fox had asked for, and received, them.

Fox stepped further into the ring, his anger flaring as Cyrus glowered at him.

"This fight is to be the official punishment of Cyrus Oates for the assault of Fox, both of the *Siren Song*. Handed down and carried out by Fox. This fight will conclude when one fighter yields." Rowan's voice rang clearly around the ring.

All he had to do was get Cyrus to surrender. Easy.

Both men dropped into a fighting stance.

"Begin!"

They circled like a pair of wolves. Cyrus eyed the crowd warily as if unconvinced they wouldn't intercede if he started to win. Did he think the rest of the *Siren* crew would jump in and beat him to a pulp to defend Fox? They might if it weren't for the presence of their captain. They all loved Fox. If Cyrus didn't know how badly he'd fucked up before, he did now.

"I don't want to hurt you, Fox."

"Should have thought of that before you did," Fox said lightly.

"Do you really expect me to fight you? Is this a trap?"

Fox's fingers twitched. "Give it your best shot, and we'll see how it goes."

"After I beat you, your monster boyfriend is just going to come kill me in my sleep, is that it?"

Every word out of his mouth just stoked Fox's anger more.

"He's not the monster here," Fox said quietly.

Cyrus lunged, but it was a halfhearted attempt, testing the waters to see if anyone would intervene. Fox dodged easily, dancing away on light feet despite the ache in his body.

"I *said* give it your best shot," Fox said, as the crowd sneered and booed. They wanted justice, but they also wanted a fight.

Cyrus turned and struck again, this time landing a hard punch to Fox's cracked ribs. Fox hissed in pain, and Cyrus hesitated for a second, waiting again for the audience to take matters into their own hands and defend poor, loveable Fox.

Fox used the momentary lapse to press his advantage. He drove his knee into Cyrus's stomach, simultaneously using both hands fisted together to clobber him between the shoulder blades like a hammer.

Cyrus collapsed with a rush of breath, and Fox retreated a few steps, waiting for him to get back up. Ready. He didn't want to finish the fight too fast—he still had some anger to get out.

Two breaths and Cyrus was back on his feet.

"You little fucker," he spat.

"That's what they call me," Fox joked, affecting a cute demeanor and poking one finger into his cheek.

"Slut," Cyrus hissed. How quickly he'd gone from insisting he didn't want to hurt Fox to outright hatred. It was obvious he'd just wanted to save his own skin. His true nature came out when he could no longer get what he wanted.

The crowd was quieter now. Fox had been intending this fight to be good entertainment, but it was clear to everybody here that it was more serious for him. Those who knew Fox knew him as bubbly and lovably annoying.

Maybe that was why Cyrus had thought he could take advantage.

But Fox rarely let this side of himself show. The side that craved pain and violence. He took no pleasure picking on the weak like Cyrus did. But a bigger, stronger opponent? That was his bread and butter.

They traded a few blows back and forth, neither gaining the upper hand.

Confident now that this wasn't a trap and the audience wouldn't intervene, Cyrus aimed his next punch directly at Fox's face. Fox blocked with his forearms, hissing as Cyrus's fist connected with bruised flesh. He missed Cyrus's other fist coming at him from the side. Cyrus's knuckles crashed against the right side of his head.

Fox's ears rang. For a moment, his mind went blank with only the memory of last night. He stumbled back, but he regained his bearings quickly. His eyes caught on Gaël in the crowd, thankfully being held back by both Robin and John. The rage and love in Gaël's eyes bolstered him.

Fox bared his teeth in a grim imitation of his trademark grin. He stalked back toward Cyrus.

"What did you hope to accomplish?" Fox said low, so only Cyrus could hear as they circled one another again, always looking for an opening. "You'd what? Rough me up? Show me what a *man* you are and I'd go back to you? Fall for you?" He laughed.

Cyrus balked, but Fox wasn't really looking for answers.

The crunch of Cyrus's already broken nose bones under his knuckles was all the answer he needed.

Cyrus reeled back, clutching his re-broken nose as blood gushed down over his lips. But Fox wasn't finished. He struck again, landing a flurry of punches across Cyrus's ribs and chest, sending him stumbling to the edge of the ring. The crowd caught him and for a moment Fox thought they might try to join the fight. But they pushed him back to his feet and into Fox's path of destruction once more.

Fox swept Cyrus's feet out from under him, grappling him to the dirt. He wrapped his legs around Cyrus's torso from behind, arms locking around his neck like a vise. His body wrapped around Cyrus like a boa constrictor, unyielding and merciless. Cyrus struggled, and Fox applied more pressure. He leaned his cheek against the side of Cyrus's head, mouth close to his ear.

"Looks like I was the monster all along," he cooed.

Cyrus grunted and elbowed Fox in the side. His hold tightened again.

"Who's the little fucker now?" Fox whispered. He ignored the frantic slapping of Cyrus's hand on his arm. Clearly yielding, but no one would fault Fox for going just a little further. "Who is whose bitch?" Cyrus's face was turning red. "Oh? Can't speak? That's too bad, really. If you answer my questions, maybe I'll let you live."

Cyrus's nails dug into Fox's forearm, real fear entering his eyes.

Fox held for another few seconds, then eased his grip. Cyrus gasped and sputtered as his airway opened again.

"I yield," he choked out when he was able to speak again.

Fox flexed his arm against his throat.

"That's not what I asked."

"I'm the little fucker," Cyrus said desperately, shame and pain evident in his face.

"And?"

"I'm your bitch."

"Very good."

Fox released him, and Cyrus rolled away from him, coughing. Fox stood, giving Cyrus a light kick in the side for good measure. The crowd was dead silent around them. Fox dusted the dirt off his trousers. Then bowed cheekily.

Approval roared from the crowd. Now that the fight was over, Gaël was released from Robin's and John's restraining hands and rushed into the ring, gathering Fox up into his arms and frantically kissing him. Out of the corner of Fox's eye, he saw a few of the *Kraken* crew members pick Cyrus up and drag him back toward the brig. Cyrus was their problem now; Fox and Rowan were washing their hands of him. Deep down, Fox knew that the Demon might decide he was too much trouble after the *Siren* left and dispose of him. But Fox resolved not to think—or feel guilty—about it. He was only looking ahead.

"I'm fine. I'm fine," Fox soothed as Gaël's hands ran over him, checking for serious injury.

"That was incredible," Gaël finally gasped.

"You should never have doubted me."

"I didn't." Gaël took his face between his hands, looking into his eyes. "I only wanted to protect you."

"We protect each other," Fox admonished.

Rowan and Yves approached slowly, allowing the couple time.

"I'm impressed," Yves said.

"I knew you could do it," Rowan added, ruffling Fox's hair.

Fox beamed. He always craved the rare praise from his captain. Praise from two captains was twice as good.

CHAPTER 22

SEPTEMBER 7TH, 1666

The sun sparkled bright and serene on the water. A soft breeze ruffled Logan's wavy blond hair, its coolness another reminder that summer had turned to autumn. Good timing then that the repairs on the *Siren* were finally complete. If they left soon, they could get a few months of sailing in before the winter storms hit. Logan smiled to himself, feeling light as a feather at the prospect of getting back to the sea.

He continued walking up the lane and spotted John coming out of the blacksmith's shop.

"John!" Logan called, raising his hand in greeting.

The other man nearly jumped right out of his skin and quickly shoved an object he'd been carrying into the bag at his side. Logan had never known John to be a nervous person, but he supposed being second-in-command for a captain like the Demon would wear on anyone's nerves eventually.

"Let's have lunch," Logan said brightly when he reached him. He clapped John on the shoulder, and a muscle in John's jaw twitched. They'd had lunch together almost daily since that day in the walled garden but nothing further had happened. Not that Logan wanted something to happen. To be honest, Logan had expected something to change afterward, that his first sexual experience with another person would alter his outlook somehow, but he found he felt the same as before. The only thing that had really changed was that he and John had become quite good friends, mostly commiserating about their captains' antics. But Logan also enjoyed sitting quietly together. He was constantly surrounded with big, loud personalities on board the *Siren*, and though he loved his crew, it was nice to be around someone with a calm disposition occasionally.

John didn't look so calm now, but he reluctantly agreed, and Logan steered him toward the tavern. In the past weeks, the tavern had been full of *Siren* crew members daily, but now that the repairs were finished, most of the pirates were busy making preparations for their imminent departure. The tavern remained relatively empty at midmorning. Logan ordered them food and ale, and they went to sit outside in the sunshine. John was quieter than usual today, fiddling with a small brown pebble that had been left on the tabletop by its previous occupants.

The tavern keeper brought their meal, and John thanked her politely before going back to his sulking, now with food.

Logan let him sulk. He didn't mind the quiet, and he didn't want to pry into whatever it was that had John in a mood. Logan took a bite of food, watching beneath his lashes as John slowly chewed his own bite. His beard had grown out a bit more. It seemed like he hadn't shaved in a while. The hair was a mixture of brown and darker red, as if the two colors that made up the hair on his head had separated as they made their way down to his chin. And then there were his lips. Logan couldn't quite get the image of them wrapped around his cock out of his head.

"You look chipper today. What's the occasion?" John asked after a few bites. Logan blinked at him, embarrassed to be caught staring at the other man's lips.

"Meanwhile you look like you swallowed a toad," Logan countered.

John shot him a warning look. "Just tell me."

"The *Siren*'s repairs are finally finished," Logan replied cheerily. John sat up straighter, spearing Logan with that intense gaze of his.

"The repairs are done? When do you leave?" His voice was tense, just like the rest of him.

"Within the week, I expect. It all depends on Rowan." Logan took a sip of ale, examining John over the rim of the mug. He was acting strange, and it was disconcerting.

"Think there's a chance he'll decide to overwinter here?"

"Slim to none."

"Yves won't be happy about that," John grumbled.

"Is that what's got you so gloomy? You think the Demon is going to be...more demon-y when we leave?" Logan asked.

"That's the gist of it," John mumbled, but he wouldn't look Logan in the eye. They finished their meal in silence. Afterward, they parted ways, John citing some work he had to get done. Logan made his way up to the manor house.

He knocked on the infirmary door before entering. He knew Henri and Robin had formed a romantic relationship, and he didn't want to walk in on any intimate moments. He had a hard enough time avoiding running into Fox and Rowan with their respective partners. Logan had always wondered what the big deal was about sex, and now that he'd had a taste of it, he still didn't fully understand why everyone was so sex-crazed. Though his recent preoccupation with John's lips was quite concerning, he'd resolved to withhold judgment on all of it till they were safely back at sea.

But Robin and Henri were simply sitting at the table when he opened the door. Robin concentrated on mixing up some greenish concoction, and Henri thumbed through a slim volume that looked surprisingly like poetry. They both looked up as Logan entered.

"Mister Crowder, what can I do for you?" Robin asked, wiping his hands on a clean cloth.

"I don't need anything. Thank you. I only came to ask if there's been any news about hiring you on to the *Siren*." Logan knew Rowan had talked to the Demon about it and gotten no solid answer. It wasn't as if the Demon couldn't spare him. He had two other physicians in his employ, though they seemed not to be as diligent as Robin.

Robin and Henri exchanged a look.

"We've had no news. Why do you ask?" Robin said.

Logan frowned. They desperately needed a physician on board the *Siren* if they were to sail within the week. Especially since Old Joe had taken a liking to the idyllic island and decided to stay and enjoy his retirement. They could try to hire one when they next made port, but it was hard to find an even half-decent doctor that was willing to throw in their lot with a bunch of pirates. So they wanted Robin. He was kind, proficient, and he and Henri were practically attached at the hip.

"Well, I wanted to tell you both that we'll be departing within the week."

A stricken expression crossed Henri's face.

"Do you think the Demon will let you go?" Henri asked.

Robin chewed his lip. "I really don't know. He seems reluctant."

"We could kidnap you," Henri suggested. "We are pirates after all."

Robin patted the back of his hand fondly. "I'd rather not get on the Demon's bad side, thanks."

They all fell silent, and Robin went back to mixing his medicine.

"Will you be well enough to travel?" Logan asked Henri.

"I'm fit as a horse!"

"They put horses down when they break their legs, love," Robin commented, not looking up from his task.

"Okay, well, maybe that was not the best comparison, but I'm completely fine." He blinked up at Logan from his seat and set the book down on the table, still open. Logan could see now that it wasn't poetry after all, but a penny romance novel about a dashing pirate who was secretly a prince that had been popular with rich young ladies a few years ago. "Can you talk to Rowan again? I really don't want to leave Robin behind."

"Of course." Logan smiled. He'd always had a soft spot for the big man, and he couldn't stand to think that he would be unhappy because of something as simple as a pirate captain's obstinance. "We can't let you go too long without a doctor nearby. You might get set on fire again." He turned to leave, smirking at the indignant sputtering and gentle soothing noises of Henri and Robin respectively.

The penny novel fell to the floor as Logan shut the infirmary door behind him. Henri bent to pick it up, but Robin beat him to it, scooping the flimsy book up and handing it back to Henri. Their fingers brushed lingeringly.

"I'm serious about kidnapping you," Henri said, only half-teasing. "I know we haven't talked about it much, but I want you to come with me."

Robin smiled and leaned over to kiss him, his lips warm and soft. Henri pulled him closer, taking comfort in his nearness. If the

Demon wouldn't release Robin from his contract, would Robin have the courage to leave?

"Do you want to come with me?" Henri asked when the kiss broke apart, a small thorn of anxiety prickling his insides. Robin's lips were still a breath away. He brushed them once more against Henri's.

"Of course I do. I just..." He sighed and withdrew, rubbing the back of his neck with one large hand. "I'm not brave like you. I don't want to cross the Demon."

Henri could see the edge of fear in Robin's round face. He wanted to gather Robin into his arms and keep him safe, to make it so he was never hurt again.

"If you don't come, we might not see each other again," Henri said. He swallowed around the lump in his throat. Robin was the first person he'd ever felt sexual attraction for and the first person he'd ever loved. He would do anything to keep from losing him. Was that really not enough for Robin to take the risk of angering the Demon? He couldn't look Robin in the eye, afraid that what he would see there would confirm his worries.

He felt Robin shift, then Robin's hand was on his cheek, lifting his head to look at him.

"Hey," Robin's smile was sweet yet sad. "I'll talk to him. I'll beg if I have to. I don't want to let you go, Henri."

Longing tugged Henri forward. He leaned into Robin's gentle embrace and kissed him again. If Robin was released from the indenture the Demon had him under, he would be free to leave not only the island, but also pirating life altogether. Would he stay with Henri when he could have a normal life instead?

Robin was like the heroine in the cheap novel Henri was reading. His gentle nature was one of the reasons Henri had fallen for him, but even if he'd chosen this over being ransomed back to his family, that didn't mean he would choose it over any other life. He was meant for peace, for healing, and no matter how much they loved each other, Henri worried that Robin would eventually yearn for a peaceful life again. What if he left Henri behind just like the heroine left the pirate in the book? That possibility gnawed at Henri like a persistent leech, sucking away some of the confidence he had in this new feeling called love. Were they destined to part? What if Henri simply wasn't good enough to compete with the possibility of a peaceful life?

Henri tried not to let the anxiety show on his face when their kiss broke. He let Robin go back to his mixing as if it were all settled, but when he picked up the book again, the story had soured.

Fox CLOSED his eyes and raised his face to the sun. It was a beautiful day, and he and Gaël had taken the opportunity to enjoy the warm sunlight before the weather turned to autumn chill. Now they relaxed on a rocky outcropping beside the water. Out in the harbor, the *Siren* was abuzz with preparations for their inevitable departure.

Fox leaned back on his hands. His body was still sore, and he suspected some of the bruises would linger for a long time after they left Illusion, and Cyrus, behind. But he didn't wince when the purple clouds of blood beneath his skin pulled painfully. His mind didn't turn to the fear and vulnerability of being at Cyrus's mercy. Instead, the memories they conjured were the passion and pain of Gaël's touch, the vicious victory of beating Cyrus in a fair fight.

"Fox," Gaël said hesitantly, breaking into Fox's thoughts. He'd been so careful with Fox since that night, but Fox no longer hated it. He'd eased into the warmth of being comforted by someone who loved him.

"Hm?" Fox hummed. Gaël had been quiet today, and Fox knew why. But he didn't want to talk about it.

"Does...does pain turn you on?"

Fox opened his eyes. A soft breeze kicked up and ruffled Gaël's black hair. His face was open and honest. Nervous. Fox had known this was coming eventually, but a spike of anxiety speared him all the same.

"Sometimes," he replied honestly. He saw Gaël swallow his discomfort, ready to graciously accept yet another messy aspect of Fox's personality. He took Gaël's hand between his. "Before you say anything, I wanted to say I'm sorry about the other night. I shouldn't have asked you to do that. I won't ask you to do something like that again."

Gaël's gaze roved over Fox's face. There was no judgment in it, and Fox felt a surge of love for him. They had only been together again for a short time, and it often felt like there had been no gap in their relationship at all. They were connected in a way that few couples were. They'd grown up together, spent every moment from the age of five to nineteen in each other's company, and they knew each other as well as they knew themselves.

But they'd been separated for six years, and sometimes Fox forgot that they were both different people than they had been when they were nineteen. As in tune as they were, as much as they cared for one another, it would still take time to work out the knots between them and learn who they were now.

"It's alright." Gaël's thumb rubbed across Fox's knuckles. His own knuckles were still scraped up from that night. "It's not that I'm against it. It's just the timing. I...I didn't want to hurt you even more. I thought it would make everything worse."

Fox bumped his forehead against Gaël's cheek, and Gaël returned his gesture with a gentle smile, still fiddling with their clasped hands.

"I want to explore so many things with you, Foxy." Fox didn't miss the glint in Gaël's eye before he lowered his gaze to their hands. "But you scared me. I don't want to be the cause of any more of your pain. So we have to talk about it, okay? You can tell me anything, you can ask anything of me, but you have to listen too."

Tears burned at the back of Fox's throat, quickly smothered by the overwhelming fondness that welled up in his heart. He'd never felt more safe than he did with Gaël. He'd tried many things, done many things. And sometimes he didn't realize his mistakes till afterward, but with Gaël he knew instinctively he would never have regrets. With a few simple words, they understood each other. Fox brought Gaël's scabbed knuckles up to his lips. Gaël had a reputation among the pirates as someone that shouldn't be messed with. Yet underneath he was gentle; all the muscle and fighting was just because he hated to see others get hurt. Fox was safe with him. He'd never been more certain of anything.

"I understand. I don't want to cause you pain either," Fox promised. He was the victim of a crime, but that didn't give him the right to exert his will on Gaël in pursuit of his own healing. Ultimately he knew that he had a long way to go before he could put all of this behind him. But he knew Gaël would be with him every step of the way.

CHAPTER 23

SEPTEMBER 7TH, 1666

"We're leaving in six days."

Yves stopped in his tracks. They were in the middle of the village, on their way up to the house from the docks. Rowan stopped too, looking back at him. Waiting.

"What?" Rowan asked when Yves didn't respond. The man seemed rooted to the spot. His facial expression remained impassive, but Rowan thought he could see a storm building behind his eyes. Rowan hoped that when the storm clouds broke over him, he'd only get wet instead of drowning.

"Why so soon?" Yves finally asked.

Why was he acting so strangely? They'd both known this was coming since the beginning. This small bubble of relative peace they'd carved out here on Illusion was just that, an illusion. It was always meant to be temporary. Just like everything in the life of a pirate, it had to come to an end. Rowan wouldn't pretend he wasn't sad about it, nor could he deny that it was necessary. Unavoidable.

"It's not soon," Rowan hedged. "We've been here for almost three weeks. The *Siren*'s repairs are done. And I think it would be better to get Fox out of here sooner rather than later after what happened."

All solid reasons. Practical reasons. But the main thing was that Rowan grew increasingly restless the longer he lingered here. He needed to get back to pirating the same way he needed air in his lungs. Being on land for so long, hour by hour, day by day, he felt like he was losing some vital part of himself. A part that needed to feel the roll of the ship beneath his feet. A part that craved action and the thrill of the hunt. Though Yves had certainly given him plenty of thrills in his time here, it wasn't enough to quench that burning call to return to the sea. He needed to leave Rowan Faine behind and become the Ghost Hawk once again.

It was a pity that meant leaving Yves behind as well.

Yves just looked at him, and behind those fathomless black eyes, Rowan saw a multitude of thoughts and emotions flicker past. Gone in an instant. As much as he thought he knew Yves—as many intimate moments as they'd shared—the man was still a mystery. And that was partly what attracted Rowan to him. He could not guess what he would do next. Yves was as changeable and dangerous as the sea.

Yves strode forward suddenly, taking Rowan by the arm and dragging him up the lane toward the manor house. Rowan stumbled after him, trying to catch his balance.

"Yves, where..." Rowan tripped over an uneven patch of road and would have fallen, but Yves caught him, arm tightening around his waist. Rowan grabbed the front of Yves's greatcoat to rebalance himself. He could feel the eyes of a few passersby on them, and his face flushed at being so publicly in such a position. But Yves's arm locked around the back of his waist, and he couldn't escape.

"What are you doing?" he panted.

Yves cocked his head to the side, his gaze sweeping over Rowan's face. Searching.

"If you're leaving so soon, we should make the most of the time we have left," Yves said darkly. The words themselves were sweet, but his tone was almost threatening. A shiver ran through Rowan's body head to toe. A sort of morbid anticipation pooling in his groin.

"Do I frighten you?" Yves asked, amusement edging his voice.

"You terrify me," Rowan confessed breathlessly. He punctuated the statement by releasing the top button of Yves's white shirt.

"Is that why you're leaving?"

The genuineness of the question stopped Rowan's fingers on the second button, clearing his head enough to realize that he'd essentially been undressing the Demon in the middle of the street. He thought he heard an edge of uncertainty in Yves's voice, but that couldn't be. Yves had no such vulnerabilities. He wouldn't be unbalanced by something so simple as his sexual fling leaving.

"I'm leaving because I have to," Rowan answered honestly.

Yves black eyes hardened to gleaming obsidian chips. He released Rowan. But before Rowan could step away, Yves bent and picked him up, throwing him over his shoulder as easily as if he weighed nothing.

"Yves! What the hell!"

The bystanders watched openly now.

"Put me down!"

"No."

Yves strode up the lane with Rowan struggling on his shoulder.

"Put me down!" Rowan demanded again, ineffectually thumping Yves's back with his fist.

"Hush." Yves smacked Rowan's ass lightly. From somewhere high above, Nephele screeched in indignation on his behalf.

They made it to the front door of the house, and Rowan felt sure Yves would put him down, but Fox happened to be exiting at that exact moment and held the door for them. He smirked at his captain.

"Help me!" Rowan ordered.

"Are you in danger, Captain?" Fox asked innocently.

Was he?

"No, but..."

"Then you're on your own I'm afraid." Fox made to close the door, then turned and added with a sly smile, "Have fun."

Embarrassed heat climbed up Rowan's cheeks. His ears burned. Fox was never going to let him live this down. All the fight went out of him, and he let himself be carried up the stairs.

Rowan's shame turned to anticipation as they crossed the threshold of Yves's bedroom. Yves dumped him onto the bed unceremoniously and began undressing him without a word. He started with the boots and socks, then moved on to Rowan's jacket. Rowan let himself be handled like a doll. He couldn't figure out what Yves was thinking. He almost seemed angry, yet there was something else there too. Rowan knew that he would never understand Yves. No matter how hard he tried. No matter how long he stayed. No matter how intimately their lives and bodies were entwined.

Rowan lay in the luxurious bed stark naked. His cock was flushed and already weeping for attention. He should have felt vulnerable with this man who'd carried him here and undressed him in silence. He hadn't been lying when he confessed his fear, but it was the kind of fear he craved. The kind he felt chasing his quarry across the water, battling a storm, fighting an enemy that was much bigger and stronger than he was.

As always, he was going to let Yves do whatever he wanted to him. Wreck him. Ruin him. Split him in half. Because their time together was almost up.

Yves shucked off his own coat. Folded it and set it aside. Rowan watched him. The way the afternoon light played across his face, the elegant slope of his shoulders and taper of his waist—no one had ever been more beautiful or more deadly. Yves unbuttoned his shirt halfway, the lace cuffs of his sleeves partly hiding his elegant hands.

Finally he looked back up at Rowan's face. They hadn't even kissed yet, but Rowan felt breathless anyway from just the promise in those eyes. Yves removed the blue silk scarf that had been hanging at his collar and knelt one knee on the bed beside Rowan. He leaned down until their noses nearly brushed, warm breath wafting across Rowan's ready lips.

"You're my prisoner again for tonight," Yves said in a tone that brooked no argument. Yet Rowan found himself nodding eagerly anyway.

"Before your imprisonment begins, give me leave to use you however I wish. You need only say the word 'siren' to stop, but until then, you are mine. Body and soul."

Rowan swallowed past the sudden dryness in his mouth. His mind whirled with the possibilities of what Yves might have planned that would necessitate such an escape. But at the same time, his pulse pounded loudly in his cock and head.

"Yes," he managed.

A small, vicious smile twitched the corners of Yves's mouth.

"What is the word?"

"S-siren."

"Very good." One hand lifted Rowan's head, and he tied the scarf over Rowan's eyes so Rowan could only see the faintest shimmer of light through the folded silk. The bed shifted as Yves left it. Rowan stayed still, listening to his own breathing.

Yves returned. He ran his hand down each of Rowan's arms

lightly, then lifted them up over his head and tied his wrists together with something that felt like another scarf.

The usual way this started was a spark of passion, moans, the sound of lips meeting. But this was so slow, so quiet, that it almost overwhelmed him.

Yves ran the backs of his fingers lightly down Rowan's cheek. Rowan twitched, startled. Goosebumps broke out across his skin. Without sight, even the lightest touch was heightened, every moment was laden with anticipation.

Yves touched him again, fingers skimming his collarbone and dancing over his ribs. Each touch satisfying and light on its own, yet together building into a sensation that left him shivering.

"So sensitive," Yves murmured. His fingers moved down over Rowan's stomach, tracing the rim of his navel.

Rowan endured this teasing for what seemed like an age. Yves's hands roamed over him, drawing close to his cock, then pulling away just before giving Rowan the relief of his touch.

"Yves, please..." Rowan finally gasped. He felt like he would burst if Yves didn't kiss him right now and end this unbearable anticipation.

"Impatient," Yves scolded. But he complied. Rowan felt Yves's breath on his face. He strained forward, longing for a kiss. For anything.

Yves's teeth sank sharp and painful into Rowan's bottom lip. He groaned at the first real sensation. When Yves captured his lips in a kiss it held the promise of the night to come. Rowan's tongue slipped between Yves's lips, exploring his warm mouth. Yves's hands roamed over his body, his touch firm and grounding now. And finally. Finally, his warm hand closed around Rowan's eager cock.

"Ah..." Rowan gasped. His back arched, already overstimulated by the lead up to this moment. Yves stroked him slowly. He relished the slide of Yves's palm on his sensitive shaft. All the while, Yves continued kissing him. Rowan's arms tensed. He wanted to touch Yves too. To make him feel good. To make him moan. Besides the few words he'd spoken, he hadn't made a sound. But Rowan's hands were still bound.

Yves broke the kiss. His lips moved down Rowan's chin to his throat and then his chest. He lingered there, nipping at his skin, then moved down to his stomach.

Rowan almost sobbed when Yves's lips finally wrapped around the tip of his cock. The glide of Yves's supple mouth down over the shaft was agonizing. His long tongue swirled across Rowan's fevered skin, and he heard the lube bottle uncork, smelled the delicate scent of coconut. Slick fingers found his entrance and pushed inside without waiting. Yves immediately set to work opening him up. His long fingers stroked Rowan's tight walls. Rowan's breathing was harsh in his own ears as Yves found his prostate and massaged circles into it. His mouth still worked around Rowan's cock, and Rowan realized that he was not going to last. After so much buildup, the pleasure coiling in his belly was already overwhelming. It was enough to make him come, but he wanted more.

He would always want more of Yves.

"I need you," Rowan gasped at a particularly deep stroke, his cock hitting the back of Yves's throat. Yves's teeth dragged lightly against his shaft. "I need you inside me. Please." He wasn't above begging when it came to Yves. But Yves didn't respond other than to press his fingers to Rowan's prostate firmly. Rowan could imagine Yves looking up at him with those hard, dark eyes, lips smirking around his cock. Rowan pressed the back of his head into the soft mattress, mouth open and gaping. This image of Yves in his mind's eye was enough to finally push him over the edge. He came hard into Yves's mouth, back arching, muscles straining against his silken bonds.

But Yves wasn't done. He swallowed Rowan's cum effortlessly without breaking his rhythm. His mouth continued to devour Rowan's softening length, and his fingers carried on massaging his back entrance. Rowan's skin tingled with overstimulation. The blood rushed to his head, dizzying, then back down to his cock as it began to harden again.

Rowan realized suddenly that Yves had no intention of letting him go any time soon. Of just having sex and going on with their day. The thought both terrified and thrilled him.

He arched his hips up off the bed, and Yves's throat constricted around the head of his cock. This was all driving him crazy, but he just wanted more. His skin was already hot and sweat-slicked.

The pleasure built a bit slower now, weaving itself sinuously through his body.

Suddenly, the warmth of Yves's mouth disappeared, and his

fingers withdrew. Rowan clenched around nothing. The air felt cold against his fevered skin.

"Yves..." he whined, too far gone to hate how needy he sounded.

Yves didn't answer. Rowan felt the bed shift as Yves left it. He was alone, and the silence was as deafening as the scarf was blinding. Rowan fidgeted on the bed. Impatient. He turned his head towards where he thought he heard the rustle of Yves's clothing. Rowan was sure he looked desperate and needy lying there naked and tied and blind on Yves's bed. He wondered what Yves thought of him right now.

The silence stretched, and Rowan grew more restless with every passing moment. He squirmed again. Was Yves watching him? Enjoying his discomfort?

The mattress dipped beneath Yves's weight again, and Rowan's breath caught. Yves's fingers gripped his hip and guided him to turn over onto his stomach. Rowan complied, propping himself up on his knees and elbows, ass in the air. He was sure he looked ridiculous, but he didn't care.

One of Yves's fingers dipped inside him, jolting him. Rowan heard the clink of a belt buckle.

CRACK!

Pain seared across his backside, and he instinctively cried out, jolting away from the pain, but Yves's fingers inside him kept him in place. And with the pain came pleasure. Yves rubbed the sore spot with one hand and massaged his soaked hole with the other.

"Y-Yves..." Rowan moaned shakily.

"Did you like that, darling? Do you want more?" Yves's voice was husky with desire. His fingers squelched as they moved in and out of Rowan at a punishing pace.

CRACK!

The leather snapped across Rowan's ass cheek again. Then again. Yves's fingers pumping deep inside him all the while. Rowan's nerves were on fire. The pain radiated through him, but he loved every minute of it. Every moment suffered at Yves's hands was exquisite.

Finally he felt the press of Yves's heavy cock against his stinging skin.

"What do you want, darling? Tell me what you want me to do to you," Yves ordered.

"Fuck me. Please. I need you inside me," Rowan begged.

Yves's fingers retreated and were replaced by the tip of his cock pressing to Rowan's throbbing opening. There was a breathless pause. Rowan turned his head to the side as if he would be able to catch a glimpse of Yves's beautiful face despite the blindfold.

Another smack landed across Rowan's ass, this time from Yves's open palm. Rowan's cry of pain turned to pleasure as Yves thrust into him up to the base. Rowan rocked forward on his knees with the force of it, Yves's hip bones hitting the sore curve of his ass. Yves withdrew and thrust in again just as hard. Rowan's cock throbbed and dripped precum onto the rumpled sheets. He bit his knuckle to stifle his guttural moans as Yves's thick length pounded into him over and over. He was breathless. Lightheaded. The intense pleasure and pain lanced sharply through his body and mingled at his core. He desperately wanted to reach back and stroke his own cock to relieve some of the pressure. But he didn't try to escape his bonds. Even though the silk now chafed his wrists, he didn't dare disobey Yves.

"F-fuck...more...please more," Rowan pleaded.

"Such a greedy little brat," Yves growled. "Who's going to fill you up like this when you're gone, hm? No one can fuck you better than me."

The buzzing ecstasy in Rowan's head muffled the words from his understanding. Any meaning behind them was lost on him. All he could do was moan Yves's name and hang on like hell.

The next orgasm crashed upon him suddenly. His cum spurted weakly onto the white sheets. Yves smacked him again and didn't slow his pace even a little. Rowan bit down on his knuckle again.

After a few more hard thrusts, Yves pulled out. He scooped a fingerful of Rowan's cum off Rowan's inner thigh and flipped Rowan onto his back. Yves's cum-slathered fingers dipped into Rowan's entrance, lubricating him with his own juices. Then his hand went to Rowan's throat, and his throbbing cock penetrated him once again. Rowan's back arched as the overstimulation hit him in waves. The sounds that fell from his lips no longer sounded like him. Yves's fingers tightened fractionally around his throat. Rowan gasped, little colorful stars spangling at the edges of his already restricted vision. His cock struggled to harden again, pathetically soft after coming twice already.

He could still breathe. Just barely.

Rowan was hit with a sudden, primal urge to see Yves's face. To look upon the man who held his life in his elegant hands while fucking him dumb. Rowan brought his bound hands down to tug at the edge of the blindfold.

Yves's hand tightened further, eliciting a choked sound from Rowan's throat.

"Leave it."

Rowan obeyed, hands shaking. Yves's hips rutted into him, and he bent low to kiss him. The pressure on his throat eased. Rowan inhaled Yves's breath hungrily as Yves's delicate fingers stroked his throat. Rowan was intoxicated by the taste of his lips, the hard heat inside him.

Even though Rowan's erection was only at half-staff, he could feel another peak ready to shatter him. He wondered if he had anything left in him. He'd come twice already, and Yves hadn't even finished once. The man truly was a monster.

Yves broke the kiss but remained close. Their strained breathing mingled between them. Then the muscles in Rowan's abdomen tightened, the strokes reaching some new, unexplored angle of divinity as Yves shifted positions. As quickly as blinking, Rowan was so far gone his own voice sounded separate from himself, moaning incoherent nonsense as Yves railed him.

More. Fuck me. Wreck me. Yves. Please. Please. Please.

He had no idea what he was begging for. He leaned forward, trying to stifle his cries on Yves's lips. But found Yves's shoulder instead. He bit down hard, tasting salt. Yves moaned in his ear, voice deep and resonant.

"Say my name," Yves demanded.

Rowan released his shoulder, sweat still salting his lips.

"Yves..." he moaned.

Yves's thrusts were getting faster. Sloppier.

"Again." His voice was husky.

"Yves..." Rowan was dissolving in a raging, rapturous sea. He said it over and over like a litany of lust. And finally he drowned in another orgasm. His semen dribbled weakly onto his stomach as Yves rode him through it. But after a few more strokes, Yves came as well, hot release gushing into Rowan's clenching walls. His hips slowed and stilled, still buried deep inside.

Shockwaves shuddered through Rowan. His whole body shook

uncontrollably, and he realized that the edge of the blindfold was wet with tears.

Yves's breath wafted hot on the side of his sweat-slick neck. He was still seated deep inside, and Rowan reached out blindly to brush Yves's cheek with his knuckles.

"Let me see you."

Yves's lips brushed Rowan's jaw just beneath his ear.

"Oh darling, we are far from done."

ROWAN DIDN'T WANT to stop. Though he was exhausted, his body hurt, and he had lost track of the hours long ago. He was keenly aware that his time with Yves was short. The *Siren* was seaworthy, and soon he would be free on the open water once again. So he wanted to savor every moment he had left in Yves's arms. Because truthfully he didn't know if they would ever see each other again. Or if he would ever return to this bed or kiss these lips again.

Another orgasm rippled through him, and he came dry. The scarves still restricted his vision and bound him. He'd run out of semen long ago. Yves however, seemed to have an endless supply of both cum and energy. Rowan was drenched head to toe in sweat and sticky with ribbons of both his and Yves's cum.

"Coming again, darling?" Yves purred as he rolled his hips languidly forward. "How many times is that now?"

"I d-don't know," Rowan stuttered. He had truly lost the will to count after the fifth or sixth time. Yves had contorted him into every imaginable position and railed him until his limbs were too weak to hold himself up anymore. So now he was on his back again, legs wrapped around Yves's slim hips. Rowan's lips were kiss-bitten, skin red and tender. He'd been whipped, spanked, choked, bitten—and done his fair share of biting in return.

But he couldn't stop. He wouldn't stop until Yves was satisfied.

"Do you want more?" Yves asked.

"I'll always want you." The words left his lips without thought. Too honest by far. But his nerves were raw, and his mind was hazy with lust and afterglow.

The tear-soaked silk was torn away from Rowan's eyes.

Silvery moonlight sliced across the darkened room. Rowan blinked rapidly, trying to clear his vision. Finally Yves's ethereal face swam into focus. He could have cried to finally see it. The pale light glinted off Yves's dark hair, his smooth skin. His obsidian eyes flashed with a wild passion, and a spark of lust rekindled deep in Rowan's core.

"You're beautiful," Rowan breathed.

Yves's hips rolled forward again, making Rowan gasp.

"Let me touch you," Rowan pleaded.

"Needy." But Yves undid the knot at his wrists. Rowan reached up and cradled Yves's face in his hands. He pulled Yves down and kissed him deeply.

Everything was encompassed in that kiss. Through the weeks he'd been here, *stay as long as you need* became *stay as long as you want*, then simply, *stay.*

And Rowan wanted to stay. He dearly wanted to live in this moment. But he *needed* to go.

Yves moved slowly and deeply within him. He took Rowan apart piece by piece until all that was left were the small, animal whimpers falling from Rowan's lips. Yves kissed them away.

CHAPTER 24

SEPTEMBER 9TH, 1666

Rowan spent the morning finalizing supplies for the *Siren's* imminent departure. A storm threatened to roll in from the east, sending cooling breezes to sway the island trees. The knee length hem of his black Kefryean skirt fluttered as he made his way back to the house. Gray clouds scuttled through the overcast late afternoon sky. Rowan was looking forward to having dinner with Yves. The other man had been gone from their bed that morning, no doubt still sulking.

The last few days they'd been arguing about Rowan's departure. And now that Rowan was ready to leave, he wanted to cheer Yves up, to give him a little going away present.

There was a spring in his step as he entered the front door of the big house. John was on his way out, looking grim.

"Is everything alright?" Rowan asked.

"Huh? Oh, yes, fine." The first mate looked distracted, barely glancing at Rowan as he passed.

Rowan hurried up the stairs, stopping briefly in the bedroom before continuing on to find Yves. He didn't bother knocking as he entered the office. Yves didn't look up from the papers on his desk, so Rowan paused for a moment to take in the sight of him.

Yves looked dashing as always. Day after day, Rowan was astounded by the other man's beauty. The overcast light slanted through the window to bathe his tan skin in a milky glow. A lock of his raven hair fell across his forehead, and his tongue pushed at the inside of his cheek as he scanned through his ledgers.

"What is it?" Yves's smooth voice brought Rowan out of his reverie.

"Is that any way to speak to your lover?" Rowan answered coyly. They'd never labeled their relationship that way before, and Yves looked up at him, startled. Yves's dark eyes traveled down the length of Rowan's body, catching immediately on Rowan's unusual attire. A small smile tugged at the edge of his lips.

"Have you been wearing that all day?"

Rowan didn't miss the huskiness in the other man's voice. He stepped closer to the desk, letting the skirt sway with his movement.

"Of course. Why? Is there something wrong with it?" he answered in mock concern. He stopped beside the desk, and Yves turned his chair to observe him. Rowan lifted the hem of the skirt slightly, revealing a small sliver of creamy thigh. "It's quite comfortable," he continued. He looked up through his lashes, seeing Yves's gaze sharpen. Rowan held back a smirk. "Don't you think it's pretty?"

"It is," Yves agreed. His tongue ran along the crease of his lips. "Come here."

Rowan took half a step closer, teasing. But it seemed that Yves was in no mood for games. His long, ring-laden fingers hooked into the waist of Rowan's skirt and reeled him in till the shorter man stood between his splayed legs. The hungry look in Yves's eyes had Rowan's cock already twitching. He'd known this outfit would drive the other man crazy, but he hadn't expected such an immediate response. It pleased him.

Rowan held his breath as Yves's hands slipped beneath the skirt, caressing his thighs and traveling up his legs, sending tingles racing over his skin. He saw the moment Yves realized he wasn't wearing anything beneath. His long-lashed eyes widening ever so slightly. It was difficult to surprise the Demon, and Rowan was proud of himself.

He didn't have long to bask in that feeling, however. Yves yanked him forward so that Rowan was straddling his lap.

"What an alluring little thing you are," Yves purred. He cupped Rowan's bare ass in his elegant hands, his rings cold against Rowan's skin.

Rowan braced his hands on Yves's shoulders and leaned down to kiss him, earrings clinking together. Yves's mouth was plush and pliant, his long tongue slipping into Rowan's mouth as soon as their lips connected.

Rowan's cock hardened further as he imagined those lips around it. That deft tongue flicking over the sensitive underside. He could feel the hardening bulge in Yves's pants and rocked forward slightly, creating friction between their bodies.

Yves hummed against his lips. His fingers massaged Rowan's upper thighs. Rowan rocked his hips again.

"So eager," Yves murmured. One of his hands moved to wrap around Rowan's cock, thumbing the precum beading at the tip. A soft moan escaped Rowan's lips. He reached down to undo the fastenings of Yves's pants.

Yves's cock sprung free. Gods, it was huge. Its size somehow always surprised him. The thought of its throbbing length buried deep inside him made his whole body shiver with anticipation. But underneath it all, he knew this would be one of the last times they slept together. He was leaving soon, and they might never see each other again.

Rowan pushed those thoughts away, determined to make the most of the situation and the unbelievably sexy man currently under him.

Yves stroked Rowan's cock slowly, his other hand moving between Rowan's ass cheeks to finger his rim. He found it already wet and primed. A slow grin spread across his face as he dipped his middle finger into Rowan's already loosened hole, one of his rings pressing against the rim.

"This was your plan all along, wasn't it, you devious minx?" Yves cooed. "You couldn't wait to have my cock inside you."

"So then what are you waiting for?"

Yves's fingertips pressed Rowan's prostate, causing his muscles to clench. He swore softly.

Then Yves was lifting Rowan, positioning him over his erection and withdrawing his finger.

He didn't even give Rowan a moment to breathe before he forced Rowan's hips down, burying his massive cock in Rowan's hole up to the base. Rowan cried out in surprise and sudden pleasure. He'd prepped himself in the bedroom beforehand, but his fingers weren't nearly enough to match Yves's length and girth. Yves gave him only a moment to adjust before he was lifting him again, fingers bruising on his hips, and slamming him down. Rowan's back arched, a deep guttural moan escaping. His head tilted back. Yves sucked a mark onto his exposed throat.

"Pretty baby," he moaned, "you wanted this, so move."

Rowan's legs were already shaking from the huge cock buried deep in his ass, but he did as he was told. He began riding Yves's cock, angling so that it would hit his prostate with every thrust. His hands tightened on Yves's shoulders, and Yves groaned.

"Fuck, you're tight." His large hands framed Rowan's tiny waist. His gaze fell to watch Rowan's perky cock bounce beneath the skirt, a small patch of wetness seeping through the fabric. Rowan was losing it. He hadn't expected this to be so hot, impaling himself on Yves's cock again and again, feeling every throb, every ridge of vein. The pleasure was already building uncontrollably in his gut, and the stretch and burn of his dripping hole around Yves's cock was addicting.

"Yves..." His hips stuttered. "Please touch me." He hated how much he craved this. How addicted he was to this man who was once his bitter rival. It was going to be so hard to leave.

Yves smeared precum down over Rowan's weeping cock and began to stroke him in time with Rowan's hips. Taking pleasure from the front and back, Rowan's moans grew louder. He was so close... only a little more and...

"Captain!" John burst into the room. "I followed your orders, but Logan's hurt—" He stopped short at the sight of Rowan in his captain's lap, clearly fucked out. "Shit."

Rowan's mind came crashing back into stunned reality in an instant, the high of his potential orgasm forgotten in the face of John's words.

"Logan's hurt?" Rowan disengaged himself from Yves's lap. A bit of wetness dripped down the inside of his thigh, but he didn't care. "How? Where is he? What happened?" He started forward, but his attention snagged. John's face was smudged with black powder, little scrapes and pin-pricks of blood dotting his cheeks and neck. Then the rest of John's words sank in. "Wait. Following orders? What the fuck is he talking about?" He wheeled on Yves who was refastening his pants over his still hard length.

"What is he talking about?" Rowan asked again, his fists clenched at his sides.

"I can explain..." For the first time since they'd met, the Deep Water Demon looked frightened. He took a tentative step toward Rowan, hand outstretched. "No one was supposed to—"

"It doesn't matter now," John interrupted. For once he wasn't his usual stoic self. "Logan is in the infirmary. It's bad."

~

ROWAN PUSHED past John without a word. Yves made to follow, but John stopped him with a firm hand on his arm.

"Leave it."

Yves wrested his arm free from John's strong grip, but John blocked his path again.

"Let me pass."

"No," John said. "We fucked up. Let him be with his friend. He needs to cool down before you try to explain."

"What happened? How did it go wrong?" Yves argued.

"I'm going to tell you something for your own good. You're prideful and selfish. You're ruthless. It's what makes you a great pirate. But it won't serve you well in love. You can try to talk him down from this. But if you love him, you have to accept his decision. No matter what it is."

All the fight went out of Yves's shoulders. That word. Love. He hadn't let himself even think about it in so long. He knew the terms of his life well, the terms of his darkness, and love was not a part of them. An impossibility. What he felt toward Rowan could never be love. Neither was it merely a continuation of the obsession he'd harbored for the Ghost Hawk from the very beginning. It was possession, the feral need to keep Rowan by his side. Yves was on the cusp of losing the one man who could be his equal. And through his own selfishness, he'd managed to push Rowan away even further than he ever would have gone on his own.

CHAPTER 25

SEPTEMBER 9TH, 1666

When Rowan made it to the infirmary door, he was met with a worried looking Henri rushing back into the room carrying an armful of towels.

"Where is he?" Rowan demanded. He felt like there were snakes squirming around in his stomach. He didn't know what had happened to Logan or how badly he was hurt. But John and Henri's urgency told him it was serious. Whatever it was, it was Rowan's fault. For complacently extending their time here. For leaving Logan alone to go for one last tryst with Yves. For ever trusting Yves and bringing them here in the first place.

"Robin's tending him," Henri said. He shifted the towels to one arm to chew at his cuticles. "It's bad, Captain."

"How bad? What happened?" Rowan felt suddenly frozen. He didn't want to go in there. Because when he saw Logan it would make his failure real.

"I don't know. I was on the docks, and I heard a boom. Then John was rowing him back—"

They were interrupted by the infirmary door opening.

"Henri, I need—" Robin stopped short when he saw Rowan standing there. "Even better, Captain, I need both of you. Now."

Rowan didn't argue. He and Henri just followed Robin into the infirmary.

Logan writhed on a waist-height table at the end of the room. His breath came out in little gasping sobs, and his clothing and face were peppered with spots of blood. His skin was pale with the loss of it.

Rowan's eyes went immediately to his right arm. The white sleeve of Logan's shirt was soaked in dark blood and black powder burns, and the arm beneath ended in a lump of red meat and gristle and bone where his hand should have been.

Rowan's steps faltered, but Robin pushed him forward.

"There's no time to waste. I need you two to hold him down for the amputation."

"A-amputation?" Henri's deep voice sounded so small. "You can't save his hand?"

Robin grimaced but got on with the business of scrubbing his hands. "It's beyond saving. Believe me, I would save it if I could, but it would be best to get it off as soon as possible." He dried his hands on a clean cloth. "Captain, you take his upper body. Henri, legs. I gave him something for the pain, and I think he's still in shock, but once I start cutting, he's going to struggle."

From Rowan's previous interactions with Robin, he'd seen the man as shy, almost demure. But here in his element, Robin was confident and capable. Rowan did as he was told. He laid his body crossways across Logan's chest, pinning his uninjured arm to his side. Henri did the same with his legs.

Logan's eyelids fluttered open, eyes glassy with shock or the drugged stupor of whatever Robin had given him.

"Captain?" His voice was dreamy. He looked like a fallen angel, all blond curls and blood.

"It's okay, Logan. Just rest. It will be okay." Rowan tried not to look at the gleaming utensils Robin laid out on the table next to him.

"Bite this," Robin instructed, placing a thick piece of leather between Logan's teeth. Logan's glassy eyes widened as if he knew what was about to happen, but he bit down. Robin rolled the bloody sleeve up to reveal a tourniquet around Logan's upper arm. Rowan averted his gaze, looking instead at Logan's face.

"It will be okay," Rowan murmured, hoping he sounded reassuring despite the rawness in his throat.

He felt the moment Robin began cutting. Logan's body bucked. He tried to spit out the strap, but Rowan shoved it back in, muffling his scream behind the leather. Rowan and Henri held him as still as they could, neither able to look at what Robin was doing. Rowan buried his face in Logan's chest, listening to the frantic hammering of his heartbeat.

"I'm sorry," he murmured into the blood-speckled fabric. His tears mingled with the blood. "It's all my fault. I'm sorry."

The minutes seemed to drag on forever, but Logan blessedly passed out halfway through.

Some time later the smell of searing flesh brought Rowan out of his guilty contemplations. His head rose to see Robin cauterizing the stump of Logan's arm, a faint wisp of smoke curling up from where the hot metal met flesh.

"Is it done?" Henri asked. He looked exhausted, face tearstained and hair disheveled. "Will he be okay?"

Robin hung the cauterizing instrument on a metal rack to cool and released the bloody tourniquet from around Logan's arm. He didn't answer till he removed the dented strap from Logan's teeth and checked his vitals. He sighed.

"As long as we can stave off infection, he should be fine." He couldn't seem to look either of them in the eye. Had he known about Yves's plans too? Or was he simply uncomfortable seeing the anguish on his lover's face? He began wrapping the stump in clean white bandages. "I'm going to give him something to help him sleep for a while, and there are a couple big splinters I have to remove. You two should go clean up." He scooped up Logan's unconscious body and transferred him to one of the empty cots near the window.

Rowan was about to protest, but he realized that there were spots of blood all over his shirt. Robin unbuttoned the front of Logan's shirt and began the painstaking process of removing several large splinters from beneath Logan's skin. Rowan pulled Henri to the side.

"Stay here," he whispered fiercely. "I know you like Robin, but this was all orchestrated by Yves somehow. We can't trust him. Don't let Logan out of your sight."

Henri looked at him in disbelief. "I-I don't think Robin would have anything to do with something like that," he whispered.

"Regardless, keep an eye on Logan. He'll need a friend here when he wakes up."

"What are you going to do?"

"Gather the crew. We're leaving as soon as Logan can be moved."

~

Rowan left the infirmary, only to find an unwelcome figure waiting in the hallway.

John.

The first mate's expression was stricken, nervous. And seeing him there made the rage that had been slowly simmering in Rowan's gut boil over.

"You," he snarled. Before John could so much as raise his hands in defense, Rowan slammed him into the wall, one hand bunched in the front of his shirt, and punched him square in the jaw.

"Tell me *exactly* what happened. What did Yves tell you to do?"

John was silent. He didn't deny it. Didn't defend himself. He knew what Rowan had heard in the office was as good as a confession.

"Is Logan okay?" He'd never sounded more uncertain, more guilty.

"He lost his hand." Rowan spat the words at him like poison. John squeezed his eyes shut, collecting himself. Did he really feel so guilty about what he'd done? If so, why had he done it in the first place?

"Yves ordered me to sabotage the *Siren* and make it look like an accident so you would have to stay longer..." His eyes met Rowan's, full of genuine guilt. "No one was supposed to get hurt. I saw you at the house, and I thought...I thought no one was on the *Siren*. I was going to..." He paused, sucking in a shuddering breath. "Logan caught me, we fought, and one of the gunpowder kegs I'd messed with went off right in his face. I didn't mean for him to get hurt. I swear."

Rowan released his hold on John's shirt, and John slumped against the wall.

"He did all this just so I would stay here?" Rowan felt sick to his stomach. It really was his fault. Yves had done this because of him, because of their relationship.

John didn't answer, but Rowan didn't need one. He pushed away and stalked down the hall just as Fox came sprinting around the corner.

"Captain! What happened? I heard—" He stopped short when he saw Rowan's blood-stained shirt, and tears began to well in his eyes. "Is Logan..."

"He's alive. He lost his hand, but he's alive," Rowan reassured him. He drew Fox closer by the hand. "Go check on him, only for a minute, then gather the crew quietly and prepare the *Siren* for departure."

Fox's tears spilled silently over his cheeks, but he nodded.

~

ROWAN HURRIED UP THE STAIRS. It was still light out; they could still make it out of the harbor and into open water if they hurried. The conditions wouldn't be ideal, but they could make it. After that, he didn't know. He supposed they would go back to their usual pirating as planned. But his mind was a muddle of confused feelings.

He'd thought he could trust Yves. He'd thought Yves actually cared for him. But for Yves to betray him like this... Even if he hadn't meant for anyone to get hurt, he'd gone too far. It was clear now whatever care he had for Rowan was purely selfish. He only cared for what Rowan could do for him, and for the conquest of getting his rival into bed.

Rowan should never have trusted him, but all that didn't mean Rowan could just turn off his own feelings. Had it all been a lie? Each kiss? Each word? Even meeting his sister and telling him about the darkness in his past? Rowan's heart couldn't quite believe that. Still, he knew he had to leave now, before Yves could ply him with more lies. Before his own heart could talk him out of it.

Rowan stopped in front of the door to the room he and Yves had shared for the past few weeks. He told himself Yves wouldn't be on the other side of this door. He would just change into clean clothes, gather his things, and leave.

He opened the door.

Yves jumped up from the bed as Rowan entered.

"Rowan!" He didn't approach, just stood there looking lost. Rowan said nothing in return. He grabbed his rucksack and began shoving clothes into it.

"You're leaving." Yves's voice was dark, and it wasn't a question.

"What do you think?" Rowan snapped. He pulled some under-garments on under his skirt. He wouldn't be changing into clean clothes with Yves here. He couldn't even stand to look at him. While he'd been riding Yves, his best friend had been hurt on Yves's orders. The thought disgusted and shamed him.

"Rowan. Please. Just let me explain." Yves took a few tentative steps toward him. But Rowan was already back at the door, his bag over his shoulder.

"John explained well enough," he answered coldly.

"Darling, all I wanted to do was keep—"

Rowan made a sound of disgust and fled.

Fox had done his work well and quickly. The crew was already being ferried out to the *Siren* in landing boats. In his haste, Rowan hadn't considered whether the ship was damaged in the explosion, but it looked seaworthy enough to get them out of here, even with the soft rain that prefaced an imminent storm beginning to patter on the docks.

Rowan spotted Fox directing the exodus and approached, handing his bag off to another crew member.

"How soon can we depart?" Rowan asked. In Logan's absence, Fox had become the de facto first mate.

Fox's lips thinned to a line. "The *Siren* will be ready within the hour, but conditions aren't great. The hold is a bit charred, and Robin says we shouldn't move Logan just yet."

He could deal with the first two, but if they took Logan and his health worsened because of it, Rowan would never forgive himself.

"Keep loading up. I'll talk to him." He spotted Gaël helping load up a boat and glared at him. Fox's lover had asked him some time ago if he could join the *Siren*'s crew, but now Rowan couldn't help but be suspicious of anyone connected to Yves.

Fox gripped Rowan's upper arm. "Whatever Yves did, Gaël has nothing to do with it. He's part of the *Siren* now."

"Fine." Rowan didn't have the strength to argue right now. If Gaël had ulterior motives, he would deal with it later. Rowan turned and ran back up to the house. He found Henri and Robin having a quiet argument over Logan's unconscious body in the infirmary. Two packed bags rested at Henri's feet. They fell silent when Rowan entered.

"We're going," Rowan said without preamble.

Henri was about to say something, but Robin stepped in front of him.

"Logan is still unstable. You don't have a physician on board, and Logan needs proper care for a wound like this."

"I don't want to leave Robin," Henri added. His voice was raw, not just from crying over Logan.

Rowan sighed in exasperation.

"If you think I'm leaving you or Logan here after this, you're crazy. You *will* be on that ship within the hour." He turned to Robin. "I don't care if Yves is willing to release you from service. He almost stole my best friend's life, so I am stealing his prized physician. Logan will be fine on the ship if you're there, right?"

Robin hesitated for only a moment before nodding.

"Good. I expect the three of you on the *Siren* as soon as possible." He turned on his heel and left without looking back.

THE RAIN FELL GENTLY around Yves as he stood on the shore, sticking his hair to his forehead. He still wore the clothing he'd fucked Rowan in earlier. Just as Rowan still wore his skirt, now stained with the blood of his friend. Yves swallowed, his mind sifting through what he would say.

The docks were all but deserted by the time Rowan arrived. Only Fox and Gaël remained on shore. A few of the villagers watched curiously from their porches, and out in the harbor, the *Siren* was lit up with activity.

Rowan stalked past him, determinedly not sparing him even a glance.

Yves grabbed his arm, harder than he'd intended. He consciously eased his grip, pushing down the part of him that wanted to pick Rowan up and lock him away forever.

"You can't leave."

"I won't be *kept*," Rowan snarled.

Yves swallowed his pride, letting the shame over what he'd done rise to the surface. That was exactly what he'd wanted to do. Keep Rowan here, away from danger. Keep him for himself and devour him whole.

But he knew now. If he did that, Rowan would only resent him. He was not a man meant for domesticity. If Yves kept him here, he would lose the things that made him. His daring. His cleverness.

They would wither in captivity like a caged bird losing its song. The only thing that would remain was his old hatred for Yves. Yves had let his own selfish desires override Rowan's needs. No matter how desperately Yves wanted to keep him here, to delay their separation just a little longer, he had to accept Rowan's choice.

He stepped closer, hesitantly reached out to cup Rowan's rain-damp cheek in his hand.

"I could no more keep you than I could keep the stars under my bed. Just..." His voice trembled. "Promise me that I will see you again. Promise that we will not be enemies."

Rowan's eyes widened. Could he not understand, after all of this, the true depths of Yves's feelings for him? They hadn't ever spoken the words, and Yves had thought himself incapable of such feelings. But somehow Rowan had broken through that deep darkness inside him and brought down the blue sky to soothe his churning waters. That hunger, that need to possess him, keep him, it all came from Yves's fear that he would lose Rowan and be alone again with only the nameless darkness for company. And even though Yves knew he was incapable of loving Rowan as he deserved, in his heart he chose to name these impossible feelings love.

Rowan didn't seem to feel the same, especially not now that Yves had hurt him so thoroughly. Yves longed to snatch back his foolish actions, to accept the fact that to Rowan, he might just be a pleasing body to pass the time until he could return to the sea where he belonged. He could accept that, if only Rowan would stay by his side. Tears formed in Yves's eyes, and he forced them down.

Rowan searched Yves's expression, blue eyes trying to reveal all his secrets and vulnerabilities. Yves wanted to give everything to him, but his heart ached in a way he'd never felt before. And that made him shrink in on himself.

"I promise we will not be enemies," Rowan said quietly, placing his hand over Yves's where it rested on his cheek. "As for seeing you again, I-I don't think I can forgive you for this."

Yves's heart fractured just a little more, the darkness within him frantically trying to mend the damage and not succeeding.

"I'm sorry. I should never have tried to keep you. I'm sorry I hurt Logan."

Rowan nodded, looking unsure of what to say.

That was all Yves was likely to get. A simple promise that they would not try to kill each other when they went back to their old lives. Yet Yves was a selfish man at heart.

He smiled his shiniest, most charming smile.

"Grant me just one more thing."

Rowan's eyebrows rose, but he remained silent.

"Don't go out in this storm." Yves could sense the tides beyond the shelter of Illusion's bay churning with dangerous potential and smell the imminent storm in the air. He could not protect Rowan from all the dangers of the world, but at least he could prevent him from sailing into this storm. So he laid it out like the terms of another truce, even though he wanted nothing more than to fall to his knees at Rowan's feet and beg him to stay.

A war of indecision waged in Rowan's eyes. Then his gaze flicked over Yves's shoulder, and he stepped out of Yves's reach. Yves turned to see Henri and Robin making their way slowly down the path. The limp form of Logan in a cart behind them.

For a moment Yves feared the man was dead, but a puff of breath escaped into the chilled air above Logan's still form.

His fear turned to shame. He had not once asked after Logan's condition when it was all his fault.

When he turned back, Rowan was looking up at him.

"I'm taking Robin and Gaël."

Yves couldn't argue with that. If that was what Rowan wanted, he would not interfere. For once, he would be unselfish. Rowan's eyes flicked to his injured friend as they passed, then back up to Yves. "He's alive. You're lucky he is. If he had died..." Rowan took a deep breath. "If he had died, nothing in this world would keep me from my revenge. But Logan is a more forgiving man than I. We will stay the night in the harbor and let the storm pass. If he wakes before then, I'll send for you so you can make your apologies in person."

He turned on his heel and strode away to the waiting boat.

CHAPTER 26

SEPTEMBER 10TH, 1666

The infirmary of the *Siren* was dark but for the flickering lantern beside the door. Robin and Henri had claimed Old Joe's cabin next to the infirmary as their own, and the pair had long since retired, leaving Rowan to sit at Logan's bedside. Robin had wanted to stay up with his patient, but Rowan sent him to bed with assurances that he'd fetch him if anything changed.

In truth, Rowan knew he wouldn't be able to sleep tonight. He had too much on his mind, and he wanted to be by Logan's side when he woke, even if he had to wait all night. So he sat in silence in the near darkness thinking about how he'd gotten them all into this mess and what they would do next.

He looked down to where he clasped Logan's remaining hand between his own. He didn't know how long he'd been sitting there, but it was late, and exhaustion clung to him like cobwebs.

"Forgive me," he murmured. "I didn't mean to put you in danger."

"You didn't."

Rowan's head snapped up at the sound of Logan's groggy voice.

"You're awake! How are you feeling? Are you in pain? Can I get you anything?" Rowan knew he was talking a mile a minute, but he couldn't seem to stop himself. "I should get Robin."

Logan's hand tightened.

"Stay, please."

"Sorry, just...does it hurt?"

Logan turned his head away, nestling his cheek against the pillow. Slowly, he raised his arm, ending in a bandaged stump at the wrist. His face showed almost no reaction, but a slow exhale seeped between his parted lips. Carefully, he rested the arm back on the cot and closed his eyes. Rowan remained silent, waiting. Logan's throat bobbed as he swallowed. Maybe the drugs Robin had given him were still in effect, blunting the impact. For this was not the reaction of a man who had just discovered he was missing a hand.

After a long while, Logan turned back to look at him.

"How did this happen?" Logan asked quietly.

"How much do you remember?"

Logan's brow furrowed. "I was doing inventory and John was there. We fought and then... I don't know. Did...did you apologize to me? I remember you saying sorry."

"There was an explosion. John said it was an accident, but he was following Yves's orders to sabotage the *Siren* so I would stay with him longer." He lowered his head, shame washing over him once again. "We had to amputate your hand. I-I'm so sorry Logan. All of this is my fault. I should never have trusted him."

"You were just going with your gut." Logan cracked a smile at the old joke. He never could stand to see his captain sad.

"My gut was wrong this time. After this, I don't think we can ever come back."

"But it was an accident, wasn't it? They never meant for me to get hurt, did they?"

"That's what they said, but—"

"But he lied to you. He tried to make you stay when you didn't want to."

"You lost your hand. You could have *died*."

"You think I don't understand that?" Logan raised his eyebrows, successfully cowing his captain.

After a moment of silence, Logan asked, "So we're leaving? Are we really never coming back?"

"I don't know. I told Yves I would think on it. I also told him I would let him apologize to you in person if you woke up before we left."

"Well? Send for him then."

A STORM RAGED in the dark, yet within the protective arms of Illusion's cove, the wind did not howl and the rain did not sting. Both the ship and the island slept as dawn approached. Nevertheless, Yves came when called. He sat in the landing boat, back straight as Gaël rowed them across the dark water. Standing at the rail, Rowan felt a sense of grim satisfaction that the Deep Water Demon had heeded his call despite the rain and the late hour, summoned in the dead of night like a real demon.

The boat drew up, bumping softly against the side of the *Siren*. Gaël ascended the ladder first, followed by John, sporting a bruised jaw, then Yves himself.

"Captain." John nodded respectfully to Rowan. Yves remained silent. Neither of them seemed like they had gotten much sleep, if any.

"Logan's awake, and he'll hear your apology before we leave." Rowan's voice sounded extraordinarily cold even to his own ears. He turned his back on them and led them to the infirmary.

Logan was sitting up in bed with Robin by his side. They both looked tired, and Logan had a faint sheen of sweat on his brow. The drug had worn off. And the pain must have been overwhelming. Rowan stayed by the door as Yves and John approached.

John spoke first.

"I'm sorry, Logan." His usually stoic voice was laced with emotion, and he knelt at the side of the cot in contrition. "When you caught me, I shouldn't have fought. I shouldn't have been there in the first place."

To the surprise of everyone present, Logan reached out with his remaining hand and patted John on the head.

"I understand," Logan said. Though his voice was strained with dregs of pain, he was comforting the very man who'd hurt him. Rowan had always thought Logan was too sweet for the life of a pirate. And once again, Logan proved him right.

"You panicked and made a mistake. I never expected to come out of a life like this unscathed. I just hoped it would come from an enemy rather than a friend."

A friend? When had they become friends?

John nodded and stood.

"If we see each other again, I hope I can make it up to you." He turned to Yves. "I'll head back first."

Now it was Yves's turn. The tall captain looked down at the injured man. From his angle, Rowan couldn't see the expression on his face.

"It was my order that caused this, and I take the blame. My actions have hurt you and..." He turned his head slightly over his shoulder as if he wanted to look at Rowan. "Caused great distress to your crew. What I did was selfish and misguided, and I am sorry. Please allow me to pay reparations to you."

Logan's eyebrow quirked up. "If that's the case, consider Robin's indenture paid with my hand, and I would have your word that we will be allowed back to Illusion if we so choose."

"Logan, wait..." Robin began as if to stop him, but Logan silenced him with a look.

"He is free to go, and the *Siren*'s crew are welcome back at any time."

Logan nodded and slumped back against the pillows.

"He needs to rest now," Robin said. Both captains shuffled out of the room.

In the corridor, Rowan began to make his way up to the deck, but Yves caught his arm.

"Will you return if Logan wants it?" he asked.

"How can we return if I don't know where we are?" Rowan said coolly.

Yves seemed to be keeping his expression carefully blank, restraining whatever emotion he might have been feeling. His grip on Rowan's arm tightened ever so slightly, and he leaned close to Rowan's ear as if they might be overheard.

"I will tell you, and only you, the location of Illusion." Rowan's stomach flipped at Yves's closeness as the taller man whispered the coordinates in his ear. "If you return, wait on the eastern side of the island, and I will come to guide you h—" He'd surely been about to say "home" but stopped himself. "To guide you into the harbor," he amended.

Rowan tugged his arm from Yves's grip. "If we're done here, you should get back." He started down the hall again, but Yves didn't move.

They stared at each other for a moment. The tension in the air was palpable, and Rowan was as confused as ever about where Yves stood in his life now. He wanted Yves to leave him in peace to collect his thoughts. He wanted to go back to his old life and forget this ever happened.

But he wouldn't forget. And he couldn't go back.

"Rowan." Yves's tone was pleading, his usual confidence gone. Replaced with wariness. "Please. Will you allow me to kiss you goodbye?"

Rowan didn't know what he'd been expecting, but it certainly wasn't that.

"How could you ask that after what you've done?" he asked tiredly.

Yves's perfect lips quirked into a sad smile.

"Because I am a selfish man Rowan. Let me have this, and I will never ask you for anything else." But he'd asked for so much already. He took Rowan's hand gently and drew him close. Rowan's lips parted breathlessly, and Yves's eyes sparkled as if daring Rowan to resist his charms. His other hand came up to caress Rowan's cheek. Waiting, Rowan realized, for Rowan to say yes.

"You could have had me for three more days, if you hadn't done this. We could've had more time." He couldn't keep the anguish from his voice. His mind whirled with warring desires. He was still angry. He still *wanted* to be angry. And he hadn't forgiven Yves, even if Logan had. Rowan was a man who could hold a grudge till his dying breath but... "I'm selfish too."

Rowan rose on his toes and kissed Yves's waiting mouth. Their lips fit together as if they'd always belonged. But unlike the intense passion of their previous encounters, this kiss was soft. Gentle in a way Yves had never been with Rowan, maybe anyone, before.

Before he knew it, Rowan was swept up in it all, and they were stumbling through the door to his cabin. The room where it all began and would now end. He let Yves undress him slowly, reveling in the way Yves's elegant fingers caressed his bare skin. He expected this to be a quick fuck. A release for all his anger and tension. In the back of his mind, he wondered why he was doing this. Why he was giving in to Yves once again.

Yves was tender as he laid Rowan on the bed. He was never like this. There was a good reason he was called the Demon by seafarers and sexual partners alike. So what had gotten into him? Was this really all because Rowan was leaving?

He let Yves's mouth move over his skin slowly, feeling some of the tension, but not the anger, melt away at this familiar yet unfamiliar touch.

Yves took Rowan into his arms. Stroking. Caressing. Their naked bodies pressed together, and Yves's erection throbbed against his thigh. Yves captured Rowan's lips in a prolonged kiss, his touch delicate and almost worshipful. He was treating Rowan's body as something precious and dangerous, with the sort of reverent defiance pirates usually reserved for the sea.

Yves palmed Rowan's cock, his kisses moving down over the fluttering pulse in Rowan's throat. Rowan's hips bucked involuntarily into Yves's hand. Yves's mouth continued to caress his body, licking and sucking, eliciting small gasps.

Yves licked a bead of precum from Rowan's slit. Rowan's moan was almost a whimper as Yves drew his desperate cock into his mouth. Rowan threaded his fingers into Yves's dark silky hair. Yves hummed, his throat vibrating and constricting around Rowan's cock.

Gods, it felt good. Heaven itself could be found inside Yves's beautiful, deceptive mouth. Yves took him deeply. Effortlessly. His tongue flicked over the sensitive underside of Rowan's cock, and Rowan realized he was quickly speeding toward orgasm. Bliss twisted through his body and prickled across his skin. The soft interior of Yves's mouth cradled him in a cloud of euphoria. Yves bobbed his head quicker, taking Rowan in from tip to base with every stroke.

Rowan's control snapped, and he rolled his hips in time with Yves's rhythm. He was so close, fucking into Yves's yielding mouth. The storm outside thrashed through its last death throes as Rowan chased down his release. He didn't care what might come after.

A few more thrusts and he was coming hard down Yves's throat. He gripped the other man's hair tight, holding him with his lips pressed around the base of his cock. Nose nestled in his pubic hair as his cock throbbed out his orgasm.

Yves swallowed it all, waiting patiently for Rowan to release him and rubbing soothing circles into his thighs with his fingers.

Finally spent, the tension fled Rowan's body all at once and he released his hold on Yves's hair. Yves retreated slowly, taking his time. He crawled up to lay next to Rowan, gathering the smaller man into his arms and kissing him softly. The taste of Rowan's cum sat heavy on his tongue. Rowan could still feel Yves's erection pressing to his skin, strained and weeping. He expected Yves to take his own pleasure now. To open him up and fill him as exquisitely as he had earlier that day. But Yves made no move to do so. He just carried on kissing and caressing Rowan's body as if committing it to memory.

Neither of them had spoken a word since that first kiss in the hallway. Neither had broken the spell their bodies were weaving together. And finally Rowan realized this for what it was. A goodbye. A farewell in the only way Yves knew how. Spoken in action instead of words. The actions of a man who thought he'd never see his lover again.

He allowed Yves one more kiss. He savored it. In this moment, his anger didn't exist. In this moment, the hurt of the world was held at bay.

Then he broke the kiss and reality pushed its way through his post-orgasmic haze.

Yves's dark eyes roved over Rowan's expression, searching for meaning. For understanding. Desperate for one last look at him.

Then Yves's arms were no longer around him, and he felt the loss of him like a skipped heartbeat. He wanted to reach out and bring Yves back into his bed. His heart. But morning light was seeping through the spent clouds. The tide was turning, and he still could not forgive him.

Yves dressed without a word, and Rowan did not move to stop him. Yves looked back at him once from the open doorway. Then he was gone.

～

THE DEEP WATER Demon met his former crew member Gaël on the rain-slick deck of the *Siren*. Waiting to bring him back to shore.

"Ready to go?" Gaël asked.

The Demon dragged Gaël forward by the front of the shirt.

"Protect the Ghost Hawk with your life. You understand?" His eyes blazed with all the violence of an inferno. "If any harm comes to him, you will answer to me in hell."

215

Gaël's sharp jaw clenched. Then he slowly peeled the Demon's hands from his shirt.

"I no longer answer to you at all," he said calmly, "but I would never let *my* captain come to harm."

There was nothing more to say between them. Nothing more the Demon could do to protect the man he...he still could not think it. What use was that word when it was already lost?

He allowed himself to be rowed to shore. He stood on the end of the dock in the sunrise as his people gathered behind him to watch the *Siren Song* depart. The small figure of the Ghost Hawk appeared on deck as the *Siren Song* rode the tide to the mouth of the harbor and disappeared between the rocks.

John materialized at the Demon's side.

"Are you okay Captain?"

The Demon didn't turn to look at him. His gaze was trained on the passage to the open water, eyes reflecting the red sunrise.

"No," the Deep Water Demon replied. "It is time we returned to the sea."

PART 3

RUINATION

CHAPTER 27

NOVEMBER 17TH, 1666

Rowan was woken silently by Logan shaking his shoulder. He was alert immediately, but the ship was dark and too quiet.

"What is it?" he asked his first mate, already scrambling out of bed and pulling on his clothes.

"Lookout spotted a navy vessel dogging us. Looks like Talva," Logan said calmly.

"What time is it?" It was pitch black outside the window, and he felt like he hadn't been sleeping long. Nephele grumbled from her perch and stretched her wings.

"Two in the morning."

"How long have they been following?" Now dressed, Rowan buckled on his sword belt and pistols on his way out the door. Logan followed.

"Two hours since we spotted them."

"And you didn't wake me?"

Logan's mouth twisted to the side. "You needed sleep."

That was true enough. Rowan hadn't been sleeping well after the way he'd left things with Yves two months ago. His bed felt empty, and every time he saw Logan a pang of guilt sliced through him for missing the man who had caused Logan's injury. He should have protected his friend. He shouldn't have gotten himself so wrapped up in Yves's charms. But he couldn't help it; awake or asleep, the Deep Water Demon was never far from his mind.

Even now with the navy ship on their tail, his thoughts turned back to Yves.

They emerged onto the deck to a hive of near-silent activity in the dark. The crew had been roused, the lamps doused. Rowan smiled to himself. He'd trained them well, and they moved like ghosts through the night, only the creaking of the ship and the shush of the waves could be heard. Fox appeared at Rowan's side and placed a spyglass in his hand.

"Five o'clock, Captain."

Rowan directed the glass toward where Fox indicated. It wasn't hard to find; even in the vast darkness of the nighttime sea, Rowan could tell it was following in the wake of the *Siren Song*. They weren't hiding; the ship was lit up like a festival, under full sail and flying the blue, green, and white five-flower flag of the Talvan empire.

Rowan couldn't help the pang of disappointment he felt. He'd half hoped it would be the *Kraken*.

"Why are they so lit up?" He handed the glass to Logan to take a look. "If they're tailing us, wouldn't they want to be sneaky about it?"

"They are quite a bit bigger," Logan said, lowering the glass. "A ship like that doesn't have to rely on stealth. But maybe they haven't marked us as pirates yet."

"Maybe they're just stupid," Fox suggested.

Rowan pursed his lips, looking up to where his flag snapped on the main mast. A skull on a field of black, framed by white hawk's wings. Could the other ship see it in the dark? Did they know who they were following?

"Think we can outrun them?" Fox asked. A few of the crew members nearby stopped what they were doing to listen. Rowan ticked over the options in his head. They could run. They probably *should* run. Slip into the darkness without a sound. Live up to the name Ghost Hawk. There was no material benefit to taking on a warship. The only thing that fight was good for was his reputation.

"What's our position?"

"A few miles west of The Teeth, Captain," the navigator answered.

An idea sparked in Rowan's mind.

"Perfect, we'll keep it quiet and dark, try to lose them between The Teeth. If that doesn't work we'll outrun them on the other side."

All was still for a moment before Logan said, "Well? You heard the captain, get to it." His calm, commanding voice carried across the deck, and the crew silently jumped to their tasks.

"I've lost their trust," Rowan muttered under his breath so only Logan could hear.

Logan clapped his remaining hand on Rowan's shoulder. "You'll earn it back in no time," he said brightly. There was no denying the crew was a little on edge about how they'd departed Illusion, and it pained Rowan to think he'd done anything that made the crew lose faith in him. They were his family. The only family he had, and he had to protect them at all costs.

~

"So fucking persistent," Rowan spat.

As soon as the *Siren Song* had picked up speed, cutting silently through the waves, the navy ship stopped their game of keeping distance. They closed in more quickly than Rowan anticipated. The fact that they weren't hiding it at all nagged at him. There had to be some other tactic at play here. The navy had certain rules of engagement, but those niceties didn't apply to pirates. If you were a pirate, you couldn't expect mercy. The navy would run you down and slaughter you in a heartbeat if they could. But that didn't mean they had to be straightforward about it.

The *Siren* banked starboard and entered the channel between the first two islands that made up The Teeth. Just like their name, the archipelago contained a smattering of small islands uninhabited even by plants. Their white rocks jutted up from the waves like punched out teeth. They were quite useless for both habitation and resources, but still, the perpetually warring empires of Marra and Talva had fought over them on and off during their various wars. Now they were littered with the debris of long ago naval battles, gull shit, and nothing more.

As the *Siren* wove between the islands, Rowan looked back to see if their pursuer still followed.

The ship was close. So close that Rowan could see the details of the figurehead and flags adorning the prow and masts. It was Talvan navy alright, and he recognized it as the *K.S. Glorieux*, a notorious pirate hunter. Good. They'd had a few run-ins with it before. He knew the ship's capabilities. Between him and Logan, they could manage to outmaneuver it and be home free.

The *Siren* still sailed in silence in the dark, but now he could hear the officers of the *Glorieux* calling orders. Rowan piped the orders for their next maneuver on his whistle, and the crew obeyed. The channels thus far had been deep enough for the much larger warship to follow, but Rowan knew that these waters could be perilous, especially in the dark. Sandbars between the islands shifted with the currents and tides, and you never knew when you would run aground. At least the islands themselves were easy to see, the white rocks almost glowed in the faint light of the waning moon.

They passed close to the largest island on the port side. Rowan knew there was a shallow sandbar between it and the next island over, one that was too shallow even for the *Siren* to pass unscathed. But if he could maneuver them just right, the *Siren* could pass through a small section of deeper water close to the rocks and come out on the other side without their pursuers in tow. Above, Rowan's crew worked in the rigging like silent unseen birds. As the bow cleared the white edge of the rocks, the *Siren* tacked sharply to port. Rowan held his breath, waiting for the telltale scrape of sand on the hull that would tell him it hadn't worked and they were beached. Beside him, Logan cocked his head to listen as well.

A faint scrape came from the starboard side, the sound of the hull rubbing against a bank of waterlogged sand. Rowan glanced over the rail, but it was impossible to see anything beneath the black water. A few of the crew dug out poles in case they had to try to dislodge the ship from the edge of the sandbar. They waited.

But the *Siren* didn't catch; it glided past the sandbar, and the faint scrape of sand fell away as they escaped it. Rowan exhaled slowly, relishing this small victory in silence, then turned to watch the *Glorieux*. The larger ship turned to follow, but it was obvious they didn't know about the sandbar. Rowan smiled as the ship first slowed, then stopped all together, listing slightly to the side as they beached themselves like a depressed whale on the hidden sand. The distant figures of the crew scuttled around frantically trying to get the *Glorieux* dislodged. The *Siren* continued on, leaving their enemy behind. Just a little while longer and they would be home free, out on the open water again. They could be out of sight by the time the *Glorieux* managed to get free.

~

By the time they spotted the second ship, it was too late.

No sooner had the *Siren* sailed free of the shelter of The Teeth than a sharp whistle of alarm split the air. Rowan's head whipped around, spotting the threat immediately. It was another Talvan warship, bigger by far than the *Siren* and armed to the gills with cannons and soldiers. Rowan didn't even have the chance to begin shouting orders before a barrage of cannon fire hit them dead on, splintering the newly repaired wood. Shit. It had been a trap after all. And he'd played right into their hands, while thinking he'd outsmarted them.

The gun ports of the *Siren* banged open, but they hadn't been ready—only one was loaded, and the cannonball did little damage as it crashed through the other ship's rail. The soldiers were already readying grappling hooks as the *Siren* pulled up alongside. Rowan shouted for the helmsman to turn. They could still make a run for it. Maybe they could double back and lose this new threat in the labyrinth of The Teeth too.

Another volley of cannon fire rocked the *Siren*, and the first grappling hook was thrown over the small gap between the two ships. It caught on the rail followed by several more.

"Prepare to be boarded!" Rowan shouted to his crew. There was no use for silence and secrecy anymore. Not when they were going to have to fight their way out of this. Rowan drew his pistols and fired upon the men who were hauling the two ships closer. He heard gunfire from the rigging and knew that Fox was up there picking off as many enemies as he could before they could get across the gap. But if there was one advantage the navy had over a band of pirates, it was numbers. The men who fell were immediately replaced by more sailors. And the two ships were inevitably drawn together like two moths to the flame of battle.

Rowan drew his cutlass as the sides of the two ships crashed together, the outer rigging tangling. His men fell upon the assailants with screeching cries, but they were no match for the waves and waves of sailors. Rowan sprinted down the stairs to the main deck and joined the fray, slashing with the razor-sharp edge of his cutlass and stabbing with the dagger in his left hand. The constant report of gunfire sounded from the rigging above.

Rowan dodged the butt of a rifle that swung at his face and gutted the man carrying it. He sheathed his knife, grabbed the gun, and fired into the face of the next enemy behind him before discarding it. The air was alive with the smell of gunpowder and blood. Flames bloomed somewhere on the ship, lighting the darkness with crackling orange. He heard the thump of bodies falling to the deck but couldn't pause long enough to see who they were. All that mattered was the next enemy, the next blood to whet his sword.

Stinging pain sliced across his thigh, and he stumbled. Hands reached out of the fray, and before he knew it, the barrel of a gun pressed cold and hard to his forehead.

"Lay down your arms, or we kill the Ghost Hawk!" a commanding voice shouted. And suddenly all was still but for the dancing flames and shadows.

Rowan locked eyes with the man who had spoken, glaring defiance at him even as his own crew was quickly disarmed. He wanted to shout. To tell them not to surrender. That it was better to die fighting than to meet your end on the gallows. But two more sailors disarmed him and bound his hands in front of him. He couldn't tell what was happening behind him, but there was yelling from below deck as the sailors tried to root out the rest of the crew.

Rowan winced as he was pushed roughly to the deck. The rope that bound his wrists was too tight, and he was already losing feeling in his hands. The cut on his thigh roared in pain, much deeper than he'd first thought. Logan's knees thumped to the boards beside him.

"You okay, Captain?" he murmured.

"For now. You?"

Before Logan could answer, a pair of shiny boots came into view. Rowan looked up at a man who looked to be in his late thirties, decked out head-to-toe in the crisp blue and green uniform of the Talvan navy. His brown hair was pulled back into a tail and tied with a satin ribbon. He looked like the sort of man who'd always had everything handed to him on a silver platter. The kind of man who thought the advantage of his birth deserved all the rewards the world could offer.

The kind of man Rowan hated more than anything.

"The infamous Ghost Hawk, I presume," the man said with a clipped Talvan accent.

"And you are..." Rowan's eyes landed on the insignia on the uniform's left breast. "A rear admiral? Pity, I was expecting at least a vice." Rowan scoffed.

The admiral's neck flushed red. From his angle, Rowan had a clear view past him into the rigging and beyond it, the night sky. Two shadows of deeper darkness flitted across the upper rigging between the two ships, unnoticed by the soldiers below.

"A filthy pirate has no right to judge his betters. We captured you with just two ships, a fleet would have been excessive."

Rowan quirked an eyebrow and chuckled. He had to put on a confident face. He would think of a way out of this. He had to. "You've captured me, but you haven't won until I'm dead. How are you expecting to achieve that?"

"No man is immortal. Least of all you. You won't be laughing when you're on the gallows in King's Square."

Rowan rolled his eyes. "You're pretty talkative for a navy man. How'd you make rear admiral so young? Your rich daddy buy it for you?"

There was a faint gasp from the officer at the admiral's side, and suddenly the tip of the admiral's ceremonial sword was at Rowan's throat.

"What do you know about my father?" the admiral snarled. "What did the Demon tell you?"

"What? The Demon?" Rowan didn't have to fake the surprise in his voice. Why was a Talvan admiral asking him about Yves? Did the authorities know they were connected? And what did Yves have to do with this man's father?

"My name is Admiral Batteux," he said as if that name should mean something to Rowan. The blade dug into Rowan's skin, and a trickle of blood slipped down his neck. "Where is the Demon?"

Rowan swallowed, collecting his wits. Logan was by his side. His crew—those who had survived—were corralled below deck as far as he knew. He could get out of this, he just needed time to think.

"Haven't met the man myself," Rowan replied, trying to inject as much confidence into his voice as possible. "But I heard he's quite vicious. If your father crossed him, good luck to the poor bastard."

"I *know* you're working with him," Batteux growled. Rowan

knew he probably shouldn't be so coy with a sword to his throat and the *Siren* captured, but it wasn't in his nature to be anything else.

But how could this man know that Yves and Rowan knew each other?

"If you want him so bad, why not go after him instead of me? I don't know the Demon, and I certainly don't know where he is." That last part was true at least. Yves could be anywhere by now.

Admiral Batteux's silence was too telling.

"You don't think you can beat him, do you?" Rowan smirked. "So what? I'm just the easier target?"

A malevolent smile lit Batteux's face. "Does that hurt your pride, little pirate?"

A few months ago it would have. Before meeting Yves, the thought that the navy considered the Deep Water Demon a bigger threat than him would have filled him with boiling jealousy. But now...now it made him miss that devious bastard even more.

Rowan couldn't help the laughter that bubbled up to the surface. It built to a full on cackle, as loud and audacious as Fox's laugh. He stared Batteux directly in the eye and laughed like a madman, the very picture of a half-crazed, murderous pirate captain.

He laughed even as the sword slashed across his cheek in an X, blood running down his face like tears.

Logan shouted, struggling against several sailors holding him back.

"I won't tell you shit," Rowan said, bloody teeth barred. "I hold no quarrel with my fellow pirates. My enemy is your corrupt fucking government. So if you find the Demon, be prepared to burn in his fire." His eyes never left Batteux's face. Though he desperately wanted to look at Logan, to make sure his friend was okay.

Batteux leaned in close and set the tip of the bloodied sword against Rowan's cheekbone just below his eye.

"That bastard killed my family in cold blood," he hissed. "It's he who will burn. And so will you. If you won't tell me the location of his hideaway, I can torture it out of you. Maybe the Demon will come running if he hears his little toy cry."

Rowan blanched. A hideaway? How did they know about that?

"He won't come for me." But his confidence was wavering. If Yves heard he was in trouble...would he come? Would he get himself captured to save Rowan? Rowan couldn't bear to think about what would happen if Yves was captured too.

"I think he will," Batteux said. "So let's make you cry." The blade dug into Rowan's cheek, and he realized suddenly what Batteux meant to do. He jerked back, but Batteux caught him by the hair and forced his head forward again. Somewhere off to his right, Logan screamed his name, and there was a commotion from below deck where the rest of the crew was being held.

"Stop—" The sword sliced a millimeter deeper into his face, slow and agonizing.

"Tell me where he is," Batteux hissed.

"No," Rowan ground out between gritted teeth.

The blade dug into his eye socket, searing pain lancing through his head like lightning. One side of his vision went dark. Rowan bit his tongue, barely holding back the scream that was desperately clawing its way up his throat. He would not show this man weakness. He would not—

BOOM!

Batteux flinched, cutting the outer corner of Rowan's eyelid as he whirled toward the source of the noise. Rowan wavered, lightheaded. Blood gushed down his face, and soaked into the collar of his shirt.

But from his one eye, even he could see the navy ship was on fire, and silhouetted against the flames were two familiar figures.

Fox and Gaël.

"Capture them! Put out the fire!" Batteux shouted, red-faced with rage. He turned back to Rowan, sword raised, but Logan broke free from his captors and rammed into Batteux, sending him sprawling. He snatched up the dropped sword and turned to kneel by Rowan's side, quickly cutting his bindings.

"Captain, you okay?" He rested the stump of his arm on Rowan's shoulder to steady him, still clutching the sword with his other hand.

"Fine. I'm fine."

But he wasn't. Overwhelming pain pounded through his head like thunder, and he couldn't see out of his right eye. His hands shook uncontrollably as he touched the wound tentatively. Fuck. His fingers came away bloody.

Behind Logan, Batteux regained his footing. He looked uncertain for the first time, his hair half falling out of the orderly tail and his uniform askew.

"Get them," he ordered, but most of his crew had abandoned their posts to fight the fire on their own ship. Shouting and gunshots sounded from below deck as the pirates rebelled against their captors. Batteux's face twisted in rage. He drew a knife from his belt and stalked toward them.

"Filthy mongrels," he snarled.

"Captain!" The shout was Fox's voice, but it was not him who jumped in front of the slashing knife. The blade cut across Gaël's broad chest, flaying open his shirt and skin. He barely flinched as he grabbed Batteux's wrist, twisting until the knife dropped to the deck with a clang. Fox rushed up behind and locked Batteux in a chokehold.

Logan tried to help Rowan to his feet but the pain in his head sharpened. The remaining half of his vision swam. He fell back to his knees on the deck. Around him, his crew was fending off the remaining navy sailors. Rowan gripped Logan's arm. "I'm fine. Go. Win."

With a last worried glance, Logan stood and began issuing orders. They had the advantage now, and they were going to take it.

"Man the guns!"

Rowan struggled to his feet, pushing through the pain as best he could. He managed to stumble to where Gaël and Fox were about to gut Batteux as the first volley of cannon fire plunged into the side of the navy ship, and other crew members disengaged the grappling hooks from the rails.

Rowan grabbed Gaël's arm.

"Stop. I need to ask him something," he panted.

Gaël lowered the knife, instead gripping Rowan by the elbow to keep him upright even though blood poured down the front of his own shirt from the gaping wound on his chest. Rowan turned to Batteux, leveling him with a steely one-eyed gaze.

"Who told you those things about me and the Demon?" he asked. "Why do you think he has a hideout?"

Batteux smirked at him. "Your men aren't as loyal as you think they are."

Rowan took a shaky step forward, taking the knife from Gaël's hand. He placed it against Batteux's cheek in the same spot as Batteux's sword had rested against his. "Who? Tell me, and I might let you live." Rowan's patience had reached its limit. He was in pain, running on only a few hours of sleep, and he felt like he was going to pass out.

The sky lightened with the rising sun as another cannon volley hammered into the navy ship at point-blank range. It listed to one side, no doubt it would sink soon.

"You're done for," Rowan said. "At this point your only hope is my mercy."

Fox's arm tightened experimentally around Batteux's throat. "Answer the damn questions," he growled. Batteux struggled for breath for a moment, slapping at Fox's arm before the pirate loosened his hold again.

"Cyrus. His name is Cyrus," he gasped.

Fox's arm went slack in shock, and Batteux bolted toward the side of the ship.

Gaël lunged forward but only managed to catch the tails of Batteux's coat. Batteux shrugged out of it and leapt over the side of the ship into the sea.

"Fuck! Sorry, Rowan. Sorry. Shit." Fox swore.

But the last of Rowan's strength was drained. He stumbled, and Fox rushed forward to keep him from falling.

"Take me to Robin," Rowan panted. Fox nodded, handing him off to Gaël's waiting arms so they could both go below to the infirmary. "Tell Logan to get us out of here before the *Glorieux* un-beaches itself."

"You okay, Captain?" Gaël asked, as if he himself was perfectly fine and not half flayed open on Batteux's sword.

"I just..." Rowan's depleted vision swam again, and the last thing he saw was Gaël's worried face as the last of his vision faded.

CHAPTER 28

NOVEMBER 17TH, 1666

For once Henri wasn't hurt. Well, no more than he was before. Robin had let him take the splint off a few weeks after they'd departed Illusion, but he wasn't quite in fighting shape. His bone still ached a bit, and his leg was weak from all the weeks of disuse. Robin had ordered that he not push himself too hard, so Rowan had reassigned him to the gunner crew below decks. And that's where he'd been when the navy sailors boarded. In the aftermath, he'd tried to help Robin with the wounded, but there had been plenty of others who weren't hobbled by a weak and aching leg. He'd just ended up being in the way.

Now he sat on the end of the bed in the physician's cabin that he and Robin shared, cleaning a rifle just to keep his hands busy with something useful. It was getting on toward evening, and the porridge Henri had procured for Robin's eventual return was rapidly growing cold. Since they'd been back on the *Siren*, Henri had been feeling quite useless. His leg would be back in fighting shape in a month according to Robin. But in the meantime, he had nothing to do. And his burn-scarred skin itched beneath his clothes like his leg was a ship's hull stuck all over with barnacles. He couldn't tell if it was because of the scars themselves or just boredom. Probably both.

Henri set the gun aside as the door opened and Robin stumbled through. He looked exhausted. Dark circles clung under his eyes, and his face and arms had several scrapes and scratches he'd received during the attack. He'd been working nonstop since early that morning, and it showed in every line of his lanky body.

Nonetheless, he smiled when he spotted Henri.

"How are they?" Henri asked. The battle had been short yet brutal, and a few men had succumbed to their injuries before they could get them into Robin's care. Not to mention the awful thing that'd happened to Rowan.

"I haven't lost anyone else at least." Robin sighed, flopping down next to Henri. "I think they'll all make a full recovery; even Gaël's nasty cut will be fine. Fox is sitting in with them now so I can rest."

"What about Rowan?"

Robin grimaced. "His leg will heal..." He sighed again and ran his long hands down his face. "Even if I could have saved the eye, his optic nerve was severed. He would have lost it eventually. The cuts on his face are definitely going to scar."

Henri placed the bowl of cold porridge into Robin's hands.

"If you couldn't save it, no doctor in the Islands could have," Henri reassured him. Robin gave him a grateful smile and a kiss on the cheek.

They lapsed into silence as Robin ate. He didn't seem to care that the porridge was mostly cold and definitely gloopy. He devoured spoonful after spoonful like he was starving. Henri supposed he probably hadn't eaten all day. One tended to lose their appetite when covered in the blood of their friends and crew members.

"Do you want more?" Henri asked when Robin began scraping the extra bits off the bottom of the bowl with his spoon.

Robin looked up, the last bit of porridge stuck to his bottom lip.

"No, it's okay."

His stomach disagreed. It rumbled through the quiet of their cabin. Robin's ears flushed red in embarrassment.

"I'll go get more." Henri took the bowl from his hands.

"No." Robin caught his arm. "Don't strain your leg. Honestly I just need rest."

Henri was skeptical but discarded the bowl on the top of the sea chest next to the rifle. Robin stretched his arms over his head and winced.

"You okay?"

"Yeah." Robin rolled his shoulder experimentally. "Just sore from bending over all day."

"Without me?" Henri quirked an eyebrow.

"I was saving lives," Robin protested, whacking Henri on the shoulder, then wincing again as the action jarred his sore back.

"Here." Henri crawled onto the bed to kneel behind him. He began to knead the tense muscles that connected Robin's wide shoulders to his neck. Robin relaxed into his touch, only wincing slightly as Henri's fingers worked out the knots.

Henri hummed as he worked, a cheerful tune he'd heard in some tavern or another.

"Is that the Seafarer's Dream?" Robin asked after Henri had hummed the whole thing and started over again.

"Hm?" Henri pressed his thumbs to the musculature between Robin's shoulder blades.

"The...ah...the song," Robin said as Henri's fingers dug into a particularly tight knot. Henri bit his lip, hoping Robin wouldn't notice that his little groans of pleasure were turning Henri on.

"I don't know what it's called. I just heard it somewhere," Henri said. Robin tilted his head to look up at him, that familiar amused smile on his lips like he was trying to hold back a laugh.

"It's the Seafarer's Dream. It's about a sailor who finds out the Kraken is a beautiful woman and seduces her." He snorted a laugh at Henri's baffled expression. "Maybe pay attention to the lyrics next time you pick up a raunchy tune from a tavern."

"Whoever wrote that needs their head checked out," Henri muttered. He resumed kneading Robin's back.

"What, you've never had a strange dream?"

"I don't typically remember my dreams. I just go to sleep and wake up." Henri reached the midpoint of Robin's back, and it was getting difficult to apply pressure from this angle. "Lie down so I can get your lower back."

"That seems like you," Robin said. He sighed as he laid down on his stomach, forehead propped on his folded hands so his neck wouldn't twist to the side. Henri straddled his legs and began working the soreness out of his lower back with long, firm strokes up the sides of his spine.

"You're shockingly good at this," Robin said, letting out a quiet groan as the heel of Henri's palm hit a tight spot.

"Why shockingly?"

Robin chuckled. "It's just that you don't have a very delicate hand with other things."

With every stroke of his hands, Henri's crotch brushed the curve of Robin's ass. Coupled with the pleased sounds Robin was making, it did nothing to aid in Henri's quest to *not* get uselessly horny when his boyfriend was exhausted from being up to his elbows in gore all day.

"Have I ever been heavy-handed with you?"

"I suppose not," Robin admitted. The light outside was dimming as the sun dipped further toward the horizon. They were sailing southeast, hoping to get out of range before the navy caught up to them again. Out the small porthole, Henri could see only gold-edged waves.

He looked back down to where Robin lay beneath him. Though Robin was a bit taller than him, he was also softer and lankier. Henri slipped his hands beneath Robin's loose white shirt to rub his back directly. The shirt had not a speck of blood on it. Robin must have washed up and changed before returning.

Despite his softness, Robin's back was sturdy. There was muscle there, not the kind that came from climbing rigging and fighting, but the kind for lifting injured people and setting broken bones. The muscle of healing, not destruction. His pale skin reminded Henri of kneading bread in the kitchen of the bakery he'd worked in as a child. The pliant dough squishing beneath his hands. He reached up to run his fingers through the back of Robin's hair, the color of wheat on a gray day.

"Henri..."

In leaning forward to touch Robin's hair, Henri's half-hard cock had pressed to Robin's buttocks, his other hand braced on Robin's bare waist for balance. He stayed like that for a moment, frozen in this unexpectedly sexual position.

"Sorry." Henri sat back.

Robin turned his head to glance at Henri out of the corner of his eye. "I don't mind." Robin pushed his hips up slightly so that Henri's clothed dick rubbed a little harder on his ass. Henri's dick hardened further. "Seems like you missed me," Robin said, amused.

Henri leaned down to kiss his cheek. "I saw you just a few hours ago. But yes, I did miss you."

Robin pushed his ass against Henri's dick again. "Want to show me how much?"

Gods, he was going to drive Henri insane if he kept this up. Henri didn't know whether to rejoice or despair at his boyfriend's increasing confidence in seduction.

"You're exhausted, and your back already hurts," Henri protested.

Over the few months since they'd left Illusion, both of them had grown more used to the physical closeness and intimacy of being together, but Henri still sometimes got nervous that he would end up hurting Robin somehow.

Robin sighed. "That's true but..." His hips wiggled again. "Now I'm turned on too."

Henri pressed a light kiss to the fluffy hairline behind Robin's blushing ear.

"So what are we going to do about that?" he murmured into Robin's ear. "I don't want you to be too exhausted and sore tomorrow. You have work to do." Despite his words, Henri's hips rocked forward involuntarily. Robin bit his lip and groaned. Henri's hands were braced on the bed on either side of Robin's wide shoulders. He trailed kisses down the back of Robin's neck to the collar of his shirt. Robin placed his hand over Henri's own and threaded their fingers together.

"Whatever it is, we better do it quick so I can go to sleep," Robin said, stifling a yawn.

"Mm, better take your clothes off then." Henri rolled to lay on his side next to Robin, running a hand down his back then slipping it under his shirt. Robin turned to face him, and Henri noted the bulge of his erection beneath his trousers. Robin moved closer and captured Henri's lips in a tender kiss. In all the months they'd been together, no matter how heated they got, nights like this always began so softly. It was in Robin's nature to be gentle, and Henri adored that about him. It was in such contrast to Henri's own rougher mannerisms, and he often wondered what Robin saw in him.

Robin's hand moved down to unfasten Henri's trousers. His mouth was warm and sweetly urgent against Henri's own. Henri moaned when Robin's hand slipped beneath his clothes and brushed Henri's cock. The pad of Robin's thumb rubbed over the head, and then his fingers wrapped around the shaft. Henri's hand tightened on his waist, drawing him closer so that their bodies couldn't help but wrap up in each other.

"I love your hands," Henri sighed as Robin pumped him slowly. Robin just smiled and continued kissing him. He slotted one long leg between Henri's thighs. Robin's breath was warm on his skin. It was as if they were bundled together in a cocoon of golden evening light, and they had all the time in the world to explore and luxuriate in each other's bodies.

Henri pushed Robin's shirt up around his ribs, exposing a stretch of pale skin. He let his hands explore at his leisure as Robin pulled Henri's trousers down his hips. His movements were slow with tiredness.

Henri pulled slightly away from Robin's embrace. Robin's eyes remained closed, but his eyelids fluttered. As Henri's warmth left him, Robin's face tilted forward, chasing the loss of Henri's lips on his. Henri brushed the corner of Robin's lip with his thumb, and Robin leaned into his touch.

"Do you want to go to sleep?" Henri asked softly.

"Mmm." Robin's round cheek was soft against his hand. Henri pinched it lightly between his thumb and forefinger. Robin inhaled through his nose and opened his eyes. His pupils were dilated wide.

"Hm? What?" Robin's thumb circled the head of Henri's cock again.

"I asked if you wanted to sleep instead," Henri repeated.

"Yes. I mean." Robin blinked, his sandy hair falling softly across his brow. "No. I just want you to touch me."

"You seem like you're half asleep already." Henri kissed the tip of his nose.

"I'll stay awake. I swear," Robin protested.

Henri realized he would have to take the lead. "Okay, but straight to sleep after."

Robin nodded.

Henri unfastened Robin's trousers and removed them slowly. Robin's eyes slipped closed again, but his breath quickened. Henri stripped his own trousers off as well so they were both naked from the waist down. He returned to their previous position, and pulled their bodies tight together. Henri flattened his hand against the small of Robin's back to hold him in place. He rolled his hips experimentally, creating friction between their skin. Their cocks slid against each other, and their legs tangled together. Robin gasped, head tilted back on the pillow, and Henri pressed kisses along his soft jaw.

Henri continued to move, watching the small expressions of pleasure flit across Robin's face. He wouldn't let himself give in to the urge to hurry. To chase down his own high. He forced himself to move slowly and savor the feel of Robin here in bed with him in the golden hour of evening. His lips lingered on Robin's skin, and Robin let out little moans with every movement.

Henri moved his hand from Robin's back to envelop both of their cocks. Robin's hips stuttered involuntarily, thrusting into Henri's hand, his velvet hardness sliding against Henri's shaft.

"Henri..." Robin whispered. Their bodies moved together, and though their pace was leisurely, the pleasure was heightened by the fact that they'd so recently escaped death. Both they and their friends were safe and alive. Henri hadn't been a pirate for long but he knew how precious this time was. For there was no guarantee the next moment wouldn't bring calamity. Henri briefly wondered if Captain Rowan understood that, or if he was still tied up in his anger and laboring under the delusion that what had transpired between him and the Deep Water Demon had been purely physical.

Robin sighed contentedly in his ear, and Henri pulled back slightly to see Robin's hazel eyes were open.

"What are you thinking about?" Robin asked.

"Just that I'm glad you're here," Henri said.

"Mm, me too." Their hips moved simultaneously, and both of them gasped. Henri rested his forehead against Robin's, and Robin snaked his arm around Henri's waist.

The pleasure that had been kindling slowly in Henri's core sprang to life. He moved faster, thrusting into his own hand with Robin alongside him. Robin's breath was warm and soothing, but it was coming faster and faster as his own pleasure built. He tilted his head back, but Henri's other hand came up to cradle it, bringing their foreheads back to rest against each other.

"I'm close," Robin panted. His back arched forward into Henri's touch, and Henri pumped his hand a little faster. Tingles raced through his core, and he felt warm all over, enveloped in the golden warmth of Robin's love.

"Henri...Henri..." Robin's voice whispering his name warmed him like the sun. He captured Robin's lips as their pleasure peaked.

Robin came into Henri's hand with a shudder and a moan. His cum slicked Henri's hand as he continued pumping for a few more moments until the rush of his orgasm fogged his head, and he came soon after.

They lay entwined in the afterglow as the day finally slipped past golden hour and the room darkened. Robin's breath grew slow and even. He dropped off to sleep quickly before the cum had even cooled on the sheets. Henri kissed the tip of Robin's nose and slipped out of bed to clean up. Robin groaned when Henri wiped him with a damp cloth but didn't wake. Henri tucked him into the warm blankets and climbed in with him, drawing Robin's sleep-warmed, naked body into his arms and resting his cheek against the fluffy blond hair.

"I am so, so glad you're here."

CHAPTER 29

DECEMBER 13TH, 1666

The damaged *Siren Song* weighed anchor in the dark waters of Wave Harbor and waited for the harbormaster to send someone out to negotiate the price of overwintering in the port. They'd anchored briefly off the north coast of Souna to assess the damage the Talvans had wrought but found that it was far less than feared. So not wanting to tempt fate by stopping too soon, they moved on to a place they could hunker down for a while, unbothered.

Though the port of Wave Harbor on the southern end of Souna was technically under Talvan rule, it was far enough away from "polite" Talvan society that many pirate crews docked there to wait out the harsh winter storms. The governor, a man large in both stature and greed, saw this as an opportunity to make a little money on the side. So he'd offered up Wave Harbor as a winter haven for pirates, smugglers, and other brigands of the seafaring variety in exchange for a tithe of a share of their season's profits. As long as they came in after the first frost and left before the fruit trees got their buds, the pirates could rest assured that they wouldn't be ratted out to the higher authorities.

Of course, this all depended on the pirates behaving themselves. Wave Harbor wasn't a lawless place, and the governor didn't want his ragtag guests mingling with the "decent folk." No matter how much the pirates spent on ship repair and alcohol, they were restricted to the eastern side of the harbor, a neighborhood unofficially known as

Pirate Alley. It was much larger than a single alley, but pirates tended not to worry overmuch about semantics.

Frost crackled on the *Siren*'s rigging as Rowan stood at the rail watching the lights in the town go out one by one until only those of Pirate Alley still blazed. He resented remaining in Talvan territory after what had happened, but it was one of the few safe ports for their kind, and he didn't have much choice. The harbormaster wouldn't come tonight. They'd slipped into the harbor just after dusk, and it was too cold and too windy to navigate safely. Any decent person would already be tucked safely abed.

But Rowan wasn't decent. He was a pirate.

Despite Rowan's cockiness, Admiral Batteux's words had shaken him. He was used to being the hunter. The hawk that swooped down on unsuspecting prey. But these past few months—ever since he'd finally met the Demon—he'd been the hunted. He was a toy to be batted around between a cat's paws before finally being devoured. He'd been willing prey for Yves, so eager to be seen by the man he'd hated and admired that he'd ignored the danger. And after that, still reeling from Yves's betrayal, he'd sailed directly into Batteux's trap.

Maybe Rowan was losing his edge, no longer fit to be captain. No longer cunning and stealthy as his reputation claimed.

Rowan touched his face with cold fingertips. The swelling had gone down, but the cuts across his right cheekbone were still tender, and his eye socket ached. Robin had assured him that the scars would fade with time, but Rowan's eye was destroyed and gone.

Rowan grimaced when his fingers brushed the edge of the bandages that still covered his empty eye socket. Robin hadn't wanted to stitch it closed, insisting they would find a fake eye once they reached land. Rowan had never considered himself vain. Aside from his magpie-esque collection of earrings, he usually went for practical over beautiful. But now he couldn't help but mourn the loss of whatever beauty he'd had. And even worse, his thoughts turned to wondering what Yves would think. Would he find Rowan's scars hideous?

Rowan shook his head. None of that mattered. He wouldn't see Yves again. Even if he did, it wouldn't matter what he thought of Rowan's looks, because Rowan didn't care. That's what he told himself. He was determined to put their unfortunate entanglement behind him.

The air grew colder the further night crept along. Rowan's breath pooled visibly in front of his lips. He turned away from the rail, intent on retiring to his cabin and attempting to sleep, but he came face-to-face with Gaël instead.

"Oh! Captain, I was just coming to get you."

It had been three months since Gaël joined their crew and despite Rowan's initial wariness of the intimidating former crewman of the *Kraken*, Gaël had proved to be an invaluable member. He fit right in with Rowan's scrappy band as if he'd always been there.

And he'd saved Rowan's life.

Rowan's gaze flicked down to where a swath of bandage peeked out beneath Gaël's open shirt collar. A twinge of guilt tugged in Rowan's chest. Because of him, Fox had almost lost the love of his life.

He forced his eye back up to Gaël's face. There was no use dwelling on things he couldn't control.

"Coming to get me for what?" Rowan asked.

"Fox has a present for you." He paused, a fond smile playing on his lips. "And Logan was worried you'd freeze to death out here 'because you don't know when to stop sulking,' sir."

Rowan snorted. It was just like Logan to tell him he was sulking.

"You don't have to call me 'sir,' Gaël. We're pirates. And besides, you saved my life, so I think you've earned more than a bit of familiarity."

"It was nothing," Gaël muttered. He turned to go belowdecks, expecting Rowan to follow, but Rowan caught his arm.

"It's not nothing. You did more than most would, and you paid for it. I didn't get a chance before, but thank you. I'd be dead if it wasn't for you."

Gaël blinked at him as if it had never occurred to him that he had the option to *not* throw his body in front of a blade to save someone else.

"Of course. You're my captain and Fox's friend and..." He stopped himself from saying whatever was next. His lips thinned to a line.

"And what?" Gaël wasn't wearing a coat, and Rowan didn't want to keep him out in the cold longer than necessary, but Gaël's sudden silence raised his suspicions.

"Never mind. We best get back before Fox gets antsy."

"Gaël." Rowan squeezed his arm. "I don't think I have to tell you that keeping secrets in this crew is not the way to earn our trust, regardless of your heroic acts. Tell me what you were going to say."

"The Deep Water Demon told me not to let anything happen to you or he'd hunt me down in hell."

Rowan released Gaël's arm as if burned.

"He threatened you?"

Gaël nodded. Yves had gone that far? Why? Did he still expect Rowan to come crawling back and wanted him to be unmarked when he did? He'd be disappointed then, that not only was Rowan not returning but half of his face had been marred by Cyrus's revenge.

Rowan's anger toward Yves built, burning the yearning away in its wake. Rowan couldn't seem to keep his feelings straight about him. One minute Rowan was reluctantly pining away, remembering the thrill of Yves's touch and the next he was full of anger that he'd ever met the man in the first place.

"Rowan, Captain Rowaaaaan…"

Rowan's thoughts were interrupted by Fox calling for him. Fox's voice, as always, held a mischievous edge.

A few moments later, Fox's head popped up from the hatch leading belowdecks.

"Why are you still out in the cold? Come on."

Fox led them to the mess where Logan and most of the crew were gathered with food and drink laid out on the tables.

"What's all this about?" Rowan asked.

Fox spun in a slow circle, his arms outstretched, nearly smacking Henri in the face in the close quarters.

"It's a 'glad we're alive' party!" Fox exclaimed.

"A what?"

"You heard me." Fox was practically bouncing, giddy with whatever else he had in store.

"Why?"

Logan raised his eyebrows.

"Because we're happy to be alive, presumably," he said. "Don't be a spoilsport."

"And we have a present for you," Fox cut in. Rowan had to admit Fox's exuberance was infectious; his mood lightened despite himself.

Fox bounced forward and draped one arm across Rowan's shoulders. His expressive face practically glowed with excitement. He drew a small box from his pocket and shoved it into Rowan's hands.

"We're glad you're alive, Captain," he said sincerely, but still with that impish sparkle in his bright green eyes. His sentiment was echoed by voices around the room. Logan gave Rowan an encouraging smile and motioned for him to open the box.

Rowan lifted the lid. Within was a beautifully made eyepatch of dark brown leather. The strap and edges of the patch were embossed with simple little flowers and curly lines that resembled waves.

Affection for his crew welled up in Rowan's heart.

"Where did you get this?"

"Henri made it." Fox bounced on the balls of his feet. "Try it on!"

Rowan lifted the patch from the box, but there was something else underneath. Nestled in the bottom on a folded up bit of cloth was a marble the size of an eyeball.

"What is this?" The milky green sphere, almost jade-like, stared back at him.

"It's your new eye," Robin said.

Rowan didn't know what to say. His hand quivered as he plucked the eye from the box. It was smooth and glassy in his fingers. The others had gone quiet, watching him.

"You don't have to use it if you don't want," Fox said quietly in his ear. "I won it from some old guy in a game of dice a few years back. I thought it was pretty."

The corners of Rowan's mouth twitched up. It was just like Fox to hold onto some useless, pretty trinket until circumstances somehow karmically aligned to make his hoarding pay off. As exasperated as Fox made him sometimes, Rowan appreciated his friend more than he ever got a chance to say.

Placing the two gifts back in their box for safekeeping, Rowan glanced around the room at all the beloved faces of his crew, feeling an undeniable love and kinship for them well up in his heart.

"It's pretty. Thank you."

"Well now that's settled. Let's party!" Fox squeezed Rowan's shoulders then traipsed off to load up a plate of food. The rest of their friends followed suit. Rowan slipped the box into his pocket and went to take an empty seat next to Logan.

"Do you really like the gift?" Logan asked, taking a big bite of food. He was still a little clumsy using his left hand for everything, and a bit of potato dropped off his fork onto the table. He sighed around the food he had managed to get into his mouth.

"It was very thoughtful," Rowan assured him. "I'm sure I'll look very fearsome."

"You will." Logan grinned. "Next season you'll be the most feared pirate in the Islands for sure."

"Unfortunately, we have to talk about the Cyrus problem," Rowan said. He'd thought for a moment, as the days grew shorter and winter crept in, that maybe Yves had released Cyrus on purpose to exact revenge on Rowan for leaving. But he'd quickly forced the thought out of his mind. Cyrus's alliance with the Talvan navy put Yves and Illusion in danger too. He must have escaped somehow, and Rowan was determined to hunt him down before he had the opportunity to cause any more problems.

"Right now? But it's a party." Logan gestured to the others with his handless arm, his sleeve pinned around the stump of his wrist. Logan realized he'd used his right arm and tucked it close to his body. Despite insisting he was okay, Rowan knew it still pained him and left him feeling self-conscious.

"It's a 'glad we're alive' party. If we want to actually stay alive, we've got to get rid of that snitch."

"Fair enough." The other crew members were well into their feast by now, chatting about all the things they had planned for their long winter in port. Logan ate a few more forkfuls of food, seeming to be contemplating the next thing he would say. Finally he set his fork back on his plate.

"I know you don't want to hear this, but we should consider going back to Illusion or at least ask the Demon for help."

The ache in Rowan's chest was back.

"Have you forgotten that he's the reason you only have one hand?" Rowan hissed. He felt a lot of guilt over what had happened to Logan, but he wouldn't let himself forget who was really at fault.

"Of course I haven't, but we need to consider what will keep the crew safe. I know your pride was hurt but—"

"This isn't about my pride," Rowan interrupted. Even as he said it, he knew it was a lie, but he continued anyway. "*You* got hurt Logan. And it was because he wanted to keep us there against our will. We'd be no safer with him than we are out here. At least with the navy, we know their motives. The Demon is too much of a wild card, and we can't trust him. *I* can keep the crew safe, and I don't need his help."

Logan turned to face him fully. "He has much more firepower than us. And the Talvans are hunting him too. We could team up, then go our separate ways."

"He threatened Gaël to make sure nothing happened to me. You think that manipulative prick is going to let us go again?"

Logan blinked at him, taken aback. "Don't you think he might just want to protect you?" he asked more quietly.

In the sudden quietness, both of them realized that those around them had stopped the revelry to listen to their argument. Rowan's heartbeat sounded loud in his ears. He stood without looking at the rest of the people in the room.

"We'll talk about this later, in private." He hurried out of the mess, hoping no one would follow. No sooner had he stepped foot inside his cabin than Logan's words fully sank in. He stopped just inside the door, staring at the same bed where he and Yves had slept together for both the first and last time. His heart pounded against his ribs.

The truth was that it actually hadn't occurred to Rowan that Yves had done what he did—the lies and manipulations, the threats towards his crew—because he actually cared about Rowan. When Gaël said Yves had threatened him, Rowan's mind had jumped directly to control and ownership, not protection.

He couldn't keep his head on straight even without Yves constantly breathing sensually down his neck. One minute Rowan was missing him, even worrying about being seen as attractive to him, and the next he was calling him a manipulative bastard and storming out on his best friends in the world.

Rowan felt like he was going insane, and the idea that Yves might actually care about him made everything much worse.

"Rowan?"

He whirled, realizing he hadn't closed the door. He'd expected Logan, but it was Fox. He stood just over the threshold of Rowan's cabin, looking nervous. He ran his fingers through his already tousled brown hair.

"Can we talk?"

"Come in," Rowan sighed. Fox followed him in and closed the door behind. He passed Rowan and plopped onto the end of the bed, patting the mattress beside him. Rowan reluctantly sat. Fox scooched closer to him so they were hip to hip and laid his head on Rowan's shoulder. Fox had always been physically affectionate with his friends, but sometimes it still caught Rowan off guard.

"I told Gaël to stop protecting you," Fox said without preamble.

"Want me dead that bad?" Rowan joked, because he was unsure what to say. Fox shook his head against Rowan's shoulder and threaded his arm through his.

"It seemed like it upset you."

"I'm not upset to be alive just...sorry that he got hurt because of me. You just found him again."

Fox lifted his head and propped his chin on Rowan's shoulder instead.

"I'm glad you're alive, Captain. I'm glad he is too. I love you both."

He said it so easily that Rowan wished that if Yves had felt that way about him, he could have just said it, and they wouldn't be in this situation. Rowan's own feelings were an ever-changing storm, but he thought that maybe, if he knew what Yves felt, the skies would clear.

"How do you do that?"

"What?"

"How can you say you love someone so easily?"

Fox laughed. "It's actually not easy. You're just an idiot."

"There's no hope for me then?"

"Maybe you can learn. I don't know. It might be harder for you to see love now that you only have one eye."

Rowan smacked him on the arm.

"Really though," Fox continued. "Do you think you love the Demon? Is that what all this is about?" He poked Rowan playfully in the ribs, trying to lighten the mood.

Again, he didn't know. He knew a thousand other things before he knew about this. Fox sensed his hesitation.

"Well, for the record. I think that demonic bastard does love you, as much as someone like him can love."

"How do you know you love Gaël?" Rowan wasn't sure what had come over him. Maybe it was the jarring thought that Yves might actually care about him for more than sex. Maybe it was the comfort of one of his best friends cuddled up beside him. But he suddenly needed to know.

Promise me that I will see you again. Promise that we will not be enemies.

Was that love? Or possession?

"You know," Fox said, "a long time ago, Gaël and I kissed for the first time in a tavern here in Wave Harbor. Well, we did a lot more than that. Anyway, ever since then, I'd been angry. I'd been trying to forget him, but I never could. Not just because he hurt me, but because he's a part of me. When he came back, I wanted to stay angry, and I was, but it was like some part of my world fit back into place. That's how I knew. And I think you know a lot more than you're willing to admit. It can be hard to forgive someone who hurt you. Even harder to forgive when they've hurt someone close to you. But it's hardest of all to open yourself up to that potential willingly."

Up until now, they'd avoided docking at Wave Harbor because of Fox's past.

"I'm sorry for bringing you back here."

"That wasn't the point of my wise words, but thank you."

His words were wise. Sometimes Rowan forgot how smart Fox was beneath his silly antics.

Rowan had only ever had very short, surface level relationships. Never anything that could have even come close to being called love. It seemed almost horrific to Rowan to share the deepest parts of himself with someone, to let them truly know him. Did he want Yves to know him that way? They'd been physically close. Done things together that Rowan had never done with anyone else. And Yves had told him of the darkness in his past.

Rowan didn't know what to think.

"You're smarter than you look, Fox."

"When it comes to this, I'm a hell of a lot smarter than you."

CHAPTER 30

DECEMBER 15TH, 1666

The wind whipped down the streets of Pirate Alley and dug its icy claws under the edges of Fox's coat. He shoved his bare hands into his pockets as he and Gaël stumbled from the warm interior of the tavern. Gaël took his arm to steady both of them on the wet cobblestones. Fox looked up at him, the alcohol in his blood softening the severe lines of Gaël's beloved face.

This was the first time he'd been back in Wave Harbor since the night Gaël had abandoned him. And while Rowan had been apologetic about coming back here, it was their only option, and they all knew it.

The two of them had started out the night drinking with a group of the *Siren*'s crew, but now they were alone together, their breath clouding before them as they made their way through the thin streets.

"I can't wait to get you back to the *Siren*," Gaël murmured in Fox's ear. The closeness of his body was the only warmth in Fox's world tonight. They'd both been a bit on edge since arriving in Wave Harbor. Neither of them knew quite what to say to the other. Gaël had apologized over and over for that night, and Fox had truly forgiven him, but that didn't mean they could forget all about it. So they'd both been covering their unease with endless flirting.

Fox giggled, drawing Gaël closer so his body heat bled through Fox's damp coat. "You think you're topping tonight? That's cute." He felt a shiver run through Gaël's body.

They walked a bit further, making their way back toward the docks where the *Siren* lay waiting. The streets were relatively deserted in this cold, but every public house and inn they passed was bursting with light and the chatter of the pirates and sailors within. There wasn't much else for them to do but drink in the winter. It was too dangerous to sail, and there wouldn't be any prizes worth capturing anyway.

"Should we go back now?" Gaël asked. Fox didn't miss the eagerness in his voice. The man was an open book, and Fox loved that he could read him so easily. Not that he could read actual books, but that wasn't the point.

"Just one more drink." He took Gaël's hand and drew it into his coat pocket to warm it. Gaël smiled at him and followed him on his winding way through the streets of Pirate Alley. Fox was much more familiar with this port than Gaël was. Neither of them wanted to think about why. Being trapped here alone was the lowest point in Fox's life, lower even than his shitty childhood, because at least back then he'd had Gaël by his side. At least he hadn't been alone.

But he wasn't alone now. Gaël's hand was in his, and the rest of their friends were either safely on the *Siren* or up to their own mischief in Pirate Alley's taverns. Despite the underlying unease, Fox was content.

Until they rounded the corner and came face-to-face with the one place in this town that neither of them wanted to set foot in again.

The Salted Snail Inn.

Fox stopped dead in his tracks, and out of the corner of his eye, he saw all the blood drain out of Gaël's face.

The front of the building was salt-weathered timber, cracked and warped. The unpainted shutters were pulled tightly closed against the cold, but laughter and the faint strains of a bawdy song drifted through them into the dark street. Orange firelight flickered through the cracks and reflected on the wet cobbles where Fox and Gaël stood.

This was the place where they'd shared their first kiss. Confessed the feelings they'd kept hidden for so long. The place where they'd lost their virginity to each other.

The place Gaël had fled from him as he slept.

Fox inhaled a shuddering breath. He let it sting his lungs and ice his blood. Gaël's fingers clutched his hand tighter in the depths of his coat pocket.

For a moment they just stood there, staring at the inn like they'd seen a ghost. Their collective breath fogged in the chilly air. Fox tried to fight it, but a bit of that old panic was gnawing at his stomach. He couldn't seem to take his eyes off the building with its blue-painted snail above the door that used to be orange.

"Fox?" Gaël tugged his hand. "Let's go. Let's just call it a night." His voice sounded anxious.

"Wait."

Fox didn't know why he said it. He wanted to leave. Wanted nothing more than to turn his back on this place and go home. But somehow that felt like defeat. And a strange idea was worming its way through the folds of his mind.

Back then, when he was all alone, he'd had nothing to do but wallow in his misery. Wallow and survive. That was it. But now he didn't have to do that. Now he'd made a life for himself. A life where he was happy, and he didn't want these old hurts to fester anymore. The memory would always be there, but the hurt didn't have to be.

Just like with Cyrus, Fox would rewrite that hurt into something new.

"Let's stay here tonight."

Gaël said nothing, and Fox turned to look at him. Their hands were still clasped together in Fox's pocket.

"Don't you hate it here? I know I do." Gaël's expression was stricken. Confused.

"I know, but we don't have to."

Gaël's brow furrowed. "How can I not hate the place where I made the biggest mistake of my life?"

Fox knew he meant leaving, but that deep down panic made the words cut all the same. He plastered on a smile.

"I know I said I wouldn't push you again, so I'll only ask once. What if we rewrote this too?"

Gaël's brow smoothed slightly in understanding. The icy wind blew his hair in front of his eyes.

"You can't just gloss over every bad memory with good sex, Foxy."

Fox stepped in close, pressing a light kiss to Gaël's lips and inhaling the steam of his breath. Then he pulled back to look Gaël in the eyes.

"With this I think I can. It still hurts both of us. But I don't want to live in the past anymore." He touched the spot on Gaël's chest where he'd been flayed open by Admiral Batteux's sword. "The present is all we have. And besides…" He leaned forward, letting his lips brush Gaël's cold nipped ear. "I want to fuck you in the same bed you left me in."

The door of the Salted Snail burst open, issuing forth a wave of sound and light and a spill of drunken pirates who hooted and hollered at the sight of the two of them embracing in the cold. Gaël's breath huffed against the side of Fox's neck as the tide of pirates passed them by. Then, seeming to make his mind up, Gaël tugged him toward the still open door.

The interior was awash with noise, and Fox was instantly warmed by the jovial mood and press of the crowd. It looked cleaner and nicer than he remembered, despite its rough exterior. Gaël dragged him to the bar and ordered them two mugs of ale, then leaned over and whispered something to the barmaid that Fox couldn't hear over a sudden roar of cheers as the song ended.

Fox sipped his ale and watched the crowd, all of whom were much drunker than he and Gaël. A jittery feeling had almost replaced the panic in his stomach. Gaël turned away from his conversation with the barmaid and wrapped one muscled arm around Fox's waist, pulling him tight to his side. He slipped something small and heavy into Fox's coat pocket.

Fox watched him out of the corner of his eye. Gaël's dark hair was wind tousled, his profile starkly beautiful against the warm firelight. This was how he'd always seen Gaël back then, before he even knew his own feelings. He'd always been at Gaël's side, stealing glances at his gorgeous face and wondering what it would be like to kiss those pouty lips.

Gaël took a drink from his mug, still watching the crowd. But Fox watched how his throat bobbed as he swallowed, how his cheek dimpled slightly in amusement at the suggestive lyrics of the next song. He felt so small in Gaël's arms. So protected and wanted. The rest of the world fell away from his perception, and there was only Gaël.

Someone jostled Fox, causing some of his ale to slosh over the rim of his mug onto the floor.

"Watch it," Gaël growled at them, his arm tightening around Fox's waist protectively. But Fox didn't mind the intrusion. He set his mug back on the bar with a soft thump. Gaël turned to check if he was alright.

He was so close, his body heat radiating through the layers of clothing between them. Despite himself, Fox's breath hitched at their proximity. This was just how it had gone that night. The memory was still painfully fresh, Gaël drawing him close out of the way of some drunkard. But his arm hadn't left Fox's waist when the danger passed. Their bodies, their lips, were so close. And then...

Fox saw the moment Gaël realized it too. His gray eyes met Fox's green ones. The jittery feeling in Fox's stomach stoked itself into full on butterflies. What was wrong with him? He was no longer that inexperienced boy, secretly in love with his best friend. But he felt just the same as he had back then.

Gaël slowly set his mug down as well, never taking his eyes from Fox's flushed face. His free hand came up to cup the back of Fox's neck, their shared memory guiding their bodies almost in pantomime of that night. His gaze flicked across Fox's face, trying to read his innermost thoughts. Then he drew Fox to him, and their lips met.

It was the same. So the same that for a moment Fox felt as if he really were reliving it.

Yet it was also different. Gaël's mouth moved slow and sensual against his, none of the sweet hesitation of inexperience. And when Fox's hands came to rest on his chest just as they had before, they found hard muscle instead of scrawny youth. The butterflies in his stomach fluttered quicker, becoming leaping flames of desire.

Gaël reluctantly broke the kiss, his forehead resting against Fox's.

"I love you, Foxy. I always have, and I always will."

The same words. The same place. Somewhere in the distance, the city bells chimed midnight. And Fox realized with a jolt, it was even the same day. But this time those words rang true, echoing in Fox's heart like the tolling of the midnight bells.

I always will.

Fox felt some fractured part deep down begin to knit itself back together with a thread of gold. The glow of Gaël's love shining over every fissure and flaw and scouring away the shadows within them so that only the fissures themselves remained. It was not that Gaël's love could heal all the damage Fox had sustained. But he knew that if he faltered, Gaël would be there to catch him.

Fox almost couldn't remember what he was meant to say. He balled his fists in the front of Gaël's shirt and kissed him again, this time with all the heat of the butterfly flames inside of him. Gaël returned his enthusiasm and didn't seem to mind that Fox had gone off script, or that he hadn't said 'I love you' back. He knew.

I always have and I always will.

~

THE LITTLE WEIGHT in his pocket turned out to be a key to the exact room from before. Fox didn't have time to think much on that as he struggled to fit the key into the lock and turn it while Gaël was busy sucking a mark onto the skin at his neck from behind. With a bit of struggle, he got the door open, and they stumbled into the room and locked it behind them. As with everything tonight, the room was different and the same all at once. The simple wooden bedframe and the purple and blue patchwork quilt were familiar, but the entire room was decidedly cleaner, and there was a freshly laid fire in the hearth that was just beginning to warm the room.

Gaël spun Fox around and pinned him against the door. His gray eyes were stormy as he took Fox's face between his hands, much gentler than Fox was expecting, and Fox could tell that Gaël was controlling himself carefully.

"Do you still want to do this?" His deep voice was raw, and Fox couldn't tell whether it was due to lust or the past emotions bubbling up. Maybe both.

"Of course," he answered.

"Good."

The kiss left Fox breathless, and the fire in his core flared and reached toward Gaël's light. Gaël's fingers dug into the sides of his face, deepening the kiss. His tongue invaded Fox's mouth, and Fox's knees went weak. A wounded whimper escaped his lips. His hands fisted in the front of Gaël's shirt. He wanted to be closer. Wanted to devour and be devoured in turn, to be absorbed into Gaël's strong body and become inseparable from him.

Fox's hips bucked forward, brushing their clothed erections

together. He caught Gaël's lower lip between his teeth, and Gaël's fingers threaded up through his brown hair, loosening the tie that held it off of his brow. The damp strands fell to brush his chin, and a shiver ran down his spine as Gaël's fingertips worked over his scalp.

They stumbled further into the room, barely breaking their kiss to shed their damp clothes until they were standing bare chested in just their trousers with a trail of clothing and boots behind them. Fox bent to kiss Gaël's collarbone. His fingers ran tentatively over the long diagonal scar that ran across Gaël's broad chest from right shoulder to the lower left ribs. It had only been a month, and the scar tissue was still new and fragile. Fox's fingertips tripped over the even marks where the stitches had been embedded in his tan flesh.

"Does it hurt?" he whispered, his mood suddenly sobering at the reminder that both Gaël and Rowan had almost been taken from him. His lips roamed over Gaël's hot skin.

"Not really." Gaël's cheek brushed Fox's hair. "Don't worry about me."

Fox's head snapped up. "How can I not? I...I almost lost you again..." He was suddenly choked up. Even when they were children and Gaël was a lot scrawnier than he was now, he'd always been the protector, the one who got hurt in the place of others.

Gaël took Fox's hand in his and moved it away from the wound. He waited till he caught Fox's eye.

"You won't lose me. Isn't that what all this is about?" He raised Fox's hand to his mouth and kissed it, not taking his eyes off Fox's face.

Fox gulped down the uneasy emotion that had risen in his throat, and it burned away in the flames of his desire as Gaël's tongue flicked between his fingers.

"Let's not think of anything but now," Gaël murmured. He licked Fox's index finger.

"Don't think this means I'll go easy on you."

"Never."

Fox pushed Gaël onto the bed and climbed on top of him. He ran a line of light kisses down the tender pink ridge of scar tissue, listening to the way Gaël's breath hitched when his lips met new skin. As he reached the end of the scar and continued down over Gaël's hard stomach, he pulled Gaël's trousers down his hips, allowing his eager cock to spring free. Fox glanced up to his face and found him watching with half-lidded eyes. Fox graced him with a mischievous smile, then flattened his tongue at the base of Gaël's shaft and licked a slow stripe up the smooth underside. Gaël bit his lip to stifle a moan. Fox's tongue reached the wet tip and circled teasingly around the head. He reached into this own trouser pocket and withdrew the vial of lube he'd thankfully had the foresight to bring along. He pressed the glass, still cold from the wintery weather, against the inside of Gaël's thigh and giggled when Gaël flinched at the chill.

Fox tucked it into his palm to warm it and continued teasing Gaël with his tongue. Gaël's breath quickened as Fox's lips met the tip of his cock, and he pressed his tongue to the underside of the shaft as he took in Gaël's cock. When he got as far as he could go, his nose nestled against the dark curls, he curled the edge of his tongue around the shaft. The prominent veins along the hard length throbbed against Fox's lips.

Fox wiggled his hips. He loved being filled with Gaël. The taste of him. The feel of him. It was almost a shame that this was the only way he was going to be full of Gaël tonight. So he had to make it count. He hummed and swallowed around Gaël's cock, wiggling his hips again. His eyes flicked up to make sure Gaël was watching. He was. His storm cloud eyes smoldered with lust.

"If you're gonna—ah—tease me like that you should take your pants off." Gaël groaned as Fox bobbed his head slowly. Gaël's hands fisted in the quilt, small gasps and moans escaping from his parted lips. Fox shimmied out of his trousers as he continued pleasuring Gaël with his mouth.

"That's better," Gaël sighed. He brushed a lock of hair out of Fox's face. "You know I like to see you."

Fox released his cock with a lewd slurp. "You just like my ass."

"It can be both." Gaël smirked. Fox giggled and smacked him on the thigh. Then, still grinning, he crawled up the bed to plant a kiss below Gaël's jaw. He rolled the now warmed vial of lube up Gaël's stomach.

Gaël spread his legs a bit wider in invitation. Fox's lips traveled down his neck, over the smattering of powder burns. He tried not to think of their source and was quickly distracted by the warmth of Gaël's body, the softness of his skin, and the pulse of his heartbeat under Fox's lips.

Fox uncorked the vial one-handed and slathered the lube onto his fingers.

"It might be a bit cold still," he murmured.

Gaël inhaled sharply but quickly relaxed as Fox's hand slipped between his thighs and began teasing his entrance.

"Foxy...ah..." Whatever he was about to say was interrupted by Fox pushing one finger inside him. Gaël's back arched off the bed.

Fox paused for a moment to let Gaël adjust to the slight stretch, watching Gaël's face. Though their sex life was robust and they switched, Fox liked to bottom more often. Despite Gaël's relative inexperience, being topped by him was an otherworldly experience. The man was practically a god.

But that didn't mean Fox couldn't take him apart piece by piece if he set his mind to it.

He pushed in deeper, the warm wet walls constricting around his finger.

"Relax." Fox nipped at Gaël's collarbone and planted several open-mouthed kisses over his neck and chest as he pumped his finger lazily, stretching him out. When he deemed Gaël ready, he added a second finger and began to scissor them to stretch Gaël further. He groaned against Gaël's skin, imagining these slick walls sucking him in, clenching around his dick. The thought had him rutting his hips against Gaël's side.

Maybe it was just the memory of last time they were in this room, but the slide of his cock against Gaël's skin and the noises falling from Gaël's lips as Fox fucked him with his fingers were driving Fox crazy. His cock was already red and weeping, and like the hopeless virgin he'd been back then, he wouldn't last long in this condition.

Judging by Gaël's expression, neither would he.

"Please..." Gaël moaned as Fox curled his fingers to hit the sensitive bundle of nerves inside him. Gaël's fingernails dug into Fox's shoulder.

Fox leaned down to nip his earlobe. "Please what?" He massaged Gaël's prostate again causing him to gasp.

"P-please fuck me. I need you." He looked at Fox with desperation. "I'm ready, just please—"

Fox didn't think he was quite opened up enough, but he couldn't resist his lover's begging. He withdrew his fingers and pushed Gaël onto his side with his back to Fox. Fox trailed kisses down the side of his neck as he lubed up his own cock. He gripped Gaël's thigh to open up his legs, and he guided the tip of his cock to Gaël's entrance between muscled cheeks. Gaël rutted his ass back, desperate to be filled, but Fox held him in place.

"Do you remember?" Fox asked, his face pressed to the side of Gaël's head. "You hesitated just like this..." His words trailed off when Gaël's body tensed. It truly wasn't his intention to make Gaël feel guilty again, or to ruin the mood, but he just couldn't shake the sense of twisted déjà vu that had overtaken him, a strange nostalgia for the way they had been and the pain that came after...

Gaël turned to look at him. "I wish we had never parted. I wish..." He gasped as Fox's dick rubbed at his hole. His eyes slid closed for a moment, long lashes resting on his high sculpted cheekbones. He swallowed. "Fox, if this is your way of punishing me, I—"

Fox silenced him with a kiss. He took his time, letting his tongue explore the hot interior of Gaël's mouth, willing his lips to memorize Gaël's pouty pink curves. If they were ever separated again, he wanted the feel of Gaël to be imprinted upon his skin.

"I'm not," he whispered when the kiss broke. "I promise I'm not punishing you. I'm just trying to remember what it felt like that night." He wanted to remember what it felt like to be in Gaël's arms for the first time. To lose his virginity to the man he loved. A deep well of nostalgia had opened up in the chambers of his heart, only stoking the flames of desire higher. He planted a kiss on Gaël's cheek and ran his hand up his inner thigh. Gaël bit his lip, head tilted back to bare his throat.

"You remember how you hesitated?" Fox murmured in his ear. "You were so afraid of hurting me. You wanted me to be sure. And I begged you to fill me up. I've never regretted that, you know. Even with all that happened after. I'm glad my first time was with you."

"Fox—" Gaël's words were cut off by a gasp as Fox finally pushed into his tight, wet heat. The head of Fox's cock caught slightly on the rim of Gaël's hole before he pushed past it. "Fuck, Fox. Fuck, you feel so good." Gaël whimpered. His back arched, and Fox's lube-slick fingers tightened on his thick thigh. Fox's lips trailed over his neck again, lavishing his skin with fervent kisses. The fires in his gut were already turning his blood molten. He was only halfway in, trying to give Gaël a chance to adjust, but damn, it felt good. His teeth latched onto Gaël's shoulder as his hips rutted forward involuntarily, burying himself up to the hilt. Gaël's tight walls clenched around him. Fuck. He really wasn't going to last if it already felt this good.

"So tight," he hissed between his teeth. He tried not to move for a moment. He knew he hadn't prepped Gaël enough. But Gaël's ass twitched back, trying to take him in more. Fox obliged. He pulled out to the tip, angling to where he knew he would hit the sweet spot dead on.

He snapped his hips forward and was gratified by the agonized moan that ripped itself from Gaël's throat.

His teeth sank harder into Gaël's skin as he thrust into him again and again, hitting that delicious bundle of nerves every other stroke. Gaël reached back to grip his damp hair. His breath was already ragged, the sweet music of his moans loud in Fox's ear. Fox's hand trailed up his thigh to wrap around his throbbing dick. He pumped it in time with his strokes, relishing the new sounds of ecstasy it pulled from Gaël's lips. He sucked dark marks onto Gaël's perfect, fevered skin and soothed them with his tongue.

"Foxy, please...I'm so close. Please...ngh...fuck. I love you...more... please, more." Gaël was babbling. His hips stuttered, as if his body couldn't decide whether to fuck himself back onto Fox's cock or thrust forward into Fox's hand.

Fox brought him to the edge, his strokes deepening until he could tell that Gaël was right on the precipice of orgasm.

He pulled out and released Gaël's weeping cock. A whine escaped Gaël's lips, and Fox pushed him onto his back, capturing his needy lips in a hard kiss. When they broke apart, Gaël gazed at him with a look of utter fucked-out devotion. He reached up to cup Fox's face with both hands and wrapped his legs around Fox's slim waist, drawing him back in. Fox lined himself up again and bucked his hips forward, watching the way Gaël's eyes rolled back in his head.

Fox couldn't take his eyes from Gaël's gorgeous face as he thrust into him. He hitched Gaël's hips higher, tucking his own folded legs beneath Gaël's ass to achieve a deeper angle he knew would hit all the right spots and drive Gaël mad.

Fox's gaze lowered to the scar again, his fingertips gently grazing it.

"F-Fox," Gaël gasped.

He looked back up to Gaël's stormy eyes.

"I'm not going anywhere."

Fox grinned, the momentary melancholy falling away. "I should hope so, considering I'm inside you right now."

Gaël's thumbs brushed over Fox's cheeks and across his lower lip, almost reverent, worshipful, as Fox took him apart stroke by stroke. Fox caught one of his hands, pressing a kiss into his palm and trailing his lips down the inside of Gaël's wrist.

Fire licked through his veins. The inevitable orgasm coiled in his gut, ready to snap and undo him too. Gaël's moans were almost choked, and Fox knew that he would soon plunge over the edge.

Gaël's gray eyes opened, heavy with bliss, and he moaned Fox's name so sweetly.

Fuck. Fox's ass clenched, yearning to be filled with Gaël's cock. He hitched one of Gaël's legs over his shoulder, then reached back to finger his own twitching rim. His fingers were still slick with lube and Gaël's precum, and an almost hysterical laugh clawed out of his throat as he breached himself with two fingers.

The sting and stretch went straight to his dick. Gaël clutched the blue and purple quilt on either side of his head, half-lidded eyes watching as Fox fucked himself back onto his own fingers then forward into Gaël's swollen hole.

"F-fuck, Foxy, you couldn't stand not being filled up could you?" Gaël teased, even as his voice was weak and raspy from screaming Fox's name. Fox could only moan in response. He snapped his hips forward harshly. He was so close, and he needed to make Gaël come before him.

Gaël's fingers twisted in the quilt, his back arching off the bed. Fox chased down his lover's orgasm, stroking into him with a reckless abandon and hitting just the right spot over and over until Gaël seemed almost delirious and fucked out of his mind.

"Let go, sweetie. Come for me like a good boy," Fox panted.

Gaël whimpered. Then with one particularly deep stroke, his mouth went wide and silent, and hot cum spurted across his belly. Fox rode him through it, his movements erratic as fire crackled through him. Gaël's insides clenched and fluttered around his cock, sucking him in.

The edges of his vision went dark as his fingers found his prostate and his hips stuttered, burying himself deep as everything finally snapped, and he spilled his orgasm into Gaël's tight heat.

Fox collapsed against Gaël's heaving chest. Breathless, tasting the salt of Gaël's sweat on his lips. He withdrew his fingers from himself, moaning at the loss and slightly wishing he'd bottomed after all.

He kissed Gaël's chest, the ridges of scar tissue rough on his lips. Gaël's arms settled heavily around his shoulders. They stayed like that for a few moments, basking in the afterglow and each other. Finally, Fox's legs began to quiver. He unsheathed himself and rolled onto the mattress beside Gaël. Gaël turned onto his side so they were chest-to-chest. He wrapped an arm around Fox's waist and pulled him into his arms, sleepily kissing him on the tip of his nose. Fox looked him over. He was gorgeous. His body slicked with a light sheen of sweat, chest heaving. His lips were parted to catch his breath. He looked at Fox as if he were the most wondrous thing in the entire world.

"You're amazing, Foxy," he sighed, his breath still a little bit shaky. "Maybe I should bottom more often."

"Oh, really?" Fox wasn't sure how he felt about that. He loved fucking Gaël into breathless oblivion, but equally—or even more—he loved being at the mercy of the man beside him, being stretched out by his deliciously thick cock. Being absolutely wrecked and worshiped, barely even able to walk the next day and...

Fox felt the stirrings of arousal in the pit of his stomach again. His asshole and cock twitched back to life at the same time.

"Gaël?" Fox drew his fingertips lightly down the center of Gaël's heaving chest and hard stomach until they almost touched his spent cock.

"Hmm?" Gaël's stormy gray eyes opened a crack.

"I'm actually not done. Are you?" He pressed their bodies tighter together so Gaël could feel his half-hard length. Gaël's beautiful lips widened into a mischievous grin, cheeks dimpling.

"Gods, you're insatiable."

"But you love me." Fox planted a playful kiss on his shoulder. He locked onto Gaël's gaze, letting his eyelids lower slightly to look up through his lashes.

"Of course." Gaël leaned their foreheads together.

"I just need you inside me," Fox groaned, rutting his hips so his cock chafed against Gaël's thigh.

"Give me a minute, you animal."

"Animal?!" Fox drew back in mock offense. "Me?"

"Yes, you, you crafty bastard."

Gaël kissed him, slow and sweet, his hand drifting down to cup Fox's ass.

"I saw you fingering yourself while you were balls deep in me. How did it feel? Was it good enough or do you want to be filled up with something better?"

Fox whimpered, feeling his cock hardening further at Gaël's words.

"I'm just making up for lost time," he breathed.

"We have all the time in the world." With another kiss Gaël pulled away to search the rumpled blankets for the half-empty vial of lube. He found it and uncorked it with his teeth. Then slathered his fingers with the sweet-smelling oil.

He pulled Fox close again, wasting no time breaching Fox's hole with one finger. Then, realizing that he was already partly loosened, added a second. Fox nuzzled against Gaël's broad chest, letting out small moans and kissing his salty skin as Gaël fingered him.

Gaël took his time with it. His fingers were slow and sure, loosening Fox up to take his cock. Unhurried. But every press of his fingers against Fox's sensitive walls had him gasping. Even the brush of Gaël's breath in his hair heightened Fox's post-orgasmic sensation.

"Don't come before I even get to fuck you," Gaël murmured against his hair.

"Not helping," Fox moaned. His dick was almost painfully hard, pink and straining to be touched. Gaël just chuckled, adding a third finger and pressing the rough pads of his fingers deliberately to Fox's prostate.

"Ah!" Fox's body jerked, arching into Gaël's touch. Gaël's fingertips massaged little circles into the bundle of nerves, sending stars shooting across Fox's vision.

"Fuck, I'm gonna come if you do that again," Fox panted when Gaël's fingers finally withdrew.

Gaël flipped him onto his back, caging him between muscled arms and kissing him deeply. Fox realized suddenly that Gaël was hard again, Fox's cum dribbling down his thighs.

There was no hesitation this time. Without breaking eye contact, Gaël penetrated up to the base, his hips smacking against Fox's ass.

"Fuck, yes!" Fox cried. Gaël gave him no time to adjust, and he didn't need it. He only needed Gaël's length inside him. Gaël pulled back and slammed in again, setting a brutal pace that quickly brought

Fox to the edge of overstimulation. But gods, it was good. More than good. Heavenly. Every tired muscle in his body tingled with sensational bliss. He was engulfed in it, drowning in Gaël's breath. His kiss.

Fox arched off the bed, wanting more. Needing more. His fingernails dug into Gaël's arms.

"Gaël. Oh god..." His own voice sounded foreign to his ears, desperate and completely gone from sanity. He realized there were tears leaking from the corners of his eyes. But he didn't care. As long as Gaël loved him, that was all that mattered.

"Tell me you love me," he gasped.

"I love you," Gaël moaned. "Gods, Foxy I love you more than life itself." He wrapped one arm beneath the small of Fox's back, bringing them even closer. Fox could feel every frantic beat of his heart through the throbbing of his dick. He threw his arms around Gaël's neck and pulled him into a kiss. Tingles spread throughout his body like a thousand stars crashing into him. Gaël's tongue licked into his mouth and swallowed a guttural moan as Gaël's cock hit his prostate.

"I'm gonna come," he moaned into Gaël's mouth. Gaël only picked up the pace.

Gaël had said that they couldn't rewrite every bad memory with good sex. But so far, Fox found that to be untrue. With every mind-bending stroke he could feel the last of the hurt melting away, the last of the cracks healing, glued together with the devotion in Gaël's eyes. The empty well of memory in the chambers of Fox's heart flooded full of new experience, old love rekindled and transformed. And in the morning when he woke and Gaël was still there in his arms, he would be healed.

Tonight had never been about the sex. It was about staying.

He blinked tears and stars both away from his vision and saw Gaël's eyes glassy with tears as well.

Fox's breath caught. Suddenly it was all too much. The love and ecstasy mingled and overflowed, and he came across his stomach with Gaël's name on his lips, pleasure beyond comprehension bursting across every raw nerve. After a few more strokes he felt Gaël shudder and spill hot and hard into Fox's clenching hole.

Gaël leaned down to kiss the tears from Fox's temples, gentle now that they were both spent. Fox's whole body trembled with aftershocks, and he clutched Gaël to him as if he would disappear. Gaël peppered kisses across his face waiting for Fox to come down.

Fox's arms and legs remained locked around him, keeping them connected as their cocks softened and sweat cooled.

"Fox?" Gaël ventured after a while.

"Mmm?" Fox had moved past the aftershocks and was now basking in a sort of heavenly golden warmth that he was half afraid meant he'd died and was in heaven.

"My arms are getting tired."

Fox huffed a laugh and released him. Gaël pulled out of him and climbed off the bed. He retrieved a water jug and cloth from the side table and wiped them both down. Fox was still floating in the warm sea of bliss. He barely even noticed when Gaël picked up his limp body and tucked them both under the familiar quilt. He nuzzled into Gaël's neck, warm and content and drifting. Eager for the morning to shine on their love.

CHAPTER 31

JANUARY 18TH, 1667

Freezing rain pattered off Logan's shoulders as he made his way down the deserted street. It was no time to be out, but he had things to do and not a lot of time to do them. His and Rowan's connections had come through with a lead on Cyrus's possible whereabouts. So here Logan was in the port town of Rose-forte on the southern coast of Talva's mainland, slogging through freezing rain and slush and trying not to be seen by the various navy men who typically hung around fort towns like this. They couldn't risk bringing the *Siren*, so Logan had booked passage on one of the few ships still sailing during the winter, and it had not been a pleasant journey.

Rowan's contact alleged that Cyrus was being kept in an inn by the Talvan navy in Roseforte. Logan had been to six different inns already in the two days he'd been here with no luck. He had to be careful in his search. If Cyrus, or the navy, heard that a one-handed man was asking around for him, he'd bolt, and who knew how long it would take them to track him down again.

Logan spotted his destination, an inn with a tavern on the main floor and a sign depicting a swan holding a pink rose over the door. He ducked inside, settling his soaked hood back onto the equally sodden shoulders of his coat. Despite the gloom outside, the interior was warm and lively. Logan's eyes scanned the room. There was a table of navy sailors in the corner, but the rest of the patrons were civilians. Logan was unsurprised to see that most of them looked like merchant sailors, probably not from around here. In this awful weather, the locals would be at home with their families. But here, the patrons gathered around mugs of ale and warm cider, chattering away the stress of the day.

Logan's eyes landed on a familiar figure tucked into a booth in the corner opposite the navy men. Not Cyrus as he'd hoped, but none other than John Hakon.

Logan couldn't help the grin that threatened to split his chapped lips at the sight of his friend. Maybe he should've held a grudge. The gods knew Rowan still did. But Logan was the type to forgive and forget. It had been an accident. John had apologized, and though the stump of Logan's wrist still ached, especially in this weather, he was happy to see John.

John seemed to have spotted him as soon as he walked in. He raised his mug in greeting when their eyes met, and Logan took that as an invitation.

"Fancy meeting you here." Logan slipped into the booth opposite him. John nodded, taking another swig of his ale. He looked tired. Dark circles rimmed his eyes, and he was thinner than Logan remembered. The only thing that didn't look worn down about him was his freshly shaved chin and cheeks.

A red-haired woman hurried up to take Logan's drink order, then bustled away again when the navy sailors called for her. Logan and John kept their faces averted till the men looked away. Logan personally wasn't well known as a pirate by sight, but he still didn't want to draw the attention of the law. Especially when he was alone and one hand short.

"So," Logan said brightly when the serving woman had left. "What are you doing here? And where are the rest of you?" He hadn't seen the *Kraken* in the harbor, but then again, such an infamous pirate vessel wouldn't dock in a legitimate port like Roseforte. Especially one crawling with navy men.

"They're not here. I'm on a special errand for the captain," John answered.

"Oh? And what is it? If you don't mind me asking. Maybe I can help you out."

"You remember our *mutual friend* Cyrus?"

Logan sat forward, his interest piqued. "You're looking for him? Seems our errands are one and the same."

The woman brought Logan's cider. Logan thanked her and paid with a generous tip. She winked at him before leaving again.

"I am looking for him," John said when she was gone. "We got word that he'd escaped on one of our merchant ships. The captain wants me to track him down before he talks."

"Well it's too late for that." Logan took a sip of his cider. The sweet apple taste burst across his tongue followed by the stark sting of alcohol, all too quickly replaced by the bitterness of the predicament they currently found themselves in. Rowan and the rest of them had completely forgotten about Cyrus in their haste to leave Illusion behind. They'd wondered if the Demon would just murder him without Rowan's moderating presence, but it seemed that he'd stayed alive long enough to escape. "We had a run in with the Talvans about two months back. We barely made it out, and we have it on good authority Cyrus is to blame."

"Little rat," John growled. "Do they know the location of..." He cut himself off before uttering the name Illusion, lest prying ears be nearby.

"I don't think so. It seemed like they just knew of its existence. Not the location."

"Probably because the bilge rat was stowed away below deck. We should be thanking the stars that he didn't figure it out."

"He's not the smartest. I don't know if he would have figured it out even if he was above deck," Logan said.

"Well he was smart enough to capitalize on what he *does* know. Yves is going to be furious when he finds out," John grumbled. "You said you fought the Talvans? Is everyone okay?"

"We lost a few crew members. Your Gaël and Robin are fine. Robin proved his skills once again." Logan tried to keep his voice neutral, but losing crew members he was responsible for always stung.

"And your captain?" John cleared his throat. "Yves is definitely going to ask."

"He's alive and well." It was true, in the strictest sense. Rowan was alive, and he'd recovered from his injuries. But he had new scars across the right side of his face, and his right eye was gone.

John sighed and slumped against the back of the bench. "Good. I don't know what Yves would do if anything happened to him."

"That bad?"

"You have no idea," John groaned. "He... Well, let's just say we're much richer and much more exhausted than we were before. And we're not docking for the winter."

"What? Why?" Sailing during the winter was madness. Even though it typically didn't get too cold in this region, winter came with storms. Lots of them. Sea traffic slowed to only essential trips and those who didn't have a port to call home. Even the most seasoned sailor would balk at the prospect of sailing during the winter when they didn't need to.

John shrugged. "Captain is pushing us. Hard. He hasn't been the same since you lot left."

Logan's brow furrowed. He didn't know the details of Rowan's short relationship with the Demon, but he'd assumed that if there were feelings involved, it would have been on Rowan's side. He couldn't imagine the Deep Water Demon mourning the departure of his lover to the point he would needlessly put his crew at risk.

A burst of raucous laughter from the navy men across the room interrupted them, and they waited in silence for the noise to die down.

"So," Logan finally said, "any luck with Cyrus?"

"Yes and no. He was here. I've confirmed that much. But he left two days ago. I don't know what ship he was on or where he was going. But Nia over there"—he pointed to the serving woman, who smiled at him—"says the bastard was bragging how he's going to make a fortune taking down the two worst pirates on the sea."

Shit. Logan must have missed him by mere hours. Now he and Rowan would have to start searching all over again.

"We'll have to find out what navy ships left two days ago. No way they're going to let an informant like that go off on his own."

Nia the serving woman materialized beside the table and set down a plate of steaming hand pies.

"Oh, uh, we didn't..." Logan began.

"On the house, sweetheart." Nia patted him on the shoulder. "You've been the only quiet and polite table all night, so I brought you a little something."

"Thank you!" Logan beamed. Nia was quite pretty, and he

hoped he wasn't blushing in front of John. He didn't want more teasing about his virginal status again. Though after that blowjob in the garden he supposed he technically wasn't so virginal anymore.

To distract himself, he reached for one of the delicious looking pies. Then paused, realizing he'd used the arm that no longer had a hand attached to it. Even after months, he still wasn't quite used to it. But thus far he had kept it resting on his lap under the table. Now it was out in the open for all to see.

"Oh my. Best not let the others see that," Nia said gently. "They'll think you're a pirate." She squeezed Logan's shoulder, then walked away, hips swaying.

While a one-handed pirate might have been cliché, it was for good reason. Marra, Talva, and even Lasland all cut off one hand from pirates they captured, even if they intended to hang them after.

Logan sighed and picked up a pie with his left hand. He bit into it, relishing the savory filling. John remained silent, and Logan realized that he was staring at where Logan's arm abruptly ended. It was clear that he still felt guilty over what happened.

Finally, John's deep-set eyes flicked up to Logan's face.

"I'm sorry."

Logan was sure he didn't strike a very serious figure with his cheeks full of pastry. He quickly swallowed and said, "You've already apologized, and I've already forgiven you. No need to do it again."

John's lips thinned to a line. "I don't know how you can forgive me so easily. You lost your hand because of me."

Logan mulled it over for a moment. He'd always been a forgiving person. Some saw that as a weakness, but Logan preferred to think that most people deserved a second chance.

"I've heard of you, you know," Logan said after a while, pitching his voice lower so the other tavern patrons wouldn't overhear. "I recognised your name when the Demon said it that first day. It took me a while to place it, but now I remember."

John had gone very still. "What have you heard?"

"You're John C. Hakon, disgraced Lieutenant of the Marran Navy. They call you the Beast of Whitestone Reef." He paused, letting the old title and nickname sink past John's shock. "You burned the northeastern flotilla to the waterline during the war with Kefrye, killing dozens, if not hundreds, of officers and sailors in the process."

John looked positively sick to his stomach. Up until now, Logan had assumed this information wasn't a secret considering John was still using his real name. But based on John's reaction, Logan suddenly realized he'd just brought up a potentially touchy subject out of the blue.

"If you know what I've done," John said at length, "why are you sitting here with me? Why are we friends?"

Logan sat forward again, his arm stump resting on the table between them, hand pies forgotten.

"We're pirates. I can no more judge you for your past than my own."

"I don't suppose I can convince you I had a good reason," John said gravely.

"I was indentured to the Marran navy until I was eighteen. I know the cruelty they're capable of. You don't have to explain yourself to me."

"Then why mention it at all?" John asked, perplexed.

Logan sighed. He'd never been a good talker. Not like Rowan was. And it seemed that he was not explaining himself very well. In fact, he realized that what he'd said had probably sounded accusatory.

"You seemed like you were brooding about my hand. So I wanted to remind you we've all done worse things than accidentally blowing my hand up." He sighed again. Exasperated. "My point is, you don't have to feel guilty after I've forgiven you. I already knew your past when we became friends, and I chose to associate with you anyway."

John huffed a laugh. "That's a bit simplistic, and reminding me of my crimes against my own country is a strange way to go about it." But he seemed to have relaxed back into the conversation now that he knew Logan wasn't about to turn around and rat him out to the navy men across the room. He still had a hefty bounty on his head, after all.

"I'm not very good at that stuff," Logan admitted.

"Fine. Just for you, I'll stop feeling guilty starting in the morning. But let me apologize just one more time."

"Okay, lay it on me."

"I have a gift for you."

"Really?" Logan perked up. He liked gifts, and it was a hell of a lot better than another gloomy apology.

"It's up in my room." John eyed the stairs on the other side of the room. He'd have to pass the navy men to get there. "Maybe it's best if you came up instead of me bringing it down."

They finished off their drinks and Logan shoved the last bits of pastry into his mouth. John left another tip for Nia on the table, then they made their way toward the stairs. Thankfully the navy men and the rest of the sailors were too deep in their cups to pay the pair much mind.

~

John's room was small but clean. A single straw-stuffed bed sat against the wall to the left with a washstand opposite. The bed was meticulously made, still showing the habit of a man who'd spent years in the military. Logan wondered if John missed it, but after his faux pas earlier, he wasn't going to pry.

There was a small window at the back of the room. In better weather, it would have looked out onto the roof of the shop next door, but now it only showed sheets of rain sluicing down its pitted surface. The rain had gotten heavier while they were in the tavern. Logan hadn't noticed due to the noise of the other patrons, but here under the gabled roof it was positively roaring. Logan wasn't looking forward to trudging through this storm back to his own accommodations.

John shut the door behind them and scooched past Logan to the bed. He knelt to peer under it.

"Here it is." He drew out a large wooden box the length of his forearm and set it on the edge of the bed. "Come look."

Logan went to stand beside him. The box was well made of a rich-toned wood that might have been oak, with brass fittings. Logan ran his fingers over the smooth lid.

"It's pretty."

"Well? Open it." John stood, dusting off his knees.

Oh. Logan had assumed this beautiful box was the gift. He undid the brass catch and lifted the lid.

Within was a stretch of sky blue cloth punctuated by compartments that fit snugly around the components of the real gift.

Nestled among the fabric was an exquisitely carved false hand made from the same wood as the box, with small metal fittings that would allow the fingers to bend. Another mechanism secured it to a leather cuff that would fit over Logan's wrist. Beside it sat an elegantly curved hook that could be swapped in for the hand.

Logan stared at it for a long time. He'd been thinking about getting a prosthetic for months, but thus far hadn't found an opportunity to go looking.

"Where did you get this?" he breathed. His fingers brushed over one delicately carved fingernail.

"I made it. Well, I carved the wood parts. Someone else helped me with the rest." John sounded pleased with himself. "What are you waiting for? Try it on."

Logan carefully lifted the hand out of the box and slid the cuff over his wrist. He tightened the straps easily one-handed, then held it up, marveling at the detail and how it fit his wrist perfectly. It was almost an identical mirror of his real hand.

"How did you do this? It's amazing."

"Look, you can even bend the fingers," John said, ignoring his question. He folded down some of the fingers so only the middle one stood, straight and proud. "See?"

A giddy giggle bubbled up to Logan's lips. "Perfect. Now I can be rude with both hands. I've been missing that."

John just smiled, pleased that Logan liked the gift. Logan experimentally moved the fingers into different positions with his real hand, admiring the craftsmanship. John had even thought to carve a delicate swirly texture into the palm and fingertips to make it easier to grip things.

A bolt of lightning flashed outside, startling him. It was followed up closely by a deep roll of thunder. He was reminded that he still had to walk through the storm to get back. And now he'd be carrying his new prized possession.

John's gaze followed his out into the rain. He winced as another flash of lightning lit the room.

"You shouldn't go back out in that. You'll catch your death if you don't get struck by lightning first."

"I don't think I can avoid it." Logan laughed. "The place I'm staying is at least half a mile away."

"Just stay here. I can ask Nia for extra bedding and take the floor."

"I can't kick you out of your bed!" Logan protested.

"We can share if you prefer." John raised a suggestive eyebrow, causing Logan to blush to the roots of his hair. John laughed.

"It's settled then. I'll ask for the extra bedding."

JOHN WENT DOWN to the kitchen by the back stairs, leaving Logan alone in the room. He sat on the edge of the thin bed, cradling the wooden hand in his lap and watching the rain through the wavy glass window. His thumb ran absently over the whorls of grain on the palm. It was by far the best gift he'd ever received, even if it was given by the man who'd caused him to lose his hand in the first place.

He held both of his hands out in front of him. Flesh and wood side by side. They were the same, even down to Logan's wide palm and short nail beds. How had John managed to make it nearly identical to his real hand?

Logan was startled from his thoughts by the door opening to admit the man in question. Logan quickly returned his hands to his lap.

"How does it fit?" John asked, closing the door behind him.

Logan held both hands up side by side again, and John came to sit beside him.

"It's amazing." After John's mild flirting earlier, Logan was hyper aware of John's body heat next to him. "How did you get the details so perfect?"

John took the wooden hand in his, and Logan could almost feel the pressure of his fingers as if it was his own flesh. His heart jumped into his throat, and not just because of the flash of lightning and the boom of thunder that rattled the roof overhead. Logan hadn't been able to forget that first lunch they'd had together in the lady's garden on Illusion. Even in the dead of winter, he could still smell the heady scent of flowers crushed between his back and the warm brick. He could still hear the bees buzzing in his head, erasing any rational thought with their droning.

The flow of Logan's thoughts caught briefly, finally connecting two things that had previously been separate. John had done what he'd done to delay them from leaving. He'd apparently been doing so all along, on the Demon's orders. And what better way to delay the repairs than by distracting the man in charge with sex?

Another thunderclap jolted him out of his thoughts, and he realized he'd been staring at his wooden hand where it was cradled in John's hand. He looked up to see John gazing at him expectantly.

"Sorry, what did you say?"

"I said I just have a good memory for detail," John repeated. Logan's gaze fell back to their joined hands. Had John really only sucked his dick to distract him from carrying out the *Siren*'s repairs? Was that directly on the Demon's orders, or had he decided that course of action on his own, hoping he wouldn't have to resort to more drastic measures? Fuck. Logan thought it hadn't affected him much, but his stomach dropped at the thought that John hadn't really wanted to do that with him.

He realized he was staring at John, and forced himself to blink. The smell of crushed flowers withered, and the buzzing of bees turned into an uncomfortable roar.

Logan didn't quite know how to ask if it was true. He glanced around the room, looking for something to distract him, and realizing John had returned empty-handed.

"Where are the blankets?"

"Oh, Nia said she would bring— Speak of the devil," he said as a knock sounded on the door. He released Logan's wooden hand and went to answer it.

"Delivery!" Nia said cheerfully when he opened the door. "I thought it must be awfully cold up here since you asked for so many, but it's not so bad. Were you just trying to lure me into your room again, Mister Hakon?" Her tone had turned flirtatious. As she handed over the bundle of blankets, John's hip bumped the door.

"Oh?" Nia peeked past him into the room and spotted Logan. "Your cute blond friend is staying? You should have told me! I would have fixed my hair." She patted her light red hair where a few tendrils had fallen fetchingly out of their pins. She really was quite pretty, with peachy, freckled skin and well-fed curves that filled out her blouse and skirt. Logan knew he was blushing fiercely both from John's recent closeness and Nia's flirtations.

John turned to put the blankets at the foot of the bed, and Nia leaned against the doorjamb, cocking one generous hip to the side and crossing her arms beneath her bosoms. The blush climbed higher on Logan's face, and he lowered his eyes respectfully.

"Quite the shy one, isn't he?" she said to John.

"Don't tease the poor man. He lives on a ship far away from flirta-tious women," John quipped.

"So do you," Nia said.

John just shrugged.

Nia pouted and leaned further into the room. "But it's your last night here isn't it, John? I was hoping I could give you a proper goodbye to thank you for all your hard work keeping me warm these last few nights."

The barely concealed innuendo was not lost on Logan. He fidgeted uncomfortably. John took Nia's freckled hand between his and kissed her knuckles.

"Sorry to disappoint you."

Nia disengaged her hand and ran it lightly up John's firm chest.

"Who's disappointed? Two is better than one, I always say."

Logan's heart skipped a beat in shock, and Nia stepped into the room. She crouched by the side of the bed to catch Logan's down-turned gaze. Her eyes were shockingly green, rimmed with thick lashes the same reddish-orange as her hair.

"So? What do you say, shy little pup? Do you want to help your friend keep a poor tavern maid warm on a terrible night like this?"

Logan swallowed around the lump in his throat. It seemed she and John had a previous arrangement, and Logan didn't want to hinder them. And he didn't want to pressure John into touching him again if he hadn't even wanted to the first time. Maybe he could go back to his own inn after all. It wasn't so far...

As if nature was conspiring against him, the rain began to beat the window panes even harder, and lightning forked through the clouds threateningly. Logan glanced at John for help, but he only raised his eyebrows. They were definitely asking him to join what-ever arrangement they had. Was John okay with this?

Logan thought about going back down to the tavern to wait it out, but the navy sailors were probably still down there. It wasn't that he didn't want to join John and Nia, but his only sexual experience was getting head from John that summer afternoon in the garden. He didn't have any experience with women, let alone two partners at once. His mouth opened, then closed again wordlessly.

John shut the door and approached, leaning down until his lips were close to Logan's ear.

"Should we finish what we started, Logan? I promised to teach you, but we never got a chance."

Logan's heart was pounding so loud that he heard John's words as if he were very far away. He found himself nodding along to John's proposition.

"Teach him? Did you bring me a delicious little virgin to corrupt, John?" Nia's hand slid up Logan's thigh, and he felt all the blood rush from his head to somewhere else, which definitely didn't help his ability to think coherently.

"I, uh..." Logan stuttered. Nia had a very sweet face; who could have guessed it hid this bold personality?

"Think it through, Logan. We won't do anything till you say yes. Right, Nia?" John assured him. But he was still so close, his body heat warming Logan's clammy skin. This time, there was no one pulling John's strings, no ulterior motive driving him.

Nia pouted, but her hands stopped their exploration. "Please say yes. It's been *ages* since I've been able to play with an untrained pup like you." Her pale lashes fluttered at him.

Logan glanced between the two of them. He'd always had a little trouble reading romantic or sexual situations. He'd often gone back to his bed alone after a night out with the crew only for them to tell him the next day that someone or another had been flirting with him the whole time. But this was clear even to him. And he was quite chilly with the winter storm raging outside...

"I...I might not be any good," he said.

Nia graced him with a warm smile. "Like John said, we can teach you." She took both of his hands between hers. "Dear lord! The fake hand is warmer than your real one. No need to be so nervous!"

Logan calmed slightly at her reassuring words. He would probably never get an opportunity like this again and even if he did he might not notice it. Besides, maybe this would put the unquiet memories of crushed flowers, buzzing bees, and John's mouth to bed once and for all.

"Okay," he agreed.

Nia's smile brightened even more. "Okay? As in you'll do it?"

"Yes." He was getting nervous again but he tried to push it aside.

"Oh, thank the gods, 'cause I'm already wet as that storm out there." She giggled and leaned forward to kiss Logan. Her lips were warm and soft and her tongue, when it slipped into his mouth, tasted vaguely of mint tea. She fitted herself between his thighs and moved his hands to frame her waist. Her tongue moved tantalizingly slowly, guiding his own tongue where she wanted it to go. She made a pleased little sound in her throat, and Logan felt the thin bed dip as John settled onto it, watching them.

Logan decided to be bold. He guided Nia off the floor and pulled her into his lap, her legs to one side and her ample buttocks nestled against his already swelling manhood. She wrapped one arm around his shoulder and began kissing him again, this time with more fervor as she felt his hardness pressing against her. Logan's arm supported her back, but thankfully his remaining real hand was free to explore. He cupped her breast and was met with a little sigh of pleasure.

"Maybe you don't need me to teach you," John chuckled. Logan glanced at him to see he was lounging against the pillows, lazily stroking his own naked cock as he watched them. This was Logan's first time seeing any part of John naked, and his pulse quickened. John's dick was massive. The two of them were of similar stature, but John was miles ahead of him in that department. It wasn't that it was especially lengthy. Logan estimated it to be of similar length to his own, but it was *thick*. Surely as thick as Nia's delicate wrist, if not more so. Logan's body shuddered at the sight.

"What a pervert you are, John. Me and..." She paused, looking at Logan with her wide green eyes sparking like chips of peridot. "Oh, I'm sorry, sweetie, I never asked your name."

"Logan."

"Very cute." She ran her fingers through his hair. "You look like such an angel; I almost feel bad for defiling you."

"Trust me; he needs it," John said. Nia shrugged and turned her attention back to Logan. She unbuttoned the top of Logan's shirt.

"I'm sure you won't look so innocent once we get these clothes off," she whispered to Logan conspiratorially. Logan's dick twitched in response, and she squeaked in delight.

Following her lead, Logan untucked Nia's blouse from the waist of her skirt and unlaced the stays beneath. His hand slipped beneath, and he took his time exploring her pliant flesh, slowly inching her blouse and chemise further up her waist as she continued unbuttoning his shirt and distracting him with mint-flavored kisses.

Before he knew it, they were both topless, and Logan trailed kisses across the freckles dotting Nia's peachy breasts. She moaned quietly, almost imperceptible beneath the sound of the driving rain. She pulled away after a moment, and Logan thought maybe he'd done something wrong. But she sank to her knees on the floor between his thighs and unbuckled his belt.

"Let's see what we're working with here." She pulled his trousers down his hips. When his cock sprang free, she all but clapped her hands delightedly. "Very nice," she cooed, and embarrassment flushed his face.

He bit his lip as she palmed his cock. Her hands were small, especially compared to John's. She stroked it a few times, smiling as an involuntary moan escaped him.

"You can let your voice out, sweetie. Otherwise how will I know what you like?"

When her warm mouth sank down around his cock, he didn't hold back the moan that escaped his throat. She cupped his balls in one hand, massaging them gently as her head bobbed, minty tongue swirling over the tight skin. John moved to kneel on the bed behind him. He ran his fingertips up Logan's bare chest, over the apple of his throat and tilted his chin up so Logan had to look at him. His deep-set brown eyes brimmed with lust and mischief.

"Do you like her better than me?" he teased, his hard cock pressing against Logan's back.

"N-no..." Logan stuttered as his cock slid deep into the back of Nia's mouth.

"Oh? Am I better then?"

"I don't... I mean...ngh..." Logan found he couldn't form a coherent sentence with Nia's mouth around him. He grabbed John by the front of the shirt and pulled him into a kiss instead. There was no question left in his mind that John wanted this. Wanted *him*. John's strong grip tightened on Logan's jaw, tilting his head further back to deepen the kiss. Nia hummed, her throat vibrating deliciously. Logan was sure he wouldn't last long this way, but he was determined to keep it together and actually see this through.

As if she had read his mind, Nia suddenly released him. She wiped a bit of saliva from her lip and sat back on her heels, observing his tilted back head, his bare chest and his aching erection. John didn't release him from the kiss as Nia pulled off Logan's trousers, boots and socks.

"Lay down," she ordered.

John finally broke the kiss but didn't release Logan. He raised his eyebrows at Nia.

"Ladies first."

"Oh, so I'm a lady now? I'm flattered." But her chest flushed pink as she stood. John released Logan's face to pull her closer. Logan was caught sandwiched between them, his face nestled in the valley between Nia's breasts and John's thick cock still pressing into his spine. Nia's skin smelled faintly of sweat and floral perfume. His mind flashed back to the flowers crushed beneath his back, and he inhaled the scent of her as John pulled her into a sloppy, open-mouthed kiss. Logan took her rosy nipple into his mouth, rolling it over his tongue. Nia gasped, and John petted the back of Logan's hair in approval.

John guided Nia to lay on her back on the narrow bed. He was still mostly clothed but for his cock poking out from his undone trousers. He bent over her and licked a stripe down her sternum, hitching her rose-pink skirts up her thigh with one hand. His eyes slid to Logan where he remained awkwardly at the edge of the bed.

"Watch and learn." He smirked. He pushed the layered skirts higher and spread Nia's thighs apart to expose the junction between her legs. Nia hadn't been joking earlier when she compared herself to the storm. The crotch of her underwear was flooded with moisture.

"So wet for me already," John teased, "or is it for him?"

Nia arched one red eyebrow. "Are you going to keep talking or use that mouth for something useful?"

John chuckled and pulled the underwear down her legs. He gripped her thighs and widened them a bit further, then ran the pad of his thumb over the edge of her soaked slit, pulling it back slightly to reveal the petal-like folds within. Logan had the feeling John was doing this for his benefit, and he couldn't take his eyes off her, observing with fascination. John's tongue followed the path his finger had taken the moment before. Nia gasped, clutching the pillow on either side of her head. John ran his tongue up the slit again and found the swollen nub within. Nia moaned as his tongue circled first one way then the other. He went slow at first, lapping at her juices with fervor and letting the pleasure kindle in Nia's core. Then he picked up the pace, varying speed and movement until Nia's back was arching off the bed, and the noises she made reached a desperate crescendo. Her legs trembled as she let out one final cry before her muscles seemed to go slack.

John sat up, not bothering to wipe the shiny juices from his lips and chin.

"Your turn," he said nonchalantly to Logan.

Logan was startled out of his concentration. "What? But I don't know how."

"You just saw how."

"Don't you want to taste me?" Nia cooed, reaching one hand out to Logan.

He very much did. He tentatively took John's place between Nia's legs. His cock was throbbing painfully, begging for touch. He kissed the inside of her thigh slowly, making his way to the furled petals of her center. He glanced at Nia, whose eyes were closed. Then at John who nodded encouragingly. Logan bent and pressed his tongue flat to her entrance and she gasped, already primed and quivering from John's thorough attentions. He gave an experimental flick, then ran his tongue up the slit until he found the pulsing pink bud.

It was soft textured yet firm on his tongue, tasting slightly of over-ripe peaches. He swirled his tongue clockwise, listening to the soft gasps and moans that fell from Nia's lips. He flattened his tongue against her clit before swirling it back the other way. He continued, varying pressure, speed and technique, repeating the ones that got the best reactions. He was so focused on the task that an extra gush of fluid against his lips accompanied by a shuddering moan surprised him. He raised his head to look at Nia. She was flushed pink from head to toe, chest heaving as if she was out of breath.

"Holy shit," she gasped. "I thought you said you've never done this before."

"He's a very diligent student," John said.

Logan sat up. "Was it good?"

"Fuck. Just come here, pretty boy." Nia grabbed him by the wrist and hauled him down to the bed. There was some shuffling as the three of them rearranged themselves on the narrow mattress, and Logan ended up on his back with Nia poised over him. She bent to kiss him, licking her own juices from his chin.

"Do you like how I taste?" she purred. Logan felt John's hand close around his cock from behind Nia, pumping him slowly.

"Yes..." Logan moaned. John placed something at the tip of Logan's cock and rolled it down over his shaft, sheathing it.

"Good. Because I'm going to absolutely fuck your brains out. Remember that sweet taste when you're screaming my name."

With one swift motion, she sank down, impaling herself on his cock, enveloping him in her wet softness. She let out a breathy exhale, and Logan almost came right then. He gritted his teeth, trying to hold himself together. Just like in the garden, he wanted this glorious sensation to last as long as possible. He wanted to make her come again, not to mention John who had barely been touched by either of them thus far.

Logan moaned deep in his throat as Nia began to rock her hips. Her skirts pooled around them like fallen petals, and her pink breasts bounced with every thrust. Logan was enveloped in her scent, the taste of her pussy still on his lips.

Logan's hips jerked up suddenly, burying himself as deep into her core as he could manage.

"Just like that," Nia moaned. "Fuck me..."

Logan did as he was told, thrusting his hips up to match her pace. John appeared by his side. He was still almost fully clothed but for that massive cock. Logan reached for it, running his fingertips up its length.

"I have a few more things to teach you," John said. He ran his fingers gently through Logan's hair, then gripped the soft blond waves tightly, pushing Logan's head into the pillow. He straddled Logan's face as Nia continued bouncing on Logan's dick.

John positioned the tip of his intimidating cock at Logan's lips. His grip on Logan's hair tightened further. Almost painful.

Logan was sure he looked terrified for a moment, then he steeled himself and nodded.

John plunged in, Logan's teeth scraping his monstrous girth. He pushed until Logan was choking on it then pulled back and plunged in again. The pulsing member cut off Logan's moans as it invaded his mouth. Logan's hips stuttered to a stop. But Nia continued to ride his dick as John fucked his face. Nia's voice filled the void that Logan's had left. Her sweet moans carried a rough edge, and somewhere in the back of Logan's overstimulated mind, he knew she was close again.

So was he. Somehow the choking shaft invading his throat was pushing him even closer to the edge of ecstasy. Drool ran down his chin. His eyelids fluttered, and he fought to keep them open. Nia cried out just as a crash of thunder shook the inn. Her supple insides clenched around him. He moaned around John's girth, and his hips jutted up to come deep in Nia's fluttering core. Logan's teeth scraped hard down John's shaft, and John growled at him. He pulled Logan's head roughly forward, forcing the entirety of his length down Logan's throat once more before pulling out completely.

John climbed off him, and Logan just lay there in a post-orgasmic daze. As soon as John was out of her way, Nia slumped down exhaustedly to nuzzle Logan's neck.

Logan felt John's fingers at the part where he and Nia were still connected. Nia lifted her hips to let Logan's softening cock slide out of her. Her warm breath feathered across his throat, and he stroked her back.

Logan watched John over Nia's shoulder as he rolled another sheath onto his own cock. Logan grimaced as he saw the angry red marks his teeth had left on John's shaft.

John knelt on the bed behind Nia, and she lifted her hips to meet him. He rucked her skirt up around her waist. His fingers ran languidly over the supple curve of her ass.

Nia's breath hitched, but she remained cradled against Logan's chest.

"John, I need you," she gasped.

John's deep-set eyes met Logan's, and he thrust hard into Nia's core. She cried out, filled to the brim with John's veiny girth. Her moan was guttural, teeth scoring Logan's collarbone as she clung to him for dear life. Logan pressed his cheek to her mussed red hair, but he didn't take his eyes off John.

John smirked as his next brutal thrust had Nia screaming his name. Her teeth dug harder into Logan's skin.

They were so different, these two people who had seduced him on a stormy winter night. John, powerful and efficient. Nia, luxuriously feminine. Yet both of them were so gorgeous and unfathomable.

John was breaking Nia apart bit by bit. Her whole body shook in Logan's embrace with every thrust. The noises she made and the friction of her soft stomach rubbing his cock was turning him on again. He cradled the back of her head with his wooden hand and reached down with the other. His fingertips found her sensitive bud.

"Mmmm, Logan..." she moaned, raising her head to kiss his throat. John smacked her ass lightly.

"You'd do well to remember who's fucking you right now," he growled.

"I can't help it. He's just so pretty," Nia whined.

John rolled his eyes and spanked her again.

"Our little pup is getting hard again," Nia informed him. Logan's fingertips were crushed to her clit on the next thrust.

"Is that so?" John smirked and pushed Nia gently forward till her and Logan's cheeks were pressed side by side. Her ample breasts heaved against his chest. John reached amongst Nia's rumpled skirts and found Logan's half-hard length. He stroked it slowly, bringing it back to its full potential.

Logan was already dizzily overstimulated as John positioned Logan's cock beside his own at Nia's entrance.

"Nia?" John asked.

Nia shivered but whispered, "Yes please."

John penetrated her first, then pushed Nia's pelvis down slightly to allow Logan to as well. Logan's mouth gaped wide in stunned ecstasy as he slid in beside John's substantial girth. Nia's walls fluttered and clenched as her body struggled to accommodate the stretch of both of them inside her. She whimpered.

John rolled his hips, and both Nia and Logan moaned in harmony. Logan's hips bucked up, relishing the pliant heat of Nia's interior that contrasted with the pulsing hardness of John's cock. Nia sucked the skin of his neck to muffle her moans.

John set a strong pace as Logan's hips stuttered again. As John pounded into her, it was almost as if he was fucking both of them at the same time. Both at the mercy of his masculine power.

Tingling ripples raced through Logan's nerves and stars broke across his vision. Nia's body shook uncontrollably in his arms, and she seemed to have lost her voice completely. Her mouth was simply open, lips pressed to Logan's sweat-slick throat in silent ecstasy.

Logan clutched their bodies tight together. Thunder rumbled as the tingles broke into a shattering orgasm.

"Fuck," John groaned. Nia's whole body clenched, and John

smacked her ass again. "Fuck, Logan..." With one last powerful thrust, his body shuddered, and he groaned as he came.

John stayed like that for a moment before pulling out and collapsing to the thin sliver of mattress not occupied by Logan and Nia's exhausted bodies.

"Now who needs to remember who he's fucking," Nia mumbled, reaching over to smack John's chest.

"Like you said. He's just that pretty," John replied breathlessly.

~

It was barely light out when Nia burst back into the room. After recovering from the afterglow the night before, she'd hastily thrown her clothes back on and left to sleep in her own bed in the attic. After cleaning up, Logan and John had climbed under the covers together and dropped quickly into sleep.

"Get up!" Nia said now, closing the door behind her. John was alert immediately, already grabbing his trousers from where they lay crumpled on the floor. Logan blinked sleepily. He rubbed his sore jaw, slightly regretting letting his first time giving head be with a man with such a massive dick.

"What's happening?" John asked.

Nia's hand was still on the brass door handle, her peridot eyes wide and frightened. "There's navy soldiers downstairs, and they're looking for both of you."

That brought Logan to full consciousness. He fought with the blankets and finally extricated himself from the bed.

"How do they know we're here?" John hissed.

"Don't know, but they have your names and where Logan's crew is holed up, and they're on their way up right now. Hurry."

Now fully dressed, John grabbed his bag from beneath the bed. He tossed Logan's hook to him and shoved its box into another knapsack. Logan strapped on the hook and pulled his coat on over it, ripping the sleeve. John gave him the bag.

"How long do we have?" Logan asked.

"Just—" Nia's words were cut off by the distinctive sound of military boots on the stairs. "Shit. I've gotta go. I had fun last night. Don't die." She winked and disappeared into the hallway.

A blast of shockingly cold air hit Logan's back, and he turned to see John with one leg already out the open window. He tossed his bag onto the roof of the shop half a story below.

"Come on." John climbed the rest of the way out the window and dropped down to the roof with a *fwump*.

Logan pulled on his boots and crossed to the window. The world below was completely changed from the night before. At some point as they'd slept, the rain had turned to snow. A thick layer of pristine white blanketed the rooftops in contrast to the streets below which were already a churned up, muddy and slushy mess.

"Toss it!" John called up. Logan dropped the knapsack into his waiting arms. Spurred on by the pounding boots which were now coming down the hall, Logan climbed onto the windowsill and jumped down after it. The snow was not as fluffy as it looked. It crunched beneath him, and his feet slipped as they hit the thick layer of ice it hid. John caught his arm, steadying him. He handed the bag back to him.

"Best to split up," John said regretfully, and Logan felt a pang of similar emotion. He didn't have feelings for John, not romantic ones at least, but parting like this after the night they'd just shared seemed too abrupt.

A crash sounded from their room as the soldiers broke down the door. John leaned over and planted a peck on Logan's cheek. "Next time, it'll be just the two of us. Good luck." He winked and released Logan's arm. Then jogged to the edge of the roof. One of the soldiers was trying, and failing, to climb out the window after them, his rifle catching on the frame. Checking that there were no soldiers waiting on the street, John dropped down into the mud without a backward glance.

CHAPTER 32

FEBRUARY 2ND, 1667

Rowan wasn't in the mood for drinks or noise or chit chat, but he found himself surrounded by people anyway. It had been more than a month since they'd arrived in Wave Harbor, and Rowan had barely left the *Siren Song* in all that time. Logan had admonished him for "brooding" before he'd left to try to track Cyrus down, and he must have given Fox the task of getting Rowan out of his isolation because that little shit had practically dragged Rowan, along with Gaël, Robin, and Henri, out to a dockside tavern that was absolutely bursting with other pirates.

Of course Fox and Gaël had absconded somewhere or another almost as soon as they got there. No doubt they were fooling around in some not-so-dark corner. He was happy for them. Really. They were in love and whatever feelings being back here had conjured up, they seemed to be handling it well.

That left Robin and Henri, who were unfortunately no better company. Rowan sipped his mead, letting the honey-sweet alcohol burn the back of his tongue as he watched Henri and Robin make moon eyes at each other. He was starting to get a headache, and his vision was playing tricks on him again, unfortunately an all too common occurrence since he'd lost his eye. Robin had said it wasn't unheard of for those who lost eyes to see things that weren't there, similar to the phantom pain of losing a limb.

Around them, pirates from all over the Islands drank, sang,

flirted, and fought. As a seafarer, there was nothing much else to do in the winter than this.

Logan was still out tracking down their leads on Cyrus, Fox and Gaël were pawing at each other, and Henri and Robin were in their own little world. Rowan may as well be alone in the crowd of his fellows.

Rowan had never really been lonely before, not even when he'd first been indentured to the navy. But he was now without...

"—eep Water Demon."

Rowan's gaze zeroed in on the woman who'd spoken the name. She was pretty, with bronzed brown skin and coily black hair that puffed up around her face like a cloud. She was dressed in black from head to toe with a red sash around her waist and a pair of ebony handled pistols at her hips. Her bare forearms were banded with the same sea serpent tattoos as Henri, and many other sailors of Yarene heritage, had. A form of protection from the ravages of the sea. She held court over a cadre of other pirates at a table not far from Rowan, her presence among them like a queen with her lowly subjects.

And she was talking about Yves. Rowan got up and sidled closer. Henri and Robin didn't notice that he'd left, too busy with each other.

"The *Kraken* is wintering at sea, and they're not slowing down either. I tell you it was like nothing I've ever seen. We were in the middle of a storm, but they still took on an Avardellan merchant. It was brutal. The Demon..." Her voice trailed off, and her eyes flicked up to where Rowan had inadvertently drifted too close, drawn by the flame of news about Yves.

The woman's gaze roved over him, lingering on the eyepatch and the still-fresh scars on his face. Then she smiled.

"So the Ghost Hawk has decided to join the land of the living finally." She took a sip of something that looked like spiced rum from a glass that was definitely too nice to have come from the tavern. "Have you come to hear about the exploits of the craziest bastard of us all?"

"Yes," Rowan answered. He'd told himself that he didn't need news of what or how Yves was doing, but that was just one of the many lies he'd been telling himself for months.

"Well then, take a seat, handsome." She snapped her fingers at one of the pirates who immediately vacated their seat. Rowan took it and set his cup of mead on the table. The woman leaned forward and held out her hand to shake. "I'm Zanta."

Ah. Splinter Zanta, the captain of the *Monsoon*. She was famous in the Sunrise Sea near Yarene and had gotten her nickname when she'd led a mutiny against her previous captain, Silver Stroud, and driven a large splinter through his heart, killing him. Rumor had it she still kept the bloodied splinter mounted over her bed.

Rowan took her hand and shook it. "Ghost Hawk," he introduced himself, even though Splinter Zanta seemed to already know who he was.

"I hear you've made some powerful enemies." Zanta swiped her thumb across his knuckles before releasing him. "By the looks of you, those rumors were right."

Rowan grimaced. It was the first time he'd been out in public since losing his eye. He resisted the urge to touch the eyepatch uncertainly.

"Unfortunately it seems that the law has caught up with me," he said, trying to play it off. "But what's this about the Demon sailing through the winter? Why?"

"Fuck if I know. I wouldn't want to be out there with that crazy bastard right now. He seemed... I'm not usually superstitious, but he seemed almost possessed. I could hear him laughing, and I don't think they even got any plunder. He just wanted to destroy the other ship. By the time they were done, there was nothing but debris floating in the waves." An almost imperceptible shiver ran through the listeners. The Deep Water Demon already had a reputation for brutality even among other pirates, but this seemed excessive.

Rowan frowned. Yes, Yves was known for brute strength, but he was also smart. Sailing into a storm on purpose and taking on another ship right in the middle of it? Destroying a ship so utterly that they couldn't plunder it? That wasn't like the Yves he knew. Yves was cold and calculated, and that served his particular brand of violence well.

So what had happened?

"That's not—" Rowan stopped himself before he could say more. But a spark of interest flashed in Zanta's eyes, and she leaned forward, propping her elbow on the table and her chin on her hand.

"That's not what? Do you know something, Ghost Hawk?"

Rowan remained silent, crossing his arms. Zanta's eyes flicked to the pirates surrounding them then back to him.

"Leave us," she said, low and commanding. With a little hesitation, the other pirates faded into the crowd. Zanta tilted her head where it still rested on her hand. "Tell me," she said quietly. "Tell me what you were going to say."

"It's nothing." Rowan tried to keep his expression neutral, but he must have given something away, because Zanta's eyes narrowed.

"You know him." It was a statement this time, not a question.

"Yes," Rowan admitted quietly. "We were...are rivals of sorts."

Zanta whistled. "Rivals... You've fought him before?"

"Yes."

"And who came out on top?"

Rowan nearly choked on his drink, but Zanta seemed not to notice the suggestive nature of her words. Of course she didn't. Who would assume that the Ghost Hawk and the Deep Water Demon had ended up in a weeks-long affair after practically destroying each other out on the open sea?

"It was a draw."

Zanta whistled again. Impressed. "I can't say that's expected. But considering you're here in front of me and not rotting at the bottom of the sea, I suppose it makes sense." Her expression grew serious, and she leaned closer to him over the table. She looked genuinely frightened. "A bit of advice, captain-to-captain, don't go looking for him now. He's...different. I don't know how to explain it, but it's like he's no longer human."

But why? Had something happened to him after Rowan left? Or was it *because* he left? Rowan couldn't quite believe that. Whatever Rowan's own feelings for Yves might be, it still felt impossible that Yves might feel the same. The infamous Deep Water Demon wouldn't be driven to extremes by something as simple as a lover leaving him.

Would he?

Rowan didn't want to know any more. His temporary curiosity over Yves was sated, and he just wanted to forget about him and move on.

"I'll heed your advice as much as possible. Maybe he won't survive the winter." A sour feeling curled in his gut as Zanta laughed.

The two of them sat talking until their drinks were finished. They traded stories about their exploits. Zanta confirmed the legend that she had stabbed her former captain with a splinter through the heart.

"I suppose the nickname is earned then," Rowan said.

"I suppose it is. Is yours?"

Rowan laughed. "I'm not sure. Do I look ghost-like? Or hawkish?"

Zanta tilted her head, regarding him. They'd gotten closer as the conversation went on, and he could see her pupils dilate slightly as she looked at him.

"You know..." Zanta leaned in further, running her hand up his thigh, never breaking eye contact. "I admire your work. And you're quite handsome. Why don't you let me keep you company tonight, and maybe you can tell me how you lost your eye?"

She really was beautiful, her tan skin and black leathers gleaming in the torchlight. His eye flicked down to her soft-looking lips which were slightly parted. Awaiting his answer.

An image sprang unbidden to his mind. Yves asleep and vulnerable at his side, pink lips still kiss-bitten. Yves in his dew-damp dressing gown in the morning mist. Yves watching him leave from the end of the dock at Illusion.

Rowan bit his lip, trying to mentally shove the unwelcome thoughts of Yves from his mind. He wasn't going to be drawn back into that devil's charms. He had to move on, and this would be a great opportunity to start. Nevermind that Splinter Zanta was another infamous pirate captain just like he and Yves. Baby steps.

Rowan placed his hand over hers, then ran his fingers lightly up her wrist. She was around the same height and build as Rowan, with added feminine curves in her hips and chest. She had a faint scar on her chin, but otherwise she was flawless from her head down to her heavy brass-buckled boots.

Zanta smiled and leaned forward, teasing him with the closeness of her lips.

"Shall we retire to the *Monsoon*? Or will you let me take you here in front of our fellow rogues?"

Blood rushed to Rowan's dick. It seemed that he was developing a taste for the bold charms of other pirate captains. That was a bit concerning, but he'd worry about that later. He closed the gap between their bodies and kissed her instead of answering. She wasted no time in slipping her hand up his thigh, her thumb pressing the head of his rapidly hardening dick. He moved his hand from her wrist to her waist, and his tongue played with hers in the confines of her deliciously warm mouth. Her tongue tasted of spiced rum and the honey cakes she'd eaten, a crumb still peppering her lip.

He let a quiet moan vibrate in his throat. The bustle of their surroundings fell away. He hadn't slept with anyone since Yves, and his body responded enthusiastically to the end of this short drought.

Fuck. He shouldn't have thought about Yves. Zanta palmed his clothed cock.

"Should we go?" he asked. He wanted to fill his senses with her. He knew this would likely be a one-night stand, or a short fling for the time they were both in Wave Harbor, but it was the first step on his road to forgetting Yves.

Zanta nodded. She took his hand and led him out into the cold, crossing the docks quickly to the pirate ship dubbed *Monsoon*. They stopped at the base of the gangplank, and Zanta captured his lips in another deep kiss. He let his hands wander over the ample curve of her ass.

They stumbled up the gangplank and down a short hall to Zanta's quarters. Rowan's gaze flicked over the room, simple like his own, with trinkets dotting the shelves and a wide shelf bed along the far wall. She distinctly did not have the bloodied splinter mounted over it as the legends said.

A shimmer like water in sunlight caught the corner of his eye, but it was just his vision playing tricks on him again. He turned his attention back to Zanta, running his fingers up her back and letting her tongue explore his mouth. She broke the kiss.

"I warn you"—Zanta giggled—"I'm a selfish lover. So I hope you're good with that tongue of yours."

I'm a selfish man, Rowan.

Rowan blinked, trying to dislodge Yves's voice from his consciousness and focus on Zanta. She was the person before him, the person touching him. And she had never had the opportunity to hurt him.

Zanta licked his bottom lip playfully before taking his hand to lead him further into the room. The shimmer flashed in his vision again.

But his feet wouldn't move. It was as if they were frozen to the floorboards. But it wasn't a problem with his body. It was his mind that wouldn't let him follow this gorgeous woman to bed.

His mind was full of Yves.

Yves kissing him. Yves's hands demanding against his body. Yves giving him pleasures he'd never known before.

The desperation in Yves's voice as he asked Rowan to stay.

He couldn't do it. Zanta was beautiful, a cunning and fearsome pirate, and Rowan had no doubt sleeping with her would be glorious. But he couldn't. He couldn't exile Yves from his mind and heart. Was this what Fox was talking about? Was this inability to forget Yves love?

No. It couldn't be something so foolish as that.

But he wasn't yet able to move on.

"Hawk?" Zanta tilted her head questioningly. She tugged his hand.

"I'm sorry. I have to go." Rowan released her hand and turned to flee back to the *Siren Song*.

~

ROWAN'S ERECTION still hadn't gone down by the time he made it back to his cabin on board the *Siren*. He couldn't get Yves out of his head. It was like he was under the spell of his seduction even when he wasn't here. It wasn't just that Yves had given him the best sex of his life over the few weeks they'd been together. It had been such a short time, but its impact in his life was proving disproportionately large. He feared that he would never be able to forget Yves's touch or the way he'd felt when they were together, the way they'd fit together. This yet-unnamed ache in his heart would persist forever.

Exactly as Fox said.

But while Fox had been able to forgive Gaël for leaving him, Rowan didn't think he could forgive Yves's betrayal.

Still, his lips. His skin. The silken strands of his onyx hair and the black sparkling depths of his eyes haunted Rowan's waking and dreaming hours.

And finally Rowan gave in. He stripped down and climbed onto his frigidly lonely bed. The bed where he'd first felt the sweet agony of Yves's cock inside him. He closed his eyes, remembering Yves's throat squeezing his cock. Rowan's hand closed over his own hard length. He began pumping slowly, letting his mind conjure up whatever images it wanted. He hadn't allowed himself this pleasure since leaving Illusion. Maybe as punishment, maybe because he knew it would make his cravings for the other man worse.

Fuck, he should have just stayed with Zanta and let her take the lead so his mind could wander back to Yves.

But no, that would have been a disservice to her. She deserved a lover who would please her enthusiastically. Not someone who was hung up on another. Besides, if Rowan was going to torture himself, it may as well be by his own hand.

Rowan's hand moved faster as a litany of images flashed through his mind. He rolled to the side and retrieved the vial of lube Yves had left from that first night. There was still a bit left. Just enough. He slicked some over his cock, then used the rest on the fingers of his other hand. He slipped his fingers into the crease and felt his puckered entrance. He pushed one finger in slowly, imagining it was Yves instead. It was tight, no longer used to the near-daily invasion of Yves's cock. Rowan gasped and bit his lip.

He continued to stroke his cock with the other hand. His fingers pumped slowly in and out of his hole. But he couldn't quite reach the right spot from this angle. He rolled onto his knees, and tried again. His fingers made a lewd squelching sound as they entered him, and he thrust in and out in time with the strokes of his cock. Yves would've already had him writhing with pleasure. His long fingers would have already brought Rowan close to completion.

Fuck. It wasn't enough. Not only were his fingers too short to reach the spot he wanted but also nothing he did to himself could compare to how Yves touched and filled him.

Rowan grunted and withdrew his fingers. He rolled back onto his back and stared at the ceiling. He continued to stroke his dick, but his heart wasn't in it anymore, and soon enough he gave up.

Would he ever be able to have sex or pleasure himself again without Yves being at the forefront of his mind? Rowan smacked the mattress in frustration. He squeezed his eyes shut, seeing Yves's cruel, handsome face behind his eyelids.

"Fuck you," he whispered. "I'm not coming back."

CHAPTER 33

FEBRUARY 11TH, 1667

"Hey you!"

Rowan stopped in his tracks, turning slowly to see none other than Splinter Zanta stalking across the docks toward him. It had been over a week since he'd backed out of sleeping with her, and he had the distinct impression that she wasn't pleased. He wanted to turn the other direction and flee. But he stood rooted to the spot as if the heels of his boots had sprouted and grown between the cracks of the dock.

"Zanta," he said, steeling himself to be berated. "What can I help you with?"

"Oh, don't give me that look." Zanta stopped just a few feet away from him.

"What look?"

She smiled, her hand resting casually on the handle of one of the pistols at her hip. "You look like you're about to be scolded by your grandmother."

He glanced down at his feet, bashful.

"You're doing it again! I'm not mad at you, you know. I think I'd be a jerk if I was."

Rowan looked back up, noting the way her breath curled in the frigid air.

"I can't say I'm not disappointed," she continued, taking a step closer. "I'm sure you had your reasons, but my offer still stands if you change your mind."

"So you're not going to scold me," Rowan teased, suddenly feeling much more comfortable around her.

"Not unless you're into that—"

"Captain!" Rowan and Zanta turned toward the familiar voice calling across the docks to see Logan sprinting toward them.

Logan slid to a stop, crashing into Zanta as his boots skidded on a patch of ice. She grabbed his arms to stop him from falling and almost collapsed along with him. They righted themselves with a lot of swearing and apologizing.

"Captain, I have to..." Logan paused, bending double and panting to catch his breath. He was windswept, exhausted, with a small pack on his back that was definitely not the one he'd left with. There was something different about him and for a moment Rowan couldn't place what it was. Then his gaze snagged on Logan's hands resting on his knees. Hands. Plural. In the place of the one he'd lost there was a beautifully carved wooden hand.

"Captain, I need to...tell you..."

"Logan, slow down. Just breathe. What happened? Did you find Cyrus?"

Logan took a few more gasps, then righted himself. "He found us. We've gotta fucking go right now. The Talvans know where we are, and they're coming."

"Fuck, how long do we have?"

"I don't know. They left before me. I got here as quick as I could." Rowan swore again.

"We have to go. Now," Logan reiterated.

"Go round up the rest of the crew at the Crown and Lion. It's two streets down on Amelia Street," Rowan ordered. Logan dashed off, and Rowan turned the other direction to return to the *Siren Song*. Zanta caught his arm.

"Wait. I don't know what's going on, and you don't have to explain now, but there are civilians here. A lot of civilians. Are the Talvans really going to attack or do they just want you? Should we go too?"

"I don't know. The Talvan navy is out to get us, and a port full of pirates would be hard to pass up. I think you should go." He looked out at the harbor full of pirate ships from every corner of the Islands resting at anchor. "And warn everyone you can on your way."

"Right." Zanta squeezed his arm. "Good luck."

"You too."

They parted ways. Rowan sprinted to the ship, his lungs prickling with winter air. By the time he got there, Logan and the crew members he'd rounded up had reached the docks as well.

They were underway quicker than they'd ever been, and across the harbor, Rowan could see other ships springing to life as well. But not enough. Either Zanta hadn't gotten to many or they'd decided to take their chances instead of heeding her call. The *Monsoon*'s fan-like yellow sails unfurled, and he could hear Zanta's voice, clear and sharp, issuing orders.

The *Monsoon* fell in line behind the *Siren Song*, riding the tide out of Wave Harbor. As they neared the harbor mouth, Rowan's heart lifted. He inhaled the wintry salt air, savoring whatever freedom he had left. Maybe they would make it out. Maybe they would make it on time.

No.

The *Siren* cleared the harbor mouth and rounded the rocky outcrop that bordered the western side, only to come face-to-face with a Talvan man-o'-war lying in wait like a lioness ready to pounce.

"Divert course!" Rowan shouted, as Logan yelled "Port! Port!" but their crew had already seen and acted. The *Siren* veered to port toward the open sea to avoid a head-on collision. They barely missed clipping the ship's starboard bow, and Rowan could see the Talvan crew swarming over the deck and lines, preparing to strike. Above them, the Talvan five-flower flag snapped in the winter wind. The sight of it sent shivers down Rowan's spine. It was a flag that meant only death for him and his kind. The ship's green lettering purported it to be the *K.S. Vaillant*, and a shaggy-maned lion figurehead graced its bow, jaws yawning wide to devour its enemies.

"Ready cannons!" Rowan shouted. He didn't want to get into a battle with an actual man-o'-war, but they might as well try to get a few shots off before they fled. The two ships passed close together, and as the *Siren*'s gunner crews scrambled to load the cannons below deck, the *Vaillant*'s gun ports opened with a bang. The cannons rolled forward, and Rowan found himself staring down the black maw of the barrels at eye level on the gun deck of the much larger ship.

"Down!" Rowan ordered, and his crew hit the deck just as a volley of cannon fire raked across them. Crew members screamed among the crashing and splintering of wood, and Rowan looked up from where he lay flat on his belly on the deck. One crew member clutched a splinter wedged in his side. Rowan sprang up.

"Get him to Beckett," he barked. Henri wedged his shoulder beneath the man's arm and hauled him below deck, one hand clamped over the bleeding wound. Rowan turned to the helmsman. "Get us out of here before they reload." It felt like it was taking forever to clear the massive ship. But they'd spent their cannons on this side. Several other pirate ships fled the harbor and turned east, away from his battle with the *Vaillant,* but with no luck—Rowan's eye snapped to two more ships flying the five-flowers closing in. The *Monsoon* had turned straight south, no doubt planning to flee into Yarene waters where the Talvans would be more hesitant to follow. It was one thing to raze a warren of pirates from their own colonies; it was quite another to invade the waters of a valuable trade partner. Good. He hoped the *Monsoon* would make it intact.

He jumped to his feet as the gun ports on the deck below him clanked open.

At the lead gunner's order, the *Siren* fired a full broadside into the lower decks of the *Vaillant.* Rowan didn't wait to see the damage it caused; he signaled his crew into silence, and all sound from his ship ceased except for the pound of footsteps and the clank of the gunners reloading as fast as they could. Daylight was fading, and he needed to take advantage of his crew's ability to operate without verbal command. Maybe it would give them enough of an edge to slip through the navy's clutches once again.

The boom of cannon fire carried across the water from the east where the other Talvan ships were in an all-out battle with the pirates who had tried to escape. No doubt those still at anchor in the harbor had heard by now. Whether they tried to escape as well or stayed in hopes that the navy wouldn't get that far, Rowan could only guess. He hoped that they wouldn't be wiped out. Different pirate crews may not be friends at the best of times, but he didn't want to be responsible for the Talvans wiping out a dozen pirate ships in one fell swoop.

The *Siren* finally cleared the *Vaillant*'s reach and tacked south away from the coast. Away from the harbor and its treasure trove of pirate ships and bounties.

"Captain." Logan grabbed his arm and pointed due west. A forest of masts dotted the waves below the horizon. "I can't tell who that is; can you?" Logan handed the spyglass to Rowan. But the ships were too far away to tell who they belonged to. The Talvans wouldn't send their entire armada, even if they did have a chance to wipe out a large amount of pirates at once. It had to be someone else. Rowan swore under his breath. There was no doubt in his mind each and every ship out there was an enemy. If they stayed to fight the *Vaillant*, it would be too late to escape when the other ships arrived. Their only chance to survive was to run. He signaled to the helmsman who banked the ship harder south. Maybe they could slip the noose and make it to Yarene waters as well. That would give them some reprieve to regroup.

But the *Vaillant* wasn't going to release its prey that easily. They turned and pursued. The *Vaillant* was no match for the *Siren*'s speed, but they were fast for a ship that size. The *Monsoon* was ahead of the *Siren* now, having spotted the armada as well and corrected course. Despite the full broadside the *Siren* and *Vaillant* had delivered to each other, neither seemed to have sustained critical damage. It was a shame; Rowan was hoping to hinder the *Vaillant* and make his getaway while they floundered in the pirate-infested waters.

There was still a chance to run, but before that, Rowan wanted the Talvans to know who they were messing with.

"Hoist colors!"

The huge flag, big enough to cover Yves's massive bed in Illusion twice over, climbed up the main mast. The white skull framed by upturned wings on a black field. The flag feared above all else aside from one. His crew whooped. Ahead of them, the *Monsoon*'s flag went up as well, a dripping red heart pierced by a splinter.

Three smaller ships bearing the Talvan flag rounded a promontory to the northwest and Rowan realized there were several more further away as well. The *Vaillant* wouldn't have to catch them after all—they just had to slow them down until the rest of the fleet arrived. Rowan swore under his breath. The *Siren* couldn't put on any more speed. They were already utilizing the wind and current to their greatest advantage. The three smaller ships gained on them with startling swiftness. He whistled for the gun crews to reload and be ready. It looked like they would have to fight after all.

The smaller ships surpassed the *Vaillant,* one veering toward the *Monsoon* and two bearing down on the *Siren.* When they had just about caught up, Rowan signaled, and the *Siren* swung around sharply, the sails slackened for a moment before catching the wind again and propelling them between the two ships. The Talvans were caught off guard as Rowan's gunners fired chain shot into their sails and rigging. Before they knew it, the *Siren* had slipped out from between them and was turning again, ready to rake them once more before either of them even got a shot off.

Not far off, the *Monsoon's* cannons thundered and its crew shouted, and further down the coast, the escaping pirates still battled the other navy ships. Something in Rowan thrilled at the idea that Yves's former homeland had sent this much firepower just to take him down. And there were more on the way. He raised the spyglass to the approaching armada. They were much closer now, and Rowan could just make out the red, black, and white flag of Marra. Its yellow sun blazed from between a bracket of red laurels.

So that was it. The Talvans had sent ships to take him out, the Marrans had seen an opportunity, and now they were stuck in the middle of yet another chapter of war between the two most powerful countries in the Islands. Rowan's cannons fired again as they passed one of the smaller ships. But this time the Talvans were ready. A volley of chain shot ripped through the *Siren's* rigging, snapping and tangling ropes and tearing holes in the sails. The ship banked toward them, intending to ram them and end this once and for all. If the *Siren* was immobilized and boarded, they were done for. Especially if the *Vaillant* had a chance to catch up.

But the *Siren* was nimble; they veered away just in time. Rowan turned to give Logan orders to send the snipers up into the rigging and stopped cold. A new ship rounded the rocky promontory. A ship that was achingly familiar from the two weeks they'd spend sailing side by side. The *Kraken's Fury* entered the fray with its colors already flying above a bloodred flag of no quarter. Yves intended to give no mercy.

Rowan pushed down the conflicting feelings that threatened to overwhelm him and tried to return his focus to the matter at hand.

But in no time, the *Kraken* came within range, meeting the *Vaillant* as it finally reached the action. Flaming arrows arched through the air to catch on the man-o'-war's sails and rigging. At the same time, another volley of the *Siren's* cannon fire punched through the hull of one of the smaller ships, and it began taking on water.

The winter sun slipped down the icy sky, plunging the battle into red and orange light. The *Siren* left the floundering ship and bore down upon the other. Rowan whistled a flurry of orders, but his gaze continually strayed toward the spot where the *Kraken* was engaged in close battle with the *Vaillant*. The larger warship was aflame now, but it still managed to pummel the side of the *Kraken* with cannon fire.

The other Talvan ship drew alongside the *Siren*. Sailors tossed grappling hooks over the rails and tried to pull the two ships together. A hook clanged against the rail to Rowan's left and he swiftly cut the rope to disengage. He sprinted down to the main deck. The crack of rifle fire sounded overhead, and he drew his pistol, aiming for the helmsman. The deck lurched as the *Siren* fired another round straight into the side of the other ship, but his bullet found its mark. The helmsman fell to the deck, blood blooming on his blue and green uniform. Rowan reloaded, and the cannons continued to bombard the side of the other ship. Hot iron shredded the wooden gunports, splinters flying. Sailors rushed around the deck, officers shouting orders till they were red in the face. Yet Rowan's crew was silent.

Until Fox let out a howl from the rigging that was taken up by the pirates on deck. The eerie sound carried across the water to the *Kraken's Fury* and was returned with full force by their fellow pirates. The sound seemed to dampen the Talvan sailors's ability to think. They hadn't fired their cannons in a while, perhaps their gunners were all dead. The *Siren's* gunners, however, were in top form. They continued their bombardment of the other ship, reloading faster and faster between every volley. The Talvans were on the back foot now. Their chain of command was disrupted, and they had no way to fight back without boarding the *Siren*.

With one last volley of cannon fire, the navy ship began listing to the side, quickly taking on water. In the winter weather, anyone who'd survived this long would soon freeze to death once they hit the water. A whoop of triumph echoed through Rowan's crew. Rowan looked to the west where the Marran navy still steadily approached. The *Monsoon* had managed to disengage from their attacker and was fleeing across the icy waves like a bird in flight, with the navy ship in pursuit. To the east, several ships were aflame but Rowan couldn't tell who was who anymore in the quickly darkening night.

The *Siren* turned to port, disengaging from the scuttled ship and ready to escape to open water. Rowan bounded up the steps to the quarterdeck. Behind them, the *Kraken* and *Vaillant* both blazed with fire. As he watched, the *Vaillant* veered to ram the *Kraken* with a sickening crunch. His gaze flicked over the deck, trying to spot Yves, but he was nowhere to be found amongst the chaos. Rowan lowered the spyglass, stomach churning.

He looked out to the open sea where they were headed, to freedom. The path was open but for the ship dogging the *Monsoon*. They could make a break for it and ride the currents to safer waters. They could leave all of this behind.

They could leave Yves and the *Kraken* behind.

He looked back.

"Shit." He stalked over to the helmsman, who backed off at the look in Rowan's eye. Rowan spun the wheel, turning the *Siren* sharply toward the ongoing battle. The two smaller ships were halfway sunken by now, the sailors either already in the freezing water or desperately clinging to the wreckage. Rowan ignored their strangled cries and chattering teeth.

Logan appeared at his side.

"Captain, we have a chance to..." He trailed off when he saw what Rowan intended. "So we're helping them then. Have you forgiven him?"

The question caught Rowan off guard. This wasn't a matter of forgiveness. He didn't have to forgive Yves to not want him to die, or worse, be captured by the Talvans and hanged in King's Square. He still respected Yves as a captain, even if he hated him.

His hand tightened on the spokes of the wheel. Who was he kidding? The world would be a duller place if Yves was no longer in it. The sea might lose its magic altogether if the Deep Water Demon no longer sailed its waters.

Besides, he'd promised they wouldn't be enemies.

Instead of answering, he said, "Stay on the ship Logan. I don't want you fighting."

Logan scowled at him. "I'm perfectly capable of fighting left-handed, and you know it. John even gave me a hook."

"John gave you..." So that's where he'd gotten the hand. And it also explained why the *Kraken* was here in the first place. He shook his head. "Doesn't matter. You're acting captain while I'm gone."

"Don't tell me you're going over there."

The *Siren* drew up to the other side of the man-o'-war, fire driving away the icy prickle of the sea air on Rowan's skin. A slow grin spread across his mouth. He drew his cutlass and raised it over his head as the *Siren* drew even with the tall side of the *Vaillant*.

"Prepare to board!" His shout rang over the crackle of the fire, stark and orange against the blackening sky. It was met with a roar from his crew. Without waiting, Rowan grabbed a charred rope that swung free from the taller ship's rigging, resheathed his cutlass, and climbed.

Pirates swarmed onto the deck of the *Vaillant* from both sides like a poison fog rolling in. As soon as Rowan's feet hit the deck he drew his cutlass again, slashing out at the first blue uniformed sailor who crossed his path. The man's eyes went wide with terror as Rowan skewered him through the gut. He yanked the sword back out, and the sailor fell to the deck. Rowan stepped over him.

The din of battle filled Rowan's ears, and he couldn't help that his heart swelled with elation and adrenaline at the sound. He slashed his way across the deck with Fox and Gaël at his back. The flames roared ever higher. Rowan didn't realize he was looking for Yves until he heard it, a sound unlike any he expected to hear on the battlefield.

Laughter.

The Deep Water Demon laughed as he killed. He cut a wide swath through their enemies, saber flashing in and out of bodies so fast it was all a blur of metal and blood. Gore coated his skin and clothes. His long black hair was slicked back with blood. And he laughed. Full and rich. A laugh of pure, maniacal joy. He was terrible and beautiful, wreathed in fire and madness.

Despite everything, desire sparked low in Rowan's belly, an unyielding urge to have those bloodstained hands caress his skin. To have those bared teeth mark him. It was a wholly illogical feeling. Rowan still hadn't forgiven Yves for his betrayal, but he was overcome by the desire to be possessed by Yves, body and soul.

Yves dispatched a Talvan officer and kicked out at another, severing the tendon at the back of his ankle with the sharpened spurs on his boots. The man's scream as he fell to the deck abruptly cut off as Yves stabbed him through the eye and moved on. Grinning all the while as if killing were the greatest joy in his life.

The smoke must have been playing tricks on Rowan's eye. For he thought he saw an amorphous shadow trailing along at Yves's back, inky dark and undulating like the sea. Rowan drifted toward Yves a few steps, heedless of the danger around him.

Someone crashed into Rowan, nearly knocking him to the deck. It was Fox, nose bloodied but otherwise unharmed.

"Get your head out of the clouds!" he barked at Rowan. "You'll have plenty of time to ogle him when we're not about to die." But there was a teasing tone to his voice, and when he smiled, Rowan could see that one of his front teeth was chipped.

Rowan plunged into the fray once more, working his way toward the center of the ship. If he could find the captain or some other commanding officer, he might be able to force a surrender. What a victory that would be. The Ghost Hawk taking down a Talvan man-o'-war in the dead of winter. Sure, he'd have to share the glory with Yves, but he found he didn't mind. He'd certainly shared much more with him than that.

"Captain, the admiral!" Gaël shouted.

Rowan turned in time to see Admiral Batteux fighting his way down the quarterdeck stairs toward them. Cyrus was nowhere to be seen. The stupid bilge rat was probably hiding below deck, afraid to face the mess he'd made.

"To me," Rowan ordered. Fox, Gaël, and several other *Siren* crew members formed up behind him. They fought their way toward the center of the deck, slashing and hacking at any blue-coated sailor who got in their way. The smoke thickened, flames spreading across the rigging and deck. It was only a matter of time until it reached the gunpowder stores, and then all of them would be fucked. He'd have to make this quick.

A knot of sailors accosted them. Rowan dodged one blade, only to be slashed across the forearm with another. Fox dispatched the man with a stab through the chest, and Gaël pulled Fox out of the way of the next man who stabbed at his neck.

"Keep going," Fox said, nudging Rowan forward. "We'll catch

up." Rowan nodded and managed to stumble out of the fray, slipping on a puddle of blood on the deck. The wound on his arm was shallow, but it stung like a bitch. He dodged a pair of *Kraken* crew members brawling with a rather large sailor and found himself at the base of the main mast. A piece of burning sailcloth dropped at his feet, and he lurched to avoid it, crashing backwards into someone.

Yves whirled, his face a rictus of violence, almost unrecognizable. He was beautiful, but it was the beauty of death, for death was all that lit his eyes. There was no recognition in them. No indication that he knew that Rowan was a friend, not an enemy. No indication that he knew him at all.

Yves swung, his saber whistling past Rowan's face. Rowan stumbled back, automatically raising his cutlass to deflect. But there wasn't enough time. Yves slashed again, and this time it barely missed slicing Rowan's cheek open. Rowan's heel caught on a piece of debris on the deck, and he landed hard. His sword clanged across the deck, out of his grasp. Yves bore down on him. He raised his sword, and Rowan tried to scramble back, but there was nowhere to go. His back bumped up against the unstable mast.

"Wait," Rowan gasped. But his voice was barely audible over the fighting and flames.

The sword descended.

"Yves!" Rowan threw his hand up.

The sword stilled.

Rowan looked up into those cruel black eyes that glittered with reflected flames. A lock of raven hair soaked in blood fell across Yves's forehead. Their eyes locked while the battle raged around them. The flickering orange flames cast strange shadows behind Yves's towering form. He was soaked in blood and gore as if he'd bathed in it, and in the shifting light, the black of his irises seemed to consume his eyes entirely.

"Yves, please. It's me." Rowan lowered his hand so Yves could see his face. The tip of the saber remained poised at his chest, ready to plunge into his heart and end it all. Yves's brow furrowed. His bloodstained lips parted as if to speak. And a little, just a little, of the murderous intent left his beautiful face.

"We promised not to be enemies," Rowan whispered.

Between one flicker of the flames and the next, recognition entered his eyes. There and then gone again. The sword lowered slowly, metal glittering, until the razor sharp tip touched the spot over Rowan's heart.

Rowan's breath hitched. As always, he was powerless in Yves's presence. But he raised his chin and met Yves's gaze. If he would die here by Yves's hand, he would make Yves watch the light drain from his eye. Even if the lust of battle had overtaken him. If he didn't recognize him. Didn't love him. Rowan could accept death if it was Yves who dealt it.

But of course it wasn't Yves that had him pinned to the deck ready to plunge a sword into his heart. It was the Deep Water Demon. Zanta had told him that Yves was fighting like a man possessed, and now Rowan could see it with his own eye. Yves didn't even recognize him. He only saw more blood to be spilled, another body to kill.

The burning mast groaned like a dying whale. Yves's head snapped up. With this distraction, Rowan batted the saber to the side and lurched to his feet. The mast groaned again, huge sheets of burning sail falling into the writhing crowd on deck. The mast was going to collapse; he could feel the death-rattle shudder of the ship beneath his boots.

"Yves," he pleaded. But Yves only gazed up at the flames high above them and past that, the black sky full of smoke and embers and stars all glittering and deadly. There was a hand-sized smear of bare skin on his cheek, clear of blood, and Rowan resisted the urge to fill it with his own bloody print.

A jagged fissure split the mast. The deck shuddered again. The mast listed toward them, then with a great *crack* it split free from its base. Rowan grabbed Yves by the front of his gold-trimmed coat and yanked him to the side just as the mast crashed to the deck in the spot they had just been. They stood face-to-face, Rowan breathing heavily. They were so close Rowan could have kissed him. But any small spark of recognition was gone from Yves's eyes now. He freed himself from Rowan's clutching hands, turned, and disappeared back into the fray.

Rowan made to go after him, but the deck lurched to the side. The *Vaillant* was going down, and he didn't want to go with it.

"*Siren!* Retreat!" His call echoed across the deck, repeated by the many voices of his crew.

Rowan fought his way back to the port rail. It was an uphill battle, the deck listing more and more to starboard, weighed down by the collapsed main mast. Fox and Gaël met him at the rail. Below, the *Siren* was drawing up alongside again. When it was close enough, they climbed over the rail and used the abandoned grappling ropes to drop down to the deck. What remained of his crew followed, but so did the Talvan sailors, desperate to escape their doomed ship.

"Round them up," Rowan ordered, before bounding up to Logan on the quarterdeck. "Get us out of here."

The *Siren* began to pull away from the side of the burning ship. Rowan hoped Yves and his crew had the presence of mind to return to the *Kraken* in time. He couldn't see anything of the other pirate ship with the sinking *Vaillant* blocking his view. More calls for retreat echoed over the chaos on deck. Sailors began jumping into the freezing sea and swimming toward the fleeing *Siren*. If they survived the plunge into the icy water and could catch up, Rowan would consider mercy.

"John!" Logan's voice cut through the noise. Rowan looked up in time to see the *Kraken*'s first mate dive over the side of the *Vaillant* which was now almost fully engulfed in flames. Logan ran to the rail, his eyes anxiously scanning the dark water. John surfaced, and Logan let out a sigh of relief. Rowan threw a rope to him, and together, they pulled John up over the rail.

John collapsed onto the deck, gasping and shivering.

"Get us some blankets," Rowan ordered a passing crew member. Logan helped John sit up. "What happened? Where's Yves?" Rowan asked.

"He's fucking crazy." John's teeth chattered, and his body shivered violently, the cold winter air coating his soaked hair in frost. "He's still up there."

No. Yves was still on the ship? Why? Rowan stood. The *Vaillant* rode low in the water now, enough that Rowan could see onto its deck. The sailors were still in a frenzy, trying every avenue of escape from the burning wreckage. On the other side, the *Kraken* still crackled with flame, but she was still seaworthy. Rowan ran to the rail, searching for any sign that Yves was alive.

Fox bounded up the stairs as Logan helped John below to get warm. He caught Rowan by the shoulders, grinning despite a splatter of blood across his face and the chipped tooth.

"Did you say it?"

"What? Fox we don't have time for whatever you're talking about. I have to—" He tried to look past Fox toward the other two ships.

"No." Fox's hands tightened on his shoulders. "This is important. Did you say it? Idiot, did you tell him you love him?"

"When would I have time to—"

A roar of flames interrupted them as the man-o'-war was completely engulfed. Rowan's gaze zeroed in on a lone figure standing still on the deck of the *Vaillant*.

Yves was silhouetted by the flames. He raised his arms as if he would embrace them. Over the roar of fire and screams of dying men, the Deep Water Demon laughed. He cackled like a madman, loud enough to carry over the water.

"Yves!" Rowan shouted. Desperate. If he could just get to him. Make sure he was alright— But Fox caught him again.

"The rest are coming. We have to go."

Rowan struggled against his hold, but Fox was right. The lights of navy ships loomed much closer, and more of the pirates in Wave Harbor had mobilized. The sun and laurel flags of the Marran navy swooped in from the west, and the Talvans approached from the east, ready to close in on the harbor like a frenzy of sharks who'd scented fresh blood. And the *Siren Song* would be caught between all of them if they didn't run. Now.

Rowan turned back but Yves was gone.

"We gotta go!" Gaël shouted from the main deck. The sails filled with wind, speeding them away from the death and destruction.

"No!" Rowan growled. He fought Fox's grip. He had to get to Yves. He couldn't be dead. He couldn't... Fox held him tight, and he sagged to the deck. The *Kraken*'s flag still snapped amongst the smoke, the grinning skull eerie in the firelight, the hourglass on its forehead proclaiming that time was up. As long as that flag still waved, he could hold onto hope. Hope that Yves would make it back to the *Kraken*. Hope that he was alive.

The *Siren Song* sailed into the vast night, slipping the noose of the law once again.

CHAPTER 34

MARCH 10TH, 1667

The blue waves beat against the side of the *Siren Song* in a lulling rhythm. Rowan let his mind wander as he gazed at them. He'd already been sitting there for an hour, his chin pillowed on his folded arms on the rail of the quarterdeck. He was fairly sure the back of his neck was red with sunburn, but everyone knew to leave him alone when he was like this. The few times Fox or Logan or one of the others had interrupted his "brooding," as Logan called it, he'd almost snapped their heads off.

It had been a month since they escaped from Wave Harbor. A month of not knowing whether Yves was alive or dead. A month of being haunted by the lack of recognition in Yves's eyes.

They'd laid low in the small fringe islands of Yarene for a while, avoiding any chance of Marran or Talvan ships spotting them. When supplies ran low, they ransomed the captured Talvan sailors back to their government.

Whenever they returned to port, Rowan asked after Yves and the *Kraken*, but all he succeeded in learning was that the *Kraken* hadn't been seen since that night.

Even as the weather warmed day by day, Rowan sank deeper into despair. After the hostage exchange, he ordered them to sail west. To himself and anyone who questioned it, he denied that they were on course for Illusion. But deep down, he knew that he had to find out what happened to Yves one way or another.

A flash of colorful light deep under the waves caught his eye. He squinted, trying to get a better look, but it was gone. He rubbed the scars next to his missing eye. Ever since losing it, he'd been seeing things. Shadows out of place, flicks of color in the corner of his vision. It was even worse when he wasn't wearing the eyepatch. He was unsettled by it, worried that maybe he was going mad despite Robin's gentle reassurances.

A shadow darkened the waves, but it was not some hallucination this time. Rowan turned to see Gaël standing at the rail by his side. They'd become friends over the winter, and now Gaël was almost as close to him as Fox or Henri was. He was an easy man to like, and Rowan could see why Fox was so smitten with him.

"Sorry to interrupt Captain, but the *Monsoon* is hailing us."

Rowan sat up straighter and looked behind him. Indeed, there was the *Monsoon* sitting upon the glittering water as if nothing terrible had ever happened to it. Its yellow sails were in the process of being furled, and the pierced heart flag snapped in the balmy spring breeze.

Splinter Zanta walked across the gangway with the self-assurance of a woman who had recently escaped death. Rowan felt a sense of camaraderie with her now. Maybe because he still felt a little bad about rejecting her; maybe because they'd faced certain death and both came out unscathed. Whatever the reason, it seemed she felt the same way.

"Lo! I'm glad you survived, Hawk!" she shouted jovially as her boots hit the deck. She strode up and clasped Rowan on the shoulder. "I was worried when we left you behind. But it seems like you made it unscathed."

Despite his melancholy mood, Rowan smiled, the bottom edge of his eyepatch digging into his cheek.

"Can't say I'd do it again. But I'm glad you made it out too. Have you had any news of the others? Is Wave Harbor officially a no-go now?"

Zanta's lips pursed. "You haven't had news?"

"We've been avoiding the main ports."

"Then you don't know." Zanta looked simultaneously sickened

and giddy at whatever news she was about to impart. The members of Rowan's crew who weren't busy with various tasks had gathered around at his back, eager to end their self-imposed isolation from the outside world. Rowan felt Logan's presence close by and saw John watching from the upper deck out of the corner of his vision.

"Heard what?" Rowan asked.

"The Deep Water Demon is dead."

Those simple words, said so matter of factly that at first Rowan thought he had misheard her. That his fears and anxieties were playing tricks on him, just like his eye was. Henri gripped his arm, steadying him. It was as if he'd suddenly plunged straight through the deck beneath his feet into the depths of the ocean. He sank down and down, the sounds around him muffled, the darkness pressing in. Distantly, he heard Gaël's voice.

"How?"

But he couldn't hear Zanta's response. Couldn't breathe. The water pressed in on his chest with all its massive weight, forcing the breath from his lungs. Yves was dead. Rowan would never see him again. Never touch or kiss him again. And suddenly, living was too much to bear. He wanted to succumb to the water that fought to claim him. He took a big gulp.

Air. Of course it was air. He wasn't sinking to the bottom of the sea but standing on the deck of the *Siren Song*. He blinked, resurfacing to reality. Henri's grip was hard on his arm, keeping him upright. And Zanta was staring at him with a look of confusion and concern.

"Ghost Hawk?" Her voice was tentative.

"How?" Rowan managed to bite out. "How did he die?" Out of the corner of his eye, he thought he saw John sit down hard on the top step of the quarterdeck, head in his hands.

"I talked to one of the crews that escaped the harbor after we left. They said they saw it with their own eyes. That big Talvan warship was sinking; the collapsed mast got caught on the *Kraken* and dragged it down with it. Even if the Demon did survive the fire and the battle, no one could have survived that cold water for long."

For the past month, Rowan had tried so hard to convince himself that Yves was alive. He'd told himself that Yves had avoided the flames and made it back to the *Kraken*, that the reason no one had seen the famous ship was that they were laying low on Illusion. But now there were witnesses. Now he knew the *Kraken* was gone, and if Yves had survived the battle, he'd gone down with his ship.

Rowan sucked in a shuddering breath. His heart clenched painfully, and he raised a shaking hand to clutch at his shirt. Fuck. Why did it hurt so bad? Why did it feel like everything was over? Why...

Why would Yves be taken away from him before he could tell him he loved him?

Rowan had spent so long denying it to himself. So long pretending the only thing between them was lust. But if that was true, why did Rowan feel like he was drowning? It was only now that Yves was gone that he could admit he loved him, but it was too late.

"Rowan... Rowan..."

Rowan realized he'd fallen to his knees on the deck, one hand pressed hard to the sun-warmed wood, and the other clawed at his chest as if he would rip his own heart out to stop this pain. Fox knelt beside him, one arm around his back.

"He could have survived," Fox whispered. "He could have. We should go back..." Fox looked up at Zanta who was staring down at them, horrified and confused. "They didn't see the Demon himself die?" Fox demanded. "They just saw the *Kraken*. He could have lived right?"

Zanta took a step backwards toward the gangplank. "I... They didn't see the Demon himself but..."

"See?" Fox turned back to Rowan, his hand massaging soothing circles between his shoulder blades. "We should go back."

The smallest hope sparked in his despair. Fox had always been good at shining a light in the darkness. Rowan squeezed his eyes shut. They were pirates, and their time on this earth was finite. What Yves had done didn't matter now; Rowan couldn't afford to hold his grudge any longer. Not against the one man he'd ever loved. If Yves was alive, Rowan needed to take whatever time they had left together and hold it close. He wouldn't waste any more of it.

His eyes snapped open, and he realized that Zanta had retreated back to the *Monsoon*. He got to his feet with Fox and Henri's help and turned to face his gathered crew.

"Set sail for Illusion."

∾

APRIL 1ST, 1667

Darkness wrapped its comforting arms around the *Siren Song* as it finally reached Illusion. Rowan hadn't expected to see any lights from the island, secret as it was, yet the lack of visible habitation spiked his worry even more.

"We'll have to wait till it's light out. I've never navigated these rocks in the dark," John said from beside him. After the initial shock, he hadn't seemed to outwardly grieve Yves's supposed death. Maybe he stood to inherit the pirating empire; maybe he just didn't care.

Waiting was something that Rowan was very bad at. But it seemed he had no choice in the matter. They anchored the *Siren* on the eastern side of the island and waited.

Rowan knew he should try to sleep, but the dark hours passed endlessly and sleeplessly. Rowan paced the deck, stopping every few steps to glance at the island. With every moment, he believed more and more that the rumors were true. Yves was dead. Rowan had missed his chance for reconciliation and the finite time they had together was at an end.

Rowan still hadn't slept by the time the sun peeked over the horizon, casting his shadow out long before him in red and gold. That was a bad omen if there ever was one. A red sky on the morning of the fool's day. And what a fool he was, to have wasted what little time he and Yves could have spent together. The crew woke around him, giving him a wide berth as they went about their duties. John appeared at his side again, calm and implacable as always.

"No one's come out?"

"No," Rowan answered. He was sure he looked a fright, the gray bags of sleepless worry hanging beneath his eyes. He'd hoped to see a boat rowing out in the morning light. To know that Yves was here. Safe. That he was coming for Rowan just as he'd promised.

"Best get to it then." John strode toward the quarterdeck where Logan stood at the ship's wheel. A look passed between them as Logan handed the wheel over to John's command then began issuing orders to the crew in the rigging. "If we don't catch this tide right we'll have to wait till evening to get in."

Rowan watched with apprehension as John deftly steered the *Siren* between the rocks toward the harbor's hidden entrance. He held his breath as they passed through, the cliffs drawing back to reveal the *Kraken's Fury* sitting at anchor in the calm water. Rowan sighed, but his relief was short lived. The *Kraken* was in bad shape. It rode low in the water, two of its masts were charred down to half their height, and the whole ship looked as if it had been chewed up and spit back out by a real kraken. But it was here. That meant Yves had to be okay too. Didn't it?

They anchored beside the *Kraken* in silence, and Rowan brought nothing with him as he boarded the landing boat. His nerves sang with dread with every stroke of the oars that brought them closer to the shore and the truth. There was no movement on the shore, not even fishermen preparing their nets. When the boat bumped against the docks, Rowan leapt out before the crew even had a chance to tie up. And he was gone, sprinting up to the manor house at the top of the lane like the devil himself was on his heels, barely noticing the black ribbons that adorned the porches and doors of the cottages, lank in the still morning air. It wasn't until he reached the main house, his hand closing around a ribbon's silky length where it was wound around the door handle that Rowan's mind even registered them.

Mourning ribbons, meant to guide the spirits of the dead and lost home.

And here one was on the door of Yves's house.

Rowan raked in a shuddering breath, then yanked open the door and sprinted up the grand curving staircase to Yves's bedroom on the second level. At this hour he might still be asleep, but Rowan didn't care. He didn't bother knocking, just wrenched the door open and...

The room was empty, the crisp white linens on the bed perfectly arranged as if no one had slept there in months.

Tears prickled at the back of Rowan's eye, and he pushed down the urge to scream. Yves could be elsewhere on the island. Just because he wasn't in his room didn't mean he was gone for good. He could be visiting Ana. He...

Rowan dashed the back of his hand across his eye, but no tears had fallen yet. He retreated from Yves's room, closing the door behind him.

He stood in the hallway for a moment, catching his breath, trying not to let dread overwhelm him. Yves couldn't be dead. Rowan would have *known*.

Rowan barely registered the click of the door next to Yves's room opening. But his gaze turned to it anyway, some instinct drawing him toward the sound.

Yves stopped short when he saw Rowan. He stared as if what he was seeing before him was an apparition. Something dearly wished for but not real. Rowan stared back. Yves was here. Alive. He had spent months anticipating, dreading, questioning this moment. Now that it was here, he was paralyzed with fear. Did Yves recognize him? Did Yves even still want him?

Yves was the first to move. He ran forward and yanked Rowan into a crushing embrace. Rowan wrapped his arms around Yves's thin waist, their bodies pressed so tight together he could barely breathe. Just a month ago, the bloody tip of Yves's saber had been pressed to Rowan's heart, no recognition in his eyes. But that didn't matter now. The feel of Yves's body against his, the sound of his heartbeat was so familiar yet so foreign to Rowan's senses, like finally coming home after a long time away.

He heard a strangled sound and realized the Deep Water Demon, terror of the seas, was crying. Crying for *him*. Tears pricked in his eye, not of sadness, but of relief. Joy. It felt so right to have Yves in his arms again. He pulled back a bit, intending to kiss the living daylights out of the taller man. Yves gasped.

"Your eye..." He cupped Rowan's face between his elegant hands, running one thumb over his cheek beneath the eyepatch. For a moment Rowan was gripped with the irrational fear that his scars made him ugly in Yves's eyes. That Yves would turn him away.

"Who did this to you? I'll..." But Rowan was kissing him, and Yves surrendered his rage to it. They stumbled into the room Yves had just exited. It was plain, with a large desk, empty shelves and a large four-poster bed in the center. The tall windows looked out onto the harbor below where the *Siren* and the *Kraken* sat side-by-side at anchor.

Rowan had Yves half undressed by the time they made it to the bed. He didn't know what had suddenly come over him. Maybe it was the months and months of missing Yves or the long winter in his own cold bed. But now he needed to be as close to Yves as humanly possible. To feel his touch again. The final realization of his feelings for Yves was still raw in his heart. He hadn't confessed yet, and he didn't know if Yves felt the same, but it didn't matter. They were here now. Together.

For once Yves let Rowan take the lead, surrendering to Rowan's whims and desires. Rowan stripped off the last of his clothes and pushed him onto the bed, leaving him clothed only in his ruby earring and rings. There was not a mark on him, besides the one Rowan had left all those years ago. How had he survived the battle uninjured when everyone was so sure he had perished?

He was even more beautiful than Rowan remembered. Ethereal. Rowan almost couldn't recall why he'd left in the first place.

He stripped off his own clothes and knelt by the side of the bed, taking Yves's cock in hand and stroking it. He leaned forward and pressed his lips to the velvety skin.

"Is this okay?" he murmured, remembering Yves's need for control.

"Yes," Yves gasped, "please..." He was already breathless, and Rowan had never seen him so vulnerable. It was almost frightening.

Rowan licked the tender underside of Yves's cock, relishing the moan that escaped the other man's perfect lips. Then he took the tip between his lips, watching Yves's long fingers twist into the sheets. He let the thick member slide slowly into his mouth. He couldn't take it all but went as far as he could, compensating with his hand around the base.

"Rowan..." Yves moaned. He seemed already lost to bliss, and Rowan wondered what had happened over the winter to make such a difference in him. He'd gone from a powerful and controlling sex demon to a whining puddle of need.

Rowan couldn't say he didn't like it.

Yves's hips began rolling in time with the bobbing of Rowan's head, pushing deeper and deeper into Rowan's throat until he was gagging. Yves's fingers tangled in Rowan's hair, holding him in place to take the thrusts until his eyes watered. He gagged again, and his teeth scraped down the shaft. Yves pulled Rowan's head back, releasing his cock from Rowan's mouth.

"That's enough." Yves's mood had shifted. He was done playing at submission. His voice was low and rough, almost like a real demon. Rowan looked up at him through tear-blurred eyes to see Yves already gazing at him with a passionate, burning fire. He pulled Rowan down onto the bed and rolled him so the back of his head was pressed into the pile of plush pillows.

"Now you're back where you belong," Yves purred, pressing his lips to the fluttering pulse at Rowan's throat. "Here. Beneath me."

Yves's words should have made Rowan feel trapped, but they

exhilarated him. Rowan tilted his head to give Yves better access to the tender flesh of his neck. His body shuddered as Yves's teeth nipped at his skin. This was where he belonged, skin to skin with Yves.

"Gods, I missed you," Rowan said before he could stop himself. He felt Yves smirk against his skin.

"There are no gods here. But please tell me exactly what you missed about me all those winter nights alone. In detail."

Yves's mouth traveled down to Rowan's pert nipple, his tongue flicking over it teasingly. He moved his hand to Rowan's already weeping cock but didn't touch just yet. When Rowan didn't answer right away, their eyes met.

"Well? I'm waiting."

Rowan wiggled his hips, but Yves withdrew his hand just beyond touch. So that was how he was going to play it? Tease Rowan until he got his answers? Well Rowan would take that challenge. And win. All he had to do was drive Yves crazy first.

He took Yves's hand in his, but he didn't try to wrap those beautiful fingers around his cock as Yves expected.

"I missed you right here," Rowan said in a low voice. He guided the tips of Yves's fingers to his puckered hole. His dick twitched at the contact, and Yves's eyes darkened. "I missed you inside me..." he continued, guiding Yves's fingers to rub circles around the rim. He kept their gazes locked, watching every little flicker in Yves's expression. "I missed you fucking me till I passed out and making me come over and over again. I missed—" He inhaled sharply as Yves slicked his own finger with spit and dipped it into him, retrieving a suspiciously convenient bottle of lube from beneath the pillows with the other hand. After months of neglect, the sensation was electrifying.

"Did you save yourself just for me?" Yves teased. But Rowan could tell he was pleased at the thought that only he received the privilege of having Rowan in this way. Of being inside him and connected to him.

Rowan didn't answer. His back arched as Yves moistened his fingers with lube and pushed another finger in too soon, the sting of it causing Rowan to gasp. His thighs fell open a little further, and Yves settled between them on his knees as he worked Rowan open. He seemed as impatient as Rowan was. They'd waited long enough and almost died, after all.

"Please just fuck me," Rowan whined. Yves smirked at him and sped up the ministrations of his fingers, never breaking eye contact. He bent to run his long tongue over Rowan's shaft.

"Is this all you missed about me?" Yves cooed, but there was an edge to it. "That I can fuck you and fill you up just how you like?" His tongue skimmed the pink rim of the head of Rowan's cock. The fire blazing in Yves's dark eyes reminded Rowan of that night when he'd come to Rowan's rescue. The orange flames against the black water and sky were still vivid in his memory. The violent power present in every line of Yves's body that night had shaken him and made him question whether he knew the man at all. It had been as if Yves transformed and was no longer just a man, but had become some otherworldly creature that held no regard for human life.

And Rowan could still see it now, the potential for unspeakable cruelty contained in that lithe and perfect body. But it was not cruelty anymore and not toward him. That flawless skin held only one mark, one sign of weakness. And Rowan had put it there with that long ago bullet. Only Rowan could pierce the armor of savagery Yves had clothed himself in to get at the softness within. Only Rowan could devour this body made for violence and strip him down to his vulnerable soul.

With every passing moment that Rowan didn't answer, Yves stretched him wider, stroked his tongue over Rowan's quivering cock. Yet his facade was cracking. Of course Rowan hadn't only missed the physical pleasure Yves could give him. He'd missed that wry smile Yves had when something amused him. He'd missed Yves's clear fealty to the sister who had raised and protected him, the slight wheeze at the end of his rare laugh. He'd missed...everything.

Rowan was the one man on earth who could wound him. But he never would.

"Stop," Rowan gasped.

Yves's body went still, poised mid-lick. He withdrew his fingers reluctantly, confusion marring his brow.

Before he could say anything, Rowan hooked one leg around the back of Yves's knee and flipped him over. Yves let out a small huff of surprise as he was pressed into the downy mattress beneath Rowan's smaller frame. Rowan gripped Yves by the nape of the neck, forcing his head up to crash their lips together. His tongue slipped into Yves's hot mouth, and his hips rucked against him, drawing a moan from them both.

"You talk as if your place isn't inside me," Rowan said. Yves gripped his hip as the friction between their bodies increased. "As if you haven't imagined this a thousand times since I left. I see you, Yves. And that's why I missed you. Not just because you can wreck me like no one else but..." He still couldn't say it. *Why* couldn't he say it even now with Yves moaning beneath him and looking at him with those shining dark eyes? It should have been simple. Only three words to change everything.

I love you.

But it wasn't simple. So he kissed Yves once more and straddled his hips. He wasn't quite prepared enough, but he didn't care. If he couldn't say those stupid simple words, he would show it.

Yves's grip tightened as Rowan positioned himself over Yves's cock.

"You're not ready," Yves protested even as his cock twitched in anticipation as Rowan reached back to guide it.

"I don't care. I've been waiting for this all winter." He sank down slowly, wincing as Yves's monstrous thickness stretched out his slick walls. The coconut scent of the lube permeated his nostrils, and he threw his head back as he sank further and further, feeling every throbbing vein. Tears pricked the corners of his eye again, not from pain but the sudden release of pent up emotion.

"Fuck, Yves. I missed everything about you. They told me you were dead and..." A noise escaped him, half moan, half sob. The tears spilled over as he finally looked back down at Yves. Would this be enough for Yves to understand how he felt?

Yves's thumbs rubbed circles into Rowan's hips. His pelvis jerked up, fully seating himself inside Rowan's body. Rowan gasped. Then Yves sat up, supporting Rowan with one hand splayed across the small of his back.

"But I'm not dead." His mouth skimmed Rowan's collarbone. "As you can see, I'm here with you." His dick twitched deep in Rowan's core as if to illustrate the point. He pulled back slightly to see Rowan's face. "Don't cry now, even though you look so pretty when you do."

Rowan let out a shaky laugh, still sniffling a bit and rolled his hips so that Yves's shaft rubbed his supple pink insides. Rowan's own cock grazed Yves's stomach.

"So tight," Yves groaned. "Just like the first time I fucked you."

Rowan began to ride him, angling every stroke to hit the spots he needed. He was quickly becoming breathless with pleasure, his hips already aching from the unfamiliar movements. Yves watched him hungrily, his hand moving from Rowan's hip to finger the place where they were connected. He slipped the tip of his pinkie inside, stretching the rim of Rowan's hole even more. Rowan cried out, his hips stuttering to a stop.

"Can't take more?" Yves pouted. "I think you can. Maybe someday I'll show you just how much I can do." Rowan didn't know what he could possibly mean, but his body shivered with anticipation all the same. Yves swirled his pinkie around his own shaft, stretching Rowan's rim and eliciting another gasp. Yves smirked. "So sensitive."

Then Rowan was on his back, with not a clue how he'd gotten there. Yves slicked more lube over his own cock and hitched both of Rowan's shaky legs over his shoulders before thrusting powerfully in again. Rowan covered his own mouth with his hand as Yves's cock hit his prostate and sent an agonizing rush of pleasure through his body. Yves thrust again and again, his hips smacking against Rowan's ass with every stroke. Rowan pressed his hand tighter to his lips, muffling his cries of ecstasy.

Without stopping, Yves grabbed Rowan's wrist and wrenched it away from his mouth, forcing it down to the bed and holding it there.

"None of that, darling. I want to hear you scream for me."

And Rowan did scream. That delicious cruelty Yves exuded poured out of him with every brutal thrust. He cried Yves's name over and over like he was once again asking to be saved. Begging for every last thought, every ounce of self-consciousness and stupidity that kept him from confessing to be beaten out of him from the inside out.

Yves delivered. He was merciless. Powerful. And his black gaze never left Rowan's face even for a moment. He drank in the sight of his ruination like the finest wine. He licked his lips as the filthy squelch of his cock created a rhythm beneath the siren song of Rowan screaming his name.

He bent and kissed Rowan's parted lips, folding Rowan in half in the process and reaching newly agonizing depths.

"Rowan," Yves groaned, his voice full of all the grief of their long separation.

His free hand wrapped around Rowan's cock to stroke him, the other taking his weight and pressing Rowan's wrist painfully into the mattress. But Rowan didn't care about the pain. Pain was part of living, and right now pleasure outstripped it tenfold. He was losing his fucking mind with sensation now coming from the front and back. It felt like being battered by waves in a hundred-year storm. His torment and salvation was Yves. It would always be him.

Rowan choked out Yves's name one last time, and the storm pulled him under. His seed spilled hot and abundant across Yves's hand. For a moment, what remained of his vision was all darkness and stars. Yves rode him through it, and after a few more overstimulating thrusts, his cock throbbed out his own orgasm deep in Rowan's guts.

Rowan's consciousness swam back to the surface as the pressure on his wrist released, and Yves cupped his cheek. When Rowan's blue eye refocused it was to see Yves smiling down at him, a sheen of sweat across his brow and black hair disheveled. He gave one last feeble roll of the hips, causing Rowan to whimper. Then pulled out and collapsed beside him.

They lay tangled and exhausted, both content beyond reason.

"I suppose we should get up before John finds us here," Rowan laughed breathlessly. The sun had risen further, and the room was lit with golden morning light. He assumed it was John's room, based on the size and bareness, and felt momentarily embarrassed. Who else's could it be but the second in command? He didn't want the stern first mate to know how they'd defiled his nice clean bed.

He felt Yves's body go very still but couldn't see his face.

"He's alive?" Yves's voice was very quiet, almost as if he dared not let himself hope. Rowan tried to sit up, to look at his lover, but Yves's arms tightened around him.

"Tell me."

"He's alive," Rowan assured him. "He's been sailing with us all this time."

The tension went out of Yves's body, but he did not let Rowan go. Then he laughed.

"There's no need to beat a hasty retreat," he said. Rowan could feel the smile in his voice. "This room isn't his; I made it for you."

Rowan pulled back to look his lover in the face, astonishment plain in his expression.

"I'm not trying to keep you," Yves assured him quickly. "I just thought..." He huffed out an exasperated breath at his own stumbling words, then seemed to collect himself. He ran his fingers through Rowan's messy hair, looking intently into his one remaining eye.

"I made this room for you, because I want you to make a home here. If you wish. I want us to be partners." He smiled, an edge of sadness on his lips as if he expected Rowan to reject him outright. When Rowan only stared, he continued, "Darling Rowan, I love you."

Rowan's heart clenched painfully. Then, when the full weight of Yves's words sank in, a curious warmth spread throughout his body. He blinked at Yves for a moment. His injured eye ached, causing dark flickers to dance in Yves's shadow, but it didn't compare to the ache of longing in his heart. Yves looked as if he was about to cry again. His thumb rubbed over Rowan's temple.

"R-Rowan." He fumbled with one of the rings on his finger, a practical, sturdy silver band studded with small sapphires and emeralds. Not the elaborate style of the Deep Water Demon at all. "Will you marry me?"

Rowan sucked in a deep breath, trying to calm himself. Again that nagging feeling that in the past this would have made him feel shackled, owned, but all he felt was a sense of peace spreading through his chest. He had a home. A true home. And it was here in Yves's arms.

"Yes," he breathed, and was gratified by the brightest smile lighting Yves's lovely face. An almost hysterical laugh bubbled up from Yves's lips, cut off before it could fully form. But Rowan wasn't done. He took Yves's face between his hands, looking into his eyes. They were a clear night on the open sea, vast and dark and full of stars. Rowan could have navigated the *Siren* by those eyes. And they would always lead him to safe harbor. "I love you too."

The tears that had been threatening finally spilled over onto Yves's cheeks. He buried his face into Rowan's neck.

"You have no idea how long I've been waiting to hear those words from you. I...I never meant to keep you. Not really. I only wanted more time to gather my courage to confess this weakness to you."

"Loving me is a weakness?" In truth, Rowan hadn't been able to bring himself to say those words first. If anyone was weak, it was him.

"Loving you is the greatest weakness in the world. I thought it was impossible for me till I met you."

Rowan let his own tears spill over. He petted Yves's hair.

"I'm sorry it took so long," he murmured, then drew Yves into a tender kiss. "Aren't you going to put the ring on me?"

Yves smiled and slipped the ring onto Rowan's hand. It was a perfect fit.

"Where did you get it?" Rowan asked, admiring the glittering gemstones.

Yves looked a bit sheepish. "I scoured the seas for it, where else?"

"Is *this* why you sailed through the winter?" Rowan exclaimed. All of that danger and death, just to get him the perfect ring.

"Yes."

"How did you know I would come back?"

"I didn't. I just hoped. And, well, I needed to keep myself busy or I would go mad with wanting you. I thought if I had the perfect ring, it might bring you back to me."

"Your death brought me back to you."

Yves chuckled. "It's fitting then, that I almost died obtaining the ring."

They drifted for a while, the early afternoon light spilling across their naked bodies from the open window. Rowan realized he could hear birds singing to the beautiful spring day. The fool's day. But the two biggest fools on the island were tucked safely into this bed.

Yves ran his fingers through Rowan's hair, then down over the barely healed scars on his face. His thumb traced the edge of Rowan's eyepatch.

"Tell me what happened," he murmured. "Tell me who did this, and I will cut out his eyes and feed them to him."

"That's sweet. But I'm fairly sure you already killed him."

"I've done quite a lot of killing since you saw me last. You'll have to be more specific."

"It was Admiral Batteux. The one you saved us from."

Yves shifted uncomfortably at the name, then seemed to collect himself.

"Does it please you to know that I killed both he and Cyrus *very* slowly?"

Oddly, it did. Their secret was safe once again. They could let this be their home.

"Do I even want to know what you did to them?" Rowan asked wryly.

"Best leave it up to your imagination, darling."

They lapsed back into a comfortable silence. Yves couldn't take his eyes off Rowan's face, as if he couldn't bring himself to believe he was real.

Yves sat up suddenly. "This isn't what I planned," he all but wailed. "I had a whole candlelit dinner planned and..." He was cut off by Rowan's chuckle. Poor Yves looked so anguished about his botched proposal.

"We can still have dinner." Rowan laughed. "It's just now I'll be attending as your fiancé."

CHAPTER 35

APRIL 6TH, 1667

Not only was there a ring, but an entire set of clothes that fit Rowan perfectly as if they'd been tailor-made for him. Maybe they had, but he balked at the thought of what it all must have cost. If Yves bought it, a fortune. If he'd stolen it, a life.

The knee-high black leather boots were polished to a high shine, with silver filigree toe and heel caps. The black leather trousers were immaculately cut to hug his thighs and ass. The white silk shirt was open at the collar, showing off his throat. There was no waistcoat, only a wide leather belt and silken sash dyed in a spectrum of blues. Its color shifted like light under the sea. But the coat was truly a thing of beauty. It was deep blue velvet, embroidered with silver thread at the cuffs and collar. Its long, wide tails reached his calves and flared out behind him like skirts when he walked. Yves had given him earrings as well, sapphires set in silver, one for each piercing and delicate silver chains to connect them.

The only old thing on his body was the eyepatch. Yves hadn't anticipated that. But it didn't matter. None of the finery mattered.

Rowan belted his cutlass beneath the coat. It felt wrong going out without it, even in the relative safety of Illusion.

The rest of the island was fast asleep when he stepped out into the midnight darkness. Fox met him on the path beneath the trees, and they walked together in silence, listening to the waves grow louder as they approached their destination. Rowan touched the ring that lay heavily in his pocket. Yves had placed it there himself, and Rowan was grateful he didn't have to go marauding across the seas to find the perfect one, as Yves had done for him.

They'd intended to do this in daylight with their crews all around them, but a storm had raged all day and delayed them. Now mist clung in the low places between the foliage, and the leaves still dripped with rain. Beyond the trees, the sea remained restless.

But the clouds had finally broken, and Rowan didn't want to wait any longer. He and Fox trudged through the dripping trees until they reached the clifftop. His friends stood along the edge of the tree line. Gaël, Logan, John, Robin, and Henri turned to smile at him. All dressed in their best clothes. Beyond them, Ana stood in a purple gown beside her brother.

Rowan's breath caught when he saw Yves. He was dressed even more immaculately than usual. He looked like a king from head to toe. The sharp spurs on his bootheels glinted in the moonlight. His trousers were a fitted black velvet, and his black shirt spilled a cascade of lace forth from the base of his throat. Over it all, he wore a white coat embroidered with deep gray swirls like smoke, and the epaulets at his shoulders dripped with onyx feathers and looping strings of pearls. In his ear, he wore his signature ruby. He was gorgeous, otherworldly. His skin shone like mother-of-pearl in the silvery light of the full moon, and the waves threw themselves against the base of the cliff below as if sacrificing themselves to be nearer to him.

Yves turned toward him as they exited the trees, and a shadow flickered at the corner of Rowan's vision. He blinked it away. Fox squeezed his arm and stepped back to take his place beside Gaël. Yves started forward, but Ana beat him to it, rushing toward Rowan and throwing her arms around his shoulders. Rowan barely registered this before she pulled away, taking his hands in hers and pecking him on the cheek.

"I'm so happy to see you again, brother," she whispered with a teary-eyed smile. She squeezed his hand, then they both turned toward Yves. Ana led Rowan to her brother's side. She took Yves left hand and placed Rowan's in it, squeezed them once more then retreated to join the others. Rowan stood there bewildered for a moment, half mesmerized by Yves's beauty.

"You're beautiful," Yves murmured, breaking him from the spell.

Rowan resisted the urge to kiss him right there and then. He looked over to their friends, who were either grinning, or in Ana's case, quietly weeping. None of them stepped forward, and Rowan realized as the captains, the only people on this island qualified to perform this marriage were the two of them.

The dark sea continued to crash below them, white caps like bits of lace floating in the tide. He looked back up into Yves's face, and a swell of love suffused his heart.

"Yves Francois LeSauvage." His voice was quiet in the face of the crashing sea and his pounding heart. He knew this wasn't Yves's full and true name, but it was how he knew him. "The Demon of the Deep, captain of the dreaded ship *Kraken's Fury*, do you take me, Rowan Faine, to be your lawful partner, until death separates us?" A flutter of nerves twinged in his belly as he asked the question, afraid even in the face of everything that Yves would abandon him.

But Yves's beautiful lips curved into a smile. He fished the ring out of his pocket and slipped it onto Rowan's finger as he said the words.

"I, Yves Francois LeSauvage, take you, Rowan Faine, as my lawful partner. By the brine in my soul and the blood on my hands, I vow to protect you and love you until we both succumb to our final rest beneath the sea." He reached up to brush Rowan's flushed cheek with his thumb, closing the small distance still between them. "Rowan Faine, Ghost Hawk, captain of the fastest ship on the seas, the *Siren Song*, do you so vow?"

Rowan leaned into his touch, blood pounding in his temples, dizzying. He took Yves's ring from his coat pocket, and slid it onto Yves's elegant finger. The large ruby shone like a drop of blood on his skin. "I, Rowan Faine, take you, Yves Francois LeSauvage, as my lawful partner. By the brine in my soul and the blood on my hands, I vow to protect and love you until death separates us." He swayed slightly on his feet, overcome by something he couldn't name, and Yves clutched his elbow to steady him. They gazed at each other for a long moment, one blue eye and two dark ones.

"Well?" Fox shouted from the tree line. "Aren't you going to kiss?"

Rowan's laugh was cut off by Yves's supple lips on his, fingers twining through his hair and waves swirling around his heart as the others whooped and cheered their approval.

~

FINALLY, blissfully, they belonged to each other. Rowan was still a little lightheaded, so he leaned on Yves's shoulder as they made their way up the stairs toward their rooms. Yves leaned down to kiss the top of his head.

"Now that we're married, will you be taking my name?" Yves teased.

"Your name isn't even real."

Yves chuckled. "Fair enough. Maybe I should take yours. Yves Faine. It has a certain ring to it."

"No it doesn't," Rowan snorted, but his heart fluttered at Yves's words. They were married. They were bound together now and only fate could separate them.

Warm light washed over them as Yves opened the door to his room. The four-poster bed was hung with garlands of foliage and spring flowers. Every surface was crowded with white candles which filled the room with a golden-orange glow. Yves locked the door and stepped up close behind Rowan. His arm snaked around Rowan's waist, and he bent to brush his lips up the side of his neck.

"Have you been looking forward to this?" Yves murmured against Rowan's heated skin. After Rowan accepted his proposal, Yves had insisted that they sleep apart until the wedding night. That meant no sex. Much to Rowan's chagrin, he found that his body was reacting quicker than usual after the long sexless winter and additional six nights of laying in his lonely bed with Yves untouchable in the next room. After all that, he'd been half hard since the kiss on the clifftop. Now a rush of blood hardened him further, his erection straining against the tight leather pants.

"I see you have been," Yves chuckled. His hand trailed down Rowan's stomach. "Were you lonely without me all those months? Did you touch yourself and think of me?"

Rowan leaned his head back against Yves's shoulder and looked up through his lashes in what he hoped was an alluring way. If he was going to be this turned on from just a little kissing, he was going to take Yves down with him. They were in this together now after all.

"I didn't—ah—" Rowan gasped as Yves's teeth nipped his neck. He arched his back so his ass would press against Yves's hard cock.

"It will be a shame to get you out of these clothes," Yves said. His hand cupped the bulge in Rowan's pants. "They suit you. You're gorgeous."

A shiver ran up Rowan's spine. No matter how long he and Yves were together in the future, he didn't think he would ever get used to being complimented by someone so astoundingly beautiful. Rowan knew he was good-looking, but Yves was angelic. Otherworldly.

And he belonged to Rowan.

Rowan spun to face him, ignoring the flickers in the corners of his vision and the brief dizziness that overtook him at the movement. The symptoms of whatever this was seemed to be getting worse since he'd returned to Illusion. But it didn't matter tonight. He would worry about it all in the morning.

Rowan fisted his hands in the front of Yves's beautiful shirt and rose up on his toes to kiss him. Yves groaned. His tongue immediately invaded Rowan's mouth. He hauled Rowan to his chest, hands framing Rowan's waist beneath the blue coat.

Yves's hands moved down Rowan's hips and unbuckled his belt, letting both belt and cutlass fall to the floor. The pearl strings on Yves's shoulders clicked softly as they moved toward the bed. The back of Rowan's legs hit the edge of the mattress, and his hands tightened in the soft fabric of Yves's shirt, popping jet buttons which clattered to the floor.

"Eager," Yves teased.

"It's my wedding night. Can you blame me?"

"It's all about you, now is it?" Yves released Rowan's hips and grabbed his wrists, pushing their bodies apart slightly so he could see his face.

"I *am* the bride," Rowan joked.

"I'm the one wearing white."

And he looked damn good in it too. Rowan's gaze swept down his body, taking in everything from his onyx hair to the sizable bulge in his trousers to his shiny boots. Rowan's dick twitched. He couldn't wait anymore. He didn't care that these clothes were probably worth a fortune. He needed Yves *now*.

Yves must have had the same thought. He pushed Rowan onto the bed, divested himself of his elaborate coat and pounced. His burning mouth found every inch of Rowan's exposed skin as he pulled Rowan's shirt hem out of its tuck and unfastened his leather trousers. The candlelight wavered as if responding to his movement.

Rowan ripped Yves's shirt open the rest of the way, exposing his muscled chest and pale stomach. Yves growled and captured Rowan's right wrist in his hand, pressing it to the mattress as his other hand dragged Rowan's trousers down his hips. Yves's mouth was hard and insistent against his, and Rowan's body already ached for more. Rowan deepened the kiss, his hips bucking up to seek friction. He felt Yves's lips curl into a smile against his own, probably still amused by Rowan's eagerness.

Before Rowan knew it, his trousers and undergarments were off, and the shirt pushed up under his armpits. Yves caressed his heated skin, leaving trails of lightning across his body. He never broke the fevered kissing. Rowan slipped his hand beneath Yves's open shirt, trying to pull him closer. Yves's palm skimmed over Rowan's cock and Rowan groaned. When had Yves slicked up his fingers? Rowan didn't know. But it seemed that Yves was just as impatient as him. He spread Rowan's thighs wide and slipped one finger into his hole without preamble. It went in easily.

Yves's brow furrowed. Rowan suddenly remembered that he'd prepped himself before the ceremony so they wouldn't have to waste time afterward.

"What's this?" Yves cooed, but there was a dark edge to it.

"I...ah...prepped beforehand." Rowan moaned as Yves added a second finger right away and began to move them in and out slowly.

"Is this going to become a habit of yours, darling?"

Rowan clutched the front of Yves's shirt, his back arching as the pads of Yves's fingers found his prostate.

"Why? Don't you like it?" Rowan's voice was breathy with pleasure and anticipation both.

Yves leaned down to nibble at Rowan's earlobe. "As much as I love to be surprised, sometimes I'd like the pleasure of opening you up myself." His fingers massaged circles into Rowan's prostate.

"I just want you," Rowan moaned.

"You have me." Yves fingers pumped into him. He added a third and opened Rowan up even more, taking pleasure in the building moans coming from Rowan's mouth. Rowan's eyes slid closed as pleasure washed over him. His dick throbbed, leaking precum onto his stomach. Yves hit his prostate again, sending a jolt through his nerves.

"Yves, please..." Rowan couldn't wait any longer. He wanted, needed, to be filled up and fucked by his husband.

Yves's fingers withdrew, and Rowan's eyes snapped open. His fingers tightened in the fabric of Yves's shirt. Yves's hand closed around Rowan's cock and pumped him slowly for a moment. Rowan pulled him into another kiss, mouth open and wanting.

Yves broke away and released Rowan's wrist and cock. He stood, shedding the last of his clothing. Rowan sat up, stripping off his own jacket and shirt and reaching for Yves to pull him back onto the bed, but Yves grabbed him by the waist and picked him up. He crawled up the bed with Rowan in his arms and dropped him back to the mattress with his head on the pillows.

Yves leaned over him, looking at him with shiny eyes full of love and lust and the warm light of the candles. Rowan ran his hands over Yves's perfectly smooth skin. The bullet wound was still the only scar that marred his body. How had he escaped the battle with the *Vaillant* without a single permanent mark? Rowan suddenly felt self-conscious about his scarred and damaged body. He swallowed the lump in his throat as Yves cupped his chin between thumb and forefinger and leaned down to kiss him again. Rowan still felt a bit dizzy, and it didn't help that all of his blood seemed to have rushed from his head to his dick. He sighed into the kiss, his hands finding Yves's hard cock and stroking him. Yves groaned and pulled back, grabbing the corked vial of lube from the pillow and dribbling it over his own cock, letting Rowan's stroking hand spread it down his shaft.

Yves's hand moved from Rowan's chin to his thigh, gripping the pliant flesh and spreading his legs. He broke the kiss, and their eyes met. Yves positioned himself at Rowan's entrance but didn't move further.

"Yves..." Rowan whined. He wrapped his legs around Yves's hips, trying to draw him in.

Yves pushed in slowly, the girth of his dick stretching Rowan deliciously.

"Fuck," Yves gasped. "I love you."

Rowan's heart fluttered. "Say it again."

Yves withdrew, then thrust in again harder.

"I love you."

Rowan had been waiting to hear those words for so long. He would never be able to get enough of them. Now he'd be able to hear them whenever he wanted.

Rowan pulled Yves back down into a kiss, threading his fingers through the soft black hair on the back of his head. Yves rocked his hips forward, the thick veins of his cock brushing Rowan's prostate and sending a rush of heat through his body. He deepened the kiss, his tongue playing with Yves's and eliciting a low groan from Yves's throat. He reveled in the sensations of their bodies moving in tandem, the push and pull of their rhythm like the tides.

Yves trailed kisses past the corner of Rowan's lips and over his scarred cheek to the edge of the eyepatch.

"I want to see your face."

"You..." Oh. He meant the eyepatch which covered Rowan's fake eye and the worst of the scarring. Rowan's fingertips left Yves's hair and touched the warm leather. Self-consciousness spiked in his gut again. He considered denying Yves's request. But Yves brushed another lingering kiss across his lips, his hips rolling sensually, pleasure washing away the doubts.

"Promise you won't stop loving me if I'm ugly."

Yves chuckled. "You could never be ugly to me. These scars show your power."

Rowan took a steadying breath. He removed his hand from the eyepatch and closed his eyes. If Yves was shocked by what he saw beneath it, Rowan didn't want to witness his initial reaction. Yves's fingers traced the line of one scar up his cheek to the edge of the patch. He paused for a moment before pushing it up Rowan's forehead and off his head. There was a beat of stillness before he felt Yves's soft lips brush over his scarred eyelid.

"Let me see," Yves prompted. His other movements had stilled, but his cock still throbbed deep inside.

Slowly, Rowan opened his eyes, one ice blue with its pupil wide, the other the milky green orb Fox had won. His vision swam for a second before focusing on Yves still poised above him.

Rowan gasped, panic and horror replacing pleasure and clawing up his ribs. Yves still gazed down at him, but with eyes as pure black as pitch, even the whites devoured by the void. Not even reflections of the candles lit their depths. Behind him, a dark mass of tentacles took the place of his shadow. They shifted and curled like undulating waves, dark and blue and terrible as if they'd been dredged up from the bottom of the sea. One languidly curled around the bedpost, while another snaked down Yves's arm as if to touch Rowan's skin where Yves's fingertips still rested.

"What the fuck!" Rowan shoved Yves off him, *out* of him. He scrambled off the bed, falling to the floor on weakened legs before stumbling away and catching himself on the far wall.

"What?" Yves was sprawled naked on the sheets where Rowan had pushed him, looking bewildered. He sat up and the shadow tentacles moved with him, undulating around his shoulders as if cloaking him, armoring him. Yves moved toward him.

"Stay where you are," Rowan threatened, holding out one hand before him as if that would stop him. It wouldn't. Rowan knew Yves could easily overpower him if he wanted to.

Yves stopped, still half on the bed. "What's gotten into you? What's wrong?" He still sounded the same. Except he didn't. His deep voice was tinged with a watery echo.

"What are those things?" Rowan spat, pointing over Yves's shoulder. Yves looked back but seemed unfazed. Either he couldn't see the monstrous shadows or he'd already known they were there. His gaze fixed back on Rowan, depthless black eyes searching his face.

"What the fuck are you?" Rowan whispered.

Yves's eyes widened. Uneasiness rippled through the tentacles.

"Rowan." His voice was deceptively gentle. "What is it that you see?"

Rowan squeezed his eyes shut for a moment. His body trembled all over. Maybe it was his eye playing tricks on him again. He'd been seeing strange shadows for months. They weren't real. Maybe when he opened his eyes again everything would be as it was.

But no, when he opened his eyes, the shadowy appendages remained.

"I...I... There are shadows...tentacles..." That was all he could manage.

Yves flinched as if he'd been struck, and it rippled through the tentacles as well. He stepped off the bed, approaching where Rowan cowered against the wall.

"Darling, I—"

"Don't call me that!" Rowan snapped. "Explain."

Yves stopped in his tracks.

"At least come sit—"

"No." The wall was cold on Rowan's bare back, but it was the only thing grounding him to reality right now.

Yves let out a shuddering breath. He looked like he was on the verge of tears, and Rowan fought down the urge to go to him. Comfort him.

Yves held his hand palm up, a smaller tentacle threading between his long fingers. "This is the only reason I am alive. I'm a demon, Rowan. Or at least I'm possessed by one. I have been since I was a teenager."

Rowan stared at him in disbelief, mouth hanging open. If the evidence wasn't here before his eyes, he wouldn't have believed him. But it wasn't a hallucination. The tentacles were moving with Yves, a part of him. No matter how hard he stared and wished it wasn't true, they were real and they wouldn't go away.

The flickering candlelight, which was romantic just a few moments ago, now seemed menacing. He flattened his palm against the wall, trying to cling to something solid and real to calm his growing panic. He was suddenly hyper-aware that he was stark naked.

"Rowan."

Rowan's gaze snapped from the tentacles to Yves's face. Rowan swallowed painfully. He didn't know what to think. Yves had lied to him again, if not by word then by omission. How had he let himself be drawn into his charms again? Was it some underlying demonic power of persuasion that allowed Yves to capture his heart so thoroughly? It was their wedding night, he'd...

Oh gods, he'd married a demon.

Rowan's already shaking legs turned watery, and he slid down to the floor. He couldn't seem to catch his breath, and he covered his eyes with shaking hands as if that would make everything go away.

"Rowan?" Yves's voice was much closer than Rowan expected, and he flinched, hitting the back of his head on the wall. He hadn't heard Yves approach, but now Yves was kneeling in front of him, horrifying tentacles writhing like a dark halo around his naked body. He raised his hands to cup Rowan's face, but Rowan shrank away from his touch. Yves's eyelids dipped over his flat black eyes.

"Trust me one more time." His voice made Rowan feel like he was drowning. "Close your eyes."

Trust. It had been the eternal question in their relationship. Yves had asked so much of him already, but Rowan's body obeyed without question.

He inhaled sharply as he felt Yves's familiar hands on the sides of his face, then the smooth leather of the eyepatch settling over his false eye.

When Rowan opened his eye, Yves was back. *His* Yves. The shadow tentacles were gone, and the blackness in his eyes had retreated to his irises, the familiar stars returned.

The relief that washed over Rowan was short lived, quickly replaced by confusion, and he pushed Yves hands away. Yves's eyelids dipped again, but now it was easier to tell what it meant. He was hurt and trying not to show it. He didn't try to touch Rowan again, but neither did he back off.

"Please let me explain," Yves said. Even his voice was back to normal. "Let's get you dressed." He stood and held out his hand to help Rowan up. But Rowan's body was still shaking, and he knew that the demonic tentacles were still there, even if he couldn't see them. He touched his eyepatch gingerly. It was obvious even to his addled brain that his ability to see Yves's demonic form had something to do with the false eye that Fox had given him. Thinking back, the hallucinations—he wasn't so sure they *were* hallucinations anymore—had only started when he was wearing it. Yves seemed to have come to the same conclusion.

Rowan didn't get up. He heard Yves retreat back to the bed, then return. The sheet from the bed settled over Rowan's shoulders, and he drew it close around him. He looked up to see Yves had settled cross-legged on the floor across from him with another sheet draped across his lap like a drift of snow. The silence expanded between them as Rowan's panicked heartbeat started to slow. His terror was turning to heartbreak and anger instead. Yves waited for him to speak.

One thought broke through the rest of the jumble.

"You tricked me."

Yves blinked at him, wide-eyed.

"I didn't..." He'd never sounded so unsure of himself in front of Rowan.

"We're married. That's a contract, and you're a demon."

Yves's body jolted. "That's not—" His jaw clenched shut over the words, muscle jumping under his skin. "That wasn't my intention," he gritted out.

"What was your intention?" Rowan's voice had smoothed out, sounding cold even to himself. Cold and collected, nothing like the pain that was slowly constricting around his heart like a vice. "Do you even love me?"

"Yes." It sounded like a plea. Yves reached for Rowan's hand before stopping himself. His fingers curled into his palm. For the second time in their relationship, Yves's eyes brimmed with tears. "Please believe me. My name may not be the one I was born with, but I made a vow on it, and I intend to keep it. I love you more than anything, and I will protect you as long as I live."

The pressure around Rowan's heart increased, cracking it.

"How can I believe you?" Rowan rasped. "Were you ever going to tell me?"

One of the tears broke the dam and slid down Yves's cheek.

"I...I don't know."

Rowan pulled the sheet closer around his naked body. He wanted to believe that this time Yves wasn't hiding anything. That this was the last secret between them. That when they exchanged wedding vows not even an hour ago, Yves had done so with no ulterior motive.

"Tell me. Now."

CHAPTER 36

ELEVEN YEARS AGO - SUMMER 1656

Yves sprinted across the deck as it splintered and broke around him. The screams of his fellow pirates echoed in the air as another barrage of cannon fire tore their bodies apart. Yves didn't even know who was attacking, just that they'd been ambushed in the dead of night under a scarlet flag of no quarter.

Yves's already shitty life had gotten unbelievably shittier when he found out what his sister Ana was really doing to keep them alive and fed on the streets of Saulès. He wanted to help, but he was just a kid, barely past his twelfth birthday. He'd found work as a kitchen boy in the home of General Batteux, but a peaceful life continued to elude him. He'd caught the general's eye.

Even years later, he couldn't think about what happened without panic rising in his chest, or what more could have happened if Ana hadn't come for him in time.

But powerful men didn't like to give up their playthings, especially when those playthings knew damning information about their sickening predilections. To protect himself and Ana both, he got a job on the next ship out of port, which turned out to belong to pirates.

He'd taken to the sea like he was born of its tides.

And now what did he have to show for it?

He stumbled as the ship shuddered and groaned. He was just a teenager. Just fifteen. He couldn't die yet. He hadn't seen Ana in three years, and he'd never gotten the chance to thank her and take care of her like he wanted to.

But there was nowhere to go. Not now. They were in open water with no land in sight. And even if Yves begged for mercy, he doubted it would be granted.

A concussive boom threw Yves backwards over the rail, plunging him headfirst into the waves.

Beneath the water, all was quiet. Peaceful. The screams of the dying were muffled and far away. Yves kicked toward the surface, but his coat and boots dragged him down. He struggled harder. He knew how to swim, but it was as if the sea itself was determined to swallow him up. Another body plunged below the surface, dead weight trailing a plume of red. It sank past him into the depths, blood and salt water invading his nostrils. Yves battled against the sucking undertow, desperate to reach the surface.

Something wrapped around Yves's ankle, yanking him deeper. His mouth opened in surprise, a string of silvery bubbles escaping with his breath toward the receding surface. He clamped his mouth shut before the sea could rush in to take its place. He kicked at the thing holding him, but it constricted, grinding muscle and bone together. He writhed in its hold, desperate to escape, but it squeezed harder, and he felt something in his leg snap. He clamped his hands over his scream, keeping whatever breath remained inside.

Yves's coat billowed up around him as the thing pulled him deeper. His hands shook as he fumbled with the knife at his belt and it slipped from his grasp, sinking out of reach past the dark and writhing shadow pulling him down and down into the depths. His muscles burned with futile struggle. He could barely hear the report of cannons or see the firelight above the surface anymore. He reached up as if that would get him any closer to the agony and breath of life. Would it be better to drown here in the peaceful dark? Or surrender to this creature, whatever it was?

Was this all he was? An abused and runaway child. Lost at sea with only one soul in the world to mourn him.

His body went slack, letting the water cradle him, giving up. He looked down toward his future grave. The massive shadowy creature waited below, a multitude of tentacles ebbing and flowing with the deep currents. He could see no face. No eyes. Only a void-like maw of sharp teeth waiting for him.

He couldn't help it. He gasped, salty water rushing down his throat and forcing the last of the breath from his lungs.

The tentacle crushing his leg shivered, speckles of light like a galaxy twinkling across its skin. It would've been beautiful if it wasn't going to kill him.

In some distant corner of his mind, he wondered if he would drown or be eaten first.

Free me.

Was he going mad in the face of his inevitable death? His oxygen deprived brain playing tricks on him?

Free me, the voice said again, deep and echoing.

I'm the one who's trapped. I've never been free, Yves thought. The three years he'd spent on the pirate ship had been the closest to freedom he'd ever gotten. And even that was tinged with violence and death.

The tentacle, with its shiny, star-like speckles loosened slightly and the shadows beneath it roiled, revealing a gargantuan black eye.

We can help each other then.

He wasn't imagining it. The creature was speaking to him.

We can make a deal, the creature said.

I'm dying, Yves thought.

You will free me from this prison, and I will free you from death.

But how could Yves free this creature? And from what? Who could be more free than a creature in the vast seas?

I have been imprisoned here for millennia. I will free you from the restraints of death. Not only this death, but any illness, any wound suffered, will be nothing in the face of my power. I will live your life beside you, and one day we will return to the sea together. You will know success and riches beyond your wildest imaginings. But you will not know love. That is a price you must continue to pay.

Love. Yves's mind caught on the word hazily, his brain oxygen starved and slowly dying. He would give up everything to live. He would even give up love if it weren't for...

*Ana...*It was impossible to speak her name aloud. His mouth and lungs were already full of seawater. But the creature heard. The creature knew.

Ana. The creature repeated ponderously, rolling the name around in the currents. It seemed to know exactly who she was, as if it were rifling through Yves's dying mind, picking apart his thoughts and memories. *Your beloved sister who sacrificed herself for your sake. And now look at where you are, dying at the bottom of the sea. Would you rather die loving her? Or survive and repay her sacrifices.*

Yves's body jerked. He was in the last throes of drowning, succumbing to the cold embrace of the sea. But all he could think was, *Cruel.*

The creature chuckled.

Say I am cruel. Curse me and rail against me with the little time you have left. Or make a decision. Will you tie your life to mine?

Yves would have laughed if he could. It almost sounded like a marriage proposal. He was just a kid; he couldn't make a decision like this.

But he didn't want to die.

What are you?

There was a short moment of hesitation. A moment in which Yves died a little more.

Demon. Monster. God. Call me what you will. I am your savior.

A demon. A deal with a demon. A deathless life with this creature always looking out from behind his eyes.

You are dying, the demon said.

Yes. I will free you. Just let me live.

The salt water churned in his lungs, the pressure of the sea pressing in all around him. He gazed into the blue blackness of the depths. Starlight twinkled in the dark as more tentacles wrapped in chains closed around him.

His body went slack, and his eyes drifted shut again, succumbing to death.

WHEN HE WOKE on the rocky shores of an unknown land, undrowned, he was not alone in his own head. And he would never be alone again. The demon was him, and he was the demon. There was no separating one consciousness from the other now. They were one. A new being. Not Yves. Not the demon.

The demon had changed him. Made him more merciless. But in turn he had made the demon more human.

It took him half a year to return to Saulès.

~

IT WAS DARK, but Yves could see everything in the narrow, stinking alleyway beside the boarding house where Ana stayed. The Batteuxs's dried blood flaked from his knuckles as he clutched the sack of money and valuables close to his chest.

The first thing he'd done upon his return wasn't finding Ana. He'd gone straight to General Batteux's house and killed every man and woman who'd known what the general was and done nothing about it. Who'd turned a blind eye to the suffering of the child Yves used to be. He'd left only the young kitchen boy alive. It was a wonder how much he could do when he didn't have to worry about dying, when the strength of a demon coursed through his veins. There was no fear left in him, only revenge. Unfortunately, one family member hadn't fallen to his violence, the general's second son who was away at sea. He'd stolen everything he could from the house and stashed most of it in a hollow on the outskirts of Saulés, but this he'd saved for Ana, his sister, the woman who'd raised him. Who'd starved and sacrificed for him.

No warmth spread through his heart at the thought of her, no loneliness or yearning to see her again. That was part of the deal. The chambers of his heart would never again fill with the flush of love. Not for Ana, his only family, and not for anyone else. But that didn't mean he'd forgotten her.

A burst of chatter accompanied the boarding house door opening, spilling women and lamplight out onto the cobbled street. Yves shrank into the shadows, watching to see if Ana would appear among them. And there she was, as pale as the moon overhead and hair as black as the night. His own face reflected back at him through feminine lines. If the human part of him had half hoped he would feel something when he saw her face again, he was disappointed. There was nothing. He remained empty.

Ana said something to one of her companions and hung back to lock up the boarding house door as the other women moved on down the street to their nightly activities. Ana slipped the key into her pocket and made to follow.

Yves's hand shot out as Ana passed by the mouth of the alley, dragging her into the darkness. She yelped, and a small knife flashed between her fingers, burying itself into the meat of his shoulder.

"Ana," he grunted, and her struggle stopped as she looked up into his wan face, lit only by the moon overhead.

"Y-Yves, is that you? Oh gods..." Her hands flew to her mouth in horror as she took in his ghoulish countenance, half starved and smeared with dried blood. Then her gaze flicked to the knife still sticking from his shoulder. "Yves, I'm sorry. I..." Her eyes welled up with tears, and even that did not move him.

Yves released her arm and drew the knife out of his flesh, a fresh gout of blood gushing from the wound.

"Don't do that! We need to get you inside. I'll get bandages—"

"No need. Here," Yves interrupted her. He handed the bloodied knife back to her, hilt first. She took it reluctantly, eyes searching his face.

"Yves..." Her expression crumpled, and she launched herself into his arms, face buried into his uninjured shoulder as she sobbed. "I'm so glad you're alive."

Yves froze, a singular ridiculous thought nagging at his mind, that she was so much shorter than him now. He'd not seen her since fleeing Saulés when he was just twelve. But after a moment, some muscle memory kicked in, and his arms wrapped around her shoulders. He let her tears dwindle into sniffles, saying nothing until she stepped back.

"We'll need to bandage that," Ana said weakly, smiling her familiar, motherly smile.

"It's nothing." He could hear the echo of tides in his own voice, but such a thing didn't seem to register with her. Nor could she see the tendrils of shadow that protruded from his back to fill the expanse of the alley.

Yves thrust the sack of money into her hands. "This is for you."

"What?" The coins clinked together and her eyes widened. "Yves, what's going on? Where did you get this?" She seemed to register for the first time that he was covered in dried blood. "I-I heard that the general and his family were murdered. Did you...?" She seemed unable to bring herself to say it.

"Yes," Yves answered without hesitation. Tears sprang to Ana's eyes all over again, and Yves reached out to grip her shoulders. "Take this money and go far away, buy a cottage in the countryside. I will find you again. But for now I must flee. I'm returning to the sea to make a name for myself, and you'll never want for anything again."

Ana placed a trembling hand over his. "And if they catch you? You'll hang."

That did cause him some discomfort. In the back of his mind he knew he wouldn't die, but he couldn't tell Ana that. He tried to smile reassuringly, but it felt wrong on his face.

"Don't worry."

He turned to leave, but she caught his arm. He did not turn back to look at her. It was too painful knowing that he no longer felt the most human of emotions. Love.

"What happened to you?" Ana whispered, her voice breaking on another sob.

Yves looked back then and met her teary gaze.

"I'll tell you when it's safe." He gently pried his arm from her grip and disappeared into the dark, trailing shadow and leaving her sobbing in his wake.

~

YVES ONLY LASTED two days before he was caught. There was no trial. He was arrested, accused, and confessed to the murders he'd committed. The young kitchen boy bore witness, and within a few days, he found himself trudging up the steps of the gallows in King's Square under an overcast sky.

The smell of imminent rain mingled with the sea breeze in Yves's nostrils. They'd taken his boots at the jail, and the wooden steps of the gallows were cold beneath the bare soles of his feet. He kept his eyes forward as the bodies of the criminals before him were taken down and stacked into a cart.

We will not be joining them in death for long, the darker part of him whispered, and he knew it to be true, but that did not keep his hands from trembling.

Yves made it to the top of the steps, and he followed the jailers to stand atop the trapdoor. He gazed dispassionately out at the hushed crowd, wondering if they knew of his crimes and the crimes of his victims. Or if he simply looked like a frightened teenager, his clothes still stiff with dried blood.

His gaze snagged on the one familiar face in the crowd as the noose was placed over his head, rough rope scraping his throat. Ana.

She had not fled yet. She would see him die. He hoped she would not mourn him too deeply.

Yves felt wetness on his cheeks. For a moment, he thought his ability to love had returned, just before the end. But it was the clouds, not his heart, that had opened up and now wept. Soft rain pattered upon the gray square as the magistrate read out his sentence. But he was not listening. He caught Ana's eye and smiled.

"Do you have any last words?" the magistrate asked, a quill poised at the bottom of Yves's sentencing papers, ready to record his final goodbye to life. The executioner tightened the noose but not enough to hinder speech.

Yves's smile widened despite himself. Every drop of rain that landed upon his skin washed the blood away little by little, along with his fear.

"You will remember me." Yves's voice rang clear over the heads of the crowd. "I have things yet to do."

It was a short drop, but his thin body lacked the weight to break his neck.

THE DARK TIDES bore him where they willed. He floated weightless in their embrace for only a short time until slowly, he awoke. First the cold rain pattered on his face, slipping down his cheeks as if the world cried for him. Then the awareness of his throat and lungs aching. His fingers twitched as if he could soothe away the after effects of hanging to death, but his fingertips met only the dead flesh of the other occupants of the cart. Distantly, he heard the scrape of shovels moving wet earth.

Yves was alive.

He sucked in a deep breath of damp air, and it burned all the way down. He forced his eyes open, blinking in the gray evening light filtering through the spindly trees of the paupers' graveyard. It was almost blinding compared to the blackness of the tides that had borne him through death. But he relished it. Even an overcast sky was a sign of life.

Yves sat up slowly, half expecting the other bodies to rise with him. But they remained still, inert, for they had carried only one being inside them, where he carried two.

The paupers' graveyard was empty but for the cart and the two men currently digging a muddy trench to place the criminal deceased. Yves climbed gingerly down from the pile of bodies, his limbs feeling clumsy as a newborn calf. He stood for a moment, watching the gravediggers until one of them turned and saw him.

The rain had washed him clean of blood, yet the gravediggers still screamed, dropping their shovels and falling over their own feet as they fled away through the trees. Yves watched them go. He did not have the energy to chase them.

Wet blades of grass tickled his bare feet, and Yves looked down at them, his toes curling into the earth. In his childish naïveté he'd thought immortality would make him deathless. Yet he was full of death. Even now he could feel it along the edges of his consciousness, trying to pull him beneath its waves. It had gone away for a while, satiated by the blood of revenge. Perhaps that was the key to keep from going under. Perhaps he could slake death's thirst with the souls of others.

Yves turned and trudged away beneath the trees, leaving the dead and his grave behind. He did not look for Ana. His steps led him to the sea.

CHAPTER 37

APRIL 6TH, 1667

Rowan was speechless. He didn't know what he'd expected. A deal with a devil maybe. A play for wealth and power.

Not drowning. Not dying and resurrecting again and again.

Without realizing it, Rowan had sat forward, letting the sheet fall down his back as Yves talked. Tears spilled down Yves's face in earnest now, dripping off his pointy chin to plop to the white sheet over his lap. Rowan had so many questions, even more than before he'd heard the story. But he had no doubt Yves was telling the truth. He could feel it in his gut and regardless of how much it may have steered him wrong in the past, he wanted to trust Yves again.

"The admiral, he was General Batteux's son, wasn't he?" Rowan asked quietly. He didn't know why these were the first words out of his mouth, but his mind shied away from the bigger, deeper questions that nagged it.

Yves nodded.

"So you finally got your revenge. I'm happy for you." He tried to smile, but it faltered and died on his lips.

They descended into silence again, the questions between them sucking all the air from the room.

"So the demon has been here all this time," Rowan said softly. He wanted to take Yves's hand, but he needed more answers first.

"You've never known me without it." Yves dashed a tear from his chin with the back of his hand. "I am... I suppose I should say *we* are like one being. You fell in love with *this* me."

"You said you love me. But you aren't really capable of it. Are you?" It should have hurt, but Rowan's heart was already in pieces.

Yves's brow furrowed. His fingers flexed in his lap as if he desperately wanted to touch Rowan but was holding back. Instead he looked Rowan in the eye.

"That's why it took me so long to realize I was in love with you."

Rowan's cracked heart stuttered, but he asked, "How can you be so sure?"

"I've died many times, but I always come back. The only scar that has ever stayed with me was the mark you left when you killed me."

A shiver passed through Rowan, raising bumps on his bare skin. He'd killed Yves all those years ago on the deck of the *Wolf*. He'd seen Yves burn to death on the *Vaillant* and not even realized it. But Yves was here and whole now. Perfect and unscarred but for the bullet wound Rowan left in his heart.

"I thought I would go through this long life without love. I can't even love my own sister. All I have is the memory of affection. But you... When I came back this time, you were the first thing I thought of. Not that I was alive. Not pain. Not revenge. This time I came back for you. We—" He paused to collect himself. The tears had stopped flowing, and his eyes sparkled with their remnants. The candles flickered, burnt low. "Our thoughts are no longer different from each other. It is not simply that the human part of me loves you, it is all of me, all of us. I don't know how it's possible, but it's the truth."

Rowan leaned forward onto his knees, letting his armor of sheets slip further from his body. He laid his hand over the small round scar on Yves's skin, feeling the living heart beating beneath. Yves looked up at him with wonder and hope in his eyes. Hesitantly, he rested his hand over Rowan's.

Rowan's heart beat faster, mending itself with Yves's touch. He was suddenly overwhelmed with a flood of relief, love, and the remnants of interrupted lust. He surged forward, their lips connecting hard. A small noise of surprise escaped Yves's throat, and he gripped Rowan's shoulders, pushing him away.

"Rowan…" His dark gaze searched Rowan's face. "If you need time…"

"I don't need time," Rowan said fervently. "You might have all the time in the world, all the lives you want. But I don't. And the only life I have is this one, and I need you. Now." He didn't want to think anymore. All he knew was that he loved Yves, wanted him, and if he changed his mind in the morning, that was a problem for the light of day, not the candlelit darkness of their wedding night. He would savor love and pleasure while he could in this fleeting life.

Yves frowned but didn't resist when Rowan pushed aside his restraining hands. He submitted to the next kiss, and they toppled to the floor together, their naked bodies separated only by the rumpled sheet. Rowan braced himself over Yves's splayed body. The kiss became more fevered, an uncontainable craving building low in Rowan's gut.

The panic had gone, replaced by fevered elation. Yves groaned. He gripped Rowan's waist, still slightly hesitant, as if Rowan would run screaming from him if he were too aggressive. But his mouth responded to Rowan's attention eagerly, warm and pliant. He pulled Rowan closer, their naked bodies pressed tight against each other. Rowan rolled his hips, creating friction between their aching cocks. Rowan's pulse quickened, and he tilted his head to deepen the kiss. Yves seemed to be holding back, letting Rowan guide his actions. Was he worried that Rowan would change his mind? Or was it something else?

Rowan pulled back, looking down at Yves's face. He was beautiful, his lips swollen and pink from kissing and cheeks flush with warmth. His dark hair splayed out across the floorboards reminding Rowan of the unseen shadows that still lurked. Yves's fingers tightened possessively on Rowan's waist as he pulled back.

"Tell me what you want," Rowan whispered. His body yearned to continue, but he needed to know Yves wanted this too.

A small smile quirked up the corner of Yves's full lips.

"Tonight isn't about me," he said quietly. "I want whatever you will give me. I am atoning for my sins."

"It is about you though. It's our wedding night."

Yves's smile widened, and through the thin sheet, Rowan felt his cock twitch. He rolled his hips forward again, watching for Yves's reaction. Yves practically whimpered, biting his lower lip. He was at

Rowan's mercy, melting into Rowan's touch, and the momentary power over him was intoxicating. Rowan's fingers pressed harder into the wood floor as he leaned down to nip the long column of Yves's neck. A shadow wavered in the corner of his vision, and he wondered if one of the tentacles was trapped beneath his hand. Could he even touch them? Were they tangible, or did they consist only of shadow?

What could Yves really do with the power of a demon inside him?

He shook off the thought and trailed his lips over Yves's collarbone and down his chest. He pulled the sheet slowly out from between them, letting the soft fabric feather across Yves's sensitive cock. His other hand skimmed over the floor beside Yves's body. He couldn't feel the tentacles, but perhaps Yves could.

Rowan threw the sheet to the side, revealing Yves's rosy cock, pearls of precum already beading at the tip. Rowan wrapped his fingers around the shaft and thumbed the slit, eliciting a sharp inhale. He glanced up through his lashes, making sure once again that Yves was okay with this. The other man's eyes were closed, his breath uneven. Rowan lowered his head slowly and kissed the silky soft tip, his tongue flicking out to taste the salty precum. Yves's eyes snapped open, but he didn't stop Rowan as he wrapped his lips around the tip and his mouth sank down over the veiny shaft. The warm heaviness on his tongue made him salivate. He couldn't wait to have it inside him again. To be stretched and fucked and devoured.

Devoured by his demon husband.

His demon husband who had a plethora of currently invisible tentacles and who knew what else lurking in the shadows. Rowan's mind spun out in a thousand different directions. A thousand possibilities. He almost choked on them. Or maybe that was the bulging cock currently being shoved down his throat.

"Out of practice already?" Yves cooed. His fingers twined into Rowan's blond hair, pulling his head down and burying his needy cock deep in Rowan's throat. Rowan couldn't take it all. No matter how much he practiced he'd never be able to. Yves was too big, but Rowan wasn't complaining. He shifted position on his knees and opened his throat as much as he could. His throat constricted around the intrusion, and Yves's hips bucked up, forcing himself deeper still. Rowan gagged but recovered, swirling his tongue around the shaft.

"Ngh, Rowan…" Yves pulled Rowan's mouth off his cock by his hair and sat up. "Stop teasing and let me fuck you."

Rowan's breath hitched, and he let Yves pull him into his lap. Yves's hands wandered down to cup Rowan's ample ass.

Rowan bent to kiss him again. His lips tasted slightly of salt. He ran his hands down Yves's muscled back, but as expected, it was bare of the tentacles he knew were there just beyond his perception. Yves shifted Rowan so his dick pressed to the curve of Rowan's ass.

Yves leaned back to look at him, palming Rowan's cock and pumping it slowly. His other hand left Rowan's ass to retrieve the corked vial of lube that had rolled off the bed when Rowan freaked out. Surprisingly it was still mostly full. Thank the gods. They still had a long night ahead of them.

Yves uncorked the vial with his teeth. He dribbled some over Rowan's reddened tip and stroked it down his shaft. Tingles spread over Rowan's skin with every stroke. He rubbed his ass back against Yves's erection. Rowan reached back to run his fingers up the underside of Yves's cock and watched Yves's already blissed-out expression, his lips parted alluringly.

Rowan loved this man. Even if he was more than just a man. Even if he was merciless and not entirely human. Rowan wanted all of him, the truth of him.

Rowan reached up to the eyepatch which blocked Yves's true form from his view. He began to push it away.

"Stop," Yves gasped, snatching Rowan's wrist away, fingers slick with sweet-smelling lube and precum. "What are you doing?"

"I want to see you." Rowan leaned down to nuzzle at Yves's neck, his words echoing Yves's own from earlier in the night. "All of you."

Yves pushed him back to look him in the eye, searching his expression. Rowan hoped he saw only love and none of the fear and uncertainty Rowan was trying to keep clamped down. Yves's fingers tightened around his wrist.

"Please. I don't want to frighten you. I don't…" He swallowed. "I don't want you to see me like that again."

Rowan's heart was breaking all over again. Even if his reaction had been understandable, he'd hurt Yves deeply. Rejected him. Called him a monster.

So even if he was hesitant, and still a little frightened, he needed to accept Yves. They had to stop hurting each other.

"I'm not afraid," Rowan whispered.

But Yves was. Fear was written all over his face. The Deep Water Demon was not afraid of death. But he was afraid of losing Rowan.

Rowan cupped Yves's cheek with his free hand. "I made a vow too, Yves. Please, let me see."

Yves hesitated, but his fingers loosened, and he released Rowan's wrist.

Rowan reached up and removed his eyepatch. He held his breath as the deep blue shadows unfurled from Yves's back, and the sparkly darkness of his irises spread to envelop the entirety of his eyes. Yves wrapped his arms around Rowan's waist and buried his face in Rowan's chest, waiting for Rowan's reaction.

The tentacles were eerily still, as if they too were waiting. Rowan tamped down the thrill of fear that threatened to bubble to the surface. He was intimately familiar with fear. Both as predator and prey. It was only natural to be afraid in the face of something dangerous and unknown. But he refused to show it to Yves, and there was something else nestled beside it. Curiosity.

His hand moved from Yves's cheek, grazing down the side of his neck and over his shoulder. He reached out, his fingers dipping into the dark watery shadows.

Yves's breath hitched, and his head snapped up. Rowan didn't miss the throb of Yves's cock against his ass.

"Can you feel that?" Rowan asked. He was genuinely curious, but he could barely keep back the wicked smile that wanted to creep across his lips. The shadow felt cool and silky against his skin. He twisted his hand, and the tentacles writhed.

Rowan's heart pounded. His blood felt hot in his veins, throbbing through his cock and making him dizzy with desire.

"Rowan..." Yves sounded breathless. The flat black of his eyes, which had seemed so soulless before, now burned with barely restrained heat.

"What does it feel like?" Rowan asked. He knew that Yves and the demon were one being. But right now he felt as if he were directly touching the demon part of Yves. And he was acutely aware that there were three of them in this relationship, not just two.

"Does the demon have a name?" Rowan asked.

"No. It just is."

A thinner tentacle quested toward Rowan seemingly of its own volition, as if the nameless demon was reaching out. He expected the cool, watery feeling again, but when it touched his shoulder, it was solid, tactile, and real. Both Rowan and Yves gasped as the tentacle caressed his shoulder, as if Yves wasn't quite in control of whether the tentacles were solid or shadow.

The tentacle in question pulsed with a smattering of blue light as a few of the candles guttered and winked out. The skin of the tentacle was the same color it had been as a shadow, smooth textured and soft. The underside was dotted with delicate suckers which gripped and released Rowan's skin like kisses as it slid up his neck, leaving faint pink marks.

Yves watched him closely as if waiting for the inevitable stroke of an executioner's ax. A recoil of disgust. A flash of fear. Yet his arms still held Rowan close.

Rowan removed his hand from the still intangible tentacle slowly and tilted Yves's chin so that their lips could meet. He took his time, letting his lips linger as the thin tentacle continued its exploration up into his messy hair.

"Can you control them?" Rowan asked quietly.

"Most of the time," Yves said bashfully. Rowan smiled.

"So tell me, what do you want to do to me, my demon? Does it feel good to touch me with them? Do you want to fuck me with them?"

Yves's whole body shivered, rippling through the tentacles and solidifying several of them. The small tentacle tangled into Rowan's blond hair and wrenched his head back to expose his throat. Yves nipped the delicate skin there as another tentacle caressed down Rowan's back.

Now it was Rowan's turn to shiver. The tentacle brushed the curve of his ass, small suckers puckering the taut flesh. A few of the suckers gripped tighter, the tentacle coiling up on itself like a snake ready to strike. The suckers adhered to both cheeks, pulling them apart. The tentacle tip delicately touched the pucker of Rowan's entrance. Rowan whimpered in anticipation.

"Is this what you want?" Yves asked, his voice roughened by the strain of barely keeping himself under control. The watery echo was still suffocating, but Rowan was too turned on to care. Rowan couldn't look down at him; the thin tentacle still held his head tilted back by his hair.

"P-please...show me what you can *really* do," he managed to choke out.

"I will," Yves promised. "Up until now, I have been gentle with you."

The tentacle slid in easily, and Rowan realized that Yves must have dipped it into the lube, or else the tentacles were self-lubricating, which he couldn't think about now. He gasped. The tentacle writhed deeper, stretching him as the thicker part of it intruded into his wet interior. The suckers brushed against his sensitive walls, sending shivers up his spine. He moaned, the sound lewd and wanton in his own ears. One of the suckers latched onto the small bundle of nerves at his core, and dark pleasure sizzled through his nerves. The sucker pulsed, milking Rowan's prostate like a suckling mouth. Filthy noises ripped themselves from Rowan's throat, and he heard Yves growl, low and dangerous and animalistic.

Yves's mouth moved over his chest and neck, leaving marks alongside the faint pink ones left by the tentacle's suckers. Rowan gripped Yves's shoulders, holding on for dear life as the tentacle undulated and pulsed inside him. He was already out of his mind with pleasure, legs shaking, barely able to catch his breath.

"Is it too much?" Yves asked. But there was a smirk on his face, and another tentacle snaked across Rowan's stomach to caress his aching cock. The coils wrapped around his shaft, twisting in contrary directions. He'd never felt anything like it before. An intense myriad of sensations overwhelmed his senses. Euphoria radiating throughout his body. His vision went dark for a moment as the tentacle constricted around his cock. He cried out, his whole body shuddering as he came. The tentacles swiped up the splatters of cum from his skin.

Yves lifted Rowan more firmly in his arms and got to his feet. Rowan wrapped his legs around Yves's waist as he was carried to the bed. The thin tentacle still cradled his head. He was lightheaded, floating in a cloud of bliss. But he craved more.

They fell into the bed, lips connecting bruisingly and bringing Rowan back to the surface. He moaned into the kiss as the tentacle still buried deep in his ass wriggled. The tentacle around his cock loosened, one moist sucker slurping up the last of the cum from the tip.

"M-more..." Rowan moaned. His bleary eye met Yves's flat black ones, and the passion he saw there was both terrifying and exhilarating. He was completely at the mercy of the demon, perfectly willing to be torn apart by mind-bending pleasure.

More candles flickered out, plunging them into wavering half-darkness. The shadow tentacles added to the gloom, undulating behind Yves like the deep currents of the sea. But the few that had taken physical form sparkled with delicate bioluminescent stars. Yves ran his hands over Rowan's shuddering naked body, drinking in the sight of him fucked into oblivion. Penetrated by Yves's tentacle and lit from within by its seductive light. He ran one hand up Rowan's stomach, fingers roving over the constellations that now speckled Rowan's skin from the inside. He licked his lips, carnal hunger dripping from his teeth. There was no hesitation now, only possession.

His hips snapped forward, plunging his cock into Rowan's dripping hole alongside the tentacle. A guttural scream ripped from Rowan's mouth. His fingernails dug into Yves's perfect skin, drawing blood. Yves didn't wait for him to adjust. He fucked Rowan hard and fast, penetrating up to the hilt with every stroke.

Rowan felt as if he was about to pass out. He could barely catch his breath between thrusts. His hole burned with the stretch of both tentacle and cock fucking into him. The tentacle twisted deeper still, pushing further than Yves's massive cock could reach. Rowan almost choked on the overpowering fullness. His back arched off the bed, urging Yves to go deeper still. Yves grabbed his hips, tilting them up for a different angle. His cock hit the spot where a tentacle sucker was still lipping Rowan's prostate.

Rowan's vision went white, divine pleasure searing through him. He could hear his own voice but didn't understand the words. Only that he was begging. Yves growled as Rowan's nails raked down his back, leaving trails of crimson in their wake.

The thinner tentacle untangled from Rowan's hair and slithered around his throat, squeezing slightly and bringing Rowan's unending bliss to new heights as Yves's appendages continued to fuck and suck him. The tentacle around his dick slurped up his streams of cum greedily while twisting around his throbbing shaft. It was all too much, and his begging had become only Yves's name. Even though his voice was hoarse from screaming and the constriction around his throat, Yves's name was still there.

Rowan forced his eyes open, stars around the edges of his vision.

Yves's thrusts were growing erratic, a vicious snarl on his face. But he was beautiful and terrifying, and he was all Rowan's. Every merciless, otherworldly inch of him.

Rowan would never beg for his mercy, only more.

Yves growled out Rowan's name, his voice like a storm on the open sea. The tentacle inside him twisted deeper beside Yves's pounding cock. Rowan buried his hands in Yves's hair, fingernails bloody, and pulled him down into a kiss. The tentacle around Rowan's cock stroked him in time with Yves's thrusts, and Rowan reached the dizzying heights of euphoria once again. Cum spurted between the coils of tentacle. In a few more thrusts, Yves's body shuddered, and warmth gushed into Rowan, overflowing his stretched and full hole to dribble down his ass onto the mattress. Yves groaned low in his throat as he rode them through their orgasms. The passion of the kiss became languid and slow, both of them savoring the bliss of their wedding night. Neither of them were ready to let go just yet.

As Rowan began to come down from his high, exhaustion washed over him like a relentless tide. The tentacles around his neck and dick uncoiled, leaving light little sucker-kisses as they slithered away. The thicker tentacle slowly withdrew from Rowan's backside until only Yves's human flesh remained in contact. Rowan wished they could stay like this forever, wrapped up in bliss and each other with no concern for the outside world.

Finally, Yves unseated himself from inside Rowan as well, bringing with it a gush of cum dribbling out onto the bed. Yves collapsed onto the mattress, the wing-like bloody claw marks on his back smearing the white sheets. After one last caress across Rowan's sucker-marked body, the tentacles receded back into their shadow forms, the blue light going out with them.

Rowan could barely move. His whole body shivered as if in shock, still trying to process the overload of sensations he'd just experienced.

Yves drew him into his arms and planted a soft kiss on his sweaty forehead.

"Thank you," Yves murmured. His voice was not a storm now, but the soft echoes of the deep ocean.

Rowan blinked at him blearily.

"For what?"

"For not being afraid."

Rowan smiled and kissed him lingeringly.

"I told you before, you terrify me. But with you by my side I don't think I'll ever be afraid of anything else."

Yves chuckled, and Rowan felt the cool, watery touch of the shadows smoothing the hair back from his sweaty forehead.

"I meant what I said," Yves whispered. "I'll protect you and love you as long as I live."

"And if you die again?"

Yves took his hand, thumb rubbing over the now bloodstained wedding band.

"Even beyond my death, across all my lifetimes, I'll love you."

CONTENT WARNINGS

ACKNOWLEDGMENTS

Writing and publishing Demon of the Deep has been nearly a two year long process, and so many people have helped me along the way. I am eternally grateful to all of them for their hard work and dedication to this project. I've put my heart and soul into writing the story of these silly, sexy pirates, and I'm so excited to finally share it with readers. Firstly, thank you to my husband, family, and friends who have supported me through the ups and downs, elation and freakouts while I waded through the unknown waters of publishing my first book.

From the bottom of my heart, I would like to thank my beta readers and friends: Emma, Lacey, Lauren, Chris, Katelin, and Johanna. Demon of the Deep would not be what it is today without their feedback, criticisms, and late night "how dare you" messages. I would not have made it through this process without their unwavering support and encouragement. I'm sorry but not sorry that I've traumatized them a bit with this book and will continue to traumatize them with the next.

Additionally, thank you to my editor, Kal Morgan, whose invaluable feedback gave me the last push I needed to get Demon of the Deep polished and publishing ready. Thank you also to Amphi at Amphi Studios for formatting, and Kelly L. Clarke at Velvet Library for proofreading.

Lastly, I'd like to thank the artists that worked on the beautiful art to accompany this book and bring my characters to life. The artist of my author portrait, Gukkhwa (Eunhye Cho). My cover artist, Maria Arteta. Typography, cover design, and interior art by Amphi at Amphi Studio, and the gorgeous spicy character art by Ana Guimarães. You were all so wonderful to work with and seeing my characters and vision come to life under your skilled hands has truly been a dream come true.

ABOUT THE AUTHOR

Briar Belmont

Briar Belmont is a spicy romance and romantasy author debuting in 2024. She's adored reading and writing from a young age and has a soft spot for fairytales and folklore. She can often be found in her garden or curled up with her pets and a good book. *Demon of the Deep* is her debut novel.

Author Portrait by Gukkhwa (Eunhye Cho)

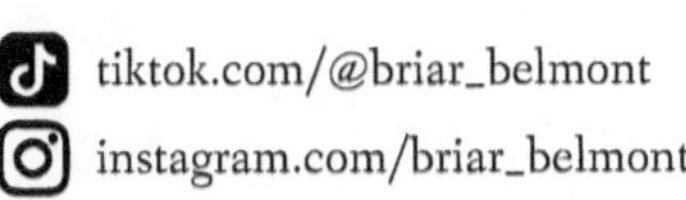

tiktok.com/@briar_belmont

instagram.com/briar_belmont